VAMPIRES OF SHANGHAI

VAMPIRES OF SHANGHAI

HOLLOW EMPIRES
BOOK 1

KATHERINE MERCER

Published by Mercerized Books

Ebook ISBN: 979-8-9940646-0-3

Print ISBN: 979-8-9940646-1-0

～

Cover design by Damonza

Serpent and lotus illustration by Eunice Chen

Editing services by Red Adept Editing

CONTENT NOTES

Vampires of Shanghai includes the following sensitive content. Reader discretion is advised.

- Graphic physical violence and bloodshed
- Extensive physical, psychological, and emotional abuse
- Non-explicit sexual situations marked by unequal power or coercion
- Death and traumatic loss
- Oppression and systemic exploitation including allusions to human trafficking
- Non-explicit depictions of substance use and addiction

生之畜之，
生而不有，
為而不恃，
長而不宰，
是謂玄德

To beget and to nurture,
to give life yet hold no claim,
to make yet not possess,
to foster yet never rule:
this is the deepest dark of virtue.

— LAO TZU, TAO TE CHING

1

"How fresh is it?" Mina asked as she churned a figure eight in the white plastic bucket of cow's blood before her. She let a measure pour from the spoon, watching as the congealed scum broke apart and reassembled. Her stomach rumbled with hunger despite the smell of the rancid liquid.

"From yesterday," the vendor said with a confident nod, hooking his thumbs on his rubber bib overalls.

Offal and tripe sat on a bed of ice with less-recognizable offerings at the stall in a wet market spanning half a block on the eastern outskirts of Singapore.

"How much?"

She balked when the man quoted double what she'd paid anywhere else.

Mina pursed her lips as she surveyed the other stalls. None appeared to cater to her specific dietary needs. Walking away from a sure meal wasn't worth the risk—not with this many people around. Switching from English to Mandarin, she haggled him down a few dollars.

The vendor portioned out the blood into a dangerously thin plastic bag before knotting it at the top. Mina handed him exact change and reached for the bag. Her hand closed around empty air as he pulled it back at the last second.

"What will you do with it?" His eyes narrowed as he thrust out his chin.

Mina hid her annoyance with a tight smile. "Haejang-guk —Korean oxblood soup. My grandmother's recipe." Her fangs itched to teach the human a lesson in customer service.

The man broke into a wide grin of sparse teeth and finally handed over the bag. Her hand seized the meal possessively.

"Just making sure you aren't a vampire lah!" he said with a hearty chuckle, his Singaporean accent tickling her eardrums. "You bring me some next time."

Mina repeated her polite smile before tightening the straps of her backpack and heading back to the main street. After a few blocks, she found a dark alcove, where she crouched and emptied the contents of the plastic bag into her metal water bottle. Trying not to gag, she chugged half of it. Rank though it was, cow's blood was cheap and easy to find as she back-packed her way down the South China Sea coast. The monster within her relaxed into the background of her consciousness, sated for the time being.

She'd been subsisting on the stuff since she escaped from Shanghai three months before. The world's only vampire-controlled territory had its perks, and access to cruelty-free human blood was at the top of the list. Mina's tongue cleaned the film off her teeth as she shoved the bottle back in her bag. Making do with such meager rations was a small price to pay to be away from a city so enamored with its own insidious pretense. Away from the vampire creator who demanded an obedient, unquestioning daughter—along with the consequences of failing to become one. Here she could be herself, whoever the hell that was anymore.

As Mina began the thirty-minute walk back to her capsule hotel—a splurge for her last night in Asia—the sidewalks came to life as the workday ended. She dodged a food cart that jutted from a narrow alley onto the walkway before her, the hawker wheeling it to a prime location before he flapped the canvas off. The sign on the cart advertised laksa, and the scent of lemongrass, fish sauce, and coconut grabbed her attention. Gods, she missed garlic, but at least she wasn't constrained to an all-liquid diet—not for another few centuries, at least.

Giving the curry cart a pass, she stopped at one selling satay instead. Mina let her fangs poke out as she tore the chicken-thigh chunks from their skewer, relishing the tang of the lime against the crunchy char of the meat. At the liminal time after sunset, before true night, she enjoyed wandering among the people, pretending to be one of them. They always seemed so content with the small pleasures. She imitated them, hoping one day she would feel like less of an imposter. A decade ago, she had been one of them. Reclaiming some of the joy of living shouldn't be too hard.

"Try some durian!" an enthusiastic auntie called, jumping off her plastic stool to offer a sample of yellow-gray lobes.

Mina dipped her head in apology as she hurried past, the ripe fruit assaulting her heightened olfactory senses.

In front of the hotel, Mina confronted the keypad lock with solemn determination. She had the code from her printed reservation document, but electronics could be touchy around vampires. Using a capped pen, she punched in the correct sequence of numbers and sighed in relief when the motor disengaged the dead bolt.

As Mina pushed through the door of the hotel, a waft of air conditioning chilled the sheen of humidity on her skin. She followed the signs to the women's half of the pod hotel and found her assigned number on a placard. The shade was pulled to the side, revealing a cubby with a single mattress and freshly turned-down white sheets. A terry cloth towel was folded at its foot. After weeks of sleeping behind garbage cans, it felt ridiculously resplendent that this entire capsule was hers for the night.

First order of business: a shower. Mina fished out a pair of flip-flops and her one change of clothes from her backpack before stowing it in the locker beneath the bed-in-the-wall. She grabbed the threadbare towel and made her way to the bathroom. Although she could hear faint rustling behind the privacy shades, the corridor of the hotel was blissfully absent of people and their voices.

The tiled room reeked of industrial cleaner, which she preferred to the alternative smells. Mina went into a shower stall and pulled the plastic curtain shut before hanging her towel on a hook. She pushed off her ball cap and yanked out the elastic tying back raven hair. Shorter tendrils fell messily around her face while the rest cascaded down her back. Mina finished disrobing balanced atop her sneakers then slid her feet into shower flip-flops.

She turned the faucet as hot as it would go before stepping into the haphazard spray. Scalding water rinsed layers of salt and dirt from her body, creating a murky puddle by a drain covered in a clump of brown hair that wasn't hers. Even for her middling height, Mina had to bend her knees to scrub her face under the showerhead. It felt wonderful. She was liberal in her use of the soap dispenser, and her skin was angry pink and gleaming by the time she toweled off.

Reclothed with her hair wound up in a towel, Mina made her way back to her pod, skirting around the women festooned in clubwear, ready for a night on the town. Perhaps in another life, she would have been one of them. Her youthful appearance still looked the part, but watching the exuberant women's excitement over a night of carefree fun, Mina couldn't have felt like a more different creature.

Her lungs still breathed, her heart still beat, and as long as she fed regularly, her skin was only slightly cool to the touch. Yet vampirism had left an indelible mark. Having freed herself from the claustrophobic social expectations of her Shanghai life, going to a gaudy club with migraine-inducing bass was the last way she wanted to spend an evening.

After crawling onto the mattress, Mina slid her travel documents out onto the bed: one economy ticket to Sydney, one tourist guide, and one counterfeit passport with a stapled pamphlet warning about the enforcement of capital punishment for drug possession and "acts of vampirism." The legalities of her existence outside Shanghai were tenuous at best, and on more than one occasion along her trek, she'd come close to being detained. The tracking dogs in Laos still haunted her nightmares. Australian laws were more forgiving than most, making it a place she might actually be able to stay and reclaim a normal life.

Mina imagined an off-the-books graveyard shift stocking minimart shelves near the beach—somewhere the radio played old pop songs and no one asked questions. A fifteen-minute break standing at the edge of the ocean, the surf lapping at her toes. She scrunched them with a small smile. That was a reasonable dream, wasn't it?

Her morning flight was the earliest available. She would ensconce herself in her dead-middle seat just as the sun rose. The window coatings would keep most of the UV rays from scorching her skin, and she'd lather on her ultra-SPF sunscreen for good measure. Thank gods for the sun-averse women of Asia and their commitment to cosmetic products of the highest standard.

Mina rolled onto her back, her wet hair splaying out around her on the pillow as she stared up at the stained ceiling an arm's length above. Ten years had passed since her arrival in Shanghai, ten years living under the stifling authority of Lian Zhang—the mastermind of the entire vampire-controlled territory... and a woman Mina had once loved.

Mina reckoned with the truth she could no longer outrun: she had asked for that life, begged for it, even. She'd so badly wanted to be cherished, to be a part of a family, that she crushed herself into the mold House Zhang demanded. Now, she realized how much of herself she'd lost in the process and how little it had given her in return.

Yet the last few months had proven Mina was capable even without the comforts afforded by Shanghai. She'd backpacked nearly six thousand kilometers while keeping herself fed and avoiding detection. She hadn't even had any accidents with humans despite the hunger—a true feat for someone still considered a fledgling vampire. Mina's solo travels had confirmed what she'd once barely dared to imagine: life existed outside Shanghai—outside of Lian. Sydney would be the finish line, the first step to a future where she could stop looking over her shoulder, where she might finally, *finally*, find something that felt like home.

THE NEXT MORNING, she was one of the first people at the airport—raised hood, dark sunglasses, and an oversized face mask for good measure. Mina felt slightly better after making it through security, her forged passport passing muster one final time. She sat at the gate on a stiff pleather cushion, hugging her canvas bag to her chest.

As the area filled up, a young family approached her cluster of seating. A boy, maybe four years old, popped onto the seat beside her.

"Hello. I like your backpack," he said, startling her with his candidness.

Mina eyed the small child, his light-brown hair and the fuzzy blue teddy bear bouncing on his lap as short legs swung freely.

His parents were bickering in hushed tones at the end of the aisle: "I told you I didn't want to stay with your parents this time."

Maybe it wouldn't be the worst thing to play babysitter for a minute. Mina angled toward the kid. "I like your bear."

"His name is Theo. He isn't afraid of airplanes," the child said with most serious conviction.

Mina's nose scrunched beneath her mask with amusement. He reminded her of her step-siblings when they'd been younger —bubbly and extroverted. She couldn't recall the last time she'd spoken to a child. She liked it more than she remembered.

"It's very nice to meet you both. Flying makes me a little

nervous sometimes, but I love seeing the fluffy clouds out the window. Do you get to sit by the window?"

"Yeah! I do!"

"Sometimes, you even get to see the airplane wing. That's really fun."

"Really?" The boy's eyes widened like he'd been let in on the most glorious secret. It made Mina's chest prickle with a strange warmth. The boy gave her an unguarded grin before going back to playing with his bear.

When planning her next move post-Shanghai, she had briefly considered finding her parents in Korea. But she couldn't imagine either would be glad to see her after over a decade of silence. She wondered if they had held a funeral for her, if her dad had remarried, if her grandmother was still alive. She wasn't prepared for the answers to any of those questions. Going back to the US, the country she'd grown up in, had been another possibility... one that seemed like moving backward. Trying somewhere new was for the best, she decided resolutely. Somewhere untainted by ghosts from the past.

When the time finally came to queue for boarding, Mina took a deep breath and got in line, documents in hand. *This is it. The last hurdle to a new life.*

She stepped up to the scanner and placed her barcode beneath the strobing red light. A two-tone rejection sounded as a larger light flashed red, stinging her eyes. *Am I interfering with the electronics?* Mina moved her fingers back to the edge of the ticket and tried the scanner one more time and got another obnoxious rejection.

"Please step aside, miss, and let the other passengers board. We'll get you sorted out at the end."

"There shouldn't be anything to sort. I have a paid seat on

this flight." She tried the scanner a third time, the end of the ticket trembling with her hands. Did she dare try to compel him to let her through?

As the air pressed in around her, feeling sticky and wrong, a floral scent met her nose: jasmine perfume.

No.

Mina's head snapped to the right as a hand rested on her shoulder, fingertips digging in with enough force to bruise.

"There you are, my love. You know this isn't where you should be."

The silken voice stole the breath from Mina's lungs as she gazed up at the face of Lady Lian Zhang. The woman stood nearly a head taller than Mina. She wore a flowy crepe suit, her chin-length hair neatly styled away from her calculating expression.

How is she here? Why is she here? After months, Mina had assumed if the woman were going to retrieve her, it would have happened already. Frozen in stunned confusion, Mina took in the calm authority of the woman's presence. Seeing Lian again was—Mina's chest constricted against the wave of warm nostalgia. *No. She doesn't control you anymore.*

"Let go of me!" She wrested her shoulder out of Lian's grasp. *I'm not going back. She can't make me go back.*

The woman gave her a look of mild irritation before reaching for Mina once more.

Rising panic spurred her to action, and Mina's fist cracked against Lian's chin—a hollow, sickening jolt of contact that didn't feel nearly good enough. Silence fell over the gate, all eyes upon them, while the gate agents exchanged nervous glances. A lock of dark hair had fallen over Lian's face, masking her expression save for a sinister-sweet smile tugging at her lips.

A shiver raced down Mina's spine as she realized the leverage she'd surrendered.

"Do I need to call security?" the gate agent interjected, the phone already in his hand. His eyes darted between the pair as though not sure whom he would be calling security for.

"There's no need for that," Lian replied with unbothered confidence, smoothing back her hair. "My daughter is... troubled, but I think she's done with her outburst now. Aren't you?"

Mina's lungs pumped with short, anxious breaths. Terror overtook her rational thoughts as she surveyed the gate for any way out. Gate agents blocked the jet bridge, and the line of irritated passengers stretched behind her. The little boy with the teddy bear hid behind his dad's legs, staring at Mina as if *she* were the violent monster. And worst of all, standing next to Lian's cool poise and polished attire, she did probably look like a problematic runaway kid.

Mina shut her eyes tightly, reconciling how close freedom felt with how impossible it had become. With a victorious smirk, Lian's fingers wrapped around her wrist with an iron grip and yanked her away from the gate. Glances from annoyed passengers followed them—their boarding process delayed for all of thirty seconds. Chancing one last look back at the jet bridge she was supposed to be standing on, Mina watched as the boy and his teddy bear were lifted into the arms of his dad, a smile on his face.

"Please, Lian. Please don't make me go back," she implored the indomitable force dragging her away. Her words were little more than incoherent babble. "I can't be a part of that city anymore. I don't want to live with y—"

Lian leaned down to hiss in her ear, never stopping their

forward progress, "*Enough*. I was patient with this escapade of yours, but it's over. You are far too young to be on your own. We can discuss it in another decade or two—for now, you are coming home to Shanghai."

A steady tremor settled into Mina's core and spread to her limbs as Lian towed her away from her dreams of a future of her own.

2

The airport was in full morning-bustle mode—business travelers with their rollaboards, tired vacationers in pajamas, and wailing infants in strollers. The odor of old grease mingled with the scent of too many humans as they passed the food court. Lian and Mina walked for at least twenty minutes to a different terminal altogether, where Mina clearly stood out as the scruffiest passenger.

The gate agent there didn't scan tickets. She waved them right through onto the tarmac with a welcoming hand. Lian finally let go of Mina to wrap a pashmina scarf around her own head and neck. The wind pulled at Mina's clothing as she squinted through her sunglasses at the early dawn light. The roar of departing jets was a deafening buzz competing with the sound of static in Mina's own mind. After so many months of successfully being on her own, this *couldn't* be happening.

Mina stood numbly as Lian proceeded toward a private plane, one emblazoned with Zhang Enterprises. The walkway and plane stairs were covered with a protective awning.

"Come along, Mina," Lian said, impatience growing in her voice.

Mina's feet wouldn't move as water gathered in her eyes. She clutched the straps of her backpack so tightly that her knuckles hurt. There was no question whether Lian could force her to return. Belying her forty-something appearance, Lady Zhang was at least seven hundred years old and quite possibly the most powerful vampire in existence. Mina, her fledgling of ten years, stood no chance. And still, she couldn't make herself move.

"I'm not going back," she said, a notable tremor in her voice.

Lian turned back around, the woman's expression unreadable. She took a step toward Mina, her gaze softening. "The night you left..." Lian started. "I regret how that evening transpired. I should not have been so harsh with you." A rare gentleness showed in her round obsidian eyes, and it tugged at Mina's heart.

Mina fought against the sensation, one Lian had manipulated into existence. "No. It's not just about the way you treat me. That... *city* you've built. Being a vampire there... I *won't* be a part of that."

Lian squared her shoulders, a frown pulling at her lips. "That *issue* is confined to House Federov, I assure you. They have been sanctioned by the remainder of the council, and ultimately, I aim to see them eradicated from the city." Lian rubbed her fingers together as she glanced toward the jet. Oblique shadows played on her cheekbones. "Even my power has its limitations, Mina," she added quietly. "Come home with me. We can make Shanghai a better place together." Lian extended a hand, palm upward in invitation.

Mina's heart thundered in her chest. She didn't believe one word of the conniving woman's apology. She had been witness to Lian's two-faced nature for too many years. And when she thought of returning to her old life, completely stifled by the stringent demands of her position in the Zhang household, breathing became hard.

"I'm not going back," Mina said plainly, determination finally evident in her voice.

A sneer twisted Lian's expression as she opened her mouth. Mina didn't want to hear it. Her feet launched her from the shadowed walkway into the searing heat of the sunlight. Everywhere it landed against her bare skin—cheeks, forehead, and backs of her hands—it sizzled with blistering force. Still, it affected her a great deal less than it would her ancient creator. Mina's only hope was that the sun would deter Lian from following. It *had* to be enough.

A baggage cart cruised by a few dozen meters away. It appeared to move in slow motion as a burst of supernatural speed carried Mina toward it. Her focus locked on that bastion of safety—her singular goal—as she willed her legs to move faster.

With a terrible lurch, she felt herself being dragged backward, first by the backpack and then by the sweatshirt. Mina's feet left the ground as she flew into the concrete of the airport wall, her head hitting it with a disorienting smack. Lian pinned her there, the woman's face inches from hers, red tinging her irises with anger. A charred hand held Mina in place. The skin had blistered and sloughed off in several places, leaving yellowish, bloody tissue exposed.

"This is *not* a negotiation," Lian snarled. "You *will* be

coming home with me. How unpleasant your life will be when we get there is entirely dependent on your compliance. You knew when you joined this family the commitment was for an eternity."

The power in Lian's presence hit Mina with a spike of adrenaline while the smell of jasmine perfume washed over her like a soporific. It had been years since Lian could compel Mina outright, but the woman's words and presence still held an unnatural sway over her psyche. Despite having distanced herself physically and emotionally for three months, Mina felt a critical part of her internal resistance crumble upon standing in front of her once more. At one point, a home within the safety of Lian's domain was all Mina had dreamed of. Regardless of Mina's waning illusions that such a place existed, Lian was right: she'd known becoming a vampire meant forever.

Dropping her head, Mina weakly muttered, "Yes, Lady Zhang."

Lian let go of Mina's jacket with a sharp exhalation, a sticky trail of plasma stringing off her grotesque appendage. With a wave of nausea, Mina was reminded of a childhood friend after an unfortunate deep fryer accident.

"Better."

Lian gestured toward the plane. And Mina went.

THE CABIN of the private jet contained a dozen beige seats. A pair to the right had a small table between them, covered with stacks of paper, Lian's reading glasses, and a fountain pen.

Twin flight attendants in matching green pencil skirts and

pillbox hats gave Mina a warm smile that morphed into something horrified as Lian stepped in behind her. Exposed bone peeked through the charred remains of the skin of her damaged hand.

"My goodness, Lady Zhang. Let me call a medical—"

"No. We're already behind schedule. Inform the captain I expect to make up the time in the air. A napkin with ice will do."

"Right away."

Mina took a few tentative steps down the aisle, unsure where to sit and starting to feel the adrenaline crash of failure. This wasn't the plane she was supposed to be on. She was supposed to—

Her backpack was torn from her shoulders, her arms contorting painfully backward as Lian freed it with her functional hand.

"Sit down."

Mina dropped into the nearest seat, her emotions a sludge of shame and regret. She watched as her bag was unzipped and the contents spilled across one of the seats. Lian sorted through the items like some lurid collection. Heat rose to Mina's cheeks as Lian pushed the shower shoes aside, recoiled after sniffing the bottle of bovine blood residue, and snorted after flipping to the first page of the fake passport. Lian even pulled out the small roll of cash from the inside of a used sock.

The spritely attendant came back with the requested first-aid items.

"Take this garbage away." Lian gestured loosely to the items on the seat before extending the wad of cash carefully held between two tapered fingers. "For your discretion."

The uniformed woman was smart enough to accept it

without comment before gathering Mina's treasures and making herself scarce.

Anger welled in Mina's chest at having her things discarded so casually. Those were *hers*—the first that weren't simply on loan from Lady Zhang in such a long time. She swallowed the emotion as she turned toward the window, its shade drawn against the daylight. Mina pulled off her sunglasses and face mask, vestiges of a failed plan. Her hair hung in sheets around her face, cocooning her against this reality: she'd lost. How she felt about it was irrelevant.

Recycled air blew steadily down on the flushed skin of Mina's face as the cabin door was sealed in preparation for departure. Lian took a seat in her makeshift office, analyzing a document with a steely expression. Already, the woman had moved on to the next problem since her errant daughter had been subdued.

The engines whirred to life, and the plane lurched onto the runway. Mina was going back to Shanghai. As she contemplated her return, her last night in the city wormed its way into her consciousness. One she'd tried to forget. The night of the Federov party.

MINA HADN'T WANTED to go, but her friend Dmitri had begged her. It was her last chance to convince the human that vampire life was not as glamorous as it appeared before he went through with his transformation. Even though she'd known him only a year, she already felt a protective impulse to keep the younger man's sweet nature from being tainted by this place and its inhabitants.

The open layout of the penthouse floor of the Shanghai skyscraper gave the voguish vampires an opportunity to be seen in their extravagant finery. Tall women in body-skimming dresses dripped with diamonds, while broody men with over-applied hair gel sipped glasses of vodka and roared at each other's jokes.

"I'll get us some drinks." Dmitri set off toward the bar, doing his best to hide a limp. Mina trailed after him, nodding her greetings to others who pretended to know her, eager to make an acquaintance with someone at the pinnacle of the social pyramid.

"Zdorovye!" Dmitri said as he handed her a highball glass of fizzy liquid garnished with a lime twist.

"Gānbēi!"

They raised their glasses, sharing a covert smile before taking a sip.

"Do you ever think about how crazy it is that we're here? You know, not just in Shanghai, but part of this society?" Dmitri took in the modern finery with an appreciative grin.

House Federov tended to embrace contemporary styles—sleek, minimal furniture and punchy, abstract art. It all clearly spoke to Dmitri's idea of luxury though Mina much preferred the traditional grandeur of Zhang Manor. The Vasa penthouse —Dmitri's prospective new home—was yet a third example of overindulgent vampire style: Regency-era gilded maximalism at its worst.

"Mmm, maybe. Probably more so when I first got here." Mina cut her eyes to Dmitri. The boy's adorably crooked teeth made him look bashful when he smiled. She could easily see why August had chosen him, if not why Dmitri had chosen August. Then again, Mina knew the head of the Vasa House could be convincingly enchanting when he wanted to be, for those who didn't see through his gentlemanly ruse.

"Where I come from, entire families sleep in a single room, wearing coats during the winter for warmth. I thought St. Petersburg was impressive when I moved there for the ballet academy. But this... this is on a whole different level." Dmitri grabbed a passing appetizer of inky-black roe dolloped on a cracker as if to emphasize the point.

"I guess I know what you mean. But Dmitri," Mina started tentatively. "Have you thought about what it will mean to never go home again? How August might change once you can't leave?"

"Ah, Mina. Not this again." Dmitri gave a dramatic eye roll as he shoved the rest of the cracker in his mouth. "August isn't like Lian," he said as he chewed.

Mina shook her head at his innocence. "He's not half as charming as you think he is. All of the old ones are expert manipulators. They had to be, to get humans to let them feed, back before Shanghai." Her tone came out more exasperated than she intended.

"Mina, you don't get it," Dmitri spat, rounding on her. "This is my only chance to fix my ankle and dance again. If I refuse his offer, I will spend the rest of my miserable life dragging this foot behind me, working a fishing boat in the Arctic. Is that what you want for me?"

Mina faltered at the intensity of his accusation. "*No, Dima.* I just... can't watch you do this to yourself." She knew what it was like to be young and enamored by this life, but unlike Dmitri, no one had warned her of the drawbacks. Mina was trapped, but Dmitri didn't have to be.

"Maybe you had other options before you became a

vampire, and you regret not taking them." A muscle tensed in Dmitri's jaw. "But I have nothing left to lose."

Mina stared, dumbstruck at his refusal to see the consequences of giving up his freedom. As heads of the Vasa and Zhang Houses, two of the eight founding houses of Shanghai, August and Lian wielded power within the city that was nearly absolute. That didn't make for the most flexible or understanding guardians.

As she opened her mouth to try to explain that for the hundredth time, a boisterous group of men approached them, greeting Dmitri in Russian with hearty handshakes. Perhaps they should take a beat to cool off anyway. Mina drifted away to a corner of the room to contemplate a different strategy to convince her friend to see what he was giving up.

Only a few minutes into her quiet contemplation, Mina, too, was approached by a group of Federov vampires. She mingled politely, inquiring about Elena's recent trip to Porto and Sasha's new venture into grain futures. In turn, Mina plied them with an informed review of the Beijing Opera's latest production and her thoughts on the tasting course at the new Parisian restaurant. She knew they all hoped for a morsel of trivia about what Lian Zhang was up to, but Mina was far too careful to reveal anything. Discretion was paramount in this city of snakes.

Out of the corner of her eye, she watched Dmitri down one shot after another with his new comrades. They were getting the lightweight human drunk on purpose, but she didn't feel particularly inclined to intervene on his behalf. She would let him have that one bad decision and the accompanying hangover.

"Have you been to see Mikhail yet?" Vladimir asked her with a sly grin.

"Mikhail is here?" she asked, surprised.

Although not the head of House Federov, he might as well have been, with the influence he held. If she left without saying hello, the offense might be serious enough to cause political repercussions for House Zhang. *Dammit.*

"I think he might be having a bite to eat upstairs." Vladimir drained the rest of his champagne before grabbing another.

Mina felt like she was being baited though she couldn't pinpoint why. "All right, but then I really must be going. Keep an eye on Dmitri while I'm gone, would you?"

Vladimir followed Mina's gaze to the inebriated human. "He has no idea what he's getting himself into, does he?"

"No. None at all."

Mina took the elevator to the upper floor. Softly thudding bass drew her attention to the end of a long hallway. As she walked along the art-lined wall, her patent heels clicked on the polished concrete. When she rounded the corner, prepared for more banal pleasantries, she froze at the sight before her.

Mikhail and his partner, Nadezhda, were both sprawled on an angular chaise lounge, fangs buried in a scantily clad woman. Between her glassy eyes and her limp posture, Mina thought she might be dead until the woman blinked slowly. Two more humans whimpered in dog cages at the edge of the room. Their expressions of pure terror mirrored Mina's own response at stumbling upon such a scene.

"Mina?" Mikhail asked in a husky voice, breaking his feed and wiping a trail of blood off his chin with the back of his hand. "I would never have expected to see *you* here."

Does he mean on this floor or at this party?

"Care to join us? This one is quite exquisite." He stroked the cheek of the unresponsive woman beneath him.

Mina did her best to hide her abject horror at the scene before her. This side of vampirism simply did not exist in Shanghai. The donation system was in place to avoid exactly this sort of depraved violence. Consenting humans and vampires might share a covert meal, but nothing here looked consensual to Mina. This was an unforgivable assault, if not outright murder.

"My apologies for the interruption." Mina lingered at the end of the hallway, her voice pitched too high, her head buzzing with alarm. "I couldn't leave without saying hello, but I must be off now. Lovely party, Mikhail. I'll be sure you receive an invite for the next of Lian's soirées." She glanced at the humans in the cages. They clutched each other's hands through the bars, silently shaking.

"I look forward to it." Mikhail gave her a self-satisfied smile before lunging at his meal with renewed vigor. A meek gasp escaped the woman as her skin was punctured once more. Mina fought nausea as she made her way back down to her own human charge. First things first: she needed to get Dmitri out of here. Second, she had to find some way to help the humans upstairs. She didn't have enough influence on her own to demand anything in Mikhail's territory, but she knew someone who certainly would. She needed to get Lian.

"Dmitri. We're leaving. Now." Mina tried to keep the concern out of her voice.

"Whaat? But we're havvving so much fun!" Dmitri threw an arm around her shoulder. "Have a drink!" The intoxicated man shoved a shot glass at her, sloshing vodka on her dress.

"Nope. Time to go. You don't want August to be mad, do you?"

Dmitri pouted. "Nooo... s'pose not."

She steered him to the car and got his jelly body into it just in time for him to pass out. When they reached the Vasa apartments, she was able to rouse him just enough to get him to the front door. The entire car ride, her head spun with visions of Mikhail and his *meal*. Vladimir had known she would encounter the unsavory scene when he sent her upstairs. He was likely using her as a pawn to bring sanctions against Mikhail, perhaps trying to clear the way for his own political agenda. Even so, Mina knew she needed to tell her creator—to try to stop Mikhail's atrocity in progress even if she was being manipulated into doing so.

When she finally arrived at Zhang Manor, shortly after one in the morning, Mina jogged up the stairs to the main floor of the residence. She followed the sound of Lian's silky voice to the sitting room. As she grew closer, she could make out two additional male voices with northern accents. Mina tensed— Lian would not appreciate being distracted from her company, no doubt an extension of an earlier business meeting.

After a bracing inhale, Mina rounded the corner, taking in the pine-green military uniforms of the men on the sofa. "Lady Zhang, please forgive the interruption, but there is something I urgently need to speak to you about." She punctuated the request with a bow. The formal gesture was anachronistic in modern Shanghai, but Mina still found herself deferring to the hierarchical traditions instilled by her grandparents.

Lian reclined in a deep chair with a glass of scotch balanced on the arm. The woman considered Mina, her relaxed demeanor lapsing into its analytical default. "General Chu, please meet my youngest fledgling, Mina Park."

The man nodded in Mina's direction with a guarded look. His gray hair was neatly parted, and his skin sagged at the jowls.

"Please, it will only take a few minutes," she entreated Lian once more.

A twitch of the woman's rose-colored lips told Mina of her growing impatience. "As you can see, I am presently occupied," the woman dismissed, turning back to the men on the couch. "Now, General, you were explaining your staffing concerns with the Beijing offices?"

"Please, Lian." Mina took a few steps into the room.

The woman's gaze snapped up with rising fury, red ringing the deep black of her irises.

"Lady Zhang." General Chu stood stiffly from the couch, tucking his hat underneath one arm. His compatriot followed suit. "I think it's time to conclude this meeting in any case, as we seem to be at an impasse. You know what our requirements are for this deal to proceed."

"Very well," Lian said, rising slowly. "Please know negotiations are still open." She gestured toward the front door and saw the gentlemen out. Mina stood transfixed at the edge of the living room as she waited for the blowback for her disruption. She would weather Lian's inevitable anger. Mikhail must be stopped while the humans might still be alive.

As the door clicked shut, Lian turned toward Mina with the calm scrutiny of a viper. "This better be good, pet." Her voice was dark with menace.

Mina swallowed, shrinking as the woman leisurely closed the distance between them. Lian's height advantage made Mina want to cower that much more.

"Well?"

"I'm sorry, my lady—"

The backhanded blow caught Mina off guard, a starburst of pain blossoming along her jaw where the woman's knuckles had struck. Mina kept her head lowered in submission as the disorientation waned.

"I have no use for apologies. Now, explain yourself."

"My lady," Mina began, hating the quiver in her voice. "I was at the Federov party tonight, where I encountered Mikhail. He was..."

The scene flashed before her eyes again, the terrified expressions of the humans whose hours were numbered if she couldn't convince Lian to intercede. Yet as she stood there, face stinging from the slap of the incensed woman, crushing self-doubt rendered her mute.

"Speak, you insolent child," Lady Zhang snarled.

"He had a human, with more in cages. And he was... feeding," Mina managed to say.

"How many were there this time?" Lian asked, her gaze calculating.

This time?

"Three that I saw, but who knows—"

"You jeopardized my entire bid for Beijing for the lives of three humans?" Lian's lips contorted into a humorless smile. "Do you have any idea the consequences and tradeoffs I face in a single day?"

Outrage coursed through Mina at the callous response. Lian had always upheld the harmonious imperative of the city at an ideological level. Enduring her volatile moods was tolerable, knowing Lian maintained the ethical backbone of the human blood-donation system in this city. *But if she can't be bothered to act when her citizens are in danger, then what good is her theoretical altruism?*

"If you already knew this kind of thing was happening in Shanghai, why haven't you stopped it?" Mina asked, a startling fury to her words. "Do you really need another city if you can't keep even one in line?" she added, her voice low with challenge.

Lian's nostrils flared in anger before the second blow sent Mina sprawling to the floor with a pained gasp. The entire side of her head, from her ear to her nose, throbbed from the repeated abuse. She fought the urge to caress the injury. Her eyes watered, more out of reaction to the physical trauma than any emotional response.

"You forget your place in this house," Lian said with a dangerous quietness as she knelt beside Mina. "If you *ever* interrupt my work again for a matter as trivial as this, I will bury you in that coffin for a month. Do you understand?"

Mina propped herself up on her arms as her dizziness settled. The threat of the coffin had her breaths coming in uneven hitches as if she were already enclosed in the dank interior of the thick wooden planks. Tears slipped from her eyes at the thought of being confined to solitary nothingness for an entire month.

Lian's hand locked around her chin like a vice, dragging Mina's face around to meet her blood-red glare.

"Did you honestly think when you became a vampire that no humans would be harmed in the process?" Lady Zhang ran a cool finger along the side of Mina's flushed cheek, her gaze raking the reddened skin with possessive lust. "Get out of my sight before I give you a real reason for those pretty tears."

Mina clung to her crumbling mental fortifications as she stood, bowed, and climbed the stairs to her room. As soon as she shut the door, her knees buckled. The darkness swallowed her tears as they rolled off her chin. *What did I do to make her hate me so much?*

When Lian invited Mina into her world—her utopian Shanghai—it was a dream come true. After living here a decade, Mina had come to realize the paradise was only a surface-level illusion. Seeing vampires attacking humans wasn't the first instance of abuse of power she'd seen in this city—it was simply the worst. For years, Mina had pretended not to notice the back-channel negotiations, the bribes, and the people who occasionally vanished along the way. This time, she couldn't.

As for Lian... Mina couldn't remember the last time the woman looked at her with anything but disappointment. Whatever traits she'd originally used to seduce the woman no longer seemed to exist in her eyes.

I have no future here, Mina realized with startling clarity. *I won't be complicit in the corruption any longer. And Lian... will be glad to be rid of me.* Mina might not be able to save Dmitri, but maybe she could still get herself out of this mistake.

A week passed before Mina had organized the forged passport and subtly skimmed enough money from her investment accounts to get herself somewhere far away. When she left, she did so without looking back.

MINA OPENED her eyes to a crystal glass of water being set on the flimsy tray unfolded from her armrest. The liquid rippled with the drone of the engines.

Somewhere in the cabin behind her, Lian's voice spoke into

the phone, clipped and efficient as it ordered the world around her: "Either reduce your emissions, or your operating permits will be revoked indefinitely."

Shanghai loomed, as did the thought of reentering Mina's old life. She could only imagine what new torments Lian had devised as retribution for her betrayal.

Mina shut her eyes once more. It didn't matter. She would endure it until she found another way out. That was all she could do.

3

Javier checked his watch and noted he'd officially been standing in the immigration line at Shanghai airport for five hours. And that was *after* the twenty he'd spent getting there from San Francisco. Rounding the corner to the customs area had been an enormous sucker punch. It contained a veritable barn of people snaking through seemingly endless lanes separated by nylon straps.

Only one row from the front, Javier drew a weighty manila envelope out of his leather messenger bag, praying that he'd made enough copies of each tedious form. The invitation letter from the Independent Territory of Shanghai government came with a long list of requirements for entry: health, legal, and finally, documentation. Any violations would be grounds for immediate deportation back to the traveler's country of origin at the traveler's expense. Javier couldn't let that happen. This was his only shot to find out what had happened to his sister, Eva, and he wasn't going home without answers.

He watched the banks of counters like a hawk for the flashing sign that indicated his turn. As soon as that light blinked, he shot forward. The middle-aged official behind the counter had a bowl cut and severe acne scarring. His gloved hand reached expectantly into the pocket underneath a plexiglass divider. Javier greeted him with a smile and slid his navy passport book over. The gold-foil eagle flashed in the fluorescent lighting as the man picked it up and scanned the first page. A summary of the relevant demographics flashed on a screen: Javier Robles, male, twenty-seven years old, born-and-raised US citizen. The picture made him look overly young with his unruly brown hair, clean-shaven face, and silly grin. Javier stood at the ready for any additional document the man might request—everything was binder clipped and sticky tabbed for easy retrieval.

However, after a cursory glance at the passport page with his stapled entry visa, complete with shimmery watermark, the man snapped the passport book shut and slid it back under the divider.

"Wrong line. New donor line there," the official said in stilted English as he waved toward the far side of the room.

Javier's jaw dropped. "The person I asked earlier said I was supposed to be in this line."

"Wrong line," the man repeated indifferently.

Javier looked back at the mass of weary travelers before turning back to the customs official. The man had already flicked on his "available" sign again. Confounded, he wheeled his suitcase back to the end of the line toward the general area the man had waved at.

Through a door, a whole new pen of people was revealed.

On the wall was a bilingual sign reading New Donor Entry. Helpful. Resigned, he filed into the new queue, the one he should've been in all along.

After only one more hour, Javier reached the next open counter. This official was younger and had a satin ribbon clipped to her high ponytail. He did not smile as he handed over his passport this time. She asked for several of the documents he'd brought, exchanging them for a new document of his own. He wondered at the splotches of red ink stamps of characters he couldn't interpret—they were his first sign of forward progress in this Kafkaesque bureaucracy.

Next, he retrieved his suitcase from a large baggage claim area. He found the bag between carousels, a nubby brown tweed with a red ribbon tied to the handle. When he asked his mom to borrow it for an extended "business trip" abroad, she'd looked so proud of her son, a successful software engineer at one of the big five tech companies in Silicon Valley, headed to open a new office in Taiwan. He didn't have the courage to tell her that he'd been laid off the month before or that he was really coming to Shanghai to find his sister. His mother had a penchant for melodrama, and she knew exactly which tears to cry to get Javier to change his mind. As much as he hated lying to her, he'd had no choice.

He fed the suitcase through a large X-ray machine that mercifully had no line. Halfway through its journey, a red light flashed above the detector. Javier shut his eyes in frustration. *What can it possibly be now?*

An inspector lugged his case over to a dented metal table and unzipped the main compartment. The man proceeded to rifle through Javier's clothes with little regard for the very careful packing job. Finally, the scrawny employee on a power trip pulled out his canvas Dopp kit pinched between his fingers. Like a magician reaching into a hat, he stuck a gloved hand in and triumphantly produced Javier's electric toothbrush.

"No electronics," the man said sternly.

"Yeah, I know. No mobile electronics. In what country is a toothbrush a mobile electronic device?" *This is getting ridiculous.*

Javier watched, dumbfounded, as the man grabbed a clear plastic bag and dropped his toothbrush inside. He applied a tamper-proof seal over the top, scribbled a signature, and confiscated it to a locked cabinet. When the man didn't return, Javier repacked his suitcase before closing it. "The bastard really took my toothbrush," he muttered to no one in particular.

At some point, Javier was going to need a technical explanation for why electronics were such a big deal here in Shanghai. Most sources cited vague "vampire sensitivities," but as an engineer, he needed more explanation than that. Whatever the true reason was, it must have been very serious if immigration was tasked with keeping dangerous used toothbrushes from making it into the country.

Javier wondered what absurd administrative dance he would have to perform next as he followed the stream of people through a hallway divided by a metal barricade. It opened to another large room with medical privacy screens and a distinct antiseptic smell. Oh joy.

He exchanged more papers with a tired-looking woman at a podium. She gave him a set of stickers with his name and several alphanumeric codes, along with a numbered plastic chip that indicated which of the privacy-screened booths he should wait at. While Javier queued outside the gauzy white barrier, he heard a pained grunt from within and winced in sympathy. Surely the worst he could expect was a few needle pokes, right?

The previous occupant must have exited out the back, because when the nurse ushered him in, the cubicle was empty. The intense smell of rubbing alcohol piqued his anxiety. A metal rolling cart lined with a blue paper towel displayed several syringes in sterile packaging. A larger contraption Javier didn't recognize sat on the tray as well. The exam started routinely enough: taking his height, weight, blood pressure, and temperature. With that out of the way, the nurse gestured toward the single plastic seat, which Javier took with uncertainty. The man hadn't uttered a word the entire time. Muted by the language barrier, Javier's palms grew sweaty with apprehension.

The nurse took two vials of blood and gestured for Javier to unbutton his shirt to provide access to his shoulder. The man's hands were cold on his skin, even through the latex gloves, as he swabbed the injection site. There was no warning before the poke or explanation of what the shot was for. Javier hoped this wasn't the point when he went to sleep and woke up missing a kidney. Or just didn't wake up.

When the nurse finally grabbed the large contraption off the cart, Javier swallowed. Next, an unexpected thing happened: the nurse ran an alcohol-soaked pad over the shell of his right ear.

"What the hell, man?" Javier ducked away from the gloved hand.

An irritated expression flashed over the nurse's face as though Javier was being the unreasonable one.

"Ear tag," he replied and pointed at a small metal square pierced through the cartilage of his own right ear.

"I'm good without any jewelry, thanks." Javier shook his head for emphasis.

"Required." The man blinked slowly, still holding the piercing gun upright as he awaited Javier's inevitable capitulation.

Javier felt an irrational level of distress at the prospect of being violated with an unwanted earring from a man he couldn't communicate with. The exhaustion and nerves weren't helping, but Javier considered leaping out of the chair and dragging his suitcase upstream until he could find someone who would sell him a ticket back to the US. *You didn't come this far to give up on finding Eva because of a silly piercing, did you?*

"Okay." Javier turned his head straight, allowing the nurse access to his ear again. At least he got a countdown this time.

"Sān, èr, yī!"

The mechanical *ka-chunk* of the gun overshadowed the actual pain of the metal post running through his ear. A flood of heat followed. The metal square the size of a fingernail made him feel unreasonably lopsided.

"Hǎo, hǎo."

Javier appreciated the man's attempt at bedside manner, or at least that's what it sounded like. He still didn't understand a word of Chinese. When the man gestured that he could leave through the back of the curtain, Javier numbly grabbed his suitcase and exited. At least that must mean he was getting close, since they'd given him his own asset tag.

In what must be the last stage of what he'd mentally dubbed the Shanghai Entry Trials, Javier entered an auditorium filled with plastic chairs facing a projector screen. "Next orientation at 19:00," it read in several languages. His watch showed 6:49 p.m. He could stay awake for eleven minutes— probably.

When the presenter walked on stage with a microphone thirty minutes later, Javier's patience with this process had grown remarkably thin. All his human wants and needs had been whittled away to something halfway familiar to eat, an enormous bottle of water, and a bed.

Javier sat up in his seat to read the English subtitles on the screen above the head of the annoyingly tall person in front of him.

"Welcome to Shanghai! We are very excited for you to join the most prosperous city in the world to fulfill the critical role of providing sustenance for our vampire patrons." The peppy voice matched the vigorous appearance of the presenter. "In exchange for your blood, donated at six-week intervals, you will be provided with free housing and an annual stipend of ¥300,000."

The crowd perked up at hearing the figure. Javier tried to run the conversion through his sleep-deprived brain. *Something like $40,000?* That wasn't much, compared to his developer's salary back home, but it wasn't hard to imagine it was incentive enough for the others here. *And you don't have a salary back home anymore. Remember?*

"However, in order to maintain our thriving city, we also need you to contribute your intellectual and physical skills to our economy. In this way, we will all enjoy the rewards of Shanghai." On the screen flashed images of diverse and attractive people working together, donating blood together, and dining together. Javier thought they were laying it on a bit thick with the propaganda—everyone in the audience was already sold, after all.

"Within the first two weeks, you will need to find employment and complete your first blood donation. Resource centers are available to help you integrate into the city. On your way out, you will collect your housing assignment along with a brochure containing information on the amenities of your new neighborhood. Welcome and congratulations!"

That's it?

The mundane orientation was a comical introduction to a place US news outlets claimed was slaughtering tens of thousands each year to feed its exploding vampire population. Thirty years ago, the pivotal port city had been infiltrated and taken over in a span of less than a week. Subversive mind control of key politicians and military leaders in China made the vampire victory decisive. After a few months of failed attacks on the vampire insurrectionists, a truce was agreed upon that guaranteed certain human rights within the city while allowing vampires to maintain control of the territory.

Despite media fearmongering and travel bans, the appeal of a place to live and a guaranteed job kept humans flocking to the city. That was almost certainly why Eva had decided to come sixteen years earlier. Javier remembered the day he'd stumbled into her unlocked social media account on her old phone. A message thread with a friend indicated Shanghai was her destination. The distress of the revelation had been gut-wrenching, both that his older sister had taken the risk of running to a vampire-infested territory and that she had felt it was her best option. Even though his sister was seven years his senior and generally kind of a dick, she was still family.

Ever since he turned eighteen, Javier had applied every year for an opportunity to come to Shanghai to search for her. And every year, he'd received a rejection—until the past summer. The letter came less than two weeks after a sweeping round of tech layoffs, and Javier decided it was now or never.

Lukewarm applause came from the front row as the projector was updated to read "Next orientation 20:00." Javier grabbed his suitcase and sprinted to the front of the room, trying to beat the fifty or so other people ambling out. He provided his name at a table and received a card with a giant number and an address. Javier accepted one of the aforementioned brochures on his way out the door and stuffed it into his messenger bag along with the mélange of other documents he'd collected that day.

The final set of doors emptied onto an asphalt parking lot filled with a horde of shuttles arranged in lines marked with giant signs numbered one through ten. Javier gulped in the sticky air and petroleum fumes. He'd never missed the cool, crisp air of California summer evenings so much in his life.

THE SHUTTLE DROPPED him off before a concrete block of apartments, one in a file of similarly shaped buildings that extended far into the smoggy distance. Multicolored laundry flapped from the balconies, and the cries of a small child echoed from an unseen location. The only greenery was a scrubby collection of bushes lining the front of the structure.

Javier had been awake for well over twenty-four hours when he shambled into the entryway of the building. Flashes of colors from a small TV screen illuminated the faces of three men sitting behind a counter.

"Shénme shì?"

Too tired to try to breach the language barrier verbally, Javier unfolded his housing assignment paper and slid it across the counter.

"Duì, duì." One of the men nodded. His head was bald on top, leaving a horseshoe ring of gray hair around the perimeter. Wild, bushy eyebrows waved like tildes. The old guy patted one of his buddies on the shoulder as he stood and remarked on the TV show, with a chuckle. From a box on the wall with a myriad of dangling copper, the man selected a key before relocking the cabinet.

"Zǒu ba!" he said loudly to Javier, pointing down the hallway. Javier mentally logged the expression: let's go. The man hummed to himself as he led the way to an elevator. Javier could've hugged the man in relief at an obstacle-free encounter.

The elevator opened on the twenty-second floor. Food smells from different dinners collided in an odd miasma of spices. Garlic and ginger were salient, but also allspice and maybe saffron. It was hard to tell over the underlying seafood odor that Javier was sure would have smelled better if he had some to sample. He wondered how many of his neighbors would be foreigners, like himself. He hoped to find someone who spoke English or even Spanish. His mute existence was becoming lonely already.

After a brief tour of the dated but spacious one-bedroom apartment, the man rambled a string of words that meant nothing to Javier before handing him the key.

"Thank you" was all Javier could think to say.

"Hǎo a." The man gave one last nod before leaving Javier in the stark space.

The invitation letter had advertised furnished accommodations, which in this case meant one couch, one table and chair, one bed, and one set of dishes. The kitchen had a two-burner electric range and an electric kettle. No oven. The bathroom was puzzling. The entire space was tiled, but it had no shower stall, just a set of fixtures sticking out of the wall next to a toilet. Javier sat on the bed and winced. The mattress felt more like a boxspring than a foam-based cushion.

At the outer limits of what his brain could process in a day, Javier unpacked his suitcase, looking for something to wad up as a pillow, and—*Dammit*. Javier gave his toiletry bag a sour expression as he remembered that he no longer owned a toothbrush. After thoroughly washing his hands, he squirted a gob of toothpaste onto a finger to scrub at the film on his teeth. It was better than nothing.

He changed into a pair of pajamas just to get out of the airplane clothes and switched off the light. A wad of T-shirts would serve as a makeshift pillow, and the two light jackets working as a blanket covered most of his body if he let his feet poke out. As soon as he lay his head down, a sharp pain caused him to withdraw with a hiss. A hand went up to touch the piece of metal in his ear that he'd forgotten about. Bitterly, he rolled over to the other side.

Javier knew his frustrations would lessen in the light of day, but as he listened to the faint noises of his neighbors, feeling sticky in the humid air, he had to wonder why the hell he'd thought it was a good idea to come to Shanghai.

Finding Eva was an admirable goal, and he wanted to honor the commitment his teenage self had made. Yet the two most likely scenarios were either that she was doing fine and would be annoyed by an intrusion into her life... or that she was dead. It wasn't like she'd been waiting all this time for her little brother to show up and save her from the circumstances that led her here. Still, part of him had to know which path her life had taken since leaving her family in California. And on the off chance she was in a bad situation and wanted to find a way home, he would help her.

Tomorrow: toothbrush, food, then start the hunt for Eva. In that order.

4

Javier's first full day in Shanghai started with a game of gestures while attempting to ask the wild-eyebrowed doorman for a map, preferably one in English. Javier even tried an expression from the previous night: "So buh." That drew a hearty laugh that made the man's eyebrows dance like wriggly caterpillars. It took an embarrassingly long time to realize the guy knew exactly what he wanted but was just enjoying Javier's bad pantomime and worse Chinese. Mr. Eyebrows's chuckles ultimately seemed good-natured, so Javier let his embarrassment go when he was finally offered a map.

The apartment building was on the northwestern side of the city, several miles from the center but only a few blocks away from the metro station. In daylight, the metropolis was larger than he'd imagined—dense skyscrapers and buildings vanished into the hazy atmosphere. As he took the underground railway to a home goods store, Javier didn't see a single homeless person or scrap of litter. In fact, people were actively cleaning walkways with brooms and hoses. The spotless modernity was a far cry from the tent cities and crumbling storefronts of San Francisco.

Almost everyone in the working-adult age range had a donor ear tag, and apparently everyone had somewhere important to be. Javier was elbowed out of the way by more than one granny before he figured out the ebb and flow of foot traffic.

Shanghai's summer heat had sweat rolling down his brow by the time he made it to the grocery store, lugging a large blue tote of home goods. Out of stamina for figuring out the city, he grabbed random edible items as he walked through the aisles, hoping a few might turn into a cohesive meal. On his way back to the apartment, he noted the location of the resource center where he could apply for a job. That could be tomorrow.

Javier lumbered down the hallway to his front door with the strap of the woven plastic bag digging into his shoulder. As he rummaged in his pocket for his key, a small mewling caught his attention. By a tee at the end of the corridor, a white fluff ball of a cat curled its feather duster tail around its body as it sat daintily on its hindquarters.

"Hello there. Are you lost?"

Like I'm one to talk.

The cat gave him a slow blink in response.

Javier set his purchases down inside the door then peeked his head out again to check on the animal. To his surprise, it was waddling toward him, tail proudly in the air.

"You sure are friendly, aren't you?" Javier crouched to give the cat some scratches under the chin. It rubbed affectionately against his legs, and soon his jeans were covered in downy white fur. As he reached for the thin red collar to check for an address, a panicked young woman rounded the corner.

"Maomao!" she called when she spotted the cat. Javier put

his hands around the animal to prevent it from running off. It flopped over and started purring instead.

"Nice cat," Javier said, feeling the need to say something although he didn't expect her to understand him.

"Ugh, he's always getting out. The latch on my door sticks, and I didn't notice it was open. Thanks for catching him." The woman's curly black hair bounced as she moved, acrylic glasses dominating her small face. Around her neck hung a flexible tape measure like the one Javier's mother used for sewing.

"Wow, you don't know how nice it is to hear English again." Javier stood as the woman picked up Maomao, cradling the docile animal in her arms. She also possessed a metal ear tag. The dull sting of his was persistent. "I'm Javier. I just got in yesterday."

"Nice to meet you. My name is Wenshi." Her eyes darted from Javier's face to his bags inside the door then down the hallway. "I studied in the US for a while. Anyway, I need to get back, but thanks again."

"Right, it was nice to meet you." Javier wanted to ask her which unit was hers and if they could get coffee sometime. But that might have been a bit much coming from a random guy she just met, so Javier let it go.

Wenshi retreated down the hallway as Javier repeated the name in his head, trying to get it to stick. It was worth remembering in case Maomao got out again.

Once more in his own apartment, Javier heaved the giant bag of purchases onto the dining table. He withdrew his most eagerly awaited prize: one brand-new toothbrush. Several minutes of vigorous brushing later, his gums tingled with minty victory, and he was ready to tackle the rest of the unpacking.

He tucked his groceries into the tiny cupboards and refrigerator before setting the shiny black pan on the stove with its coordinating dinky spatula. He felt like he was moving into a dorm all over again, except ten years too old.

He carefully slit the plastic wrap on the thickest bed topper he could find and flopped it out over the "mattress" that came with the apartment. The foam slowly expanded as Javier shook out the fitted sheet to cover it. The cotton was scratchy and smelled of chemicals, but he wasn't up to deciphering the pictographs on the balcony's washing machine just yet.

After a single, albeit large, sack of items, the space was already starting to feel cozier. He wouldn't necessarily invite anyone over, but it was livable while he searched for Eva, as long as that took. *Two months,* he told himself. *Three at most.* Javier eyed the corded phone, wondering if he should call his mom to tell her he'd made it. With a twinge of guilt, he decided against it.

Javier withdrew a pocket-sized notebook and a basic ballpoint pen he had snatched on a whim at a checkout register, thinking he could use them to gather information. He sat down at the table and opened the blank notebook to the first page, pressing flat the crease along the binding. *How do I find one person in a city of thirty million?*

With no cell phones or widespread internet in Shanghai, all of Javier's usual information-gathering methods were inaccessible. Eva's old phone had contained no additional clues about where she might head once she arrived. If the immigration process had been the same back then, she wouldn't have even known her new address until she arrived. Perhaps the resource office would have records he could request. Javier jotted down the idea.

What occupation would she have pursued? She had always talked about becoming a veterinarian, but how relevant was that dream in a vampire-controlled territory? Then again, Maomao must have a vet, and surely he wasn't the only house cat in Shanghai. Javier made another note.

He spent the better part of an hour with his notebook before the rumbles of his stomach convinced him to put the pen down. Javier felt good about the beginning of a plan to find Eva. He'd also jotted down a few pages recapping his experiences so far. The customs official's war against oral hygiene, Mr. Eyebrows's amusement at his bad Chinese, and meeting Wenshi and her fluffy cat. Maybe one day, he would recount the memories to someone else or, more likely, just read them and laugh at the crazy time he went to a foreign country on a ridiculous quest for his long-lost sister.

JAVIER PLANNED to be at the job center first thing in the morning. Instead, after staring at the ceiling until the sky started to lighten, Javier fell asleep, awaking with only an hour left until closing time. Fantastic. Javier threw on his wrinkled office attire before walking the few blocks to the resource center.

The office was a white-walled room staffed with at least twenty uniformed workers, all sitting behind desks arranged in a grid. Several were busy with clients.

"English?" Javier asked the person checking him in. She nodded and escorted him to a scuffed laminate desk with a man wearing two name tags, one with Chinese characters and another that read Kevin.

"How may I help you?" the man asked fluently.

Thank God. Javier took a seat and withdrew a folder from his messenger bag containing the documents he anticipated needing. "Good evening. I arrived a few days ago on a donor visa, and I'm hoping you can help me find a job. I have experience in cybersecurity and agriculture." Javier handed his resume to the man, who skimmed it before handing it back.

"Any hospitality, maintenance, or manufacturing experience?"

"Uh, not really. On my parents' vineyard, I occasionally helped run the tasting room. And I was in charge of checking the irrigation system and repairing leaks."

Kevin gave him a quizzical look.

"Never mind. No, no significant experience in those areas." Javier wiped away the sweat beading at his temple. *Is it always this humid here?*

Silence stretched as Kevin leisurely turned the pages of a binder, and Javier's knee started bouncing with impatience.

"Can I tell you more about my programming experience? I was a senior developer with—"

"No need. There are very few vocations in Shanghai requiring computer skills."

"Oh." Javier had specifically chosen his career path for the purported job stability of the tech industry. Between the dejection here and the layoff back home, that advice was proving massively inaccurate.

"Here." Kevin tore a sheet of paper from the binder and handed it to Javier with a dismissive wave. "Go to this address and ask for Arvind Patel."

Javier read the hiring manager's name along with his job

title: facilities manager. An address for the Eternal Twilight Bank Headquarters in the financial district was also listed.

"Okay, do I need to prepare anything for the interview?" Javier had worn a button-up shirt, slacks, and a pair of uncomfortable leather oxfords. The outfit was much more formal than what he'd worn to work back in California, but that was better than being underdressed. Mom had always harped on him about first impressions.

"No interview. Show up, and the job is yours."

"Really? What is the position? And what can I expect for my salary?" The ease of this process roused his suspicion. *Is the city so desperate for workers that any human will do?*

"This is a janitorial assignment, and for this grade of position, the salary is fixed at..." Kevin's index finger traced down the left-hand column of a chart taped to his desk before veering to the right. "One hundred thousand yuan a year."

"That's only a third of the stipend..." *and not even minimum wage in the States.* Javier's hands tightened on the bag in his lap. At that rate, he wouldn't even be able to cover the cost of his plane ticket with the money he earned.

"If you had maintenance experience, you could apply for a higher-grade position. Or..." The man leaned back in his chair. "We did receive some new requisitions this morning that haven't been processed yet. I might be able to find something more suited to your skills for a nominal finder's fee." Kevin interlaced his fingers behind his head as he waited for Javier to bite on the bribe.

A flash of an old memory jetted through Javier's mind—a trip to a government office with his dad in Mexico City when he was six years old. His dad had pressed crisp peso notes into the hands of several officials as a matter of course. Javier's expression hardened at the thought of giving this person a single unearned yuan.

"No, thanks. This is fine." Javier stashed the card in his bag and stood. He didn't bother asking for information on Eva, predicting Kevin would double down on his finder's fee.

At least he was leaving with a job. Javier wasn't above mopping floors and cleaning toilets if that's what it took. He was here to find Eva, not to build his résumé.

WITH HELP from the patient metro workers, Javier figured out that he needed to take a combination of the brown and the light-green lines to get to the bank. From the bustling Nanjing Road station, it was a few blocks' walk to the bank building. Navigating without a phone map was unexpectedly satisfying. He still felt phantom vibrations in his pocket, but they were lessening over time. It might actually be a nice break to not be beholden to the random texts from his mom or work at all hours of the day.

Javier's head tipped back as he tried to find the top of the buildings, windows glowing orange with the sunset. Steel girders decorated smoky glass in triangular patterns. Each of the towers in the central district had a unique architectural flare while reaching terrifying heights as if in competition with its neighbors. The traditional buildings were tucked between the skyscrapers like colorful gems.

With a sigh, Javier waited at the last intersection until the red man on the sign switched to a green countdown. He stepped onto the painted white lines crossing the road, along with a few other pedestrians. The light drizzle had only turned the sidewalks into a steam oven, and his shirt was damp where the strap of his bag rested. As he readjusted it to let the material breathe, a black SUV careened around the corner against the light. It headed straight for him.

Javier leapt back as the car came to a screeching halt where he'd stood milliseconds before. He braced himself on the hood of the hulking car, locking eyes with the frightened driver wearing a chauffeur's cap. The metal boiled against his palms as he drew in deep breaths, trying to steady himself after the near-death experience.

A passenger car door opened, and a person in high-end security guard attire emerged. He approached Javier with heavy footfalls.

"Look, no harm done. I'll just be on my way." Javier backed a few steps.

The security guard's fist closed around the front of Javier's shirt and pulled him nose-to-nose. A spew of angry Chinese assaulted Javier as he tried to shove the guy off. He could have been fighting a boulder, for all the good it did.

"I don't understand!" he tried.

The man flicked Javier's ear tag painfully while continuing the verbal barrage. Regardless of language, the message from the bodyguard was clear: "Stay out of the way, you ignorant human blood bag."

"How, how!" Javier yelled, trying to imitate the Mandarin word he hoped meant "all right" or "fine."

The click of a second car door sounded before a slender man emerged, his umbrella angled against the sun's fading rays. The guy looked like he'd been carved out of candle wax—pale, pristine, and not quite alive. Something about his stillness unnerved Javier more than the shouting guard. He had a sneaking suspicion he was looking at a genuine Shanghai vampire.

The guard instantly let go of Javier's shirt and stood at attention. Javier gawked openly at the supernatural creature before him. The vampire finally gave him a queer smile that sent chills down his spine, before beckoning the guard and walking toward the front doors of the bank building. The bodyguard gave Javier one last sneer before following his boss.

It took a horn honk to snap Javier back to reality. He stumbled out of the way as expensive foreign cars resumed their routes.

Great. Kevin had sent him to work in a vampire's nest in return for not paying his crooked bribe. How much of an occupational hazard would it be, working in close proximity with these creatures? Before then, the whole vampire thing hadn't really registered in any meaningful way. He would have to be more careful.

Javier straightened out his shirt the best he could before climbing the stone steps to the entrance. Plenty of other humans were here, not getting eaten. Javier just needed to figure out a way to blend in better.

"Hi, I'm here to see Arvind Patel about a janitorial job," Javier said to the woman at the front desk, voice still shaky from his close call outside. Her crisp white blouse made him feel even shabbier in his rumpled, damp clothing. She snatched the job-requisition form out of his hands, told him to wait, then disappeared behind a door.

Javier surveyed the lobby for other potential vampires as he waited. In the few minutes he stood there, he noticed one more potential bloodsucker: a woman in a sleek blazer, her heels rapping sharply on the marble floor. Her skin was pale, sure, but the tell was in her body language. She crossed the lobby like it was her divine right to do so, people scattering to clear a path, except for a solitary woman in a sweatshirt trailing behind her. Another vampire? Javier hedged no—the hoodie didn't exactly have that "architect of darkness" vibe. However, the welcome orientation really should have covered methods for spotting— and avoiding—vampires.

The receptionist returned with Arvind, a scrawny man in his fifties wearing coveralls. After brief introductions, he escorted Javier to a stairwell, which they descended.

"The job is simple. You will punch in by eight in the morning and out at six at night. Thirty-minute lunch break. Monday through Friday." Arvind scribbled "Javier Robles" atop an elongated manila rectangle and demonstrated how to insert it into an antiquated clock apparatus that stamped the time. It was almost six in the evening already.

"Locker rooms are in here. Can I have a copy of your visa documents?"

Arvind gave him his own pair of coveralls then showed him where to obtain a cleaning cart and which floor of offices he was responsible for. Since the primarily vampire executives came in around sunset, he should have free rein during daylight hours to tidy. If an office happened to be occupied, he should aim to be neither seen nor heard. That sounded okay to Javier. He had no desire to interact with the inhuman beings any more than he had to.

The cleaning tasks themselves were straightforward, but Arvind insisted on describing in precise detail how he should dust surfaces—including the plant leaves—then collect the trash and only vacuum at the end, making sure to start at the farthest corner and back his way out of the room. Over a dozen private offices were on the floor, along with two large conference rooms, each of them with incredible westward views of the Huangpu River and Shanghai evening skyline. A few distinctive buildings stood out among the others: one that had a round ball at the top and another that looked like a bottle opener. Javier wished he had his phone to take a picture and look up the names. Ah well, he could probably find them in a tourist guide. Maybe working downtown wouldn't be all bad.

"There shouldn't be anyone on this floor tonight. If you don't mind staying late, it could use a clean." Arvind was so obviously overworked that Javier couldn't bring himself to say no. Besides, he was going to be wide awake for quite some time.

"Sure thing, boss."

"Good. One more thing: don't go up to the top floor tonight. There's a high-profile meeting, and they don't like to be interrupted."

Javier gave a brief smile. "Understood. No need to tell me twice."

5

s the jet made its approach, gliding down through the foggy haze of early evening, condensation beaded against the windows before streaming backward. The droplets blurred the distinctive skyline of the city beyond: Shanghai. Three months of backpacking to get to Singapore and one day to end up back where she'd started.

Mina followed Lian to the car waiting on the tarmac, missing the familiar weight of her backpack. Lady Zhang gripped her briefcase with the previously ruined hand. It had entirely healed, her ancient blood thick with regenerative power. Conversely, Mina's cheeks still felt flushed from the UV exposure. The paltry cow's blood had left her supernatural strength depleted in a way that suddenly seemed to matter so much more.

They drove toward the city center, Mina's insides reeling as they passed the turn to Zhang Manor. Lian said they were going back home, right? When the car pulled up to the curb outside the Eternal Twilight Bank, Mina's confused worry only grew. She could think of no reason Lian would bring her here, except to maybe rub her nose in the fact that her bank accounts had been subsumed by the family for her desertion.

The chauffeur opened the door of the car to a sidewalk buzzing with pedestrians, an oppressive plume of city musk invading the cool interior of the car. Lian stepped out of the car and waited expectantly for Mina to follow.

"What are we doing here?" she croaked, fearful of the unknown reason for their bank visit. Mina could deal with Lian's verdict on her crimes in private. The thought of facing some sort of public trial made her insides squirm.

Lian's face was placid and unreadable as ever. "You'll see soon enough. Now, out."

Mina clenched her jaw. Was she really going to just fall back in line? Accept the withheld information and brusque commands defining Lian's regime?

What's the other option? Throw a tantrum in the middle of downtown Shanghai so the paparazzi can drum up any number of salacious reasons for your disappearance and now return?

Mina slid out of the car, pulling her hood up over her head petulantly. A tabloid scandal was the last thing she wanted to deal with. Small raindrops landed like cool pinpricks against her cheeks as she marched up the travertine steps to the skyscraper, dreading whatever awaited her inside.

As she caught up to Lian in the elevator car, the woman checked her watch pointedly. Mina tucked herself into a corner. The elevator lurched downward, a sickening challenge to her equilibrium. Doors swooshed open deep beneath the surface level to reveal a cavernous antechamber, the arrival chime echoing off its walls. Opposite them, a large circular vault door was propped open, and light spilled out of it like an ominous promise. Mina's hands gripped the railing of the elevator as she imagined being locked inside indefinitely. Lady Zhang strode out across the floor while Mina stayed firmly in the elevator car.

Halfway across the space, sensing that her progeny had not followed, Lian turned with a sigh. "You've already wasted enough of my time today—I warn you, my patience is growing thin." The side lighting cast stark shadows, emphasizing the scowl drawn on her face. A hot surge of anger gathered in Mina's stomach. Lian was an indomitable force to reckon with, but Mina was done cowering on command. That was the version of herself she'd vowed to never be again.

"*You're* the one who chose to drag me back here. I was doing *fine* on my own," Mina spat. She took one, two steps out of the elevator, if only to confront Lian on even footing.

"Is that so?" Lian folded her arms over her chest, giving Mina a head-to-toe visual appraisal.

"*Yes!* I didn't attack anyone, I stayed out of trouble, and I was free to make my own choices for once in my life. Why couldn't you just let me have that?" Her voice reached a crescendo bordering on shouting, a terrifying satisfaction tingling down to her fingertips at having stood up for herself.

Lian's brow rose a few millimeters, enough for Mina to know she wasn't impressed. "You slept on the streets. Ate poorly. Would have been arrested on three separate occasions had I not intervened."

Mina swallowed a queasy thought: *She was having me followed the whole time?*

"And besides those very basic failures"—Lian stalked closer until she was within arm's reach—"you nearly boarded a transoceanic commercial flight. Did you even consider your effect on the electronics aboard? The repercussions of a critical system failing midflight?"

Confusion rippled through Mina's mind as she grappled with the contradiction.

"We were just on an airplane, and it worked fine to bring me back to this prison." She gave her best look of righteous indignation. It shriveled under the pitying one she received in return.

"We were on a *private jet* with shields over essential systems." Lian pinched the bridge of her nose. "You have never been one to consider how your actions impact others around you—no doubt your Western upbringing is partly to blame. However, by now, you should have known better."

Mina's chin dipped as she desperately tried to find a way to discount Lian's logic. All her attempts were short-circuited by a single thought: that boy and his teddy bear plunging into the ocean because she'd been too focused on her own escape to stop for a second to think about the realities of her life.

You really are a selfish monster, aren't you?

Mina's stomach twisted as her lungs pumped in short, unproductive breaths. The room swayed dangerously, and her foot jumped forward to help steady herself.

Another exasperated sigh came from Lian before the woman gripped her tightly by the shoulders.

"Breathe. Fainting won't fix your mistakes."

Mina's hands locked onto Lian's forearms. She didn't want to breathe. She didn't want to be here. Yet she clearly couldn't be trusted to be on her own. A deep, shuddering breath washed into her lungs, then another. The mental fog was finally waning when Lian's hands withdrew.

"Now, come. We're overdue for a talk." Lady Zhang disappeared behind the heavy vault door.

Mina steeled herself, all fight replaced by a profound resignation. This was the life she'd asked for, and she'd gotten every bit of it.

Within the chamber, Mina squinted against the clinical lighting. The room was lined with numbered and locked panels. A gleaming metal table stood in the center, and atop it sat an ornate wooden box. A brass clasp and a tasseled pin kept the two polished halves neatly sealed.

Lian gestured toward the seat as she took a chair on the opposite side. The relaxed drape of the woman's taupe suit gave her an air of casual elegance, making Mina feel more shabby and unworthy as she sank into the cold metal seat. She gripped the edge of the chair so tightly that the metal buckled beneath her fingers. Mina focused on the ache in her knuckles so that she didn't have to face the truth of her farcical runaway attempt.

"You are still young—it is expected that you will occasionally misstep." Lian waved her hand as if dismissing a petty crime. "I have chosen to view your disloyalty in such a context, and I am willing to use corrective measures to address your behavior instead of punitive ones." The woman leaned forward and clasped her hands together, resting her forearms on the table. "That is, if you give me reason to believe you are receptive to overcoming your mistakes."

"Yes, Lady Zhang." Her mouth dry, Mina worked up the nerve to ask the question that hung in the balance, since she was firmly back under Lian's power. "What are you going to do to me?"

Lian gave a small grin, sitting back in her seat once more.

"To start, you will be accompanied by an escort anytime you leave Zhang Manor for the foreseeable future."

Mina's eyes lowered. She'd expected as much, yet the thought of never having a moment outside Lian's surveillance made breathing hard all over again.

"Second, you will drink no blood. Not until I'm satisfied you've reflected on the privileges of your position in my household."

Lian had rationed her meals for offenses in the past, but being denied blood altogether was a new extreme. Mina slid her tongue over her retracted fangs, wondering how long that might be. Still though, this all sounded like the lead-up.

"And?" Her gaze dipped down to the box on the table.

Lian gave a humorless smirk. "That's all. For now."

The woman slid the wooden box to the center of the table, the polished teak a mesmerizing chaos of knots and veins. "However, I've brought you here to show you what punishments *could* befall you—a promise for if you *ever* betray me like that again." Her voice carried a venom behind it that made Mina grow achingly still.

Lian slid the pin out of the brass clasp before slowly unhinging the box. Inside, a dull metal circlet was nestled in a burgundy velvet cloth, crushed and creased from age. Mina studied the shape until the grotesque form of it became clear— a serpent etched with fine overlapping scales worn with the sands of time, the end of its tail caught in its mouth. She felt compelled to run her fingers over it, yet fear kept her hands firmly anchored to the edge of the seat.

"Magicians forged this collar over three hundred years ago to enslave vampires," Lian said with the smallest twitch of a nostril as she spun the box to gaze upon the artifact herself. "It erases the self and demands obedience. A grim existence, I assure you."

Tension tugged at the older woman's jawline as she punctured the skin of her thumb with an incisor. A deep-crimson bead swelled on the surface. After a brief hesitation, she placed the digit against the snake's scaly head, leaving a wet streak trailing along its spine. Mina watched in horror as the dull metal absorbed the blood like a sponge, its body erupting with a shiny, lifelike set of black scales. The enervated serpent writhed within the confines of the box, searching for more nourishment, unable to release its own tail.

After only a few seconds, Lian snapped the lid closed and slid the clasp back into place. "Its dark magic is insidious, which is why I keep it locked deep underground in this vault. It is not something I would subject you to lightly," Lian said more softly, raking her hair behind her ear and clearing her throat. "And yet, I will not allow this kind of disobedience to persist. Do you understand, Mina?" The woman looked at her with blood-tinged eyes, a true question lingering in the air.

Mina looked at the box one last time. Even with the serpent sealed away, she could still feel its hungry soul searching for more power to consume. Any remaining rebellion shrank away from the threat of confinement with the magical collar. Mina couldn't imagine anything worse than having her little remaining autonomy taken from her.

"I understand."

"Good." Lian stood and crossed to Mina's side of the table. Gentle fingers eased beneath her chin, tilting her head up. "I hate to see you suffer unnecessarily."

Mina didn't know what to say. The sentiment sounded so genuine, but she knew how quickly it could flip to something hurtful, how Lian would indeed watch her suffer if it served her purpose. If she deemed it *necessary*.

"It's been a long day for both of us," Lian continued, easing her hand down to rest on Mina's shoulder. "One more meeting, and then we can go home."

Home. Mina flooded with relief. She would get to go home instead of remaining trapped in this vault. Words escaped her before she could think better of them: "Thank you, my lady."

Lian inclined her head, her expression softening further. Her thumb stroked Mina's cheek, and despite herself, Mina leaned into it. The first gentle touch she'd had in months.

"Now, we do need to improve your attire before we go up." Lian looked at her sweatshirt sternly. "I can't have you representing our house looking like a street urchin."

Mina looked down at the thin hoodie, the one that said I ♡ New York, which she'd found in a dumpster in Hanoi. It was the last remnant of her time outside Shanghai. Slipping it off her shoulders was a regretful acceptance that she had no business pretending she could make it on her own.

Lian shrugged out of her blazer and held it open. Mina stood and reached her hands awkwardly behind herself to meet the armholes. The silky fabric slid over her skin, enveloping Mina in a swath of warm wool and the scent of jasmine and ink —the scent of Lian. The sensation of once more being in the woman's domain was one of both safety and suffocation. Mina shivered as Lian's cool fingers brushed against her neck, gently tugging the ends of her hair free.

"I'm glad you're back, pet," Lian murmured in her ear.

Mina gave the closed box on the table one last look, promising herself it wouldn't end up around her neck. She couldn't let it.

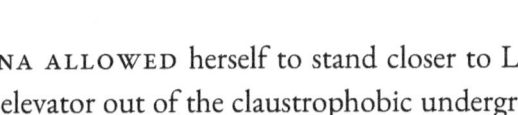

MINA ALLOWED herself to stand closer to Lian as they rode the elevator out of the claustrophobic underground. She knew the shape of her penalties, which made it easier to come to terms with her new reality—she was to become Lian's kept pet once more. *You signed up for this, remember?* Bitterly, Mina tried to focus on anything but the spiral of self-recrimination spinning in her mind.

They got out on the top floor, where a conference room with a panoramic view of the twinkling city lights held a vampire even more guileful than Lian: Lord August Vasa. Mina tried to keep the sour expression off her face as the man leapt from his seat at their arrival, a devilish grin playing at his lips. Why did the meeting have to be with this man?

"Älskling! What a delightful surprise." Lanky legs carried him to her side of the table, where he grabbed Mina's hand and laid a delicate kiss on the back before she could avoid it. If there was ever a night she did not have the patience for his theatrical antics, it was tonight.

Lian bypassed the man's greeting altogether and took a seat where a bound document awaited her. Removing her reading glasses from her briefcase, she casually remarked, "Do stop harassing my fledgling, Lord Vasa."

"*Me?* Harass *your* fledgling? Nonsense," August said in dramatic protest before turning back to Mina conspiratorially. "Dmitri is quite upset that you 'ghosted' him—a peculiar term, considering how clingy ghosts can be. Where on earth have you been, child?" His prim English accent carried only the slightest lilt of his native Swedish.

The mention of her friend churned up a bevy of guilt, and

she found herself at a loss both for how to address it and what to say about her absence. Thankfully, Lian answered for her: "She was abroad for a diplomatic engagement."

"I see." August quirked a brow in Mina's direction, clearly not convinced by the explanation.

"Is Dmitri…" Mina hesitated. She'd left only a few days before his transition—the timing couldn't be helped. "Does that mean it went all right?"

"Of course. As well as it ever does, that is." August gestured Mina to take a seat before resuming his own. "I know Lady Zhang has always preferred traditional ceremonies to ease the process spiritually. However, medicine has made significant advancement in improving mortality rates. A team of physicians monitored the entire progression, and I have to say, Dmitri was the smoothest fledgling I've ever borne."

As she sat, Mina noted the purple beneath Vasa's eyes and a certain gauntness to his cheeks, making him look a good deal older than his usual mid-thirties. The transformation was never easy on the fledgling or the creator—upward of one in three humans died, and even a fully mature vampire had only the magical stamina to procreate once per decade. Part of her hadn't wanted to admit how worried she was that Dmitri wouldn't survive the process.

"These are not the terms we discussed," Lady Zhang said flatly as she leafed through the document.

"Yes, but I've expanded your stake in the pharmaceutical division," August replied impatiently. "Our recent breakthroughs require more resources to fully develop, and it's a smart move to capitalize on the opportunity while we have a first-to-market advantage."

Lian tapped a finger on the table, her gaze unwavering. "In

that case, I would like to read the revised prospectus. Vasa Laboratories is overleveraged as it is—no, don't argue; you're the one asking for an investment—and the plan for overcoming existing debt lacked clarity. Now you're saying you've expanded the scope of the research and incurred even *more* risk?"

With nothing to add to the conversation, Mina stared at a pallid monstera plant in the corner as Lian and August continued to haggle over contractual clauses. Its leaves dithered perpetually underneath a ceiling vent, the constant agitation having tattered the edges of the variegated foliage to a crisp brown fringe. Mina scratched at the edge of a cuticle, trying to keep her thoughts from wandering back to the ornamental box in the basement and what it contained. When she looked down, the nail bed was slick with blood. The other two vampires had gone silent, both their attentions turned to her as that distinctive rusty scent hung in the air.

"Sorry," Mina murmured, squeezing the finger tightly in her other hand.

Lian's eyes narrowed in calculation. After a few seconds of uncomfortable scrutiny, she turned back to her document. "Perhaps you'd like some coffee while we work through these details. I believe there's an espresso machine one floor down."

"Of course." Mina stood, her legs prickling from a day of stillness.

"Lovely! Make mine a double," August said, giving her a cheeky wink.

Mina ground her teeth together. She was fairly certain Lian had offered the errand as an excuse for her to step out, not a suggestion that she serve coffee. *But now that His Lordship has interjected...*

"Cappuccino, my lady?"

Lian gave her the briefest nod while casting a disdainful glance at Vasa.

Mina left them to it, trying to perk herself up with the thought of an americano. It would be warm, at least. Yet her stomach rumbled, craving a different type of liquid. If things had gone as planned, she would've been in Sydney, wandering Chinatown for her evening meal.

With a sigh, she let the image go and pressed the down arrow for the elevator. Revisiting the dashed dream was too exhausting. Even if she had boarded that flight, she wouldn't have made it to Australia, anyway. At least this way, the humans had.

THE FLOOR below had only a smattering of signs of life. A vacuum droned somewhere, but the lights were dim. None of the offices were occupied; it was both too late in the evening for humans and too early for regular vampire working hours.

Mina skulked down the hallway until she found the cutaway that served as a coffee closet. The espresso machine was a top-of-the-line Italian model, not the same brand as the one she'd learned on in Seattle but close enough. Mina turned on the power and leaned back against the counter as it heated. The abstract art on the wall was a series of bland lines dragged through white plaster. Mina traced them with her eyes, wishing the soulless office decor offered more of a distraction.

She shook her head. After everything, she found herself back in Shanghai, making coffee for Lian Zhang, no less. Her sixteen-year-old self would have been ecstatic. Every time the charismatic, confident woman frequented the tiny coffee shop where Mina worked, her heart skipped. After pouring the most intricate latte art she could manage into the frothy cappuccino foam, she would deliver the beverage to Lian's table with a modest smile. The day she'd received one back was the highlight of her entire life, up until then.

A giggle bubbled out of her throat at the uninvited memory—the absurdity of the life that was supposed to be her happily ever after. The chuckle grew to a full-scale laugh, the noise ricocheting off the walls of the small room. She laughed until the noise cracked, splintering into a sob. Mina gripped her forearm, letting the tips of her claws dig into the skin.

Don't fall apart now. You've done this before, and you can do it again.

Taking a deep breath, Mina set herself to the task at hand. The act of making coffee calmed her: the mindless meditation of grinding the beans, tamping them into the basket, and pulling the shots of creamy espresso. She inhaled the familiar aroma, letting it soothe her. In an act of generosity, she even made the requested double for August. With the three drinks readied in glass mugs, Mina assembled them on a tray with accompanying saucers, spoons, and sugar. Everything was better with coffee.

She was halfway down the hall, mid-step, when her foot caught on something. The tray lurched, coffee flying. With her ankles tangled, her body tipped forward in a slow, graceless descent. Coffee splattered the low-pile carpet as Mina came down hard on her knees and elbows.

"Motherfucker!" she ground out, turning to see what had tripped her. An electrical cord lay innocently on the ground. Her reflexes should have compensated faster. *Are you so inept that you can't handle something as simple as walking?*

"Are you all right?" asked a man in blue coveralls as he appeared at the door. He had a straight nose and wavy hair that the humidity had done no favors. "I had no idea anyone else was here. I'm so sorry."

Fucking humans.

"I'm fine," Mina grumbled, collecting her knees underneath herself. "Do you have something to clean this up?" She surveyed the damage to the carpet as she collected the shards of glass from the mugs back on the tray. She felt a poignant tug at the waste of good espresso, for some reason.

"Yeah, of course." The man scurried back into the room he'd come from.

Mina looked down and noticed a brown stain on the cuff of the borrowed jacket. *Fuck.* Maybe if she ran it under water, Lian wouldn't notice her clumsy mishap. Yes, she would get this cleaned up then deal with the splotch and, somehow, make more coffee. As she hurriedly collected the glass, one of the pieces bit into her finger, leaving a deep gash in its place.

"God dammit!" Mina threw the piece on the tray, trying to keep the dripping blood from getting anywhere near her already soiled clothing.

"Whoa, here, let me help you," the man said as he knelt on the carpet. He grabbed Mina's wrist with warm, calloused hands and gently pressed a cloth to the laceration. "You really don't need to worry about this. I'll get it cleaned up—it's my fault for tripping you. Hey, don't cry! This is no big deal. Everything will all be all right."

Mina scrubbed at the tears with the palm of her uninjured hand, furious that they chose that particular moment to afflict her. She had no reason for the emotion—the cut didn't hurt, and the spilled coffee could easily be replaced. But she still took several minutes to get herself back under control. Meanwhile, the man sat next to her on the carpet, patiently pressing the cloth to her finger as her mental breakdown played itself out.

When her tears finally subsided, she mumbled, "Sorry," feeling fragile and raw.

"No worries. Sometimes, you have to let it out. Kinda seems like you might be having a rough day."

"You could say that," Mina said dryly.

"I'm Javier, by the way." His amber-brown eyes radiated a kind sincerity.

Mina guessed he hadn't been in this city very long, especially since he'd had the audacity to introduce himself to her. *You've already wasted too much time. Stop dallying with the help and pull yourself together.*

"That name doesn't work well in Chinese." She pulled her hand out of his grasp and stood.

"Oh. Really?" he asked with a small frown.

"I should get back upstairs. Please take care of the mess, if you would." Mina smoothed her clothing, regaining her composure. She wasn't a nobody in Shanghai—she was a Zhang vampire, and reputations mattered here. She couldn't be found tearfully mopping up dirty floors, even if it was her own damn fault.

"Sure, but hey." He chased her toward the elevator. "I don't think we're supposed to go up there. There's some fancy vampire meeting happening or something."

She turned on him, incredulous. *Who the fuck does this man think he is?*

"*I* am a vampire," she said, feeling dangerously on edge.

He pulled his head back, looking her up and down. "Um, are you sure? You don't really look like a vampire..."

"Yeah. I'm pretty fucking sure." Her fangs itched to give him a demonstration. She started to let them descend... but then forced them to retract once more. He had made a simple mistake, and she wasn't a monster. With everything else out of her control at the moment, she could at least keep herself from crossing that line.

The man put his hands up in surrender. "Sorry, sorry. No offense intended. I will get out of your way, Miss Vampire."

As she watched him retreat down the hallway, the ding of the elevator sounded behind her. Mina turned to see a humorless Lian glaring at her from the car while August raised an amused brow at the mess. *Arrogant prick.*

"Mina. Come." The woman's sharp command left no room for misinterpretation.

Irritated that she'd let Lian find her in this disheveled predicament, Mina strode to the elevator door and filed in at the woman's side. She could feel the woman's displeasure simmering below the surface, and her shoulders inched up in response. In the periphery of her vision, she watched Javier kneel and dab at the carpet. As the elevator doors were shutting, he glanced up, catching her eyes one last time before she was staring at her own blurred reflection in the brushed metal.

What a forward human.

He wouldn't last long in this city.

6

As the elevator doors shut on the strange trio of vampires, the image imprinted itself on Javier's brain: the finance-bro who had almost run him over, the severe woman with the astronomical ego, and Mina the mystery. Between her American accent, jeans, and excessive profanity, she definitely didn't fit the gothic vampire aesthetic he'd been picturing for a creature of the night. In fact, Mina exemplified the term "hot mess" more than anyone he'd ever met—like someone who had stumbled into the vampire world after a night gone wrong and had been paying the price ever since. He'd seen the sadness lurking behind her hostile pretense and the chilling way she'd been beckoned like a border collie to her—*mistress?* Javier shuddered, praying Eva hadn't gotten herself tangled up in that crowd.

Javier did his best to blot up the coffee stain before sprinkling it with baking soda he found in the freezer. After finishing the rest of his janitorial work on the floor, he came back to vacuum it up. *Good as new.* Satisfied with his first few hours on the job, he went back to the locker room to clock out and get out of this jumpsuit. On his way out, Arvind handed him an official document of employment, complete with red stamps and a signature. All that was left to extend his visa was donating some blood. Then he would have the peace of mind to focus on the reason he came here.

By the time Javier reached the metro station, the clock was pushing nine in the evening. Only the dregs of overworked corporate drones filed into the train as the doors whooshed open—he even got a seat. As he zoned out, staring at the tunnel lights as they strobed by, Javier's stomach gave him an angry rumble. *Did I eat anything today?*

As he contemplated, the doors opened at the next stop to let in more tired passengers. Among them, the curly-haired woman with her giant glasses shuffled in.

"Wenshi!"

The woman jerked her head up, a startled look on her face.

"Hey, I thought I recognized you. It's Javier, from the apartment," he reminded her when her confused expression didn't fade.

The doors closed, and Wenshi took a seat on the bench opposite him with a weary smile. "Right. Sorry. I picked up some overtime, so it's been a long day."

"No worries. Hey, I was thinking about grabbing a bite to eat before going home. Care to join me? Or at least give me a recommendation for where I can find food this time of night?"

Wenshi rubbed her eyes. "Sure, why not? There's a night market by the apartment, if you're okay with cheap street food."

"That sounds perfect."

When they got off the metro, Wenshi navigated the

lingering crowds with such a brisk pace that Javier had to hustle to not lose her. Food vendors lined the busy street she led him to, each with a walk-up counter and a small kitchen tucked into the side of a building. The plethora of colorful dishes emerging from each of them made Javier salivate with anticipation. It killed him that Wenshi kept walking past so many delicious options, but he trusted she knew what she was doing.

Without consulting him, she ordered from an unassuming stall tucked between two others with garish advertisements. The aproned chef threw a clump of slippery white noodles into the well-seasoned wok and followed it with practiced squirts from several sauce bottles. He agitated the ingredients with a large ladle while shaking the pan above a sizable open flame. Every ten seconds, a new ingredient was added—Javier spotted thinly sliced beef, slivers of a green vegetable, bright-red chilis, and an egg.

Wenshi dragged him to three more stalls before they finally sat down to their meal, which included lamb skewers, steamed buns, a stir-fried vegetable dish, and two cans of Coke. Wenshi handled all the ordering and payment before Javier could even reach for his wallet.

"I hope you can handle spice," Wenshi said with a sneaky smile.

"Oh, I can handle the spice," Javier boasted. He was nowhere near the biggest chili-head in his Mexican-American family, but he also wasn't backing down from a challenge.

They sat down at a banquet-style community table, shoulder to shoulder with other hungry humans. People laughed and shared conversations in at least three different languages within earshot. It gave Javier the first warm feeling of belonging since his arrival.

"So, how long have you been in Shanghai?" he asked as Wenshi levered food onto his plate with long chopsticks.

A petite golden cross necklace glimmered in the warm street light.

"A little over three years. After my boyfriend and I graduated from university in the States, we decided it made sense for me to come here while he does his four years of mandatory service. To save up so we can start a family—after we're married, of course."

"It must be hard keeping up a long-distance relationship." Javier took his first bite of the noodle dish he'd been craving since its steaming mass was plated. Flavor exploded across his tongue, sweet and salty, before the fire of the chilis hit his palate. He moaned involuntarily as the first bite slid down his throat. "Oh my God, this is delicious."

Wenshi gave him a knowing nod before continuing, "Yeah, it hasn't always been the easiest being apart, but I have faith it's all for the best." A wistful smile crept onto her face. "Hopefully, a year from now, we'll both be back home and planning our future." Wenshi took a crunchy bite of raw chili before a chunk of lamb. "What about you? There aren't many Americans in Shanghai."

"Actually, I'm here to look for my sister. She left home sixteen years ago, and we haven't heard from her since. But I'm a little stumped about how to search for her without the internet. Like, is there a phone book, or how else would you find someone with only a name?"

Javier took another sip of Coke, the fizz temporarily intensifying the numbing heat in his mouth before the sugar tamped it down. Wenshi definitely had him outclassed in heat tolerance, but he was still enjoying the meal immensely. His eyes watered, but he was mindful not to touch them. Maybe it was time to eat one of those buns.

"Hmm, that's tough. The phone books are organized by region, so if you don't know where she lives, that'd take a while. The library might have a computerized system to speed it up. If you want, I could go with you."

"Really? That would be amazing. Seriously."

"No problem. I can't do tomorrow—I have Bible study—but how about the evening after?" Wenshi finished the last bites of beef before shoveling a second helping of everything onto her plate and his. Javier, despite himself, was starting to get full. He didn't know where Wenshi could possibly be putting all that food.

"Yeah, that would be great. I don't exactly have a buzzing social calendar at the moment."

Wenshi considered him. "I'd be happy to introduce you to my church."

Javier almost choked on his food at the thought. Religion was great and all for some people, but he wasn't really sure what he believed in these days, and attending church only made him feel like an imposter.

"I appreciate the offer, but I might have to work my way up to that one." Javier wiped his mouth with a napkin. "Out of curiosity, though, how does your church feel about, you know, *vampires*? I was raised Catholic, and well, you know their thoughts on the subject. Do the churches here not mind?"

Wenshi nodded. "Yeah, we get that question a lot. Vampirism itself is not viewed as a Christian path, but giving blood as an act of compassion and forgiveness isn't a new thing for the church. Jesus sacrificed His blood for His disciples, after all."

"Huh." Javier quirked a grin. "I never thought about it like that before." *Kinda makes a lot of sense though,* he had to admit.

By the time they finished the meal, Wenshi looked even more exhausted than he felt.

"Did you like the food? Beef tendon is my favorite, but sometimes, foreigners won't try it when they know ahead of time."

"Everything was incredible. Thank you so much for ordering. I feel like I finally got a real taste of the city," Javier replied, absolutely stuffed. He gave Wenshi cash for his half of the meal, which wasn't even ten dollars, and the two of them lumbered back to the apartment with their bellies full.

The tingle of the spices clung to his lips as the night air finally reached a pleasant temperature. He'd had one good meal and made one new friend—someone who would even help him look for Eva. That sure felt like progress in a city that made you work for it.

AFTER ENDURING the next two monotonous workdays, Arvind gave Javier a tip on which nearby donation centers to use. Apparently, the corruption problem in this city didn't stop with the employment offices. If you went to the wrong blood bank as a nonlocal, they might not give you a legitimate receipt for the donation so that they could sell it on the side. Javier had never seen his even-tempered boss get so fired up as when talking about the increase in expected bribes over the last few years. It made him like the man that much more.

When Javier arrived at the miniature medical office—little

more than a check-in counter and a few chairs—he was quickly seated and stuck with a needle. Paperwork was handed to him to complete while the red, viscous liquid dribbled from his arm into a collection bag. It all felt very ordinary, but Javier still didn't know what he thought about the fact that his blood would be nourishing some unknown vampire in the city. They would drink his blood then perhaps remark on the minerality or terroir like they might with a glass of wine. It kind of gave him the creeps.

Afterward, he double-checked the donation certificate for the watermark in the upper right corner and the correct date stamp. Between that piece of paper and his employment status, he was officially permitted to stay in the city longer than the initial two weeks. It was a bigger relief than he thought it would be. It bought him time—something he suspected he was going to need.

On his way to meet Wenshi at the library, Javier treated himself to honeydew bubble tea. Although not on the official list of recommendations for postdonation recovery, he figured it was close enough, with bonus points for deliciousness. As he completed the walk from the metro station to the university, he stabbed at the last few reclusive boba amongst the ice. Spotting Wenshi waiting on the front steps, Javier tossed his empty cup into a waste bin and jogged the rest of the way. After a brief greeting, Wenshi led the way to the information desk and spoke softly with the young woman staffing it, translating for Javier.

"She says that the directories are on the second floor. Also, if we write the name down, there's an electronic catalog in the back she'll search."

"That would be fantastic." Javier scribbled "Evelina

Robles" on a scrap of paper in his most legible script, which wasn't saying much.

The second floor of the library turned out to be almost all directories. There were even directories of directories, which Wenshi dutifully paged through as Javier stood by uselessly. Even if he had enrolled in a language class, he wouldn't be able to learn enough characters to be literate in any meaningful way by the time he left. However, he was enjoying trying to pick up common expressions from the subway and food stalls. Javier tried them out with the front doorman, Mr. Eyebrows, who would correct his pronunciation and try to act out the meaning of the phrase. Knowing just ten small expressions—how to say excuse me, sorry, thank you—had smoothed his daily interactions considerably.

Students ringed the edge of the room at individual study desks, each with a large stack of books and a notebook. It was a bizarre contrast to the laptops and bulky headphones of his own university days.

Wenshi went down the row until she came to a tabbed plastic divider. "You start here, I'll start at the other end, and we'll work our way toward the middle."

"What, of this whole section?" The shelves of tomes between them seemed to stretch a mile. No way would they get through them in a night.

"Yeah. This is where the Latin-character names are, assuming she hasn't taken a Chinese name."

That was a scary possibility to consider—that his sister might not even be using the same name. Perhaps she had adopted a Chinese name or even a married name. Something else itched in the back of his mind—that snarky comment from Ms. Mina, *La Vampire*, the other day.

"Hey, Wenshi? How would you say 'Javier' in Chinese?"

She looked up at the ceiling for a few seconds, biting her lip. "Usually, names only have two syllables, and the 'v' sound doesn't exist, so you'd have to work around that and then consider the meaning of the characters. I can help if you want..."

"Oh, no. That's okay. Just curious." He wouldn't really be there long enough for it to be worth the trouble.

He pulled down his first book and flipped to the *R* listings. The translucent pages of the volume gave off the smell of well-aged dust. Something about that scent, paired with the search for Eva, brought to mind a memory he hadn't thought of in years—the last day they'd worked the vineyard together, the last time he'd seen his sister.

THE FIRES HAD BEEN bad that year. Each morning during the summer break, Eva and Javier would wake early to join the workers, blowing away the fine layer of ash that had settled on the vines from the previous day. Everyone wore handkerchiefs tied around their nose and mouth to help keep the smoke out, but by the end of the day, Javier's lungs burned from inhaling the acrid air. He tried to hide his developing cough from their mother, but she was growing suspicious.

The crew completed their work by early afternoon. Javier, Eva, and a group of a dozen workers washed their caked hands in a galvanized basin with a pumice soap. After they'd spent all day among the fruit, seeing its stunted growth and withered leaves, a disheartened quiet hung between them all. They would have to work hard during the harvest to sort the viable grapes and then even harder to wash the remaining fruit without damaging the skins. Likely, they would yield a smoke-tainted wine. An eleven-year-old Javier learned these details from conversations he'd overheard, unsure what it all meant. None of it sounded good.

As Javier dried his hands, he caught sight of his mother descending from their home. Her dark-brown hair had gray streaks in it. Her faded linen blouse was tucked into jeans, and her worn leather boots kicked up puffs of dust as she trod the gravel path.

"I think we should wait another week," Roberto said once she was close enough. He'd become the stand-in vineyard manager in their father's absence and Gabriella's confidante for the important decisions. "Rain would give them a good rinse and maybe perk up some of the vines," he offered hopefully.

Gabriella pursed her lips at the report, seeing through Roberto's optimism. "It's already two weeks past our usual harvest, and the forecasts are conflicting. The rain might not come. The crusher is being delivered tomorrow, and I don't think they'll let me reschedule again."

"What if we reach out to the Santa Clara winery? They might be able to fit us in. I really think they need more time." He glanced out over the vines, his brow creased.

Wind whipped Javier's mother's hair as she followed his gaze. A hazy smoke hung in the air, obscuring the usually prominent crests of the Sierra Nevada mountains.

"Pedro would know what to do," Gabriella murmured. Two years after their father's death, hearing his name on their mother's lips was still a painful reminder of his loss. So much had gone with him: the joy that used to surround mealtimes, the good years of the harvest, and his warm voice telling leyendas by the fire at night. All those things had disappeared, together with Javier's childhood.

"Los tacos están en la mesa," Gabriella finally said with a short smile, dismissing the workers for their lunch. They all nodded their thanks as they trudged to the shed, its picnic tables laid out with tortillas, seasoned meat, salsas, and a pitcher of agua fresca. Javier's stomach grumbled at the scent of food, but he hung back in order to talk to his mother alone.

"Mamá," Javier started, clearing his throat after an inopportune voice crack. "I want to be here to help you with the harvest. Maybe I can skip the first week of school."

"Skip your first week of middle school? I thought you were looking forward to it." Gabriella licked her thumb and rubbed at a spot on Javier's temple. With a frown, Javier brushed her hand away.

"I am... but the vineyard is more important. Seriously, Mom. I'm strong now. Let me help."

She took his face in both hands, smiling down at him with glassy eyes. "I know you are, mijo. Pero no te preocupes. Everything will be fine." Gabriella placed a kiss on his forehead before turning to join Roberto. The man was hosing down the wheels of the ATV as he tried to keep the wind from taking his wide-brimmed hat.

Javier glared at her back. What else did he have to do to show her he was capable? He hadn't complained once that year about getting up early, and he could carry just as much as Eva could—well, at least at the beginning of the day.

"You think you're the man of the family now, don't you?" his sister mocked, drying her hands off on the rough blue towel. "Well, you aren't. You're just a little kid. Why don't you run off and play with your toys?"

Javier thought of the bin in his room containing action figures he hadn't touched in six months, and his fists balled at the unfairness of it all.

"Why are you such a bitch, Effie?"

The profanity caught both of them off guard, sounding especially crass juxtaposed with the childhood nickname. Javier glanced nervously over his shoulder to make sure his mom hadn't heard. She hadn't.

Eva's mouth twisted into a scowl before she grabbed a hose off the washtub and shot him in the face with a blast of frigid water.

"Eva!" he screamed.

She looked at him with a satisfied smirk that ignited a fire in his chest. He closed the distance between them before popping Eva in the jaw with his fist. The reverberations of her teeth clacking together rattled through his knuckles and down to his elbow. She glared furiously at him as she spat blood. Javier blinked, paralyzed by the shock of his actions.

"You're dead."

Her words hit him with an icy dread—he was pretty sure she would make good on the threat. Gabriella jogged toward them, issuing stern reprimands. Javier wasn't listening. His feet carried him deep into the vines and out the other side into the stand of oak trees before he finally stopped. He had to brace himself as a coughing fit wracked his body. His lungs burned from the impromptu sprint in the polluted air.

When the hacking subsided, Javier found a shady spot under one of the trees and squatted, wrapping his arms around his knees. He examined his reddened knuckles, picking at the scuffed skin. He'd never hit anyone before, much less a girl. It didn't matter that Eva had totally deserved it—hitting people was not how problems were solved. Javier imagined the look of disappointment his father would have given him. In the end, Pedro would make Javier apologize to Eva and take some of her chores for the week. Then they would all eat dinner together.

That wasn't how things were dealt with now, though. His mother would cry and ask God why He'd given her such unruly children. They would sit through a tense dinner, and the next day, Eva and Javier would go back to bickering as they always did. Javier hated the silence. It was even worse than the crying and the yelling. Silence is what happened when nothing was left. It was the sound of a casket being lowered into the ground. It was the sound of grapes dying on the vine.

He stayed under the oak trees until the sun went down and then some. The screech of something large pierced the air, and Javier looked into the sky instinctively. Only dim stars poked through a haze. For a terrifying second, he wondered if he'd been transported back to the time of the dinosaurs, like in that one comic book. *No.* He shook his head. That was silly, something a little kid would think. However, it was probably time to get back anyway and apologize to Eva. He didn't want to, but it's what his dad would have wanted him to do. As he shuffled back through the vines, he hugged his arms against the evening wind, trying not to jump at the small animal noises around him.

As he was passing the small shed, light peeked out through the cracks of the wooden siding. One of the workers must have left it on accidentally. Javier diverted his course to turn it off but stopped in his tracks when he heard a voice from inside. *Eva?*

Javier crouched down outside the building, peering through a knothole in the boards. Inside, Eva knelt in front of a low table draped with a white cloth, chanting something. Candles in tall glass jars flickered while rosary beads and dried leaves kept them company. Javier pressed his ear against the hole, trying to make out the words.

She spoke in Spanish, a language that had surrounded him his entire life, but he had a difficult time piecing together the meaning of her sentences. It seemed like she was asking for something, like a prayer. She kept repeating the word "lluvia," but why was she trying to talk to God about rain out here in the barn? She hadn't even been to Mass in over a year—yet another great lament of their mother's, along with Eva's eyeliner usage and college-aged boyfriend.

Javier was pondering that when a piercing screech sounded behind him. He spun at the abrupt noise, pressing himself flat against the building. A colossal bird stood before him, beady amber eyes glaring from a bald head of pink-and-yellow mottled flesh. It clicked its beak threateningly.

It's a dinosaur after all!

The vulture tilted its head to the side and gave another ear-piercing bellow before extending its black-and-white wings. The wingspan was at least twice Javier's height, and he sucked in a breath, preparing for the worst. But instead of eating him, the bird launched itself back into the sky. The gusts ruffled Javier's hair as it left him stunned and plastered to the side of the barn.

Eva came around the corner.

"What are you doing here?" Her chin showed a yellowing bruise, and a pang of genuine regret overrode Javier's shock of the encounter with the dinosaur-bird.

"I'm so sorry, Effie." He ran to her and threw his arms around her middle. She stiffened at first but eventually relaxed into the embrace, putting her arms around him as well.

"It's all right, Javi." Eva smoothed the puffy hair on his head, which was caked with dust. "Come on, let's go find Mom. She's been worrying about you all day."

Javier received the expected scolding along with being sent to bed without supper. The strange thing was Eva didn't seem too upset. She even came to tuck him in that night—something she was definitely too cool for on any other day. Javier dreamed of a Jurassic world that night, and when he woke up, his sister was gone.

It rained every day for the next week.

NEAR CLOSING TIME, Javier and Wenshi finally met in the middle of the directory section. They both had nothing more than strained eyes and dry fingers to show for the night's efforts, with no hint of Eva's name to be found.

On their way out, they stopped by the front desk one last time to see if the woman had found anything in the back. Javier's ears perked up as the conversation progressed with affirmative tones. A printed document was passed over the counter, and Javier's fingers felt numb as he picked it up. The pages were photocopies of a scientific journal, the title of the article nearly incomprehensible: "Quantifying the Impacts of Blood Consumption on Recovery Rates in Sanguivores." But underneath it was Eva's name, Dr. Evelina Robles, listed first in a team of researchers.

Javier's mind buzzed as he flipped through the dense article, and at the back, he was greeted with a picture of a grown woman. Her face was fuller, with light creasing at the corners of her eyes, but it was undeniably her. A short bio on Eva was listed below her picture—educated at a local university in Shanghai and currently working for Vasa Laboratories as of the publication date, which was two years prior.

"Xiè xiè," he said to the woman behind the desk as he choked back the tears of joy threatening to spill. Library staff ushered them outside, and the doors clattered behind them as the library closed. The rain poured, but it did nothing to quell Javier's jubilant mood. Eva was actually here. She wasn't dead in an unmarked grave but practicing medicine for nonhuman creatures after all. And Javier held actual proof that he hadn't come to Shanghai for nothing. His odds of seeing Eva again had risen from minuscule to substantial, and the joy within him was difficult to even process.

"I take it that's her?" Wenshi asked tentatively, readying her umbrella.

Javier laughed heartily. "It's her. It's really her." He threw his arms around Wenshi and gave her an enthusiastic hug. "Eva is actually here. I'm actually going to find her!"

Wenshi cleared her throat as she recovered from the hug. Javier's head was too abuzz to actually read the words of the paper, so he stuffed it in his bag for a more thorough review when he got home.

"I'm really happy for you," Wenshi said, clearly unsure what to do with a man expressing so much emotion.

Javier couldn't help himself. He grabbed one of her hands and squeezed it in his.

"Sincerely, thank you for all your help. I couldn't have done it without you. When I find her, I'm cooking birria, and the three of us are having dinner together as a thank you."

Wenshi smiled back at him. "As long as you make it spicy."

7

The first few days after Mina's return, she didn't leave her room. From the southern-facing window, she could see the inner courtyard, its sweeping paths, fish ponds, and sculpted greenery—they were all the company she could bear as she internalized the reality of her circumstances. She was trapped here for the foreseeable future.

On the fourth day, she mustered the courage to join the evening meal. Mina's hand gripped the banister as she descended to the main floor of Zhang Manor. Her slippers met the plush hand-knotted rug of the foyer, which covered lustrous dark hardwood planks. A central table held an artistic arrangement of gnarled stems and spindly blossoms, each one painstakingly placed to appear as organic as possible.

The scent of green tea, spiced pork, and blood hit Mina's nose simultaneously, eliciting a pang of hunger so severe she braced herself against a credenza to keep from doubling over. Even while backpacking, she hadn't gone for so long without a meal, catching rats in her most desperate moments of hunger.

Knowing the imposed starvation wasn't due to lack of food but rather intentional deprivation somehow made the emptiness of her stomach all the more sour.

Mina crossed through the double doors to the dining room. Inside was a round table laden with an array of elegantly plated, steaming dishes. Lian occupied the seat farthest from the door, with a newspaper unfolded before her. Flanking her were Shenye and Guolong, the eldest and most trusted of Lian's offspring—each forgoing their own family for a life together supporting their creator. They ignored Mina as she entered, continuing their conversation on exchange rates between the Hong Kong dollar and the yuan.

Mina silently took her customary seat nearest the door. She portioned rice and vegetables onto her plate, an ascetic meal that might help relieve a small part of her hunger. She chewed slowly, trying to keep her eyes from wandering to the carafes of crimson liquid.

"Oh. It's back," an unctuous voice called from behind her. Mina winced, and the mushroom held in her chopsticks tumbled to her plate with an unseemly *splat*.

"Good evening, elder sister," she replied, scowling at her plate.

Yuxi waltzed in to take her seat to Mina's right, a colorful silk robe covering her loungewear—a stark contrast to the business formal worn by the remainder of the family. Flipping her luxurious platinum-blond hair over one shoulder, Yuxi poured a healthy measure of blood into a crystal tumbler. She gave Mina a cruel smirk as she swirled the liquid nonchalantly before taking a thirsty drink. Resentment and hunger mingling in her stomach, Mina bit down on the inside of her cheek to keep her fangs from descending—a serious breach of etiquette amongst vampires in Shanghai society.

"I heard you made it all the way to Singapore. Such a long way to scurry for such a little mouse," Yuxi said, amusement in her voice designed to rankle. It worked.

"Not all of us are content to attend dinner parties as a full-time occupation," Mina replied, taking a sip of her own hot water and imagining it was something more fulfilling.

Yuxi snorted. "No? In that case, you won't mind that I declined the Vasa brat's Hundred-Day Celebration on your behalf."

Mina choked on her water. "I missed it?"

Yuxi shrugged. "I don't recall the date."

"I need to see him," Mina said absently.

The pages of Lian's paper rustled as she set them aside to take a sip of her tea, an arched brow aimed across the table.

"If I may, that is," Mina amended quickly. "Perhaps after dinner—"

"No."

Heat rose to Mina's cheeks at the dismissal. Would Lian really cut her off from her only friend in the city? Mina set her chopsticks down, her appetite gone.

"You've forgotten what day it is."

Mina wracked her mental calendar for the reason Lian would deny her leave. It was late summer... The perfumed scent of incense spurred an association, and she closed her eyes in recognition.

"It's the Hungry Ghost Day."

On the night of the new moon of the seventh lunar month, it was said that unfulfilled ghosts roamed the earth, seeking revenge for the wrongs done to them. While the human population of the city observed the custom by burning joss paper and offerings to the deceased, Lian insisted her family remain inside for the night when the ghosts were supposedly most active.

"I recommend you pay your respects this evening. They don't look kindly on those who break their promises."

Mina's breath caught. The night of her turning ceremony, she'd prayed at the ancestral altar for a chance to join the Zhang family in exchange for honoring their legacy—a prayer she assumed no one else had heard. The accusatory depths of Lian's obsidian eyes said otherwise.

She wanted to object—a Chinese folk custom shouldn't stop her from visiting a friend she'd sorely neglected. Yet part of her felt an equal measure of guilt for failing to uphold the vow she'd made the night of her ill-omened turning. The ancestors had given her what she asked—that she no longer wanted it was beside the point.

"Yes, my lady," she murmured, her hands bunching the black linen napkin in her lap.

AFTER DINNER, Mina approached the altar with reverent trepidation. A tiered display of marble ancestral tablets greeted her—a jury of unforgiving spirits in her trial for betrayal. She knelt before them, the hardwood floor unyielding against her knees.

With a deep inhale to calm herself, Mina selected a fresh stick of incense, lit the end with a match, and placed it in the censer. She pressed the pad of her thumb against her sharpened incisor until the skin gave way with a piercing sting. Mina smeared a streak of her blood on the onyx orb resting between the tablets. The bloodstone quickly absorbed the liquid, and Mina bowed her forehead to the floor three times in ritual obeisance.

The house was quiet around her save for the rustling of the servants attending to the manor. The void of activity provided an uncomfortable space for reflection. After an inauspicious start to her vampirehood, she'd floundered at integrating into the society. Lian discouraged her from pursuing any serious external commitment, insisting her time was better spent at home. Mina had taken up a series of hobbies—languages, calligraphy, and even poetry over the years—hoping to make herself useful or, at the very least, to impress Lian. All of it had been trivial in the end, accomplishing neither goal.

"If you have some plan for me, I'd appreciate a hint at what it is," she whispered to the engraved stones. She received no response from the tableau of remembrance.

With a sigh, Mina gathered her legs beneath herself, pins and needles poking sharply at her toes. As she lay one hand on the newel of the banister, a whispered word tickled her ears.

"Mi-na..."

She spun around, her face draining of color. Mina hadn't heard that voice since she was a child.

"Mi-na." The disembodied word floated through the foyer once more, seeming to come from nowhere and everywhere at once.

"Halabeoji?" she called in return.

A soft light pulsed from the window near the front entrance. Her chest tight with anticipation, Mina glided toward it, drawn by the glowing aura. Beyond the glass, a spectral form floated, its body turned away from her. She pressed a hand to her mouth to suppress the gasp—it *couldn't* be. Yet even from the back, she could make out the curve of the old man's shoulders and the details of his white hanbok.

"Mi-na. Come home," his voice said in Korean with a yearning that brought a wave of emotion crashing down on her.

Mina held out her hand and pressed it against the glass. "I'm sorry, Grandfather. *I can't*," she replied in the same language, the language he had taught her.

The ghost spun slowly to face her, the face of her grandpa smiling warmly. Tears gathered at the corners of her eyes as she remembered refusing to attend his funeral all those years ago. Had she gone, maybe her family would have convinced her to move to Korea with them. Maybe she would never have even met Lian.

Mina glanced at the locked front door of the house. She longed to see the ghost without the separation of the glass, to throw her arms around her grandfather and beg him to help her. The ghost continued to bob under the portico. Then slowly, its broad smile began to gape open. Mina stared transfixed as the ghost's jaw unhinged beyond its natural limits. Rows of pointy teeth emerged as the creature's resemblance to her grandfather dissolved into a ghastly form of bulbous bones and saggy flesh. It lunged at the window, banging its head against the glass with a wet *smack* before its pocked tongue tried to wriggle its way through.

With a small yelp, Mina drew her hand away and jumped back. Her back met with a solid barrier. A person. Lian.

She spun, lowering her head to hide her terrified expression, hoping the woman hadn't been standing there long.

"Lady Zhang, forgive me." Mina flinched as another thump landed against the glass, refusing to turn and look.

Lian grabbed her hand and turned it over to reveal Mina's palm. Sooty flesh showed everywhere her skin had contacted the glass. A contemplative look came over the older woman's face, rare uncertainty clouding her eyes. "What did you see?"

"Nothing. It was nothing." The words came out too fast. Mina refused to believe that was truly her grandfather.

"You are young to see them," the taller woman murmured, stroking Mina's palm with her thumb before dropping her hand. "It's good you are back where I can protect you."

A sharp emotion stabbed Mina between the ribs, denial clashing with genuine fear.

"Are they really who they appear to be?" Mina wiped her sticky palm against her thigh. She scarcely dared acknowledge the true question that plagued her thoughts: *Is Halabeoji haunting me because I abandoned my family?*

Lian inclined her head, her cool obsidian eyes searching Mina's face. "They are capable of impersonation though typically, their representations are true."

Mina bit down on her lip, trying to keep the shock of sorrow from showing. The remorse felt like it would burst from her chest if she took one more breath. Lian closed the distance between them and lifted Mina's chin gently with her willowy fingers.

"It is a heavy thing, confronting the ways we've disappointed others."

Tears gathered at the corners of Mina's eyes before tumbling down her pale face. Lian's gaze darkened, a predatory possessiveness glinting in her expression as she caught one of the falling droplets with a tapered finger.

"You know, I really thought you would return on your own. If I gave you space," the woman said softly. Lian's cropped hair neatly framed her face, the calm authority of her presence never wavering despite the turmoil Mina could sense beneath it.

It made her feel like a mouse being watched by a raptor, and she stilled under the observation, stifling her tears. "If you'll excuse me, I think I'd like to pray some more," Mina said, infusing her voice with false confidence.

For a second, she thought Lian might say something more —*do* something more. In the end, the woman nodded her approval before withdrawing up the stairs to her expansive suite at the top.

Mina took an exhausted breath of relief before returning on shaky legs to the altar. She sat before it until the sun came up, never letting her gaze wander to the window again. Every so often, a ghostly "Mi-na" floated through the foyer, driving a spike of contrition through Mina's heart each time.

Mina prayed to the ancestors for another chance—not forgiveness, just survival. *Don't let the ghosts eat me alive. Don't let Lian eat me alive.*

THE NEXT EVENING, Mina was granted leave to call on the Vasas. She stood before the pale wooden door of the penthouse, waiting to be let in. One of the trusty Zhang security guards—once a colonel in the unstoppable Mongolian cavalry, now her dutiful escort—cleared his throat as she knocked gently for the second time. Even though Mina confirmed she hadn't missed Dmitri's party, maybe he'd spurned her as a shitty friend anyway. Mina braced herself for the embarrassment of being rebuffed, but a young butler finally opened the door.

"Welcome in, Miss Park. Masters Dmitri and August are taking tea in the solarium, if you'd like to follow me."

Mina's security detail took up a position beside the door instead of insisting on accompanying her inside, and she was relieved for the small amount of privacy.

Stepping into the Vasa apartments was like stepping into seventeen-hundreds Stockholm. Crown molding and elaborate chandeliers hung above furniture from a European salon. Mina had always thought the decor gaudy compared to the elegant simplicity of Zhang Manor. The solarium, at least, featured a domed glass roof with a lush assortment of tropical plants, as peaceful as the courtyards back home. In the early days of their friendship, Mina and Dmitri had dubbed it the "lunarium," accounting for the fact they never used it while the sun was actually out. There, the two men sat on tufted sofas separated by an ornate tea service.

"Älskling!" August beamed. "I'm glad to see my sister has let you out of her clutches for the evening." The man dabbed at his pencil-thin mustache with a lace serviette before standing.

"Lord Vasa," Mina greeted him cooly, dipping into a curtsey. The sunken look of Dmitri's diminished visage was startling, and Mina tried to keep her concern from showing. The glow of his human vitality had vanished, his dancer's musculature atrophied. Despite living in a vampire city, new turnings were surprisingly rare. Dmitri was the first person Mina had known before his transformation, and seeing the physical toll was astounding.

"Don't worry. I will absent myself and let you two reconnect. Give my best to Lian and congratulate her on her latest acquisition, won't you?" August patted her on the shoulder before gliding out of the room. Mina tentatively approached the sofa where Dmitri sat.

"Hey, Dima, it's good to see you." Mina slid in next to him on the couch.

A servant cleared August's plate while another poured her a fresh cup of tea, the smell of bergamot potent.

Dmitri gazed blankly at the table, the steam long gone from the surface of his untouched teacup. "You left me," he said distantly. "I knew you didn't want me to go through with it, but I thought you would at least be there for me." His raspy voice cut Mina to the bone.

She opened and closed her mouth a few times as viable excuses came to the tip of her tongue. Mina couldn't say any of them. She was the only person in Dmitri's circle who could remember the agony of her soul being transfigured into an entity fueled by blood.

"I'm sorry. I—" Mina bowed her head, picking at her cuticles. "I should have been here. I just had to get out of the city for a while."

She tried to balance a truthful explanation with one that wouldn't burden him with her problems. He didn't need any added stress right now.

For the next several seconds, the only sound was the tick of the long hand of the grandfather clock. With a labored sigh, Dmitri scooted closer to her. He rested his head on her shoulder while putting a hand over hers. It was as cold as a corpse.

"At least you're here now," the younger man finally

conceded. Even the scant forgiveness gave Mina waves of relief. She still had at least one friend in this world, and right now, that meant more than Dmitri could know. Mina snaked her arms around Dmitri's torso, feeling his prominent rib cage as she squeezed.

"How are you? How is August? Has he been feeding you? You know it's critical for your development the first year," Mina asked, all her concerns competing for answers simultaneously. The transformation process required bringing the human to the brink of death, far past what a body could naturally recover from. Only in this liminal state might the blood of the vampire graft successfully to the soul—a delicate transplant of paranormal energy.

With an exaggerated eye roll, Dmitri responded, "Yes, Mom. I'm eating. August has been... He's everything. I didn't know the attachment, or bond, or whatever, would be so strong. I can hardly stand being in a different room from him." Dmitri's gaze trailed over to the door where August had departed.

"I know." Mina smoothed the man's wheat-brown hair. "It will lessen with time."

"The weird thing is I don't want it to. It's like my whole life has been leading to this moment where I am his fledgling. It's like I'm not even my own person anymore."

Strain set into Mina's jaw as she ardently hoped August wouldn't take advantage of Dmitri's utter vulnerability. There wasn't much she could do about it, even if he did. Within each house, order was maintained through a strict hierarchy. Most fledglings at least had a grandparent of sorts that would keep their makers in line. The original ancient—the one that spawned each of the eight Heads of House—was no longer present, leaving both August and Lian with unchecked power within their domains.

"Try to keep your head clear. Do the things you used to enjoy, like dancing, as soon as you have the strength."

Dmitri's lips cracked into a brittle smile. "My ankle. It doesn't hurt anymore." He emphasized the point by rolling his foot in an exaggerated circle. Mina winced at the pops the joint emitted.

"That still doesn't sound normal, but if it doesn't hurt, then that's something."

"August set up a barre and flooring in front of a mirror so I can do some light exercises. He said I can work up to joining the Shanghai ballet in a few months if I'm diligent."

That was an ambitious recovery plan, but hope was more important than a realistic timeline, and she didn't fault August for giving that to him.

"You'll be premiering as Prince Siegfried in no time," Mina added with a warm smile. "I'll be hollering for an encore in the front row with an embarrassingly large bouquet of roses."

"There are no encores in ballet, and you know that."

Mina nabbed a cucumber sandwich square off the tiered serving tray. "Show me those fangs of yours. I know you want to show them off."

Dmitri extended his canines with a wolfish grin. Mina tilted his chin this way and that to admire the ivory teeth, enjoying the adorable way his crooked dentition had caused his fangs to grow inward slightly.

"Very debonair."

"Show me yours! I bet mine are bigger." Dmitri's did have an impressive length, but Mina restrained herself from telling him that it had a certain walrus effect.

"Don't you know size doesn't matter?" Mina teased. "Plus, it's not polite to flash fang in society."

Dmitri shoved her shoulder, and she shoved him back, basking in the comfort of their friendship.

"My Hundred Day celebration is next week. Promise me you'll be there."

"Of course I will."

The next hour was filled with gossip and giggles, Dmitri slowly recovering his old verve as they chatted. When his energy levels clearly faded, Mina rose. She squeezed his hand before leaving the one person in this city she could be herself with.

AS SHE ASCENDED the stairs from the parking garage to the main level of Zhang Manor, laughter resonated from the sitting room. Mina tried to slink by the opening to get to the staircase, but she was stopped in her tracks by Lian's voice.

"Come, pet. We're celebrating."

With a swallow, Mina turned to face the room. Shenye was curled up on the sofa with Guolong's arm around her. Their monogamous devotion to each other was a rarity in vampire society, most individuals accepting the inevitability of losing partners and gaining new ones. Yuxi sat on an upholstered stool, fingering the delicate neck of the erhu with one hand while levering a bow across its strings. Sonorous music filled the cozy room. Lian, sitting in her armchair, tilted her head at Mina with an inquisitive smile.

Mina sidled into the room along the periphery. She took a seat in the matching chair beside Lian. In the middle of the sitting area, a low oval table held a decanter and four poured glasses. The smell of wine and blood suffused the air, and Mina's stomach cramped hollowly.

"What is the occasion?" Mina asked, doing her best to return the pleasant smile. She didn't want to squander her good mood from reconnecting with Dmitri.

"We finalized Hong Kong."

Mina blinked. "As in another vampire city?"

"Precisely." Lian simpered, taking a drink from the large Bordeaux glass. "It's thanks to these two that the paperwork was signed this week." Lian gestured to Shenye and Guolong. The pair shared a smile with each other before acknowledging the accolade.

"Everything we do is for the honor of this noble house, Lady Zhang," Guolong said, his deep voice simultaneously servile yet smug.

Lian lapped it up.

The comment from August finally clicked, and Mina interjected, "Lord Vasa also congratulated you on your latest acquisition."

Lian snorted. "Of course he did, the ponce."

Mina shot Yuxi a glare as she dominated the attention of the room with a particularly high-pitched finale to her solo. The woman was born in the 1910s to a wealthy silk merchant, growing up not far from Zhang Manor itself—perfect Yuxi with her cultured, classical Chinese heritage. Mina could never compete with her. Honestly, it was a mystery why Lian had ever agreed to let her join the family, a fact that Mina hadn't fully grasped until well after it was too late to matter.

"Will the same methods of governance and blood donation be used for Hong Kong?" Mina asked, shoving aside her insecurities.

"That's the best part—Hong Kong will be House Zhang's alone. The humans will more or less be managed in the same way, but we will have the capacity to grow. We needed the eight houses to come together for the initial takeover, but Shanghai was never a long-term solution for all of us. As soon as the other houses relocate, we will have the Middle Kingdom to ourselves, as it should be."

"Including the Federovs?" Mina couldn't help but ask.

"Especially the Federovs," Lian said with grave sincerity. "They've been underreporting their birth rates and supplementing their blood allotment to cover it for years now. Despite the raids against their... *facilities*, the Federov operations have been troublesome to quell. I won't have them undermining the reputation we've spent decades cultivating among the humans."

Shanghai imposed strict limitations on vampire reproduction to maintain a sustainable ratio between vampires and humans. It hadn't occurred to Mina that some houses might try to circumvent that rule. It soured her stomach to think that Mikhail's depravity was linked to his family's greed for expansion. In addition, Lian's sincerity in dealing with the Federov problem only furthered Mina's unease; if the woman truly was trying to keep Shanghai a safe place for everyone, it undercut Mina's reasons for leaving that much more.

"I suspect the other cities in China will soon realize how much better off they'd be under your control, Lady Zhang. Or should we call you Empress Zhang now?" Yuxi giggled coquettishly, making Mina want to throw something at her.

"A toast to Empress Zhang!" Shenye played along, raising her glass.

Lian rolled her eyes with a smile. "Perhaps after I secure Beijing," she stipulated but lifted her glass to the toast anyway.

As the smell of the sloshing liquid hit her nose, Mina imagined how a taste of the red blend might flood her mouth with briny tannins. Her fangs descended involuntarily at the phantom blood covering her tongue.

"Please, Lady Zhang—" Mina bit her words off vehemently. She wouldn't beg. "How much longer will you make me wait?" The elongated incisors felt foreign and obtrusive in her mouth, like a relic of a feral legacy.

Lian tapped her wineglass with her fingernail pensively. "You know I could have chosen a blunter punishment—one that would have hurt more. Why do you think I chose this instead?"

Mina's insides churned with a nauseous fear along with something darker. "You wanted me to reflect on my privileges."

A corner of the woman's mouth tugged downward. "Where does this blood come from?" she asked, swirling the glass. "How does it reach this table? How many humans does it take to feed you personally? You are quick to condemn the Federovs, but you do it from a place of ignorance. Even outside of this glass of blood, this city was designed for you in ways you have yet to understand."

Mina blinked, unable to give the questions more than a cursory answer. The mechanisms of the blood donation system were like plumbing or prepackaged meats—a convenience most individuals took for granted thanks to infrastructure and the work of the few who maintained it.

Mina considered the inky crimson liquid in the carafe. "I understand what it is to feed myself now," she said deliberately.

"What if I prefer that to accepting meals that come with conditions?"

Lian inclined her head. "Is too much asked of you here, Mina?" A darkness underlined her words.

The conversations of the other family members subsided, leaving the room in expectant silence. Mina felt a flush at her cheeks, but she refused to submit to Lian's twisted logic. "*Nothing* is asked of me here. I'm a pointless decoration. All I wanted was a chance to be myself."

"There's no one stopping you from doing that here. Running away from your choices isn't a future—it's lack of character masquerading as individualism." Lian took a deep drink from her glass, a sadistic glint in her eye. "Now, be a good pet and put those fangs away. We'll see how this petulance of yours fares after another week or two without sustenance."

Mina's face burned with humiliation as the rest of her family chuckled in amusement. Calming herself enough to force her teeth to recede took serious concentration—she was *hungry*, and the blood on the table was all too tempting. Her fangs itched ferociously within her gums, eager to take a meal by any means necessary, but Mina refused to become a slave to the hunger. Lian couldn't withhold blood forever, and Mina would prove she was strong enough to not break under the denial.

8

Javier spent the next two nights at the library, tracking down as much information as he could on Vasa Laboratories and Eva's research. The medical journal that the original article had come from had an additional five papers with Eva on the authorial list and many more that cited the original titles she had written.

By the fiftieth mind-numbingly scientific article, Javier had developed enough context to understand the central theses she explored with her work. She was trying to prove that blood from certain human donors was denser in the magical energy that vampires needed to function. Many of the articles called this magical density "potency." While the experimental data suggested that the effects of the potency could be measured after it had been consumed, she had yet to measure potency in vitro. Javier had to admit the concept was intriguing, and he could understand the desire to know how things worked. But why the hell she'd moved to Shanghai and made it her life's mission... Well, he would just have to ask when he found her.

However, Javier's most critical discovery in reading her research papers was not in the conclusions section but rather in the acknowledgments. More than once, the "Sanguis Institute" was attributed for having provided access to clinical patients and laboratory resources. With some more digging, Javier discovered the elusive institute was just a fancy hospital for vampires located downtown, just a few blocks from the bank. Javier was willing to bet that Eva worked there.

The next evening after work, he approached the glass facade of the Sanguis Institute with trepidation. Javier had spent so long focused on the singular goal of finding his sister that he hadn't thought about what he would actually say to her in person. In addition, the initial relief at learning Eva was alive had slowly soured over the course of the week. If she was doing so well, why hadn't she at least let her family know she was okay? Javier wanted to give her the benefit of the doubt, but he couldn't help but feel the sting of abandonment.

Frosted glass doors whooshed open, revealing a tranquil lobby. A sheet of glistening water gurgled behind the front desk, and opalescent terrazzo floors were polished to a mirror-like finish. Javier realized his error as soon as he stepped through the entrance. Like the bank, it was clear this was a space made for the upper echelon of the city, which did not include him.

"Excuse me, sir. I'm going to need to ask you to leave." A pair of security guards corralled him before he was even halfway to the front desk.

"I just need to get some information. I'm trying to find someone."

Maybe they could be reasoned with.

"Human guests are not allowed in this facility," the guard stated, ushering him toward the door.

Javier's mind worked quickly, trying to come up with a convincing argument for them to let him through. Hell, if his encounter with Mina had taught him nothing else, it was that vampires couldn't necessarily be identified by appearances alone.

"What makes you think I'm not a vampire?" Javier said coldly, trying to imitate the voice Mina used.

"Yeah, nice try." The guard grabbed hold of his ear tag and promptly marched him to the sidewalk beyond the front door.

"Jesus, ease up!" Javier cried through gritted teeth, feeling like his ear was about to be wrenched off. In hindsight, that was a pretty stupid oversight, claiming to be a vampire while sporting a very obvious "human support staff" badge.

"Look, I'm not trying to bother anyone. I'm trying to find my sister. Eva Robles. Dr. Robles?" Javier said after the guard finally released him.

"Dr. Robles is far too busy to be bothered with the likes of you. Now get lost, and don't let me catch you back here."

The guard had said her name. He had said, "Dr. Robles." That had to be her.

A small grin spread across his face as he regarded the building.

Oh, I will most certainly be back.

THE NEXT EVENING after his shift ended, Javier rolled the dial on the padlock of his locker, fingers tingling with excitement. Inside hung a brand-new blue suit—"cerulean," the sales associate had called it. It had cost him a generous chunk of change, more than he'd earned in his time as a janitor, but if he was going to portray a suave vampire, he needed the costume to go along with it.

"Special event tonight?" his boss asked as he wiped a smear of grease from his brow.

"Not really... but kind of?" Javier suppressed a laugh at the absurdity of his plan. "Can you keep a secret?"

"I prefer to avoid them," Arvind said with a hint of judgment.

"Well, it's not really a secret," Javier hedged, struggling with the two buttons at his throat as he donned the shirt. He wished he'd insisted on the half size up. "I'm trying to get past some security guards to see my sister. They won't let me in if they think I'm a human."

Arvind's eyebrows shot up. "You know it's illegal to impersonate a vampire in Shanghai, yes?"

Javier swallowed the consternation that bubbled up. "Like, how illegal?"

"You'd likely face deportation, which would be a shame. You're one of the more dependable janitors we've had."

Javier frowned at his reflection in the warped mirror on the far wall. Even from here, he could tell the Windsor knot on his tie was horrendously lopsided. He tore it out and redraped the russet silk to start over again.

"That's a risk I'm going to have to take. I came here to find my sister, and this is the only way I can do that." His second attempt at the knot was no better.

With a sigh, Arvind wiped his hands on the rag before approaching Javier. He grabbed the ends of Javier's tie authoritatively, and after a few expert twists, he snugged the symmetrical knot against the band of the shirt collar. The man helped Javier into his suit jacket next.

"Thanks. I—I never learned how to do that."

Arvind clapped him on the back, his eyes twinkling behind the folds of droopy lids. "Just come back to me in one piece tomorrow. I wish you luck on your journey, my friend." His boss left him alone in the locker room, the paternal reassurance imparting an odd warmth in his chest.

With a bracing inhale, Javier seated a black felt fedora on his head and took one last gander in the mirror. Staring back at him was a dapper figure that looked like the villain from a telenovela. If that didn't translate to smarmy vampire, he didn't know what did.

Javier strode out of the locker room with a confidence he hoped would carry his disguise.

Here goes nothing.

JAVIER LET the chauffeur of the rented limo open the door for him before sliding out of the car in the parking lot underneath the Sanguis Institute. After reflecting on his first failed attempt, he realized in addition to the ear tag mishap, walking in off the street in broad daylight was a pretty dumb thing to do before claiming to be a vampire. Subterranean parking was the way vampires in Shanghai got around during the day. The right transportation would lend some much-needed credibility to his guise.

Javier held his chin high as he strode through the doors to the lower-level reception, a mirror image of the one from above with less natural light.

"Good evening, I have an appointment to see Dr. Robles," he intoned, angling his face to keep the ear tag hidden in the shadow of the hat brim. When he'd called to schedule, he'd insisted he be seen the next day in his most haughty vampire impression. To his surprise, it worked.

"Of course, sir," the demure woman behind the desk said, consulting an appointment list. "Please follow me."

Javier felt woozy with relief. As he followed the woman's clicking heels to the elevator, he kept his head straight ahead, ignoring the armed security guards entirely. While Javier, the human, might have nodded genially, arrogant vampires did not acknowledge hired help. Or at least, that's the impression he got from the way they'd acted around him at the bank.

Nearly there. Just keep it together a little while longer.

The elevator jetted up to the eleventh floor before sliding open. A pleasant aroma wafted from the roses kept on the glass accent tables dotting the airy hallway. Javier couldn't imagine what medical care at a place like this would cost in the States.

Javier took a fortifying breath as the woman knocked on the solid wooden door of the office. A gleaming plaque on the door read Evelina Robles, M.D. His stomach clenched, and he was sure he was going to be sick as the door swung the rest of the way open. Javier took two steps into the office as the woman from the reception excused herself.

Tall cherry bookshelves lined the wall behind her desk, filled with weighty books, certificates, and tasteful stone sculptures. The walls were painted in a soothing sage tone, and the desk was orderly with leather folios. All of this Javier took in peripherally as his eyes fixated on the woman who rose from the high-backed leather chair on the other side of the desk.

"Mr. Diaz, it's nice to meet you. House Quezada, I presume?"

Her smile was wide, with teeth as white as the string of pearls she wore. Her long, wavy hair was worn down with the top section clasped to stay out of her face. A pristine lab coat covered a purple dress. Eva's figure had matured into one that resembled their mother's, and Javier tried to reconcile his mental images of a scrawny teenager wearing cutoffs at the vineyard with this sophisticated doctor in an office building in Shanghai.

"Eva." His voice trembled with emotion as he tore off his stupid hat. "Effie, it's me."

The polite smile slowly fell from her face as recognition dawned on her.

"Javier?" Eva whispered. "How... how are you here?"

He closed the space between them with two large strides and threw his arms around her. The familiar smell of lavender shampoo filled him with warmth, and his cheeks were wet with emotion by the time he pulled away. Eva placed a hand on his face as if to convince herself that he wasn't a figment of her imagination.

"I've been searching for you. I had to find you. All these years, not knowing if you were alive or dead. Why didn't you let us know where you were?" That came out more accusatory than he'd intended.

Eva let her gaze drift down and to the side, a small frown tugging at the corners of her mouth.

"I..." She paused. "Maybe we should sit." She crossed the room to a pair of accent chairs, smoothing her dress as she dropped into the seat.

Javier obliged her, taking the adjacent chair while Eva looked distantly out the window.

"When I left, Mom and I were not on good terms. As you probably remember," Eva started. That was one way to describe the yelling and door slamming that occurred nightly. "I needed a clean break. For myself. After Dad died..." Eva pinched the bridge of her nose, her eyebrows drawing together with grief.

Javier placed a hand on her knee reassuringly. "It was rough on all of us."

With a sharp breath, Eva leapt back out of her chair, pacing the office as she crossed her arms in front of her.

"What are you doing here, Javier?" she asked, her voice suddenly clinical.

Javier opened his mouth to respond, but the words took several seconds to come. Why was she questioning *his* motives? He wasn't the one who'd inexplicably abandoned his family.

"I needed to know what happened. My dad died, and then my sister ran away from home. My family fell apart, and I needed to know why." His throat felt tight as memories surfaced from that sorrow-filled era of his life: the depression he had nursed his mother through, the loneliness of his adolescence, his family halved.

Eva's shoulders rounded. "I'm sorry," she said, her voice uncharacteristically vulnerable.

"It's okay, Eva. I just... Why? Why couldn't you let us know you were okay?" He stood and took a tentative step toward her. Some piece of him needed to assign a reason to his grief, his mother's grief.

"I wanted to. I've written dozens of letters to you. To

Mom. But I couldn't send them. Not after..." Eva buried her face in her hands. "Not after I killed our dad."

Javier's head felt hot and heavy as he tried to process her words. He stuck two fingers in his shirt collar and tugged. "Eva, no. You didn't," he said, his words slow and measured. "Dad died in an accident. There was a storm."

His sister and his father had been tending the vines when the unseasonable electrical storm blew in. Lightning struck—a freak accident. At least, that's what he'd been told. Had they kept something from him?

"Unless... that's not true?" he probed.

Eva's face contorted into a pained expression, lines creasing on her forehead. "There was a storm—that's true enough. But I should have... I should have..." She buried her face in her hands, her shoulders shuddering with silent sobs.

Javier let out his held breath. *This is just her survivor's guilt.* She'd been sixteen at the time—far too young to witness the death of a parent, to have to wrestle his body onto the four-wheeler and drive him back to the house through torrential rains.

He went to Eva and embraced her, rubbing her back reassuringly. Her stiff posture gradually relaxed as she cried on his shoulder. Assuming a comforting role with her felt foreign to Javier. She'd always been headstrong and downright hostile at times. As her kid brother, he spent more time avoiding her moods than he did trying to console them.

This was not how he expected their reunion to go at all.

"Hey, you were just a kid. I know whatever happened was an accident. I didn't mean to dredge up the past. I just wanted to see that you were doing okay," he said, trying to pull her out of her nosedive.

This probably wasn't how Eva imagined her workday going either.

Javier pulled the silk square out of his breast pocket and handed it to her, feeling incredibly sophisticated as he did so. As Eva dabbed at the corners of her eyes, she sniffed a few times before seeming to regain her composure.

"Yes, I'm doing all right," she said, her voice subdued.

"I was pretty dang impressed when I found your research papers at the library."

"Oh yeah?" Eva smiled. "Doing some light reading?"

"Man, I wish. I mean, I always knew you were smart, but jeez. That stuff is way over my head." Javier hoped a little levity could recover the conversation.

"My little brother, all grown up and flying halfway around the world to find his sister." Eva shook her head. "You look... so blue." The corners of her eyes crinkled in amusement.

"Hey, this is your fault for working someplace so fancy that security guards are posted at the doors to keep human riffraff like me out. This is the only way I could get in to see you."

Eva considered his outfit. "So, you don't normally dress like a member of a bossa nova quartet?"

"I'll have you know this color is very on trend for the fall season," he shot back, striking a model pose. He was sure he looked absolutely ridiculous.

Eva covered her mouth as she laughed.

"So how is it, working with the fanged menaces? I've only had a few interactions, but they all seem like jerks at the best of times." Javier tugged at his shirt cuffs. He couldn't imagine putting this much effort into clothing on a daily basis.

"Yeah, pretty much," Eva admitted. "It helps when you have something they want. Like exclusive medical treatments."

"I suppose. But how do you even treat a vampire? I thought they all lived forever."

"There is emerging research suggesting the aging process continues, albeit about a hundred times slower than humans. But just because things heal doesn't mean that they heal correctly or that old injuries can't cause pain. That's mostly what we do here. A few rare blood diseases have been discovered, which we're researching now. You can't believe how exciting it is to be forging treatments for an entirely new species. I've been out of medical school for a decade, and I've only begun to scratch the surface."

"Seems like it pays pretty well too," Javier said, admiring the spacious office.

"Heh, yeah, that is one benefit. Their money comes with certain expectations for levels of service and care that can be difficult to meet, but overall, there are worse ways to make a living."

It was heartwarming to hear her talk so passionately about her career and job. Maybe she had made the right choice, getting out of California. She hadn't exactly been on the best path as a teenager, and this was a hell of a leap from where most runaways ended up.

"Speaking of, I have a full schedule of clients this evening that I need to prepare for. I assume you're in town for a little while longer? Let's get dinner. Catch up."

"Of course, anytime. Tomorrow?"

"Clinical work tomorrow... Maybe Friday. Wait. I have a party for a fledgling I helped deliver. I could cancel—I hate these things, anyway."

"No, don't cancel!" Javier said with a jolt of excitement.

"Let me come with you. It's not every week you get a chance to attend a fancy vampire party."

"Well..."

"For *most* of us, at least."

Eva hesitated. "Are you sure? They really are stuffy."

"Yes! I want to soak up as much of Shanghai as I can while I'm here."

She gave him a questioning glance. "It's black tie, meaning you're going to need a tuxedo."

Javier grimaced. His shopping budget had already been blown for the entire year. Hopefully Arvind knew how to do bow ties too.

"It's a date," he said smugly. "I will see you there, Dr. Robles."

After one more embrace and the party details scribbled on heavy stationery, Javier left the Sanguis Institute, his emotions raw from the encounter, but feeling more content than he had in years. Not only had he found Eva, but he would actually have the opportunity to get to know her, the real her.

The party was just the cherry on top, but secretly, a small part of him wondered if he might run into a particular vampiric hot mess from the bank.

9

By the day of Dmitri's party, Mina's hunger had far surpassed any notions of stoically enduring this torture. Her entire torso convulsed with spasms of emptiness at least twice an hour. When she stood, the only way to overcome the dizziness was to keep a hand connected to a stationary object. She'd attempted to be docile in Lian's presence, providing the expected complimentary commentary at the right times. But the hungrier she got, the more it seemed like Lady Zhang was ignoring her altogether. The time had come for drastic measures.

Mina dragged herself through the double doors to the dining room at the evening meal, ignoring the urge to lunge at the crimson carafes on the table. Instead, she focused on Lian, who calmly perused the daily paper with her tea, like always. Pacing the perimeter of the room, Mina got as close to Lian as she could before going to the woman's side directly and dropping to her knees.

"Please, Lady Zhang," Mina said, bowing her head deeply.

"Please, may I have blood?" The stiff sound of a newspaper folding resonated in her ears as Lady Zhang shifted to consider the destitute vampire begging at her feet. Mina held her breath, awaiting the verdict.

"No. Get up."

The refusal was like a spool of barbed wire tightening around her stomach.

"I promised Dmitri I would be at his Hundred Day celebration," Mina whispered, hoping against all odds for a speck of compassion. The newspaper rustled again as it was reopened.

"A careless promise and certainly no concern of mine," Lian commented.

Mina remained on her knees, glaring at her warped reflection in the patent leather of the woman's shoes. *When will this end?*

With heavy determination, Mina rose to her feet and took a seat at the table. She couldn't let Dmitri down again. All she had to do was make an appearance. Dmitri would be so busy socializing that he wouldn't notice her slip out. Mina hardly noticed the stares from her other siblings as she scooped large helpings of rice, vegetables, and meat onto her plate. As unappetizing as it all looked, perhaps it would help distract the true hunger enough to keep her going.

"I recommend the lotus root soup," Lian said, amusement clear in her tone. "It may help with the cramps."

Mina helped herself to the soup as well, slurping with dogged resolve. She would be there for her friend, then she would figure out a way around the blood injunction. Maybe she could raid Vasa's stores while she was there—her desperation had eclipsed the risk. Hell, part of her even suspected Lian was daring her to thwart the punishment.

"Disgusting," Yuxi muttered as she shifted herself away from Mina's enthusiastic soup eating.

A feral growl emanated from a place deep within Mina's core—it was a noise she wasn't aware she could make. It reverberated in her ribs with a satisfying threat of violence.

"Oh, please." Yuxi smirked. "As if I could possibly be intimidated by a little mouse like you."

Mina fantasized about pinning Yuxi to the floor, swiping her claws across the woman's throat, then basking in the blood that poured from it. Her fingernails grew to jagged protrusions at the thought.

"Enough, Mina," Lian finally cut in, sensing the escalating tension. "If you want to go to the Vasa party, you need Yuxi to chaperone. So play nice."

"But I have tickets for the opera tonight." Yuxi pouted.

One sharp look from Lian was all it took for Yuxi to withdraw her complaint.

"Of course, I would be happy to escort my younger sister tonight." Under her breath, she added, "As long as she can still fit in her dress."

Mina glowered at Yuxi, weighing the consequences against her desire to pummel the insipid woman. *You are a person, not an animal,* she schooled herself. *And you need to be there for Dmitri.* Reluctantly, she forced her vampire aspect to recede into the background—a feat that was getting more difficult every day she went without feeding. Mina shoveled another bite of food into her mouth and chewed, trying to distract herself with the thought of attending a celebration.

The rest of the meal passed uneventfully. Lady Zhang consulted with Guolong and Shenye about the business of the Hong Kong takeover. The pair would fly there shortly, and Lian would join them in the next few weeks to assist with the transition.

The food actually did help buoy Mina's energy levels to the point where she could dress herself and make it back down to the car in high heels, albeit slowly, clinging to any and all handrails along the way. She slid into the back seat, pulling the flowy floor-length skirt in behind her. The gown was one of her favorites: a strapless ebony bodice with an ombre skirt that transitioned from purple to a vibrant orange at the hem. It reminded her of the sky just before sunrise.

Yuxi kept her waiting for over a half hour before dropping into the seat next to her. Her bleached hair was slicked back into a high ponytail. False lashes made her look like a doll, the effect only exaggerated by her pink taffeta column dress with its giant bow at her waist.

"Let's get this over with," the woman said with a sigh as the car shifted into gear.

THE VASA PENTHOUSE was decorated with lanterns and other nods to the traditional celebration of a child's first hundred days. It had become popular in the last decade to throw such parties for fledgling vampires. The incongruity of the Asian custom in the Vasas' penthouse was stylistically jarring and perhaps borderline cultural appropriation, but Mina was happy for her friend regardless. Just as the original occasion was meant to celebrate the end of a historically tenuous time in a newborn's life, the first few months of a vampire's life could be equally harrowing. The fact that he'd made it this far was a good indication he was over any serious complications with the process.

Dmitri was impossible to miss in his bright-red satin suit, standing in the corner. Mina began the work of sidling through the crowd, forced to stop and acknowledge every person who greeted her. She sensed the gossip building in her wake as she belatedly realized that she'd been out of the social sphere just as long as Dmitri had been a vampire. The speculation about her whereabouts would have run rampant in her absence. Whatever. Tonight, she was here to support a friend. Repairing her reputation could come later.

"Hey, handsome." Mina casually took Dmitri's arm, bracing herself against a sudden wave of dizziness. "Nice suit. Very vampire-vogue."

"I know, I know." Dmitri made a face. "August insisted."

"Of course he did," Mina teased.

The last week had done Dmitri some good. His cheeks had a rosy flush to them, and his eyes were less sunken than before.

"How are you enjoying your party so far?"

Dmitri looked down bashfully. "It's so strange to have all of these people here, congratulating me. I don't even know most of them."

"Yes, but they know August. Like it or not, you're vampire royalty now, so you'll have to get used to the attention."

"Oh, grace me with your wisdom, Princess Mina."

Mina shouldered him for the jibe.

Around them, the party buzzed with lively conversation. Violin music floated in from a distant room, where Mina imagined some old-timey European social dances were happening.

Dmitri grabbed a pair of champagne flutes from a passing server and handed her one.

"Zdorovye," he started, raising a glass in his half of their usual bilingual toast.

"Yes, cheers to you. It's hard to believe my little Dima is actually one of us now."

Dmitri cleared his throat expectantly. "You have to say it."

Rolling her eyes, Mina relented. "Gānbēi!"

They clinked glasses before she took a small sip. This night didn't seem a good time to test her alcohol tolerance, but she did relish the normalcy of drinking at a party. Damn Vasa for not offering any blood—a courtesy to avoid human offense in mixed company, Mina presumed. Still, escaping the gloom of Zhang Manor for the evening was a boon, one that Mina intended to enjoy.

Dmitri's innocence and excitement reminded her of a time when she, too, had been an eager newcomer, excited to be entering a lavish and exclusive world she could call her own. The promise of home and belonging was powerful to a displaced young human. And who knew? Maybe Dmitri's experience would be better than hers. Just maybe, August would prove to be a supportive and loving mentor. On this festive occasion, that was the wish Mina held in her heart for him.

A deep voice sounded behind her. "Älskling, you made it."

She turned and indulged Lord Vasa in the double-cheek-kiss greeting. "I wouldn't have missed it for the world. Congratulations to you both." Mina raised her glass once more.

Up close, the man seemed thinner than when she'd seen him last week. Creating a fledgling took a significant toll, as she understood it, but Mina expected them to have both turned the corner by now.

"I hate to be rude, älskling, but there are some people I'd like to introduce to Dmitri, if you'd excuse us."

"Certainly," she said, returning the false pleasantry.

"Thank you for coming. It means a lot to me." Dmitri hugged her tightly. She squeezed him back before he took August's arm and was escorted away.

As the pair left, Mina's energy deflated just as quickly. Yuxi had disappeared, and she suddenly found herself very alone in a sea of stares. Holding her champagne, she expected someone—*anyone*—to inquire as to her whereabouts that summer. She'd even rehearsed Lian's excuse from earlier: a diplomatic engagement abroad. Many glances cut her way, but no one approached. Had her social standing vanished that quickly?

No matter—she'd done her part, in any case. Dmitri had been congratulated—mission accomplished. Mina just needed to find Yuxi, then she could go home. *Where did that damn Barbie doll run off to?*

"Why, look who it is."

The hairs on the back of Mina's neck stood in response to the rumble of the Russian-accented voice, the consonants of his English much harsher than Dmitri's.

"Mikhail."

Mina's eyes scanned the crowd quickly for Yuxi or even August, anyone to save her from this encounter. No one was there. She squared her shoulders against Mikhail, trying to manifest a shred of energy to face him with. By the look the Federov vampire gave her, it was evident he knew exactly who was to blame for the recent censure against their house.

"Take a walk with me." The man put a hand around her

waist and led her away from the main party, toward the closed rooms of the private residence. A spike of fear coursed through her at the thought of what the older vampire might do once he got her alone. Even if she'd been well fed, Mikhail had several centuries on her. There was no question he could overpower her.

"I was actually about to leave. Another commitment, you understand," Mina tried, her voice breathy with fear as she tried to pull away. Mikhail's grip changed to the back of her neck as he steered her down the hallway.

"Oh no. You and I have a score to settle."

10

_____

When Eva picked him up from the front of his apartment, Javier was dazzled by her sienna-orange dress. She could easily have passed for one of the wealthy bloodsuckers, and part of him wondered if she'd ever wanted to be one of them. He hoped not.

"You look amazing," he said as he climbed into the car. Her glitzy earrings caught his attention before his eyes fell to her neckline. "That necklace." Javier examined the black stone pendant hanging from a twisted gold chain. "Is that a condor?"

"Oh, this?" Eva's fingers brushed the outstretched wings of the etched figure. "It might be. After your visit the other day, I was feeling a bit sentimental—found this in a box of my old things," she said with a small smile. "Anyway, shall we?"

Javier hooked a finger around his collar, trying to pry an inch of breathing room. The memory of that feathered menace screeching at him the night before Eva's departure had him discombobulated. He shook it off, focusing instead on the mundane discomfort of his stiffly starched tuxedo. *Why the hell do people wear these penguin suits?* He was already glad this would likely be the most formal occasion he attended in his entire life.

As soon as the elevator door opened on the party, Javier quickly forgot about his sartorial discomfort, overwhelmed by the opulence of both the people and the decor. Buffet tables of delicacies stretched the entire length of the room while gowns of all different colors floated by them.

"What did you say this party was for, again?"

"I was one of the advising doctors during a vampire transformation. This party celebrates one hundred days since that night."

"Huh." Javier grabbed a toast with a piece of smoked salmon on top and ate it in one bite. "The food is good."

"Enjoy. Vasa goes all out for a party, especially one of this significance. I think he's quite smitten with his latest fledgling."

"I'll say." Javier snagged a champagne flute. "Out of curiosity, what does one have to do to entice a wealthy vampire patron? Think I have a chance?" Javier chased the salmon toast with a lettuce boat of shrimp. It probably had a fancier name than that. His cheeks puckered from the sour hit at the end. "Ugh, lemony."

"Come on, you," Eva said before tugging him through the crowd.

For the next hour, she introduced him to an endless string of her colleagues, most of them old Asian men, which he supposed made sense. Their stuffy conversation was dry but tolerable until it switched to Mandarin. Javier listened for the few words he knew and tried to smile at the appropriate times but otherwise was even more bored than when he was dusting the leaves of ficuses at the bank.

The people watching proved to be the saving grace of an otherwise insufferable event. A truly international crowd graced the main hall. Saris and kimonos appeared next to haute couture, and he'd lost track of the number of languages he'd heard spoken.

Javier was in the process of grabbing his second glass of champagne when he saw her, standing next to the man in the obnoxiously red suit.

Mina.

A broad smile crept over his face. She was actually here. Javier brushed Eva on the shoulder to get her attention. Before he could excuse himself, the man in the red suit was walking toward their group on the arm of none other than the vampire from the bank, his blond hair slicked back with a high shine. Why the hell did he keep running into that guy?

"Dr. Robles, I'd like to officially introduce you to Dmitri Basmanov. I know you two didn't get a chance to meet before the transformation started."

"Very pleased to meet you, Mr. Basmanov. I'm glad to see you looking well." Eva shook Dmitri's hand.

Javier took the chance to locate Mina again. She was still in his sightline. Good.

"Have we met before?" the taller man suddenly asked, looking Javier up and down.

"Not formally, though I am well acquainted with your front bumper." The joke was met with a blank stare. "Javier Robles," he said, extending his hand. "I work at the bank."

"A pleasure, I'm sure." The returned handshake was all fingers, and Javier got the distinct impression the man was loath to clasp hands with a commoner. Whatever.

"Nice to meet you. Though actually, I was about to go say

hi to someone else. I hope you don't mind." August looked at him with that same queer smile from their first encounter in front of the bank.

"You have other acquaintances here?"

"Just one. If you'll excuse me." Javier slipped behind Dmitri before he lost sight of Mina. She had moved to the periphery of the room, at risk of disappearing altogether.

As Javier made his way toward Mina, another man approached her. Javier stilled to watch their interaction, angry that he hadn't gotten to her first. However, between the visible points of the man's teeth and the way Mina stiffened under his touch, Javier was instantly on alert. *Like hell I'm letting that slide.*

The pair was halfway down the hallway by the time he caught up to them.

"You can't be leaving already." Javier's voice boomed after them. "Not before I've gotten the chance to ask you for a dance."

"Who—"

"Yes, I'd love to," Mina said quickly, taking advantage of the male vampire's distraction to squirm out of his grasp. She half jogged down the hallway and latched onto Javier's arm as soon as she drew near, like she was trying to anchor herself to him. The electric sensation of having her so close caught him off guard.

A small smile tugged at the other man's lips as he put his hands casually in his pockets though the look in his eye said, *I'll kill you.* "You sure she's worth saving, human?" he asked.

Javier blinked as he processed the man's words, not sure which was more offensive, the threat to him or the insult to Mina.

"Have a good night," was all Javier said before escorting Mina back to the main party.

"Thank you... Juan, was it?" she said when they were firmly back in the middle of the gathering.

"Javier," he corrected. "The name that doesn't work well in Chinese, remember?"

"Oh, right," she said with a small frown. "Now, I just need to find my sister..." Javier regretfully let her go as she pulled away to scan the crowd.

"I was serious about that dance," Javier said, hoping to tempt her back.

"What?" Mina looked back at him, her gaze questioning. She looked absolutely dazzling with diamonds glinting on her earlobes, complimenting the sparkle in her warm brown eyes.

"I would be honored if you would join me for a dance." He offered his hand to her, holding the other behind his back like the sophisticated gentleman he was dressed as.

"I... All right?"

It wasn't the most resounding affirmative he'd ever received, but Javier would take it. She laid her hand atop his, and he led her toward the sound of violins. Her skin was decidedly ambient in temperature, but that didn't make it any less exhilarating to touch.

"I recognize this song!" he said as they drew nearer to the musicians. Partners twirled about the ballroom in grand, sweeping patterns, and Javier watched for an opening to lead them into the mix.

"Everyone knows the Strauss waltzes," Mina said dismissively, her gaze wandering to the opposite side of the party.

Javier stopped, turning to look at her. Her glossy black hair framed her face perfectly. She'd kept her makeup simple: a smudge of kohl at her lash line and a rose tint to her lips. Mina was stunning, but that wasn't a free pass to be a jerk.

"Look, I get it. You're probably used to company far more refined than a farm boy from California. Like that guy in the hallway—total class act. Say the word, and I won't bother you again. But if you do take me up on a dance, do you think you could possibly be a skosh nicer?"

Mina looked up at him with that questioning tilt to her eyebrows again. Javier half expected her to walk away without so much as a goodbye.

"All right," she finally conceded, pressing her lips together. "I'm sorry. I'm just really hungry."

Javier snorted. "You're hungry in the middle of all this food? That's a little silly." *Women and their diets.*

Mina already looked borderline too thin, but he knew better than to share his opinions on a woman's weight, in either direction.

"Yeah, I agree," she replied softly. "Anyway, shall we?"

"I thought you'd never ask."

Javier found his break in the couples and led Mina onto the floor, easily melding with the experienced crowd. The parquet floor was perfectly polished for easy pivoting, and the space was wide enough that he could gather enough speed so that Mina's dress flared out as she made the outside turn. Mina was an easy partner to dance with, providing adequate tension with her arms while still letting him lead their momentum. By their third pass around the room, he was feeling brave enough to send her spinning underneath his arm. Javier caught the hint of a small smile of surprise on her lips, and he relished in her enjoyment.

"Where did you learn to dance like that?" she asked, somewhat out of breath.

"Quinceañeras. So many quinceañeras." At her inquisitive look, he explained, "It's a fifteenth-birthday party for girls. She dances a waltz with her court, and if you're a guy that can even halfway keep a beat, you get recruited for every single one."

In between songs, Mina grabbed two glasses of sparkling water and handed one to Javier. "So, how does a janitor from the bank end up at one of the most exclusive Shanghai social events of the season?"

"Ahhh. That's thanks to my sister. I guess she was a doctor who helped this guy, Dmitri, become a vampire? What about you?"

"That 'guy, Dmitri,' is a good friend of mine."

So many questions sat at the tip of his tongue, about Mina's past and what had led her to Shanghai: *Where are you from? What century were you born in? Do you have a vampire lover who will eviscerate me for talking to you?*

Instead, what he said was "I was trying to get my sister to tell me how one goes about enticing a vampire suitor. Any tips?"

Idiot.

Mina gave him a truly incredulous look. "I'm not sure you have the stomach for it. Though I admit, you are quite forward for a human, so maybe you do have what it takes."

The suggestive tone to her voice, combined with a sly smile, made Javier's breath catch.

"You've definitely gotten people's attention by dancing with me," Mina added, their eye contact finally breaking.

Javier glanced around the room, noticing for the first time

the number of whispering couples staring at them. "You know all of these people?"

"More like they know me." Mina gave him a strange smile. "In any case, I really should be going now. Would you mind staying with me while I look for Yuxi? It was impressive how you dealt with Mikhail."

"You think I'm impressive?" he flirted, trailing after her as she cut into the crowd. Either she didn't hear, or she simply ignored that last comment. Fair.

The lap around the room took at least five minutes, the number of bodies packed into the space only growing as the night progressed. Javier kept an eye out for Eva as they navigated the crowd, but he couldn't locate her either. He felt a small twinge of guilt at having abandoned her, but it wasn't like she didn't have other people to talk to. He could catch up with Eva over dinner, but waltzing with a beautiful, apparently famous vampiress wasn't an opportunity one passed up.

Mina led him to the far end of the penthouse, where a glass rooftop gave an impressive view of the Shanghai city skyline. The few other couples there dispersed as soon as they arrived, and Javier was acutely aware of the quiet intimacy it afforded. He wondered if he could get Mina to postpone her search for a few minutes so they could chat a while longer—he had so much more to ask.

"Where the hell did she go?" Mina muttered to herself. "I guess I'm just going to have to go home alone."

"Or, what if we…"

Mina doubled over, clutching her stomach. Javier rushed in to catch her, easing her to the ground as she groaned in pain.

"Whoa, are you okay?"

"I'm fine," she said through gritted teeth. "You need to go now." The urgency in her voice frightened him.

"What? I'm not leaving you here like this." He put a hand on her shoulder, crouching next to her on the ground. *Eva is a vampire doctor, right?* Maybe she could help with whatever the problem was.

"I'm serious, Javier. Get. Out of here." Mina groaned as she curled into a ball around her stomach.

"No. I—"

When Mina looked up, her irises burned crimson as long canines descended from between her full lips. When Javier tried to back away, he found himself fixed in place, unable to look away from those eyes. With a sensuous smile, Mina pried his hand from her shoulder and brought his wrist to her mouth. A voice inside told him to run, but neither his arms nor legs responded to the thoughts. The points of her teeth settled sharply against his skin before her jaw clamped down, his bones creaking under the pressure. She gave an ecstatic moan as his blood pooled in her mouth, and finally Javier was able to clearly see what was happening.

"Mina, stop!" he said with a bewildered fear, the ache in his arm astonishing. As he grabbed her hand to attempt to dislodge her, she stilled him with her eyes once more before a heavy hand against his chest shoved him to the ground. Javier's head knocked into the floor with a dizzying *thud*.

"I guess you meant the other kind of hungry," he mumbled groggily.

Mina continued to drink from his wrist. Her tongue lapped gently against his skin, distracting him from the pain. Maybe he could let her have a few minutes. His limbs had turned leaden, but his chest swelled with a strange affection. *She needs this. I can share this with her, can't I?*

Javier blinked. No. That was the compulsion talking. His pulse fluttered wildly as his body compensated for the reduced blood pressure. The edges of his vision blurred. His grasp of time had slipped, but he clearly felt his body shifting into survival mode. Time for her to stop.

"Mina, that's enough now," he said, mustering as much authority as he could.

She didn't respond. Her monstrous alter ego was unmoved by his human plight, single-minded in its hunger. He was outmatched and fading fast. Javier turned his head, vision swimming, and spotted a smudge of red near the solarium entrance. Foggy recognition hit him.

"Hey, Dmitri! Little help over here."

"Oh—oh my God," the man stuttered as he drew nearer. "I don't know how to stop her. I'll go get August."

"Yeah. You do that. Get my sister, too, would you?" Javier knew he should feel afraid, but a warm calm flooded his system instead. For some reason, all he could think of was how gorgeous Mina looked tonight, and how lucky he was that she'd agreed to a dance.

By the time the group returned, Javier was having trouble keeping his eyes open. August snatched Mina around the middle while digging his fingers into the pressure points of the hinge of her jaw. As soon as she let up, August wrenched her off Javier's arm. Mina flailed against her captor as Javier's arm fell limply to the ground.

"Don't hurt her," Javier said weakly as Eva pushed up his sleeve. His sister's face appeared ashen as she efficiently tore a strip of fabric from the lining of her dress and wrapped it around his arm. Javier grunted as she cinched down the tourniquet though his arm felt oddly dissociated from the rest of his body.

"Do you think you can stand?" Eva asked as she put a hand on his neck to check his pulse. The fear in his older sister's voice was totally uncalled for.

"Sure, no problem." Javier propped himself up on his elbows and rolled to one side before the tension vanished from his limbs and he dropped to the floor once more. Eva's hand caught his head before it bashed into the ground again.

"Um, I guess not," he amended.

The trio of vampires had disappeared when he wasn't looking, leaving his sister and him in the solarium alone. He hadn't even had a chance to say goodbye.

Eva yanked his shirtsleeve back down over the bite marks, nodding at the men in black suits who approached. "First time drinking with vampires, and I'm afraid he got a little carried away," she said, her tight voice infused with false merriment.

"Where'd Mina go?" Javier asked, his words coming out slurred before he was unceremoniously thrown over the shoulder of one of the men. That was the last thing he remembered before the night went dark.

11

Even before Mina opened her eyes, the migraine threatened to cleave her skull in two. She peeled back her eyelids and groped at the bedding beneath her— her own bed in Zhang Manor. The duvet and sheets were turned down—whoever had placed her there had simply left her on top, still wearing the dress from last night.

Fragments of memories floated back like a dream sequence out of order. Dmitri's red suit, Mikhail's menacing snarl, and waltzing with a stranger. A human.

Javier.

A body on the tile of the lunarium, limp and pale. Hot, salty blood filling her mouth with the divine taste of life. Any thought of stopping, any pleas from her meal, met with fierce denial from the monster unleashed within her.

Why didn't I stop? She had never lost control like that before—hadn't thought it possible. *I didn't even try to stop,* Mina thought with crushing guilt then, fearfully, *Did I kill him?*

Nausea roiled her stomach as she realized she couldn't answer that question. A pained gasp escaped her lips as she dragged herself from the bed to the bathroom. Her head felt like it would explode from the pressure in her temples. Mina fell to her knees in front of the toilet bowl, prepared to eject the meal she'd possibly committed murder for. Nothing came up. Her body was unwilling to let go of the nourishment it had so badly needed.

She replayed her shattered memories, trying to find a moment when Javier stirred. Every time he had, she'd pushed him back down and kept drinking. His heart had still been pulsing when she was pulled away—at least, she thought so. The artery at his wrist had filled her mouth with crimson nectar in large spurts at first, but by the end, the flow had become an erratic dribble.

Had she left enough for him to survive? All he'd wanted was one stupid dance. A single, tearless sob escaped her, and she clamped her hand over her mouth. Lian *couldn't* find out about this.

The sounds of breakfast floated up from the floor below. Mina was already late for the mandatory family meal. She scrubbed the errant droplets of blood from her jawline before exchanging her gown for a simple black shift dress.

Shoving down the fresh wave of guilt, Mina bounded down to the dining room to find Yuxi sitting alone. Servants tended to the fine porcelain of untouched platters of food from the table.

"Too much to drink last night?" Yuxi asked, a sly smile decorating glossed lips.

"You were supposed to be watching me," Mina hissed, gripping the back of her chair so tightly that the wood creaked beneath her fingers. "This wouldn't have happened if..." Hitching breaths filled her lungs as her vision clouded with halos of light.

This is your own damn fault, you vile monster.

Something wet smacked her in the forehead before tumbling to the floor. A green bean.

"Pull yourself together before you get us both in trouble," Yuxi said, collecting a blackened century egg quarter with her chopsticks. "Pathetic child."

"Is he alive?" That was the only thing that mattered now.

"How should I know?" Yuxi answered with a shrug. "Vasa said you were 'indisposed'—I found you passed out in the limo, covered in—"

"All he wanted was a stupid dance," Mina said distantly as she slumped in her chair. "And I *attacked* him." A heaviness weighed on her chest like an entire mausoleum worth of stone.

Yuxi gave an exaggerated eye roll. "You're a vampire. Get over yourself already."

Mina's hands curled into fists in her lap before going limp with despair.

"I should confess."

I should be punished.

A hand smacked her on the back of the head.

"Don't be an idiot. If he isn't dead already, Lian would make sure of it. Do you realize the scandal this would cause after she so publicly went after the Federovs for human rights violations?"

"She'll find out anyway. Lord Vasa—"

"Wouldn't dare tell on his precious *älskling*."

"The driver—"

"Bribed. You're welcome."

Mina finally met Yuxi's gaze, her conniving older sister who never passed up an opportunity to point out her mistakes. "Then there's *you*. Why haven't you already turned me in?" Then the puzzle clicked together. "You were also up to something. That's why I couldn't find you."

Yuxi gave her a sweet sisterly smile before placing a hand on Mina's shoulder. The woman's pointed nails prickled at her skin. "Careful, little mouse. Don't provoke a fight you can't afford."

As she stood and spun to leave, Yuxi's silk robe hit Mina in the face, a sobering sensation. *I need to find out if he's alive. I can deal with Yuxi later.*

Javier worked at the bank—Mina could start there and work her way out, maybe take a page out of Yuxi's book and bribe someone for his address. *He has to be all right.*

MINA KNOCKED SOFTLY on the open door to Lian's office at the top of the stairs. The woman stood behind a stately desk, dark polished wood inset with a leather writing surface, as she loaded documents into a briefcase.

"Yes?" Lian said, scanning her. "You look remarkably well rested after a late night."

Mina's heart jumped as she bowed her head. Could Lian tell that she fed? "It was invigorating to be back among our kind last night. In fact, it reminded me it's been several months since I reviewed my investments. I might visit the bank this evening to remedy that."

"On a Saturday?" Lian quirked an eyebrow, a wave of black hair framing the skeptical expression.

"I lost track of the week," Mina mumbled, her eyes dancing around the room as she scrambled to cover her clumsy mistake. "Monday, then, if that's all right with you?"

Lady Zhang finished packing the sleek leather bag before shifting her scrutiny to Mina.

"I'll have an advisor stop by tomorrow if you are so keen."

"No," Mina said in frustration before she could catch herself.

"No?"

Lian crossed leisurely to Mina's side of the desk, bag in hand, looming.

"I mean I was hoping to get a chance to..." Mina's cheeks flushed as she fumbled. This was a disaster—time to back out while she still could. "Never mind. I'm sorry for interrupting you." As she turned to leave, a hand closed firmly around her elbow.

"Tell me why you want to go to the bank."

Mina gazed down at the flower arrangement in the middle of the foyer at the base of the stairs. She imagined the field that the spindly chrysanthemums had been grown in before they were harvested to be put on display. Yuxi's warning floated back to her mind: if she didn't come up with an excuse, the question of whether Javier lived would become moot once Lian found out.

Mina took a steadying breath, digging to find a kernel of truth to ground her lie.

"I just want something, somewhere outside of this house that I can go to feel like I have a purpose in this society." Mina turned back to Lian, boldly meeting her gaze. "Yuxi maintains social connections with all the other houses, Guolong is a mastermind at corporate law, and Shenye's work on infrastructure has made Shanghai what it is today." Mina's throat tightened as she added, "I'm tired of only holding value as your pet." The words were more earnest than she intended, if still not an answer to the original question.

The fingers around her arm slackened.

"Why now?"

Give her an answer she wants to hear.

"My time away... You were right. It was hard to live outside this city. Outside of your generosity. I see that now, but it's also hard to live here, feeling like a constant disappointment. I... I want to fix that."

Mina held herself still as Lian considered her with those calculating eyes for several long seconds. Had she bought it?

"What was your degree in? International business, wasn't it?"

"Yes." Mina didn't bring up the minor in East Asian studies, which felt ineffably irrelevant now.

"It's a shame you didn't choose a more rigorous school." Lian frowned. "If you were from a subordinate clan, seeking employment at Zhang Enterprises, your resume wouldn't even make it to my desk. You know that, don't you?"

Mina dropped her eyes to the baseboards. Yes, she knew. Even living on her own from age sixteen, working to support herself, Mina had always made excellent grades. But she'd never had the time for extracurricular activities or pushed herself with the advanced coursework required for acceptance to a more prestigious university. At the time, the state school felt like a very sensible choice. Lian never missed the opportunity to make her feel inadequate for her unremarkable scholarly achievements.

"However," Lian drawled. "You are not from a subordinate

clan. You are *my* fledgling." The woman's fingers smoothed a section of hair behind Mina's ear. "I will allow you to shadow me for a trial period. If you prove yourself diligent, we can identify a long-term placement that suits your... skill set."

Mina blinked away her surprise, both that Lian bought the excuse and that she was being given an opportunity to apply herself to something actually useful—an unexpected and exhilarating prospect after so many years of idleness.

"Thank you, Lady Zhang. I won't disappoint you."

"Very well. Get dressed and meet me in the car. You have three minutes."

"Right now?" Mina spluttered, quickly realizing her misstep at Lian's narrowed eyes. "Of course, Lady Zhang." She bowed deeply before scurrying down the hallway back to her room.

Mina threw a blazer over her dress, hoping the formality of the ensemble was sufficient. Two swipes of makeup were all she dared. Her appearance in the mirror caught her off guard—clear eyes and a flush of color to cheeks that had been sallow for so long. Even her ragged cuticles had healed.

As a vampire growing up in Shanghai, she found it startlingly easy to forget her own monstrous nature. Vampire abilities once necessary for hunting were now gauche to show in public. Yet the stark difference in her appearance after finally having fed served as a solemn reminder that she was a creature that not only desired human blood, but *needed* it. Eventually, if that creature wasn't fed, its voracious appetite would take over. Mina shuddered at the memory of her control slipping away. She couldn't let that happen again—never again.

She raced to the garage with a pair of suede heels in her

hands. For the first time in a long time, her supernatural speed kicked in to get her to the bottom in seconds.

Admittedly, it was nice to not be starving.

~

THE HEADQUARTERS for Zhang Enterprises were located in the tallest building of Shanghai. At over a hundred stories up, the building swayed with the atmospheric gusts. Opaque clouds pressed against the windows of the palatial office of Lady Zhang. Lian's silk blouse billowed as she crossed the expanse to an imposing steel desk, the asymmetrical onyx tabletop curving to meet the floor on one side. Mina hovered near the door.

"I start every evening by reviewing House Zhang internal affairs. Any deaths, new progeny requests, or other resource issues in the city. Tell me, Mina, how many members does our house consist of?"

"Five thousand," Mina answered, fairly confident.

Lian tipped her head in acknowledgment. "Managing a household this size requires efficient reporting and alignment on priorities." Unpacking her briefcase, Lian arranged three neat piles of documents alongside a fountain pen.

"I'd like you to gain more familiarity with the internal workings of our house. Down the hallway, there's an archive of records of all intrahouse petitions and reports. For the period of your absence, I'd like you to summarize all that was asked and granted."

"A written summary?"

"Don't be daft. Yes, a written summary. And none of those crass, simplified characters."

Mina swallowed the hard lump in her throat. As part of the vampire takeover of Shanghai, Lian had reinstituted the use of the more complex traditional hanzi as a point of cultural pride. Most of mainland China still used the simplified version, which also tended to be taught abroad. Mina had never mastered the elaborate radicals and their placements. But Lian already knew that.

"I never learned to write the traditional ones."

"No time like the present. I can't use you if you're illiterate."

"Yes, Lady Zhang," Mina said with a small bow, anxiety welling at the impossible task.

"And Mina? Do you think you could manage a cappuccino without spilling it this time?"

Mina's cheeks flushed with heat, recalling the embarrassment of that day in the bank along with the gentle man who had the misfortune of crossing her path.

"Of course, my lady."

"Excellent. You better get going, then. I expect that report by dawn."

With one last bow, Mina was out the door and jogging down the stairwell to the floor below. As the espresso machine warmed up, she located writing supplies along with a dictionary. When she returned to Lian's office, the woman was already mired in papers, her spectacles slid halfway down her nose. She didn't acknowledge Mina as the coffee was set on her desk, and Mina bowed herself out of the room once more.

Outside of the sole occupied office on that floor, an eerie stillness permeated the corridors. Normally, Guolong and Shenye would be there as well, but with those two away in

Hong Kong and the human office staff off for the weekend, most of the floor lay dormant and dark. Motion lights illuminated as Mina shuffled down the corridor, hugging her notebook to her chest. Even though she thought it unlikely that any ghosts haunted the modern high-rise, the undulating motion of the building, combined with the unprompted illumination, put her on edge.

Musty air hung like a fog in the records room. Beneath dim reading lights, Mina found the latest collection of ledgers and hefted them over to a poorly lit worktable over the course of five trips, careful to maintain their chronological order. With a sigh, she shrugged off her jacket and got to work.

"Deaths and births" had been a brusque oversimplification of the information Lian received from the subsidiary branches of her family. As she read, Mina kept a tally of the events covered and began to sketch a family tree as she pieced together who was the offspring of whom across several generations.

Lady Zhang's sign-off seemed to be required for most major dealings of the family, including real estate transactions, any foreign travel, and resolving conflicts with actual duels to the death. Quarterly financial statements accompanied the reports, with astronomical balance sheets on income and expenses. The revenues were reported in billions of yuan, much of which was paid in tithe to the house proper to cover the expense of human donors. Mina did some quick tallies in the back of her notebook. *Nearly a million yuan per vampire per annum to cover blood supply?* She gaped at the sum.

Mina was surprised to find herself engrossed in the details of the house dynamics. Reading between the lines, she got a sense of which branches were allied, which ones provoked friction, which were thriving, and which ones barely met their minimum dues. She had always thought of the Zhang House as a monolithic entity, moving as a unit at Lian's direction. The woman's steadfast governance clearly masked the churn of the subordinate factions beneath the surface.

By the time Mina compiled the details she hoped were most relevant into a single summary report, her dawn timeline was nearing. After arching the creak out of her back, she hurried to Lian's office. The clouds had lightened to a dirty dove gray, and Lady Zhang still sat behind her stark desk.

Mina laid her report on the edge of the desk, a full four pages of dense characters. She massaged the overworked palm of her hand as Lian silently flipped through it. Finally, the woman removed her glasses and stood with a menacing glare. Mina shrank under the unexpected reaction to an entire evening's worth of work.

"Aside from your atrocious penmanship, I've counted twenty-six blatant errors. Did you honestly think this an acceptable quality of work?"

Mina's cheeks burned fiercely at the censure. An apology sat on the tip of her tongue. "I—"

"Hold out your hands. Palms down."

Mina's eyes flickered up in worry as Lian strolled to a vase in the corner of her office. There, the domineering woman withdrew a slender reed of dried bamboo from the arrangement. Surely, she couldn't intend to—Lian gave a few test strikes to the palm of her hand, the sharp impact echoing through the office.

So, Mina was to be punished like a miscreant schoolchild in a Confucian-era classroom. A deluge of icy shame engulfed

Mina as she extended her hands, trying to keep them from trembling.

Lady Zhang came to stand by her side and held the report in front of her face. As Mina surveyed the handwriting, it blurred into a myriad of disorganized chicken scratches, despite how much effort she'd put in.

"Read."

Mina took a deep breath, bracing herself for the trial. "'During the summer months, the Zhang House received over three hundred reports, which included financial—'"

Thwack.

The bamboo came down across her knuckles, the exquisite intensity of the pain radiating from the backs of her hands down her fingers. A single welt appeared as a raised line of puffy pink skin. She closed her eyes as the sensation abated. *Fuck, that stings.*

"Continue."

A pronounced tremor set into Mina's outstretched hands.

"'—data which shows a strong position in real estate, healthcare, and the blood donation—'"

Thwack.

Mina bit back tears, trying to disconnect from the physical sensation. *You asked for this. You deserve this. Stop pretending like any of this is unfair, you ignorant, useless pet.*

Mina read the remainder of the report aloud, her mistakes each punctuated with a new stripe on her hands. The initial pink welts gave way to angrier white lines, their edges demarcated with a vibrant purple. Tiny dots of blood decorated the ridges of the abraded skin. By the time she read the last words, Mina didn't even recognize the ruined appendages she held before her.

"Now," Lian said, landing the cane prominently at the top of her desk with a final thwack that made Mina jump. "Care to tell me why you really wanted out of the house this evening?"

Mina deflated—this hadn't been a genuine opportunity to prove herself, only an exhausting task for Lian to break her on before interrogating her. Mina opened her mouth to beg for forgiveness... then closed it again. That's what the old Mina would have done, the one who didn't have the courage to leave. She wasn't that person anymore.

Mina forced her own hands down by her side as she straightened her posture. *Figure out a way to use this to your advantage. Javier had a sister, right? A doctor. Dmitri's doctor.*

"I... At the party last night, Lord Vasa was discussing advancements in medical research with a doctor. I believe it's the same research you are considering investing in. It made my own lack of contribution all the more apparent. I sincerely want to correct that, for myself and for our family. I'm tired of being complacent and useless." Mina tried not to wither under Lian's unwavering gaze.

"Well, this is certainly a new philosophy from you." Lian paced a wide circle around her.

Mina ignored her throbbing hands, refusing to fidget. "Please allow me to shadow you, as you suggested. I—I've lost my way. Please help me find it again."

Lian considered her for what felt like several minutes before issuing a verdict.

"I will not shift my standards to accommodate your ineptitude. If you fail to meet them, I will simply motivate you to try harder." Her eyes flicked to the cane.

"I would benefit from the structure and discipline." Even

though the words were designed to play into Lian's desires, Mina hated how hopeful they made her feel as well. If she followed Lian's strict rules, maybe she could carve out a small place for herself in this world once more. Finding out if Javier lived was a short-term goal. Either he lived, or he didn't. Mina still needed to figure out how to survive herself.

A small smile tugged at the corner of Lian's lips. "Very well. Prove the sincerity of those words, and I may even let you attend a scheduled meeting with Vasa and his doctor. But I warn you, whatever lenience I have for your moods and misbehavior at home do not extend to this office. At the first sign of insubordination, you will lose this privilege."

"Thank you for the opportunity, Lady Zhang," Mina said with a deep bow held for two seconds.

"You can thank me by demonstrating some improvement," Lian replied, her expression cold once more. "I expect the rewritten report on my desk by the time you leave."

"Yes, my lady." Mina accepted the original papers from the woman before backing out of the office. She didn't know how her destroyed hands could accomplish anything legible, let alone the impossibly high standards of Lady Zhang, but she would figure it out somehow. She was in too deep to back out.

MINA HELD her hands in a bowl of ice water for a full ten minutes, until all the skin from her wrists down was the same angry shade of reddish pink. She alternately flexed and closed her fingers, trying to regain their function. They felt somewhere in between numb and on fire.

Before starting on the second draft, Mina lingered in the supply closet, finding a pen with the finest tip and a smooth glide. She chose a heavier weight paper, hoping it would hold crisper lines. By the time she sat back down in the records room, Mina had found a calmer headspace. All she had to do was copy a report, like she was back in finals week, staying up late to finish an assignment.

With a sad chuckle, Mina recalled another night a lifetime before, handwriting an essay at the quartz kitchen island of the Seattle apartment—no laptops while Lian was in town.

"Do you regret following me that day?" the ancient vampire had asked.

"Never," Mina said without pause. She felt the woman appear behind her, a languid hand stroking her hair.

"Your tenacity intrigues me—reckless, ruinous thing that it is," Lian said.

Mina turned, smiling up at the magnetic woman. "I needed you in my life, and I succeeded, didn't I?"

Lian had pressed her lips to Mina's forehead. "You did. I only wonder how long before you discover the danger in my affection. Don't disappoint me, my love."

The words haunted her. But even if she could personally travel back in time and tell her teenage self to run, Mina knew she wouldn't have listened. Had bravery fueled her early obsession with Lian? No, she decided. Perhaps it had just been the kind of stupidity born from being young and unbearably lonely. And no cure existed for that but time.

Not that the past mattered. She'd made those decisions just like she'd made the decision to dance with Javier. Convincing Lian to give her a job might have been stupid—her swollen hands certainly suggested as much. But it felt like a step in some direction. Perhaps it was a chance to confront Javier's sister, perhaps just a reason to leave the house.

If she had killed Javier... there was no undoing it. The only thing she could control was her reaction—placating Lian, staying useful—until she could face what came next. So that was what she would do.

12

J avier awoke enveloped in a fluffy cloud, the single most comfortable piece of furniture he'd encountered since his arrival in Shanghai.

If this is heaven, I do not mind the accommodations.

His eyes opened to dappled light thrown on sumptuous white bedding. *Seriously, though, where in the hell am I?* He propped himself up against the headboard as he traced a tube from the back of his hand to an IV bag hanging on a brass reading light. The other wrist was wrapped in more bandages than a mummy. *Huh.*

"Javier?" an anxious voice sounded in the doorway.

Eva. This must be her apartment. "Man, Eva. Nice digs," he said. "Bet it comes with a nice salary, too, being Shanghai's premier vampire doctor."

"Don't you ever scare me like that again!" Eva said, her voice shrill. She sat down on the edge of the bed, crowding his space as she wrapped a blood pressure cuff around his bicep.

"Watch the—"

Eva extended a stern finger to shush him as she settled a stethoscope into her ears and placed the cold metal amplifier against the crook of his elbow. She pumped the rubber bulb of the cuff, inflating it to a snug squeeze. Purple bags underlined her eyes as if she hadn't slept in days. Javier watched in dumfounded fascination at seeing Dr. Robles at work.

"You're stable for now," Eva declared after releasing the pressure on the cuff. "I've replaced the fluid loss, but it's going to take a while for your body to restore your red count. You don't have an upcoming donation, do you?"

"What are you talking about?" Javier's mouth tasted gummy and stale. "How did I get here? We were at that party, and then..." All he could remember was dancing.

Eva looked at him shrewdly, and when he failed to finish the statement, she filled in: "And then I find you with fangs buried in your wrist—Mina Park's, of all people. Care to explain how that happened? A fetish of yours, perhaps?"

"No! Jesus, Eva." Javier's brow creased as the night came back to him in pieces: waltzing with Mina one minute then on the floor the next. "I was helping her look for someone, and then she snapped into beast mode."

"They don't *attack* people. That's the whole point of the donation system: to obviate the need to take unknown quantities of blood from unsuspecting human victims." Eva's eyes narrowed. "Just tell me. Did you ask her to do it because you were curious? Because you thought it'd give you a chance with her?"

"Why are you blowing this out of proportion? I'm fine. So what if a vampire drank a little blood—that's the whole reason I'm here, right? To feed vampires?" Javier ran his hand through his hair, admitting only to himself that yes,

Mina was a hell of an intriguing woman. But he was almost positive he hadn't been the one to instigate whatever happened.

"Javier Emilio Robles."

"You sound like Mom," he said, sticking out his tongue.

Eva's nostrils flared before she smacked him across the cheek hard enough to push the boundary of playfulness.

"You hit like her too," he grumbled, rubbing his face, taking stock of the stubble that had grown along his chin. It was more than his usual morning shadow.

"How long have I been here?"

"You've been asleep for a day and a half." Eva stood and went into the attached bathroom before returning with two large pills in her palm and a glass of water. "Take these."

"This isn't some experimental protocol, is it?"

"They're iron pills, smart-ass."

Javier downed the horse pills with consecutive uncomfortable swallows.

"Listen, Javier. You *cannot* let anyone know about what happened. Do you understand? It would be catastrophic for you, for my career, and probably most of all for Mina."

"Is she... Is she okay?" Whatever Eva's conjecture about the nature of their entanglement, something about Mina hadn't been right. Her actions felt desperate, like it was a matter of life or death.

"She will be as long as you stay the hell away from her. I don't even know why she was with you in the first place."

"Rude. I'm not a bad catch, you know," Javier replied matter-of-factly.

Eva looked at him like a sprat coughed up by a flea-bitten alley cat. Then, after the visual castigation, she went to a bookshelf and withdrew several magazines before tossing them on the bed.

"She's Lian Zhang's youngest fledgling—not only way out of your league, but also probably the least eligible vampire in Shanghai."

Javier pawed through the glossy tabloids, reading the garish titles: "Princess Mina blunders again," "Lady Zhang exasperated with fledgling antics," "Where is Princess Mina?" Unflattering pictures of Mina graced the covers, often with a black-suited undertaker of a woman hovering in the background. No wonder she got up to trouble, with that kind of overlord breathing down her neck.

"You actually read these rags? I thought these would be beneath the educated doctor," Javier remarked snidely.

She bristled. "It helps me relate to my clients if I keep on top of current social dynamics."

"Uh-huh."

She swatted him over the back of the head with a folded magazine.

"Christ, Eva. When did you become so violent?"

"When my baby brother decided to terrorize my life after sixteen years of relative peace and quiet." Eva threw her hands up and stormed out of the room in dramatic fashion. She definitely still had a mannerism or two from their mother, whether she wanted to admit it or not.

Javier prodded at the bandages on his left wrist, trying to peek underneath them to see the extent of the damage. The skin looked bruised as hell and shiny from some kind of ointment. Couldn't vampires magically heal their victims' bite wounds? Obviously, Mina hadn't read that page of the playbook, or she hadn't cared enough to bother.

No, he thought firmly. She'd been too out of it at the end to have consciously done any of this. And she'd tried to get him to leave before her transformation into Mrs. Hyde. *Note to self: when a vampire says they're hungry—listen.*

Out of curiosity, Javier flipped through the magazines, skimming article after article, hoping to learn more about the "Princess of Shanghai." When it became clear that the stories all sensationalized Mina's every move into some ridiculously consequential event, Javier quit bothering with the text and just looked at the pictures, trying to imagine what she was thinking.

Javier surreptitiously tore out a photo of Mina emerging from a restaurant in a particularly slinky dress. He quickly folded it and tucked it into his wallet on the nightstand, feeling like a naughty boy looking at the underwear section of his older sister's catalogs.

All right, enough lollygagging. Time to get out of bed and get a cup of coffee and something solid to put in his stomach.

Javier shifted his weight as he pushed back the covers, feeling a disconcerting tug from down below. He lifted the elastic of his boxers, his eyes going wide with horror before he let it snap back in place. He banged his head against the wall with a groan.

Eva had catheterized him.

AFTER THE THOROUGHLY MORTIFYING ORDEAL OF allowing Eva to remove the offending tubing, Javier walked stiffly to her kitchen. An impressive granite island stood before stainless-steel appliances and a massive gas range. Javier took a seat on one of the leather barstools tucked beneath the counter, the aftereffects of major blood loss and lying in bed for thirty hours taking a toll.

"Hey, look, Eva. I'm sorry about the way things went at the party. Can we start over again? Tell me about your life. Like, do you seriously have this incredible apartment all to yourself? Rent must be a fortune."

Eva snapped off her latex gloves and let them drop into the kitchen garbage.

"Heh, it would be. Perks of working for Vasa. Here, drink this." She set a tall glass of orange juice in front of him. "I'll cook something for you."

"You really don't have to. I've already put you out too much." Javier drained half of the juice in one long gulp.

Eva had already pulled out half the contents of her fridge. "You'd say no to a home-cooked meal? I bet you're living on nothing but street noodles."

Javier's stomach chose that opportune moment to give a mournful growl of emptiness. "Something simple, then, and at least let me help. I've actually become quite the chef since you left. Mamá started letting me help in the kitchen."

Eva paused with her hand resting on the open fridge door as if she was pondering the remaining contents.

"I'm sorry I never let you know where I ended up," Eva said after a beat. "You're right—that was a shitty thing to do even if you were a punk-ass little brother." She half sniffled, half chuckled as she turned to face him.

"I'm just glad I found you. Not going to lie though, I'm still your punk-ass little brother."

With a smirk, she rolled a red onion and bell pepper over to him and pulled a knife from a magnetic strip on the wall. "Get chopping."

By the time Eva had stopped placing things beside him, Javier felt like his arm was going to fall off. He watched her work with the calm precision of a doctor in an operating room, her tools sharp and clean and her ingredients neatly arranged in glass bowls. Her hair was piled on top of her head in a messy bun, a few silver threads amongst the mass. She looked so much like their mother that it was uncanny at the right angle. Javier opened his mouth to say so then thought better of it.

A pang of nostalgia hit him so sharply in the sternum that it was almost hard to breathe. He pined for a time when they were all together, eating dinner at that rickety wood table on the patio. He liked to think that before their father died, they had all been happy. Keeping the vineyard running was always demanding work, but at the end of the day, Papá always had a joke to make the kids laugh or a compliment for Mamá to make her smile. How cruel that a single accident could have taken that from all of them.

"Javier? Everything all right?"

"Yup. Onions got to me."

"Sure." Eva passed him a napkin. "This will take five minutes to come together. Maybe you can set the table? I might have a few beers in the fridge too—just don't tell your doctor."

Javier ambled about the kitchen to find place settings as Eva rolled a dash of oil around a sizzling wok. Once she started throwing things in the pan, the crackling pops sent an aroma of blistered vegetables and caramelized meat throughout the kitchen. By the time she plated the stir-fry over a pile of garlic cilantro rice, Javier's hunger was in full force.

They clinked their green bottles in the only premeal deference before digging in. Javier shoveled through half of his plate before even looking up.

"So, tell me about yourself. Did you go to school?" Eva asked as she politely forked reasonable bites into her mouth.

"Uh, yeah," Javier said after a giant swallow. "I studied computer science at Berkeley. I have—well, *had*—a pretty decent tech job. The last round of layoffs finally got me." Javier took a swig of beer, washing down the salty heat of the food, with its interesting blend of Mexican and Asian flavors. "It's cool, though. I got a sweet job as a janitor at the Eternal Twilight Bank now."

"Janitorial?"

"Yeah, the douche at the placement center wanted a bribe. I wasn't interested."

"Ahhh, yeah, that happens here," Eva said with an air of inevitability that chafed. "If you want, I could look for something better around the clinic."

"Nah, that's okay. I actually don't mind it. It's straightforward, you know? And I'm not sure how much longer I'll be here, anyway. I got a pretty decent severance package from the tech job, but I'll still need to find another one pretty soon if the vineyard has another bad year."

Eva frowned. "You've been supporting them?"

"When they need it. The vineyard is my home. The people who work there are my family. I'll do whatever I can to keep it going."

A sour expression crossed Eva's face, but instead of giving a contrary reply, she simply changed the subject. "So, is there a special lady back home? Or guy? I'm sure Mom has been hounding you for grandkids."

"That's a hell of an understatement," Javier said with a chuckle, scraping the last of the food into his mouth.

Before he'd even set his fork down, Eva stole his plate to reload a second helping. "My last serious girlfriend was back in college. Haven't had much time for dating since then, though." His treacherous thoughts flashed an image of Mina into his mind, her sparkling laughter after finishing their dance. *Okay, if you're looking to give your mom grandkids, that's definitely not going to get the job done.*

"You're still young. Plenty of time to find the right person."

"And you?"

"You know, it's strange. Ever since I left, I haven't found anyone even remotely compelling enough to give up my independence for." She said this with an air of defiance, as though she expected to be challenged on her choice.

"As long as you're happy, Eva. That's what matters."

Javier was glad to see the hardness in her expression soften at his response.

After they finished eating, Javier was more full than he could remember being in a long time. He insisted on doing the dishes while Eva sipped a second beer. Finally, he slipped back into his tuxedo pants and shirt, folding the jacket over his arm. Eva pressed a bottle of iron pills into his hand.

This is a very interesting walk of shame, Javier thought wryly. He could only imagine what Mr. Eyebrows was going to say when he sauntered through the lobby wearing the same thing as when he left two days before.

"Thanks for everything, Eva. Can we do dinner again next week? I can cook, but I'll warn you, my place isn't anywhere near this nice."

"I'll do you one better. It's the Mid-Autumn Festival, and the streets will be full of lanterns and people picnicking under the moonlight. We'll go together—eat mooncakes and be festive."

"I would really like that." He gave her a hearty hug. "Love you, big sister."

"Javier," Eva said, her voice suddenly serious. "I need you to promise me something."

"Um, all right?"

"Promise me you won't go looking for Mina. When they get a taste of human blood, you know, straight from the source, they can become... well, *attached*, I guess is the word."

Javier frowned as he thought of the purloined photo in his wallet. He hadn't consciously thought to seek her out, but part of him really didn't like the idea of never seeing Mina again, even if the last time hadn't gone so well.

"I think I learned my lesson on that one." Javier chuckled, hoping to get Eva to drop it.

Eva raised her fist, pinky extended. "I need a definitive answer on this one."

Javier ran a hand through his hair with a sigh, knowing his sister was right. He had no business chasing after that kind of trouble even if she was the most thrilling thing that had happened in his life.

"All right. I promise."

EVA INSISTED on paying for the cab back to his apartment, a good twenty-minute drive in the quiet traffic of a Sunday evening. Mr. Eyebrows made the expected wolf-whistle-laden commentary about Javier's bedraggled appearance after a weekend away.

"Tā hǎokàn ma?" Mr. Eyebrows asked in slow, overenunciated Mandarin. *Is she pretty?*

"Hǎokàn," Javier replied in the affirmative with a saucy wink, leaving out the part that the woman he'd spent the weekend with was actually his sister and that no debauchery had occurred. *Unless you count the catheter,* he thought with a shudder.

Back in his apartment, the light switch echoed as he snapped it on. Javier set his jacket on the back of a chair and the pills on the table, the space feeling so thoroughly empty after a weekend spent with others. Even though he'd never found a romantic partner to share his life with, living alone had never suited him. Being around family, sharing meals and house chores, was much more fulfilling.

Javier fished one last beer out of his fridge before taking a seat at the table. Even though Eva had told him to wait until the next day, he slowly unwrapped the bandages from around his wrist.

Oh my God, I've been mauled.

Not two clean puncture wounds, but several pairs littered his arm, each circle of white, dead flesh ringed in cherry. Green-and-blue bruising permeated the underside of his wrist. It hadn't felt that grisly when Mina had been biting him, but queasiness gripped him as he surveyed the damage. Maybe the attack had been more serious than he'd originally thought.

A memory surfaced—ferocious red eyes locked on his as she pushed him to the ground, draining him with terrifying intensity. She wouldn't have stopped if no one intervened.

Maybe Eva's reaction wasn't off base after all. The danger was real—that much he couldn't deny.

Still, he didn't regret asking Mina to dance. Javier fetched his wallet and unfolded the stolen magazine clipping of her. Christ, she was beautiful, but the photo showed only the surface. The contradiction was what captivated him: a haughty princess trying desperately not to let her damsel in distress show. That impossible tension had him so head over heels that he didn't know what to do with himself. And the monster lurking beneath it all only made him want to understand her more.

Would he see her again?

Doubtful.

You sorry bastard. Consider yourself lucky to have even met her. Be grateful your patient sister is a talented physician, and get your head out of the clouds.

Javier stood to fetch his silly little notebook. He flipped through it, reviewing the trail of information that had eventually led him to his sister. Since finding Eva, he'd had no need of the notes anymore. But for some reason, he felt compelled to keep writing about his time in Shanghai. After finding a comfortable position for his arm, he set pen to paper.

"Dear Diary," he started with juvenile delight. "Mina the Vampire agreed to dance with me, and that's only the beginning." Javier laughed heartily into his empty apartment at the sheer absurdity of events.

Even if he never saw Mina again, he still had that one night. Memorializing it with an entry in the notebook felt like the proper send-off to a relationship that would never be. Hell, maybe one day he would give his mother those grandkids. He would slyly tell them about his crazy adventure in Shanghai, getting attacked by a gorgeous vampire, as he searched for their tía.

Then again, maybe that wasn't such a kid's story after all.

It all kind of depends on the ending, doesn't it? he thought as he finished his beer. In any case, his time in Shanghai was making for some of the most fascinating weeks of his life so far, and he was morbidly curious to see what the city had in store for him next.

13

The next evening, Mina came to the breakfast table to find a half measure of blood poured in her glass. Her eyes met Lian's over her newspaper for a questioning second—*Am I allowed?* The woman twitched a smile in approval, and Mina drained the liquid in one continuous gulp before even sitting. It tasted thin after the decadence of Javier's blood, but perhaps the hunger had embellished the memory. For the time being, the starvation penance had ended, and thank the ancestors for their mercy.

Her work at Zhang Enterprises continued, where Mina had no title and no official desk, just a list of reports to write, numbers to calculate, and meetings to attend. At the end of each night, Lian critiqued her written work and drilled her on the affairs of the day.

"What was the biggest obstacle to establishing the blood supply chain in Hong Kong?" "Why did I reduce the fledgling allotment of the Ma clan while increasing the Li's?" and

"Which foreign heads of state are most receptive to negotiation with our kind?"

Mina's responses generally earned her additional stripes from that damnable bamboo cane. Lian paired the physical correction with readings in political theory and passages of classical text to copy—either to illuminate the answers Mina failed to give or to elaborate on why her failure had been especially disgraceful.

By the end of the week, Mina's answers improved markedly, and Lian took to assigning morally ambiguous topics drawn from the Analects:

"The Master said: 'When those above are correct, those below will not dare to be incorrect.' In light of this teaching, compose an essay evaluating the role of centralized vampire governance in maintaining order and moral harmony in contemporary Shanghai. In your analysis, consider the ethical responsibilities of rulers and subjects alike. Cite examples from current administrative reforms and donor-management protocols to support your argument."

Mina's answer had started well enough but devolved into something she had to scratch out.

"This teaching underscores the foundational relationship between moral authority and political order. In the case of Shanghai's current vampire governance, centralized leadership ensures that human donors, fledglings, and subsidiary clans operate with stability and reverence. ~~Or at least, that is the intention. In practice, correctness becomes indistinguishable from compliance. When the~~

~~ruler cannot be questioned, what remains of virtue but obedience?"~~

Mina fell asleep on top of the report and awoke with ink staining her cheek from the half-finished draft. Lian made Mina stand next to her desk for hours the following night in order to observe "efficient and cleanly work habits." When she was finally dismissed, Mina still had to finish the original report plus a new topic.

Sleep became elusive. Each of her failings was mocked or criticized. And yet in this building, she wasn't *pet*. She was Mina. And she continued to receive some small amount of blood despite her mistakes. Sometimes, Lian would even incline her head in mild acceptance of some trivial answer or piece of work. It made Mina's heart soar with pride.

As draconian as Lian's instructional methods were, Mina was undoubtedly learning *something*. Perhaps the knowledge was more suited to a Ming-dynasty civil service examination than modern business practices, but either way, she obeyed, and she was rewarded with a continued position at Lian's side. What more could she hope for?

By the following week, Mina felt confident enough in her office duties that she had opened her mouth in a meeting. The administrative assistant to the CFO had quoted an incorrect figure as a primary reason for acquiring a new building.

Mina interjected, "Actually, I ran those numbers this morning, and you're off by about ten million yuan."

The man blinked, first at her then Lian, who had the courtesy to dismiss him before calmly pouring a scalding cup of tea over Mina's head. The woman's voice was even as she said,

"You will draft an apology to Mr. Wu, which will be delivered during tomorrow's board meeting. From your knees."

Mina assumed that some of her social cachet would have translated to the office setting. *Wrong.* Whatever pecking order existed, Lian made it clear Mina's place was at the very bottom. Mina read through her apology kneeling, eyes fixed on the floor. She avoided opening her mouth after that.

The night of the meeting with Vasa and Eva at the Sanguis Institute, Mina found excuses to work close to Lian, afraid the woman would leave without her. When the time approached, Lian packed her bag and walked out the door without a word. Mina stood, defeat liquifying her insides.

"Are you coming?" Lian snapped from beyond the threshold.

Mina let out a shaky breath, grabbed her notebook, and scurried out of the room after her austere creator. Her insides, however, remained an anxious slurry as the dread dawned on her that she would soon face the sister of the man she'd mortally wounded. *Please let him be alive.*

AT THE SANGUIS INSTITUTE, Lian and Mina were shown to a resplendent conference room on an upper floor. High-backed leather executive chairs surrounded an expansive glass table perched on sculptural wooden legs.

Dr. Robles and Lord Vasa both rose when they entered, her white lab coat contrasting starkly with his charcoal business suit. Eva glowered at Mina for a terrifying second before properly greeting Lady Zhang. August hid his chagrin better but only gave her a terse nod before lavishing his attentions on Lian. None of that eased Mina's fears for Javier's well-being.

Lian took the prepared seat before a spiral-bound report and bottle of sparkling water. Mina slinked into the seat beside her, wishing Vasa and Eva would quit glancing her way. *Gods, this was a mistake.*

"Apologies," Eva started. "I only printed three copies of the literature. Should I call for another?"

"No need," Lian said, crossing her arms. "As I told Lord Vasa, I am dubious about the financial risk of researching this theoretical 'blood potency' at such a scale. He insisted I give the 'talented young physician' heading his team a final chance to convince me otherwise."

"Certainly." Eva cleared her throat, remaining impressively composed in the face of the formidable Lady Zhang. "During my doctoral research, we experimented with a direct feeding protocol for critically injured patients. While that pilot proved unsustainable, it elucidated an interesting connection between certain individual blood donors and reduced healing times. I requested the donation bank provide unmixed blood to continue tracking this correlation. If you'll turn to page seven in the report..."

Eva flipped through her own spiral-bound report. When Lady Zhang didn't move, she spun the book around to show off the figures. Mina peered distantly at the graphs, wishing she could grab Lian's untouched copy to look closer.

"These scatter plots show injury severity along the Y-axis and healing time along the X-axis. As expected, the general trend shows increased healing times for more severe injuries. However..." Eva flipped to the next page, which showed the same chart rendered in colorful blotches of data points.

"There are statistically significant clusters of data when evaluating the diet source by donor ID. For example, blood from Donor B2—shown in orange—produced a mean healing time difference of five days compared to Donor G9—shown in green—when normalized for injury severity." The doctor's eyes twinkled with scientific fervor as she pointed at clumps on the graph. Even Mina could see the rainbow delineation of each slanted swath of color.

"There are only ten human donors considered in this data," Lady Zhang stated dismissively.

"While longitudinal data is limited to ten complete profiles due to stockpiling needs, over fifty donors have partial metrics included in the complete dataset—strong enough to establish a working hypothesis." Eva's tone was conciliatory but firm. "With more resources—"

"This is an anecdote, not an analysis—hardly a sufficient basis for a multibillion-yuan investment." Lian's polished nails drummed against the glass tabletop.

Eva's eyebrows drew together. "Certainly, there were limitations in the quantity of data we were able to gather, which is precisely why further investment is required. However, this case study, combined with the other data contained in this report, provides a clear picture that whatever factor in blood contributes to the well-being of your species is present in different quantities in different samples.

"I aim to first quantify that potency and then determine the cause for individual differences. This way, the donation process can be made more efficient, further harmonizing the existence of our two species."

Eva's eyes radiated with clarity as she gave her well-rehearsed speech, while Mina tried to process the implications. If there were such drastic individual differences in donor potency, that would be masked by the pooling of the donor blood in the city's supply chain. As someone who had no—well, *little*—experience drinking directly from a human, Mina didn't have much of a point of comparison. Yet something about Javier's blood had been different, denser, more fulfilling.

"Honestly, this seems far-fetched—even for you, Vasa," Lady Zhang stated plainly, gathering her briefcase. "Keep my offices apprised of your work if it advances past the feasibility stages."

"Be reasonable," August finally interjected in his syrupy voice. "You cannot keep all of your investments in real estate forever. Technology is how we ensure a better future. The Singhs and the Temuroğlus are on board, and I assure you, you won't want to be left out of this one."

"You say the same thing every time you try to convince me to invest in your wild technological advances," Lady Zhang said, flourishing one hand. "Like your disastrous diversion with airships—"

"A fundamental flaw in execution, but the *concept* was sound."

"Or direct current electricity—"

"If Edison and Tesla hadn't squabbled so much..."

"Vasa," Lian said with finality, standing. "I will not be swayed by your outlandish ideas this time."

"Lianna, this is different." Vasa stood as well, his double-breasted suit jacket flapping open. "Of all the research I've sponsored over the years, this is one that could actually benefit *us*. This is the first time we've had access—*as a species*—to medical inquiry of this caliber. You know as well as I do that human blood is getting weaker. We need to investigate the cause, or we're heading toward a catastrophic collapse of both populations." August gripped the back of his chair, knuckles white, as he stared intently at Lian.

What did he mean that human blood was getting weaker? Mina felt about two centuries too young to understand the full extent of the conversation.

"There are plenty of humans in this world," Lian replied coldly. "What we lack is dominion, not another contrived excuse for science." The words dripped with danger. "Come along, Mina. We're leaving."

Eva opened her mouth as she looked at August, but the man shook his head, a strained set to his jaw.

A thread of panic rose in Mina as, once again, her chance to find out about Javier threatened to slip away. She'd let herself get drawn into the scientific conjecture, but faced with the potential conclusion of their meeting, Mina's motivations recalcified. Improvising, she slid the copy of Eva's report over to herself.

"My lady, if you'll allow me, I am curious to hear the remainder of Dr. Robles's pitch. Perhaps I could relay a digest to you later, at your convenience?"

Lian shot her a dark look—one that told her she would pay dearly for her defiance later.

"If you wish to waste your time, I won't stop you. However, a substantial amount of work awaits you at the office, which I still expect you to complete by morning."

Lian strode out of the room without further comment, leaving Mina in the company of two scowling faces. As soon as Lady Zhang was out of earshot, she was the first to break the silence.

"Is he alive?"

"Yes," Eva said curtly, taking a sip of her own water.

Mina let out a relieved breath. Javier was alive. If Eva hadn't looked so exquisitely annoyed, Mina might have crossed the table and given her a hug.

August stroked his pencil mustache, looking down his nose at her in derision. "That stunt you pulled was incredibly reckless, älskling. What were you *thinking*?"

Mina's eyes dropped to the gleaming tabletop under the censure. Explaining the extenuating circumstances of Lian's punishment didn't negate the truth that she *had* attacked a human. In some respects, even her famished condition had been her own fault.

"I lost control of myself, and for that, I am deeply sorry," Mina said, a buzzing sensation in her head making her feel dissociated from her body.

Dr. Robles stared at her with a calculating expression, making no indication of forgiveness. The clinical lab coat made Mina feel like a specimen being studied.

"This sort of thing happens amongst fledglings of poorer breeding, but I would expect much better from you." August continued his reprimand, hand on his hip as though he expected an explanation. Mina smothered her irritation at his presumed paternal attitude in the interest of self-preservation.

"Thank you for not telling Lady Zhang," she said, not quite keeping the bitterness from her voice.

The lanky man scrutinized her from across the table with humorless ice-blue eyes. "If I ever hear of you attacking another human, I will personally see to it your fangs are filed."

Mina's head snapped up in surprise—could he really do

that? Her fangs tried to shrink even farther into her gumline at the threat. Of course he could.

"Lord Vasa," Eva cut in. "I believe the gravity of the mistake is understood. However," she continued more softly, "Miss Park, I would be grateful if you would allow me to examine you and test for diseases that may put my brother at risk."

"Do it," August said, waving his hand at Mina dismissively.

"Wait—" Mina shot up from her seat at the table. An unreasonable fear coalesced into a knot in her stomach. What would Eva do to her, alone in a room?

"Vasa," Eva said, a bit more sharply, clasping her hands in front of herself as she glared at the man. "As you know, I require the consent of each patient seen in this clinic, despite whatever hierarchies you maintain elsewhere. Miss Park, it is entirely your decision."

To Mina's surprise, the vampire lord backed down, stalking away from the table toward the window.

"I don't f-feel sick," Mina stammered, trying to guess the woman's ulterior motive, if an exam wasn't an excuse for medically justified retribution.

Eva gave her a tight smile. "Diseases don't often present with the same symptoms in vampires. However, you could still carry certain vectors that would make a human very ill. Malaria, tularemia, certain viruses, for example."

"Oh." Mina frowned. *Yet another way you endanger people with your ignorance.*

She glanced toward the door. Mina could walk out and never think about Javier or Dr. Robles again. He was alive, and she'd apologized the best she could. What benefit was there in subjecting herself to a science experiment?

You owe him at least this, after what you put him through. After what you put his sister through.

Mina balled her fists in her lap, claws digging into the soft flesh of her palm.

"All right. I'll do it."

14

The examination room had little room to maneuver between the physician's countertop, two seats, and the hip-height exam table with a crisp sheet of waxed paper pulled across it. Dr. Robles gestured toward it, and Mina begrudgingly climbed atop, feeling childlike amidst the cacophony of crinkling paper.

"May I ask how many people you've direct-fed from in the last sixty days?" Eva asked as she palpated the lymph nodes in Mina's neck.

"None," Mina said quickly with a swallow against the pressure. "I mean one. Your brother, he—that was my first time with a human..."

Flustered, Mina trained her eyes on the nameplate pinned to Dr. Robles's lab coat as the woman motioned for her to open her mouth. The invasion of the tongue depressor triggered a gag reflex, but Mina forced herself to sit still while Eva completed the inspection. Growing up, traditional remedies had been preferred over visits to sterile offices—those were only for the really bad illnesses. The association lingered.

Yet Eva's hands were warm and efficient as she took Mina's vitals, along with saliva and blood samples. The doctor had the same light-brown skin tone as her brother and the same gentle wave to her hair, the same downturned shape to her eyes. Mina recalled Javier's face from that night, the way the right corner of his mouth pulled slyly before each witty remark, the way he looked at her as though she were the sole thing occupying his attention. As though she were special.

"Miss Park?"

"Hmm?"

Dr. Robles flipped through her notes before looking up again, a slight crease to her brow. "I don't mean to be insensitive, but for a vampire who had a substantial meal last week, and one who should be getting regular meals besides, your vital signs all suggest extreme malnutrition. Can you think of why that might be?"

Mina kept her expression neutral, her hands flat on her thighs as she responded, "No. No reason I can think of." Allowing the exam was already wildly outside her comfort zone; sharing with an outsider—a human, no less—the inner politics of House Zhang was borderline blasphemous. *If Lian knew I was even sitting here...* Sweat prickled at Mina's palms as she pointedly avoided Dr. Robles's studious gaze.

Eva tapped a pen on her notebook, finally giving her a crisp nod. "I will let you know if the labs turn up anything unusual. All of this is off the books, of course. I appreciate your cooperation. Should we go back to the conference room to discuss my research in more depth?"

Confusion blanketed Mina's mind. "Your research?"

"You told Lady Zhang you would give her more information on my proposal. I realize you weren't serious, but it's probably a good idea to at least cover your lie."

"Right." Eva's jab cut through the clouds in Mina's head. *It's not like you would understand any of it anyway.* "I've already taken too much of your time, Dr. Robles. I'll tell her I couldn't grasp the nuances of your work in any detail, which is likely the truth." Mina hopped down from the table and smoothed the wrinkles from her clothes. "I apologize for interrupting your meeting," she added softly. "I just had to know if Javier was okay."

Mina thought of his warm smile and of his sureness guiding them around the dance floor—his face the one constant in the twirling background of the ballroom. He'd gifted her with that moment, uncomplicated and joyful. She knew better than to hope to see him again, yet she yearned for it, longed to hear his laughter, craved the taste of his blood.

Mina felt her fangs descend at the memory, her irises burning with red.

No, no, no. Not again.

She shut her eyes tightly as she backed up, bumping into the doorway with a thump. Her fangs refused to retract, and her lungs clawed for short, choppy breaths. Should she make a run for it before the bloodlust took over? Her hand fumbled for the doorknob. Maybe Vasa was still in the conference room —he would help restrain the monster she'd become.

A coppery scent filled her nose, and Mina's eyes snapped open.

"Drink this."

A plastic pouch nudged her hand, and Mina snatched it before placing the spout against her lips and draining the entire half liter in seconds. She lowered her shaking hands to her sides, terrified by the ravenous demon she could no longer keep from taking over her body.

"I'm so sorry," she said, wishing she could melt into the floor and disappear. Mina flinched as a hand rested on her shoulder.

"It's been a long time since you've had regular meals, yes?" Eva's voice sounded genuinely sympathetic.

Mina clenched her jaw, nodding her head. The hunger had been a compounding debt since she left Shanghai months before. The small meals she'd been allowed the last week only staved off the worst of the immediate hunger.

"And that's not the only way she abuses you, is it?" Eva took Mina's hand and held it up to the light. The back was still littered with yesterday's welts.

"You don't understand," Mina said hoarsely, pulling her hand back from Eva's. "You couldn't understand. I *asked* for this... all of it."

Mina knew that Lian harmed her in ways most modern humans would find egregious. Yet framing Lian's treatment as abuse, when it was her *right* to treat her fledglings however she saw fit, was the critical misbelief that precipitated Mina's current circumstances. But how could she explain all of that to Eva? The educated doctor would write it off as the delusions of a victim. Mina swallowed the lump that had formed in her throat.

Eva gave Mina's shoulder a reassuring squeeze. "Domestic violence is unfortunately common in the vampire community —something I truly hope will change as our societies continue to integrate. For now, if you need someone to talk to or if you need a meal, know that you can come to me. Lord Vasa, as well—"

"You won't tell him about this, will you?" A jolt of panic clutched at her chest. The thought of him knowing the sordid backstory behind her attack on Javier was somehow much worse than having him think it an accident.

Eva sat back on her heels as she gave a concerned sigh. The pity was worse than the sympathy. "It is dangerous for you to be this hungry," the doctor finally said.

"I know," Mina whispered. *Gods, do I know.*

Eva pressed her lips together in a thin line before standing and offering a hand to Mina. "Can you promise me you'll stay away from humans until you're less famished?"

Mina nodded vigorously as she took the hand. "Yes, I promise."

"And next time you feed directly, get consent first. And stay away from the arteries until you practice healing."

Mina was chastened by the rebuke, but curiosity got the better of her. "Can I... do that?"

"You should be able to," Eva said with a smile. "The healing 'spark,' I've heard it called, needs to be transferred via skin contact, and it generally only works on bites you've personally inflicted. It might have to do with properties of your saliva—we're still in early-phase trials with the research."

Mina examined Eva once more, judging her to be at least a few years older than she herself would be. She couldn't help but wonder if she might have pursued a career like Dr. Robles's in an alternate life. Certainly, Mina wasn't intelligent enough for medicine, but she could have ended up in an office building like Zhang Enterprises. Mina tried to imagine that life, going to the office during the day and returning to her own home afterward. But the vision felt watery, impossible. Her only viable skill was keeping Lian happy, and most days, she even failed at that.

Eva moved toward the door. "I really would like to go through my research with you. Some of it might even interest you. Does that sound all right?"

Mina took a deep breath. It might be nice to have a reprieve to compose herself before returning to Lady Zhang anyway.

"Yes, I'd like that," Mina conceded quietly.

Back in the conference room, one hour turned into two as Eva thoroughly explained the details of her research, tying the narrative together strand by strand. Eva was patient, pausing to explain medical concepts and how to read the various charts. The underlying theory fascinated Mina: the component of human blood sustaining vampires not only differed between people but also was likely declining in quality. This certainly seemed like an area worth investigating. Why had Lady Zhang been so quick to dismiss it?

Eva also impressed with her knowledge of the mechanics of being a vampire. She could pinpoint what conditions caused a vampire to enter stasis—a hibernation-like state—and the precise biological processes that turned their eyes red when they were angry. Although she hadn't identified the pheromones involved in compulsion, she had strong circum-stantial evidence that they existed. Eva possibly knew more about being a vampire than Mina did.

"Thank you for your time, Dr. Robles, but I do need to get back to the office now." The clock was pushing ten already, and Mina could imagine the insurmountable mountain of work accumulating for her.

"I do hope you'll share the information with Lady Zhang.

Perhaps she'll be more receptive to hearing it from one of her own. We have enough funds to start work, but the longevity of the program could depend on her financial backing and support."

"I will." Mina collected an array of papers in her arms. A thought occurred to her, one she barely dared acknowledge. *And still...* "Dr. Robles? I know I shouldn't ask, but do you think it would be possible for me to see Javier again? To apologize?" Knowing he lived, she couldn't imagine not seeing him again.

Eva pursed her lips. "I'm afraid that's not a good idea. Direct feeding can encourage certain feelings of attachment. For both participants. The sensation should significantly reduce after a few weeks, but you will likely feel some connection to him for a good deal longer. Especially with your increased hunger, it's likely you'd end up feeding from him again.

"Of course, you are both adults, but Javier is still incredibly naïve to the ways of vampires. I trust you understand my concern that Lady Zhang might take issue if you develop feelings."

"I didn't realize," Mina mumbled, the truth painfully obvious since Eva had spelled it out. To think that her involvement in his life would bring him anything positive was foolish. "You're right—I don't want to put him in harm's way again. Just tell him I'm sorry."

~

As Mina rode the multiple elevator cars to the upper floors of Zhang Enterprises, her mood darkened in anticipation of the required groveling for her dalliance at the Sanguis Institute. When she discovered Lady Zhang had already left for the night, her apprehension only deepened, envisioning the reprimand awaiting her at home.

Mina remained at the office well past dawn, completing her assigned tasks as well as a formal report regarding Dr. Robles's research. That was the least she could do to repay the kindness the woman had shown her. When she finally returned to Zhang Manor, Mina tiptoed up the staircase so as to not wake the household.

But as she turned to pass Lian's central suite, the woman called out in her silky voice, "Mina?"

Of course it was too much to ask that retribution wait until tomorrow. Mina backtracked, pushing through the open door to Lian's room with a cautious bow. This was the first time in years Mina had entered the woman's private quarters, a palatial room of minimalist restraint.

The bed was covered in a decadent taupe duvet, crisply tucked in along the sides. A chest of drawers and an armoire lined the walls, their teak wood richly browned from age. Above them hung a vibrant rendering of a pair of sparrows on a blossoming dogwood. Next to that scroll hung a long, curved sword, its scabbard trimmed with red braid.

As Mina's eyes lingered anxiously on that blade, Lian said, "Come sit with me."

Mina shuffled to the opposite end of the room, where Lian occupied the settee. An elegantly wrapped box lay on the low table next to a short tumbler of viscous black liquid on ice. The outline of intricate tattoos on Lian's shoulders and arms showed through the white silk robe, reminiscent of delicate watercolor paintings.

When Mina moved toward the armchair, Lian patted the cushion next to herself with a devious smile. Mina clutched her materials more tightly against her chest as she perched on the edge of the seat.

She cleared her throat. "I apologize for the late hour—it took longer to apprehend Dr. Robles's presentation than I expected. Would you like to hear the details?" Mina shuffled through her papers, her fingers fumbling the edges of the paper.

"That won't be necessary." Lian took a sip of her inky tonic, ice tinkling in the glass. "Set the work aside—I have a gift for you."

Mina frowned, reluctantly placing her papers on the table next to the box. It was white and bedecked with a black gros-grain ribbon—nothing like the box in the bank vault. Yet worry churned in Mina's stomach that it might contain the serpent collar.

"My lady, if you'll permit me a question first. The blood potency decline... At first, it confused me why you wouldn't want to investigate this phenomenon. You architect societies with economics, policy, and infrastructures, and this seems like critical knowledge to inform the longevity of those systems. The more I thought about it, though, I realized... it's because you already know about it *and* its cause. Don't you?"

Lian inclined her head magnanimously, short locks of hair falling to frame her face. "Perhaps you've learned more working for me than I've given you credit for." The woman gave Mina an appraising look that sent a shiver down her spine.

"'Blood potency' they're calling it." Lian snorted. "There used to be an inherent understanding of these things before codified medicine. Qi—life force—blood potency. They're all the same. Humans have lost touch with the harmony of this world. They eat things that bear no resemblance to food, they preoccupy themselves with technological mindlessness— they barely *live* anymore. It's no wonder their qi is declining."

"Qi is distilled in human blood..." Mina said, pieces of understanding clicking together for the first time. "And by consuming it, we gain a concentrated version of that energy." Mina's eyes landed on the viscous liquid in Lian's tumbler. "But modernization—urbanization—those aren't things you can stop."

"Humans have always had a propensity for self-destruction —they allow myopic gluttony to guide their decision-making. With the correct policies, even the worst of human avarice and sloth can be rectified. You'll see," Lian declared as a challenge, obsidian eyes glinting with mirth.

Mina didn't dare ask the repercussions of policy that aimed to staunch all technological development. What modern human would elect to live in that world? Furthermore, Mina was dubious that moral turpitude constituted the entire problem.

"I'm wondering with respect to Dr. Robles's research," Mina started tentatively, now certain a better understanding of the problem—and its potential solutions—was necessary, ideally by someone who might balance Lian's supercilious views on humanity. "Even if you don't expect to learn anything from the work, might it be worthwhile to monitor the find- ings? To learn the basis of the other houses' strategic decisions?"

"That is a genuinely well-reasoned point." Lian swirled the drink in her glass. "If I do make this investment, I would hold you personally responsible to oversee and report on their work. Would you accept that accountability?"

Mina's eyes went wide as her insides tingled. "Me?"

Lian reached a hand up to Mina's face, and she instinctively flinched before she could catch herself. With a smirk, Lian simply brushed a stray strand of hair away from her face. "It will be a good excuse to use your new gift, in any case. Any further philosophical musings you'd like to discuss, or will you finally open it?"

With a fierce blush, Mina picked up the box and brought it to her lap. The bow yielded with a gentle tug, and the heavy lid slid easily away. Nestled in the plush felt was a black tote of her own, the sleek leather burnished to a high shine. Mina ran her fingers over the engraved initials on the inside flap.

"My lady is too generous," Mina whispered before looking up, her eyes glazed with emotion—it was more recognition than she'd ever dared hope for. "Thank you."

Lian shifted closer to Mina on the couch, tipping her chin up and pressing their lips together in a gentle kiss. Mina's breath caught as she closed her eyes, confused and elated in the same moment. Did she want this? Either response terrified her.

The woman shifted the briefcase from Mina's lap, as she pressed forward, deepening the kiss. Mina's eyes fluttered as her own hand went to Lian's arm to stabilize herself. Was this— could this be real? *How much more will she ask for?* Mina wondered with a jolt of fear.

"However..." The woman's tapered fingers slithered to the back of Mina's head. "I get the sense you have an ulterior motive for involving yourself with this Robles woman." As Mina opened her mouth to protest, Lian's fist tightened painfully in her hair and wrenched backward. Mina grappled for the edge of the sofa, trying to relieve some of the strain as her pulse raced.

"No, don't speak. Consider this your one and only reminder that I will learn all of your secrets eventually. The longer they stay hidden"—the fist tightened further—"the worse your punishment will be." The woman leaned forward, and Mina closed her eyes as sharp fangs scraped across her throat in bright lines of unexpected pleasure.

"Please..." she moaned involuntarily.

Lady Zhang knew her weaknesses—her *desires*—all too well.

Lian laughed breathily against her neck before the woman struck as fast as a viper, two-inch-long points sinking into the soft skin at her throat. Lian's arm snaked around her torso, pinning Mina in place as a wash of jasmine perfume rolled over her. The pain was transcendent, morphing into an ephemeral pleasure that Mina had all but forgotten. A delicate whimper escaped as she relaxed into Lian's hold.

In that moment, she was entirely Lian's; as she ceased to exist as her own being, she could let go of all the fear, regret, and loathing that plagued her always. As long as she complied, Lian would ensure everything was made right in the world. In that trust, a profound calmness absolved Mina's misdeeds. For several minutes, they existed in that spiritual state, earthly concerns fading to nothing.

When Lian withdrew, a trail of crimson marked the corner of the woman's mouth. *My blood,* Mina thought with pride. Lian brushed her knuckles across the puncture marks, sealing them, before her hand closed around Mina's throat. She squeezed lightly—just enough to make Mina's head feel heavy as Lian leaned in and kissed her deeply. The brackish taste of herself on the woman's tongue made her moan once more.

"My love," Lian murmured.

Delirious emotion overtook Mina before tears slipped from her eyes. Maybe—just maybe—Lian's feelings toward her were still in there somewhere. Maybe there would be some redemption for her in this life after all.

Lian cradled Mina's head as she held the glass of black liquid up to her lips. "Drink."

Mina spluttered at the first sip, the condensed blood burning like cheap whisky.

"I know it's awful, but you need the energy. Now, drink."

Mina obeyed, the reward of Lian's satisfaction overcoming the bitter taste. Her mind wandered with the abstract thoughts of presleep: *Is this what I've been missing?* When Lian slipped her arms beneath her listless form, Mina stirred. She didn't want to be alone after the ragged extremes of the day.

"Could I sleep here tonight? On the sofa—or on the floor if it pleases my lady." It was a kindness that Mina hadn't dared ask for in years. For a moment, Lady Zhang considered her, even pausing to brush a lock of raven hair out of her face. When the woman continued to scoop Mina into her lean arms, Mina tried not to let her disappointment show. At least Lian was helping her to bed—Mina wasn't entirely sure her rubbery legs would carry her at that point.

When Lian carried her a mere few meters before pulling back the covers and laying her on the mattress, the shock sent a wave of panicked thrill through her.

"My lady?" Mina questioned, still not daring to believe she'd earned the favor of such closeness. The dim light of the bedroom disappeared altogether before Lian actually slipped in beside her. The woman's body was pleasantly warm after the meal, curled around Mina's back, their limbs tangled.

"My Mina," the woman hummed into her ear as her grip tightened.

Those words hit Mina with a flood of warmth, and she settled into the embrace of her creator. Within a few minutes, Lian's body temperature and respiration rate fell dramatically as the stasis of sleep took her. Yet Mina remained awake, the hard-fought feeling of comfort replaced by unease. The night had been a good one—she wasn't a murderer after all, and for once, Lian had shown some measure of approval.

So why, lying in her arms, did Mina feel like she was drowning?

15

ugust Vasa stared intently at the Shanghai skyline from the top floor of the Sanguis Institute. Dusk nestled into the city's byways as it transitioned from the domain of one species to the next. He trained his mind on the movements of the vehicles below, a necessary distraction from this so-called "modern medicine."

The needle pierced the back of his neck, penetrating his cervical spinal column, and he grimaced through the pain, avoiding his own translucent reflection in the glass. As the fluid flooded into the canal, August repressed the sensation that the back of his head would burst from the unbearable pressure like an overripe tomato in the summer sun.

"Just two more to go, Lord Vasa. You're doing great," Dr. Robles said.

"I would be doing better if you let me smoke," August quipped with a strained voice, adjusting himself in the procedure chair between injections. Common synthetic anesthetics weren't compatible with vampire biology, but the opium-laced cigarettes he'd relied on for centuries worked just fine. Unfortunately, the effects of the one he'd had before entering the Sanguis Institute had all but worn off.

Eva snorted once before the sting of the needle returned. Vasa endured the rest of the procedure in stony silence as he had every two months for the last five years. It was godawful medical torture but arguably better than the alternative of succumbing to the madness of the end-stage disease, which surely would have happened by now had Robles not implored him to give the experimental treatment a chance, damnable and brilliant doctor that she was.

"All finished," Eva noted in a cheery voice as she snapped off her nitrile gloves.

"Fantastic." August stood from the chair, rolling his neck with a grimace. He collected his collared shirt from the coatrack in the office's corner and slipped it on with stiff aplomb.

"Your recent lab work is back, and I have to say I'm concerned that your levels haven't recovered by now."

August waved his hand. "It can take a year or more to regain full strength after a new fledgling."

"If you had followed the advice of your doctors—"

"Yes, you elaborated on the risks quite clearly. But Dmitri is healthy, isn't he? That's what's important. My foreshortened timeline is my own business. As grateful as I am for your continued dedication to this treatment regime, it's not a cure."

Eva set her clipboard down and gave him that disdainful sympathetic-doctor expression. "You may have years, or even decades, left of relatively normal function. Don't discount that time."

August turned to face her, reclothed in some manner of dignity. He'd postponed this conversation until Dmitri was out of the woods, but it was past time that he broached the topic with his physician.

"Dr. Robles."

"Lord Vasa?"

August schooled his expression into aristocratic indifference. "This was the last treatment I will accept from you. Dmitri and I will be moving to Buenos Aires shortly, and I shan't inconvenience your work further. With our new venture fully funded, you should be dedicating all your energies toward the potency research."

Eva's eyes grew wide with objection. "Don't give up on me, Vasa. We've worked too hard over the years for you to quit now."

August looked away to avoid her teary emotions. By God, he would not be swayed by her wanton sentiment. He grabbed his trench coat and fedora from the rack and opened his mouth to bid her farewell.

"Fine," Eva said dolefully. "But since you brought it up, we should discuss Lady Zhang's late contribution to the research effort." She took a seat on the pleather spinning stool and gestured for him to sit as well.

With a scowl, he indulged her, perching on the edge of the procedure chair with a rigid posture, lest she think him amenable to persuasion. "My sister obviously came to her senses upon further reflection on the strength of your work. What more is there to discuss?"

Eva tapped the pen on her clipboard. "She left the conference room that day adamant that the research was insufficient, and she doesn't seem like someone who changes their mind after the decision has been made."

"Lady Zhang can be unpredictable. But for as long as I have

known her, she has worked fiercely to defend the existence of our kind and the continuity of humanity on the whole. I am sure it is with these motives in mind that she reconsidered her position."

"My impression of her, albeit limited, is less altruistic than that," Eva issued combatively, folding her arms across her chest.

August fiddled with his uneven collar stays. He wanted to tell the stubborn woman to be grateful for the money and move on, but Dr. Robles was too astute after years working amidst political games. And this wouldn't be the first time he softened his sister's icy demeanor after the fact.

"All right," August acquiesced. "Perhaps I can tell you a story that will change your mind. You know your history, don't you? The truly baleful events of the early twentieth century?"

"The wars in Europe and Asia were certainly horrific," Eva ventured cautiously.

"'Certainly horrific' indeed." August gave a half smile at the tidy summary. "At the time, Lianna and I lived in Stockholm. Investments were stable, society loved our curious coupling—allt var bra. That is, until the Second Sino-Japanese war broke out."

"There can't have been many repercussions all the way in Stockholm."

The corner of August's mouth twitched at the interruption. He needed another cigarette. "My dear, wars do not contain themselves so neatly. Besides, information at that time had started to travel faster. Society heard broad details from the radio and discussed them—in a distant kind of way, you understand. Terrible news, but what could be done? Not my Lianna, though. She insisted we go to the heart of the conflict to help her people. Surely two vampires might make a difference." A wistful smile tugged at August's lips.

"Alas, I refused. Why would we leave the safety of Stockholm to go to a war-torn country on the other side of the world? Not to mention the war brewing on the continent, which I fully intended to avoid. In my cowardice, I feared the persecution of homosexuals. I selfishly wanted her to stay with me for the cover she provided as my partner... among more sentimental reasons," he acknowledged.

"You two were... together?" Eva's eyebrows danced incredulously.

"Married, if you can believe it," August said with a grin at the utter chaos and thrill that woman had brought to his life. "Of course, she left me—as she was right to. When we reunited, she refused to speak of her experience. That alone is a chilling reflection of what she must have witnessed. Those atrocities changed her into something sharper, more focused."

"What did you do instead?"

"I continued my spineless existence in Stockholm, of course, utterly convinced that the wars were not my problem to solve. This remains one of the biggest regrets of my life. The closest Nazi death camp to Stockholm was only four hundred kilometers away. Auschwitz? Only a thousand. Yet I deluded myself into thinking those weren't my people."

"Surely, it was a difficult time..."

"I do not seek absolution, child. I will live with my inaction until I die. However, especially with my prognosis, I feel compelled to make the most of my wealth and power to ensure the future for our civilization as best I can. Lady Zhang came to that realization a great while before I did and has enacted a plan to bring a divided world under vampire hegemony for the betterment of all. While I've never had her political mind, I do have an aptitude for technology and science. This work—*your* work—is my contribution toward that peaceful future that might exist in my absence."

Eva remained quiet, and August stood with a sigh.

"In any case, I'm sure you will make the best of her investment, and you would be wise to follow any advice she provides as well." August donned his hat, ready to be done with medical offices and memories.

"Vasa, if you're trying to punish yourself for the past or somehow repent by not accepting further treatment—"

"Damn it all, woman. My decision is final, and I will not discuss this with you further," he said, restraining his urge to put a fist through the wall. The irritability had intensified to the point where he almost distrusted himself to be alone with humans. He had hoped to avoid sharing that detail with the good doctor, though.

August wrenched open the door and stalked out before he lost all control of his temper. On the sidewalk outside the building, he fumbled for his cigarettes with trembling hands, nearly spilling the lot of tightly rolled black sticks from their filigreed clamshell. The first drag hit him like a wave of cool water over the blistered shards of his psyche.

Unfortunately, Eva was only the first of those who needed to be informed of the move to Buenos Aires. August had a feeling Dmitri would be less understanding. Although the Vasa takeover of the city had been under negotiations for several years, the final clearances had come through several months earlier than he anticipated.

Buenos Aires wasn't home and never would be, but August didn't know if he could rightfully live in Europe again.

Argentina would be a solid home base for his family for the time being, and he hoped the legacy would persist long after he was gone.

August decided to walk the several blocks home in the dusky twilight, blotting at the perspiration that dotted his brow with a translucent handkerchief. At least the move would mean getting away from this hellish tropical climate, a small mercy for his final days.

As the elevator doors opened on the floor of the Vasa penthouse, August's eardrums were assaulted by synthpop blaring from the gramophone Dmitri had commandeered for his makeshift dance studio. As much as Vasa enjoyed eighties music, a dull headache throbbed with increasing intensity from the injections, and the loud bass was not doing it any favors.

He handed his coat and hat to the butler before striding through several sets of French doors to the source of the cacophony. Dmitri grasped a metal barre in the center of the room, facing away, one leg extended in a paltry développé devant. August folded his arms and leaned against the doorframe, taking a moment to observe the young man before sharing the news of their move.

Knowing his mortality loomed, he felt the secret of his illness weighing on him as it never had before. August had kept the diagnosis between himself and Dr. Robles for years, hoping that an eventual cure would preclude having to share his circumstances with family and friends.

He would be forced to tell them all, including Dmitri, when the symptoms began to show. At least by that time, the end would be near. While Eva had always been reluctant to give him a direct answer, August guessed that would happen inside the year without her intervention. He dearly hoped Dmitri would be strong enough by that point, but he had already started freezing his blood for backup meals in case the disease took him sooner than expected.

"August. How long have you been standing there?" Dmitri asked when he turned to repeat the exercise to the second side.

"Long enough to see you've been neglecting your stretching." August smirked as a bashful blush crept to the boy's cheeks. He was utterly adorable with his neon headband, spandex shorts, and the single ratty leg warmer pushed up around one thigh. While August had always preferred the classical simplicity of the white shirt and black pants of the academy uniform, Dmitri always gravitated toward eccentric attire when he could get away with it. Over time, August came to view the style choices as endearing.

"You said I should take it easy, getting back into shape," the boy said.

"I suppose I did." August crossed the floor to the record player and lifted the needle with a screech.

"Ah, August, come on. You never want to listen to modern music anymore."

"Indulge me for thirty minutes of something quieter." He slipped a second disc of vinyl out of its tattered sleeve and centered it on the spinning plate. Replacing the needle, he smiled as the warmth of the clicks and pops overlay the opening string sequence of Glazunov's "Raymonda."

"Old man," Dmitri muttered under his breath in somewhat derogatory Russian.

"You wouldn't have had the gall to call me that at the academy. Put your leg on the barre, boy," he said in his more authoritative teaching voice. August had to admit he sometimes missed the simple days of instructing in St. Petersburg. Still, this was where they were meant to be now. After the accident, he owed it to Dmitri to offer this life to him.

"Whatever would I do without you, Ballet Master Vasa," Dmitri mocked as he hoisted a leg onto the waist-height rail and casually draped his torso over it.

"The cheek you've developed." August clucked his tongue as he approached the younger man. "And where did your turnout go? Must I reteach you all of the basics?" He hooked his heel on the toes of Dmitri's standing foot, nudging more external rotation, while pulling back on his outside hip to square the position. Dmitri tried to compensate as the stretch became significantly more demanding, but August placed a palm on the boy's lower back, encouraging him into the deeper position. Resistance faded as Dmitri willed his muscles to relax, his head eventually coming to rest against his shinbone.

"Honestly, August," Dmitri said through gritted teeth. "You're worse than the Russians."

"Where do you think they learned their methods? Now, focus on your breathing."

He made the boy hold it for several minutes before switching to the other leg, enjoying the closeness, feeling the lithe muscles beneath the thin fabric, smelling the gentle musk of Dmitri's exertions.

"August? Do you think I can start taking class with the Shanghai Ballet again soon? My ankle feels fine, and I think, with a few more weeks of conditioning, I'll at least be strong enough for barre."

August allowed Dmitri to come out of the stretch with a sigh. This was the part he'd been avoiding.

"Unfortunately, you will not be joining the Shanghai Ballet."

"Why not?" the boy asked, and August could sense the rising mix of anger and hurt in his voice.

"Because we won't be in Shanghai much longer. We are moving to Buenos Aires next month."

"What?" Dmitri spluttered. "I just got here. What do you mean we're moving to Buenos Aires?"

August walked over to the record player and turned off the music, which had become unbearably mawkish.

"Exactly that. The city has been claimed by the Vasa family, and as its head, I must oversee that ownership. It will be at least another nine months before you can be apart from me, so you are required to come as well." August took a breath, trying to mitigate the unwarranted harshness in his voice. "Don't worry. Argentina has one of the best companies in South America, and I have already approached them about a soloist position for you."

"But all of my friends are here!"

"You'll make new ones."

"But August—"

"But nothing!" he shouted, surprising himself with the volume. "This is happening whether you like it or not. As much as I won't enjoy dragging you there, I will if I must."

The look in Dmitri's eyes broke his heart, coming as close to loathing as he'd ever seen. August knew the unrestrained adulation of early fledglinghood wouldn't last forever, but he was sorry to have the honeymoon over so soon.

Dmitri stormed out of the room without another word,

the leather of his ballet flats slapping against the hardwood flooring. August remained at the small gramophone table for another minute, willing a sudden onset of dizziness to dissipate. He fumbled for a cigarette and let a long inhale of smoke calm his frayed nerves.

As miserable as Dmitri was, August comforted himself with the fact that the boy would have a long life and a long career in Argentina, surrounded by family. Dmitri would eventually see that the move was for the best, especially once August was gone.

16

The next week of work at the bank was interminable as Javier battled lingering exhaustion from his unplanned donation, along with a growing sense that his time in Shanghai was coming to an end. If not for the spike in ticket prices, he might have already booked the flight. As it was, a few more weeks of wages would be beneficial in covering the expense without eating into the savings he'd set aside for the vineyard. Plus, spending more time with Eva would be nice—he had come all this way, after all, and likely wouldn't see her again for several years.

It still baffled him that she'd chosen life in a foreign city over one close to her family and hometown. Already, the endless concrete had depleted the energy he got from working outdoors, immersed in living plants and restorative mountain air. Javier dreamed of the vineyard he was missing back home— the heat of the day yielding to the chill of evening. He'd finally gotten a chance to call his mom. The harvest had gone well, but she hadn't been shy about guilting him for not being there and demanding to know when he would be back. The reminder of home made Shanghai feel all the more transient.

When he arrived for his last workday of the week, Arvind was waiting for him by the clock.

"Javier, you said you had experience with electronics, yes?"

"Sure, yeah. I was a developer back home. Mostly backend but some cybersec as well."

"How about IT?"

Javier tried to keep himself from making a face. Although he didn't like to judge, IT professionals were a special breed. "Not specifically, but I could work out the basics."

"Good, follow me," Arvind said, looking on impatiently as Javier stashed his messenger bag and clipped on his badge. The man took him on a brisk walk through the service byways of the bank to a room deep underground, protected by layers of biometric screenings and access codes.

"Our lead IT employee walked out last night, but not before unplugging half of the server room. It'll be weeks before we have a proper replacement. With the expansion of the Eternal Twilight Bank systems to several Hong Kong branches, our infrastructure has been pushed to its limit already. If you can get it back up and running, I'll see about bumping you up a pay grade."

Javier surveyed the cable spaghetti surrounding the banks of server racks. The place was a downright mess, even by his sloppy software-developer's standards, not to mention the noticeable lack of operable cooling. A trickle of sweat was already rolling down Javier's temple.

"I can definitely take a look. Is there a console I can use to access the system? A list of server host names and some credentials? Do you know what OS these machines are running?"

The tension in Arvind's shoulders noticeably relaxed as Javier asked the questions that validated his ability to do the job.

"Yes, I will get you all of that information. My sincere thanks for stepping in."

"Of course, no problem at all."

Truly, the prospect of touching a keyboard again already had his fingers twitching. While Javier compartmentalized his career into something that enabled the better parts of his life, writing elegant, purposeful lines of code was uniquely fulfilling. IT wasn't really in the same category of work as engineering, but if he could use his knowledge to fix the outage for the biggest bank in the city, that would certainly be a win for the day.

Once Arvind furnished the information he needed, leaving him with a walkie-talkie and a flashlight, Javier set to work detangling the mess that the former employee had left. After the first thirty minutes of trying to establish a network topology of the equipment through pings and ARP table sleuthing alone, Javier realized he was going to have to do the tedious groundwork of tracing the physical ethernet cables first.

Feeling safely alone for the morning, Javier shed his long-sleeve shirt to air out his dampened undershirt. Although the puncture marks on his wrist and arm had scabbed over, the discolored bruising drew attention in a pretty obvious vampires-were-here sort of way. Besides having the uncouth injury, he'd taken Eva's warning to heart about hiding his indiscretions with Mina. After replaying that night in his head too many times to count, he'd convinced himself Mina hadn't intended to cause him injury. The attack had been a mistake, plain and simple.

By lunchtime, he had seventy percent of the servers reporting links up with reasonable CPU and network usage. Arvind brought his wife's pork vindaloo in a dented metal container, insisting Javier not take the time to go out for lunch. Javier refused at first, knowing his boss was giving up his own meal. But when Arvind popped the latches on the tiered containers and the complex aroma of the spiced dish hit his nose, Javier couldn't resist trying a bite. At least he got Arvind to split it with him as they sat at a table in the desolate hallway outside the server room.

"You don't know how big of a help this is. I've been here since last night, trying to clean up the damage Terry did," the man said.

"For sure. It's actually pretty nice to flex my brain. I mean, no offense to janitorial, but this is much more my speed in terms of a job."

"Would you be interested in the full-time position?"

Javier took a large bite, chewing to buy himself thinking time before answering.

"I appreciate it, but no. I'm happy to help as long as you need me to, but to tell you the truth, after finding my sister, I'm not sure how much longer Shanghai will be home. I hope that's not too much of an inconvenience."

"I appreciate your honesty, my friend." Arvind nodded in understanding. "It will take a while to fill the position. I refuse to pay into the corrupt placement offices, and they penalize me by moving my requests to the bottom of the pile. Would you mind filling in until your departure?"

"Of course—no problem."

A pang of guilt hit Javier. He wanted to help Arvind out long-term, especially if it meant thwarting a bureaucratic entity that disadvantaged honest people. However, ultimately, that wasn't a good enough reason to prolong his time in the city.

Javier finished his curry along with a side dish of an unpleasant vegetable Arvind had called "bitter melon." That one would have to grow on him.

"Hey, Arvind? I've been wondering. Do you know why this city is so against mobile electronics? This"—Javier hoisted the walkie-talkie—"is the first thing I've actually seen that can walk away from a wall."

"I've heard that the frequencies irritate their ears and that the screens are too bright for their eyes. I suppose it's easier to prevent electronics usage altogether although there are some exceptions for work-related purposes in restricted areas."

"Hmm, I guess I could see that." Javier knew that even human hearing could detect ringing noises from oscillators on some PCBs. If those were the equivalent of a dog whistle to vampires, that could get pretty irritating. Maybe Eva could confirm the hypothesis.

"Well, thanks for sharing your lunch, and tell Mrs. Patel that she is an exceptional cook."

"If I tell her that, she's going to start sending food for you too."

"Twist my arm," Javier said with a laugh, oddly comforted that his older boss had a person to go home to, one that lovingly portioned multicourse lunches for him each day.

He spent the rest of the day and a few hours into the evening sorting out the server room. At the end, it was over ninety-five percent operational with some suspect equipment quarantined in the room's corner. Cables were neatly zip-tied to the racks with labeled tape at each end. Whoever took over this project next was sure to find it a lot more maintainable than when Terry left. Until then, maybe he could convince Arvind to let him sort through the quarantine pile to figure out what was useful. Javier wasn't quite ready to go back to emptying trash cans, despite the sweltering server room conditions. Maybe Arvind would let him see to the heat dissipation problem as well.

JAVIER SHOVED a sandwich into his face on the walk back to his apartment. He would need to pack a lunch and possibly dinner the next day if he was going to keep up this frantic pace. His mind was preoccupied with architecting a way to better track server equipment when he walked through the front doors of his building.

Mr. Eyebrows made a dramatic statement in Mandarin as he held a hand up and rubbed his fingers together in the recognizable gesture for "pay up." With all the work drama of the day, Javier had completely forgotten about the bet they'd managed to make on the Mexico-China soccer game. Clearly, Mr. Eyebrows had not.

After wadding up his sandwich wrapper and tossing it in the trash, Javier fished out a hundred-yuan note from his pocket and tossed it on the counter. "Fine, you old codger, but Marquez was cheated out of that last goal, and you know it."

Mr. Eyebrows made a showy demonstration of putting the bill in his worn leather wallet as Javier shook his head and trudged off down the hallway. Admittedly, he would miss that guy when he left.

When the elevator opened on Javier's floor, Maomao looked up at him innocently. This was his third escape attempt this week. Javier scooped Wenshi's cat up in his arms before he could dart off. "Come on, buddy, let's get you home."

"Mao."

As he adjusted the cat, his fingers encountered an unpleasant stickiness matting its belly fur. Javier's hand came away slick with a dark-red liquid. Had the scabs come off his bite wounds? Nope... With mounting unease, Javier jogged down the corridor, cat tucked under his arm. Wenshi's door was ajar, and Javier knocked only once before pushing it open.

"Wenshi?"

The woman's apartment was an explosion of half-completed garments. Wenshi often took home piecework from her job for extra cash, but her place was out of control. Every piece of furniture was festooned with a rainbow of cloth. When Javier finally spotted her amongst the mounds of fabric, alarm coursed through his body.

The petite woman reclined on the couch, eyes closed and blood trickling down from the crook of her elbow. A half-full donation bag sat in a puddle on the floor, a coil of tubing spooled around it.

Maomao yowled as he was tossed to the ground. Javier grabbed a dish towel and crashed to his knees by Wenshi's side, pressing it against her arm to staunch the bleeding.

"Hey, Wenshi. Wake up. It's Javier."

"Shénme shì?" she replied groggily, her eyelids fluttering before sealing tightly once more.

Oh, thank God, she's conscious.

"Good question. Do I need to call a doctor?" Javier asked,

wondering if Eva would be home from work by now. He had a feeling his sister stayed late at the office more often than not.

"No. No doctors," Wenshi moaned. She pushed herself up, caught sight of the mess on the floor, and promptly threw her head back down on the couch. "I'm so *stupid*. There's no way they'll take a half-full bag."

"Who's *they*?" Javier pinched the bag at the top between two fingers and propped it up against the couch leg.

This city definitely wasn't for the squeamish. What the hell had Wenshi gotten herself wrapped up in that she was giving even more blood on top of regular donations?

"They... Oh, it doesn't matter. Unless... Do you think I can stick the needle back in to top it off?"

"Jesus. *No.*" Javier stared at the needle glinting through the accumulated blood on the ground. Maybe he could find something to mop it all up with and dispose of the medical waste. He stood and went to her kitchenette to grab a roll of paper towels. When he turned around, Wenshi already had the needle poised above her vein. She slid it back in with a hiss, and Javier heaved an exasperated sigh.

"Are you serious right now? Losing this much blood wrecks your body, Wenshi." *Ask me how I know,* he thought cynically. A few weeks had passed since Mina fed from him at the party, and he still got dizzy when he stood up too fast. He made a mental note to bring Wenshi the leftover iron pills Eva had prescribed him after the accident.

"Are you selling your blood too? How much did you get paid?" Wenshi asked, her eyes intent through her large spectacles.

"Dammit, Wenshi. No. I'm not selling my blood—at least

not outside of the normal exchange with the city. Is that what you're doing?"

Wenshi frowned, sadness creeping into her expression. "I overheard that some of the women at the factory give extra donations for cash. If I do this, then I'll finally have enough that I could leave. I haven't seen my family in four years, Javier. *Four years*. I just want to go home."

The quiet desperation in her voice tugged at his heart. If it were his sister in Wenshi's place, he would hope someone would help her get back home. Javier tossed the blood-soaked towels in the trash and rinsed his hands in the sink. Arvind had mentioned that the blood banks sometimes sold donations on the side. Why the greedy bloodsuckers would need extra when the city supposedly provided all their blood was beyond him.

"Javier, I need to ask a favor. I need to get this to the drop point by midnight." Wenshi looked up at him with pleading eyes. The clock on her wall already showed ten.

Javier wanted to refuse, to not endorse the reckless behavior, to not endanger himself in the process. Hadn't he already done his good deed for the day?

"Fine. Just this once, I'll help you out because of your help finding Eva. I'm not going to watch you do this to yourself, though. As your friend, I can't."

The bag now full, Wenshi sealed off the spout and withdrew the needle from her forearm.

"You won't have to. Not after this."

As she handed him the sealed blood bag, Javier grimaced at the way the warm liquid sloshed as he tucked it into his jacket pocket.

Great. I came here to find my sister, and now I'm a mule for an illegal blood trade.

Javier had her write down the address. It was in the industrial part of town, probably extra sketchy this time of night. Fantastic.

"Don't even think about doing more work tonight," he said. "Rest. I'll check on you after I drop this off."

Wenshi gave him a guilty look as she dropped the shirt she'd just picked up. "All right. Thank you, Javier. Sincerely."

JAVIER EYED the darkened warehouse through the windows of the taxi, feeling extra sleazy as the bladder of Wenshi's blood squished against his torso. Besuited clientele entered through an unmarked door at the front. They all looked like mobsters or vampires—or both.

Don't pretend like you didn't know exactly where her blood was going.

With a sigh, Javier had the driver pull around the corner at the end of the block. He tried to tell the man he would be back in five minutes before stepping out into the night and jogging across the road. Wenshi had said the door was on the western side of the building. The single streetlight was quickly swallowed by the murky atmosphere of the small alleyway. Halfway down, a red bulb showed dimly above the drop-off door. Javier scanned the road one last time, looking for an ambush, before plunging into the shadows.

The paint on the steel door curled at the edges, leaving bare metal to be colonized by rust. Javier banged out the passcode pattern precisely, the gongs ricocheting between the building walls. Some seconds later, a small panel on the door slid aside with a sharp screech, and a bin grated its way through the opening. Javier withdrew the pouch from his inner pocket, and after a moment's hesitation, he placed it in the tray. That was what Wenshi had told him to do.

The bin receded mechanically, and the trapdoor snapped its metallic jaw shut. Javier waited for the money to emerge. A pit in his stomach slowly formed as the door remained silent. Finally, Javier banged out his secret code again. An empty drawer emerged again.

"Hey!" he shouted. "Where's my money? Yuan!"

The drawer retracted with no further comment.

Well, that was just great. He couldn't leave empty-handed after Wenshi had risked so much to get her blood here. If the expected payment wasn't so egregious, Javier would already have dipped into his personal savings and skipped this little adventure.

Time to get creative.

He didn't dare to impersonate a fanged menace and sneak in through the front, not in his khakis and tennis shoes. He would have to find a different way in. *Maybe as a delivery guy?*

Javier pushed deeper into the alley and veered toward a collection of dumpsters. He held his jacket sleeve to his nose against the pungent stench as he lifted the lid on one and fished out the least-damp cardboard box. After folding it into passable shape, Javier traced the perimeter of the building until he met the corner to the back. Between two loading docks, light spilled from a propped-open door illuminating two blond women in trench coats on a smoke break. Perfect.

They were grinding out their butts with their platform heels by the time he reached the door.

"Hi—hi there. I'm a little late with this delivery, and the

guy at the side wouldn't open the door. Mind if I sneak in this way tonight?"

Both women looked down on him before exchanging a snide comment in Russian.

"No" was the curt response. They moved to slip through the door as Javier pulled out his wallet.

"Just this once, help a guy out." He held out the few bills he had left.

The taller woman sneered as she snatched the cash out of his hand. Her long ponytail nearly hit him in the face as she spun, but she did give the door an extra shove as she went through—the only invitation he was going to get. Javier sidled in behind them. Now, he really needed to get Wenshi's money, if only to pay the cab fare home.

As Javier's eyes adjusted to the bright interior of the building, the women shrugged out of their coats, revealing rhinestone-studded triangles of fabric covering only the bare essentials of their unnaturally tan skin. A few other women sat before banks of lighted mirrors, touching up makeup and snorting—*Is that cocaine?*

Javier ditched the box as he skulked through the exotic dancers, keeping his hands firmly in his pockets and his gaze averted. The dense cloud of perfume stung his sinuses.

The delivery guy character had been fine outside the building, but he didn't know how he was going to justify his presence inside. He took stock of himself in the mirror—yup, still an average Joe in the wrong place in the middle of the night.

Scanning the counter, Javier found a tub of what he hoped was hair gel and scooped out a slimy smear before running it through his hair, flattening out the waves and giving them an unctuous shine. Better. He popped the collar on his jacket and rolled up his shirt sleeves over the cuffs, but he was still missing something. Javier surveyed the room for the talisman that would get him through unscathed. A black boa, feathers interspersed with silver strands, hung off a mirror. Perfect. He wound it around his neck with the whimsy warranted by the drunk, rich asshole guise he was going for. Fully accessorized, he stepped out the door.

The corridor was clinically lit, the cinder blocks the same beige as the exterior walls and the doors painted a dull gray. Orienting himself, Javier turned right and headed toward the corner, wondering what chances he had of finding where he'd dropped Wenshi's blood.

He threw his shoulders back with false bravado as he passed a uniformed server carrying an ice bucket of champagne. She didn't look up. As he ventured farther down the long hallway that ran parallel to his original alleyway, Javier's ears perked at the metallic screech of the bin from up ahead, the bin that had denied him Wenshi's money.

He turned the corner to find a hulking man in a maroon tracksuit hunched over a rolling cart full of blood packets. The giant's hands moved methodically, injecting each plastic pouch with a syringe of clear liquid before slapping a blue star sticker onto the front. *Designer drugs and a meal in one? Awesome.*

The guy worked without looking up once, each movement unhurried but precise. Javier stared at the uncanny motion, trying to figure out what about the guy's vacant stare bothered him so much.

Whatever—task at hand.

A pleather zip pouch sat on a shelf behind the guy, and when a thudding on the door drew the meathead's attention, Javier dashed the twenty feet to it. His heartbeat pounded in his ears as he grabbed a stack of bills, erring on the generous side.

When Javier looked up, he was confronted with two beady eyes glowering at him from the pink, bald head of the doorman.

"Hey, man," Javier said, backing up a few steps. "There was a misunderstanding earlier, and I..."

The man turned wordlessly and went back to his blood-doping routine, the same robotic motions. Javier opened his mouth quizzically but shut it a second later. *Not the time to ask questions. You got what you came for.*

Shaking his head, he shoved the cash into his pocket and began his retreat. The hallway stretched as Javier retraced its length, catching the soft thud of techno music emanating from beyond several doors. A scantily clad woman emerged from one, where Javier caught the briefest glimpse of a vampire getting a lap dance from another vixen dressed as a naughty nurse. Original.

By the time Javier made it back to his original door, he was more than glad to be leaving this place. But on the other side was a space quite different from the dressing room he'd expected: a grid of bare stained mattresses each held a derelict woman, the air musty and chill. Half of the women looked up at him in horror, while the other half maintained their lethargic trance. One woman wasn't even sitting—a blanket was draped over her sprawled form, her face turned away.

"What is this place?" Javier asked dumbly. "Are you being held against your will?"

Someone halfway down the row scoffed at the question. As she shifted, Javier saw the bite marks that littered her body— neck, arms, and thighs—some looking fresher than others.

"Are you paid to be here and... provide services?" he tried again, hoping the reality was less appalling than at first glance.

"They say they send money back home," the woman replied with a shrug, her bony shoulder jutting unnaturally. She had light-brown hair and an accent Javier couldn't place. "They promised us careers as fashion models. The reality is less glamorous." She rubbed her forearm with tense hands. "You should leave."

Feeling a sick spike of injustice, Javier unwrapped the boa from his neck and tossed it aside—even pretending to be a client of a place like this was too much. "I can help you get out. I know there's an exit through one of these rooms."

The woman shook her head, a bitter anger creeping into her voice. "It's not that easy. The thralls watch for us, and even if we did make it out, none of us has an ear tag giving us rights independent of the house sponsoring our entry. A girl got out once, but the police returned her to the Federovs the next day." The woman's face contorted into a wretched grief, her voice strained and raw. "They made us watch as they mutilated her body, drained her blood. A lesson so that none of us would repeat the mistake. For us, there is only one way out." She jerked her head toward the unresponsive form lying on the mattress.

With growing concern, Javier crept to the other side of her mattress. Milky eyes met his. Her cheek was dark with bruising, her arm riddled with track marks. Nausea gripped his stomach, but before he could be sick, heavy footfalls sounded from beyond the door, growing closer.

"Hide behind the cabinet," the woman bit out in a whisper before burying her face in her knees. Javier hopped across the space and ducked behind the corner of the industrial cabinet.

He pressed himself against the cold metal as the door opened with a bang.

The man marched through the rows of mattresses, scanning the girls wordlessly. His polished shoes clicked with menace that made most girls flinch—hell, Javier too. The girls all condensed themselves, trying to appear invisible. A trickle of sweat beaded on Javier's neck before rolling beneath his collar. His hand cupped the bulge of cash in his pocket. *If they catch me, would they turn me into a thrall or just kill me?* Javier swallowed, unsure which option was worse. Probably neither. These women were living the worst fate of all.

The jailer's shoulders angled toward an especially small woman. Girl? She didn't look old enough to be out of high school, her unpainted face still round and rosy, a single braid dangling over her shoulder. As the man approached, she squirmed away to the back of the mattress. A toothy grin darkened the vampire's face. Javier's throat tightened with the urge to defend her.

"Leave her be," a voice called—not his own. It came from the woman Javier had spoken with earlier.

Ominous steps carried the warden toward the speaker. He tutted his tongue. "Jealous, are we? Lord Federov wanted a fresh one, but I could be persuaded to find a use for you too."

She squared her shoulders, but the tremble in her body was visible even from Javier's vantage point.

When the vampire's hand closed around her arm, the woman spat at him—a last line of defense. With a snarl, the man delivered a heavy blow to the side of her head, knocking her sideways. Her shoulders hitched with silent sobs as she drew inward, her thin tank top hanging askew.

The man retrieved a silk handkerchief from his dress slacks

to wipe the spittle from his brow. "Act like a wretched whore, and that's exactly how you'll be treated."

He hauled her off the mattress roughly, and this time, she didn't resist. A curtain of hair hung around her battered face, and her bare feet slapped against the concrete floor as she was marched to some grim destiny.

Am I really going to let this happen? Javier lifted his foot... and he set it back down. Challenging the vampire was as futile for him as it was for any of the others. This wasn't a room. It was a system—one designed to detain and disempower. If he made it out, he stood a better chance at helping them. At least, that's what he told himself.

Once the door banged shut, Javier crept from his hiding place. He took one last glance at each and every woman, burning their faces into his memory. At least he might be able to help identify missing persons. None of them moved or spoke as he slipped through the door once more, and a cowardly shame burned in his chest at leaving them there.

The sound of those heeled shoes was all the warning Javier got before he was slammed against the cinder block wall. A fist gripped the front of his jacket—the same one that had hauled the woman away. The man's close-trimmed beard and shiny forehead sparked a recognition: this was the same vampire who'd harassed Mina at the Vasa party.

"Who are you, and why are you sneaking around my club?" The eyes of the vampire undulated in an odd pattern, one Javier couldn't look away from. He felt a weird sense of detachment as his limbs went slack, and the world narrowed to answering the man's question.

"I was here to complete a blood drop." Javier tried to tear his eyes away from the purple and reds of the man's irises but failed—like the "thrall" at the drop door, he realized with a sinking sensation. It felt nothing like when Mina had attacked him. This was a vulgar invasion of his mind that he wanted no part of. He fought against it with the entirety of his awareness.

"You... I know you." The man's accent was Russian. "You're the foolish human who interrupted my business with Minka."

"And I thought you were an asshole *before* I discovered your human trafficking operation. Tell me, this habit of harassing women—does it make you feel powerful somehow? Or is it just a way to make up for your tiny—" Javier gasped as a shooting pain in his skull blurred his vision, like someone had driven a spike through his brain.

"Careful, human." Mikhail's meaty hand patted him twice on the cheek. "In this city, your only value is as *food* for those above you." The voice dripped with threat.

Javier's psyche beat against the compulsion, a roiling anger in his chest. He willed his fist to punch this arrogant asshole. Then, suddenly, the mental straitjacket was no longer there. He stumbled forward into a gust of cologne-laden air.

Mikhail was already halfway down the hallway, whistling a tune that sounded like an antique music box. "When you see Minka again, tell her I'm not finished with her yet," he called over his shoulder.

A deep breath inflated Javier's lungs as he shook away the leftover fog in his brain. He touched his upper lip—blood ran freely from his left nostril. His instinct told him to pummel the living hell out of that asshole. But the equation was still the same as before. He couldn't best a vampire one-to-one, especially not one who could control his mind. *Time to get the hell out of here before you lose the chance.*

Javier tried two more doors before he found the original dressing room. Ignoring the offended looks of the tired dancers, Javier shot past the rows of mirrors and back out into the night. The sprint back to the taxi left his legs burning and a damp sheen beneath his clothing. The driver yelled at him in angry Mandarin until a wad of cash convinced the man to drive. Javier's hands shook throughout the entire ride.

Back at the apartment, Wenshi opened the door, and Javier was relieved to see her upright, if awfully pale. At least she wasn't another weight on his conscience. He shoved the rest of the cash at her, glad to be rid of the money earned from the exploitation of others.

"Promise me you won't go back there. It's not safe."

"Javier, are you all right?" Wenshi asked as her eyes grew wide at the crumpled wad of bills. "This is three times as much... Did something happen?"

Javier turned back to his own unit without giving her any more information. He couldn't. Not while it was still an angry jumble in his own head.

He locked the door of his apartment and wedged a chair beneath the knob for good measure. He turned the shower as hot as it would go and scrubbed the top layer of skin off every inch of his body. The interaction with Mikhail felt like a residue he couldn't wash off. Even now, the violation of that prick controlling his mind made him feel impossibly dirty. And even that was only a fraction of how those women must have felt. Javier swallowed the nausea he felt at their entrapment and his inability to do a single thing to help.

What's more, the mention of Mina disquieted him. He had no reason to see her again, yet Mikhail spoke as though it were an inevitability. Worse yet, the connection between Mina and

Mikhail gnawed at him. He wanted to believe she wasn't the kind of vampire who exploited humans, but a scab from a puncture mark reopened and left a red stain on his towel.

Javier sat on his bed in the dark for a long time, thinking about the women still sitting on their dirty mattresses in that warehouse. The cryptic conversation with Mikhail. The systematic cruelty of the whole operation. He wanted a plan to help—something actionable to save even one of them. A plan to warn Mina about Mikhail. But he wasn't naïve, and loath as he was to admit it, Mikhail was right about his place here— Javier was a human blood bag in a city designed for the benefit of the elite species. Just another powerless human in Shanghai.

For how much longer was he willing to remain that way?

17

A week had passed since the briefcase gift, and Mina moved through the halls of Zhang Manor lighter, better fed, and back in favor—but none of it felt secure. Lian was warmer in private but more detached in public. Mina's role at the office had expanded to encompass oversight of the investment in Vasa Laboratories. It was one thing to convince Lian of an investment in the bedroom and another entirely to justify the financial risk to the board of senior leaders at Zhang Enterprises. The due diligence paperwork alone had left her hand cramping for days. Every time Mina left the office, she ran her fingers over her initials on the black leather briefcase, the small recognition still making her heart sing. The aftershock of guilt lessened each night too.

The evening of the kickoff meeting for Dr. Robles's research was the same day Lian would leave for Hong Kong. Since House Zhang had acquired the city, Shenye and Guolong had managed much of the transition, but several high-status handoffs with the local dignitaries required Lady Zhang's personal attendance. After accustoming herself to Lian's constant presence, the prospect of her absence made Mina feel adrift. As much as she resented the woman's totalitarian regime, Mina had fallen back into the habit of relying on Lian to steer nearly every action she took. It was a faulty habit, but then, what difference did it make? Why batter herself against the bars of the cage when she could accept her reality and find happiness where she could?

Sitting at the breakfast table that evening, Mina savored the crimson glass of blood with its dry piquancy. A bowl of congee sat before her, unseasoned and untouched.

"You're not eating, pet," Lian commented over her newspaper.

"I will. I was thinking about the meeting this evening is all." She set down her glass, picked up her porcelain spoon, and dutifully swallowed the bland porridge.

"Yes, I read your report on the research plan. Dr. Robles's goals seemed sound, but there was no timeline given for achieving those milestones. What are your thoughts on this?" Lian glanced up through black-rimmed glasses.

"Because the Singhs wanted their own physicians involved, Dr. Robles decided to wait until the team was assembled to commit to dates. Ascertaining those is one of my primary objectives for tonight, along with vetting their feasibility."

"Very well." Lian returned to her newspaper, and Mina relaxed, having passed the test. "And Yuxi, what will you occupy yourself with while I'm away?"

The blond woman looked up from studying her nails, blinking away the hurt expression.

"The Singhs' Mid-Autumn gathering is tonight, but you've

known about that for months. You were supposed to go with me," Yuxi added with a note of bitterness.

"You know my time is subject to the demands of the family." The newspaper snapped shut. "Perhaps you ought to follow your younger sister's example and find a way to contribute to this household instead of focusing on social frivolities. Zhang Manor has an upcoming maintenance and staffing assessment, which I will have the head maid appraise you of. And while you're at it, practice your instrument. Your artistry has grown stale."

Yuxi's eyes fluttered wildly. "As my lady wishes."

Mina sipped her oolong tea. Hearing Lian reprimand Yuxi used to feel like winning. Tonight, it was an empty victory. Yuxi hadn't done anything different to warrant the censure. Lian was simply using Mina's successes to make Yuxi appear lazy by contrast. Soon enough, the tables would turn back on Mina again.

After breakfast, Mina stopped into Lady Zhang's office as the woman slipped a navy blazer over a cream blouse, her briefcase packed for the flight.

"Apologies, I was hoping to get your signatures on these forms before you leave." Mina proffered two separate documents, and Lian took them with a raised brow.

"You should have had these ready for me yesterday."

"Yes, my lady." She bowed her head, hands clasped neatly, as Lian signed the papers and handed them back. Mina clutched the documents, something keeping her stuck in place. An unspoken thought on the tip of her tongue. A worry.

"I imagine you'll be in Hong Kong more often, now that the city is under Zhang control."

"Not any more than usual. Shenye and Guolong are

capable emissaries. They'll be presiding over the city for the foreseeable future. Why do you ask?" There was a note of curiosity in her voice. Another test, this one more complicated.

"I—I'll miss you."

As soon as the words left her mouth, a wave of regret washed through Mina at the vulnerability of the sentiment. She hadn't known what she meant to say, but it wasn't *that*.

"Don't look so downtrodden, pet," Lian said gently, her fingers coaxing Mina's chin up. "Focus on your work and listen to your sister. I will be back to terrorize you in a few short days."

A jolt of aroused panic tingled in Mina's throat.

"Perhaps I'll let you accompany me on the next trip. Would you like that?"

"Very much," Mina murmured.

"Good." Lian placed a light kiss on Mina's forehead before pulling away. Interpreting this as dismissal, Mina retreated from the office, her insides a slurry of mismatched emotions.

MINA SULKED in front of her wardrobe with an hour to kill before the meeting. The house already felt empty, and she wasn't eager to deal with Yuxi's wounded pride. At least she had somewhere to be tonight.

A devious thought crossed her mind. Lian was taller and a bit thinner, but maybe with the right pair of shoes, Mina might find a suit that would fit. And why shouldn't she look every bit as imposing as Lady Zhang in a room full of doctors? She tiptoed down the hallway and let herself in through the bedroom. The walk-in closet gleamed with every cut and color of suit imaginable, along with an impressive row of gowns. Mina let her fingers wander over the sumptuous fabrics—the charmeuse silks, brushed cashmere, and crisp linen. These weren't garments. They were armor. What if Mina could borrow their power, if just for the evening?

Her hand stopped on one of Lian's classic black suits. She slipped it on with a pale-pink cowl-necked blouse. If Mina held her hair back and angled her chin just right, the image in the mirror looked hauntingly like a young version of the Zhang matriarch. *Would Lian approve?* Yes, Mina decided. The likeness was fine as long as she remained tractable.

Before she left, Mina paused in front of the altar on the main level. Traditionally on this Mid-Autumn Day—Chuseok as she'd known it, growing up—her family arranged a table for their ancestors. Grandmother would set out fruits and sweets, and Mina would twirl around in her hanbok. Tonight, she didn't have a table, but she paused before the altar nevertheless.

After looking to make sure Yuxi wasn't present, Mina bowed to the low table and murmured, "I hope you're resting now, Grandfather." She bit her thumb and streaked the blood across the bloodstone. It was a far cry from his favorite, yakgwa cookies, but it was the sincerest offering she could make as a vampire.

Mina arrived for the meeting at the Sanguis Institute fifteen minutes early and took a seat of prominence at the conference table. She was the reason for the sizable Zhang investment, after all, and she needed to represent it with the stateliness it merited. As the room filled in, she flipped through the spiral-bound report in front of her, already thinking through what commentary or questions Lian would have: where the logical gaps were, where a vague overview should be replaced by more specific conjectures, and where an overly optimistic promise should include a risk analysis.

"Good to see you again, Miss Park," Dr. Robles said as she sat at the head of the table.

"And you. I'm excited to see how you address the challenges you brought up during the investor meeting."

Eva gave her a tight smile. Maybe Mina was laying on the corporate ooze a little too thick. Over twenty different lab-coated professionals were there, the majority at least a decade Eva's senior. Yet the woman at the front of the room looked undaunted and eager.

"Thank you all for joining me here today," Dr. Robles began, her voice ringing loud and clear. "I'm excited to embark on this research initiative with all the great minds in the room. Dr. Her, your work on antidepressants for sanguivores was inspired."

A puffy-haired man near the back nodded appreciatively.

"And Dr. Yang, I've been following your research on the relationship between stasis and aging for some time. I can't wait to hear the results of your latest study."

Eva took a measured pause as her fellow doctors also looked around the room at who was amongst them.

"We are all accomplished researchers in our field, and yet it's going to take all of us working together—combining our individual specialties—to crack the secrets of blood potency. Together, we will produce what may be the most influential work of our careers—perhaps even the most influential work of our time. Figuring out the most efficient and symbiotic way for vampires and humans to coexist will be of paramount importance as the vampire population expands itself to more cities: three already, with rumors of up to ten in the next year... but I don't need to tell you that." Eva smiled, catching herself. "Let's dig into the fun stuff, shall we?" she said, flipping open her booklet.

"I'd like to start by brainstorming the scalability issues of my original experimental setup. My method of observing the recovery of patients required large reserves of blood from single-source donors, extended periods of time for healing, and last but not least, gravely injured vampires. None of these factors lend themselves to large-scale data collection."

The room chuckled.

"So, the first issue we need to solve is how we can measure a vampire's physical response to blood potency with a smaller dose of donor blood, ideally on a shorter timetable. Oh, and I think we'll find more study participants if we find a way to do this without injuring our test subjects."

More chuckles.

Eva moved to a whiteboard. "Let's go back to basics about known vampire abilities, aside from accelerated healing. What other specialized traits do they exhibit?"

She uncapped her marker and held it poised above the surface. The room was silent, save for rustling papers and a muffled cough.

With a sigh, Eva turned to face the room again. "Look, I know we've never worked together. In addition, I know we're generally encouraged to keep our work internal to our respective sponsor houses, especially related to their unique inheritances. I'm not asking you to break your nondisclosures, but we need to set aside suspicion in order to make headway."

Inheritance. Mina filed the word away to ask about later.

"Dr. Her," Eva continued. "You've characterized sanguivore compulsion and how its power correlates strongly with depressive symptoms in both the compeller and the compellee. Tell me more about that."

Dr. Her sat up in his chair as if surprised by the question. "Well, as you say, we were able to observe a difference in the strength of compulsion among our study group, where they convinced humans to partake in activities they normally wouldn't, such as someone with acrophobia climbing a ladder."

Dr. Yang shook his head. "How are we going to measure that quantitatively, though? That experimental setup is virtually unreproducible."

Murmurs of agreement spread throughout the room.

"While I appreciate your input, Dr. Yang," Eva started, "right now, I'm only looking for constructive ideas. Don't worry—we'll go through a winnowing stage once we have everyone's initial thoughts. Maybe you can tell me more about your observation of vital signs—heart rate, body temperature, and respiration—and how you used those to 'age' a vampire. I know all of those are affected by a large meal in addition to other metabolic markers. How might that inform our study?"

Eva scrawled on the board in streaky blue marker as the conversation amongst doctors grew more animated and the ideas started flowing. A few times, she had to break up spirited debates between colleagues, but mostly, she let things play out, filling up the whiteboard with a bevy of unique vampire attributes.

Mina, for one, was astounded by the wealth of knowledge amongst the group. Half of these things she had experienced but never actually discussed with anyone. The other half, she hadn't even been aware of—for instance, that a vampire's sensitivity to silver diminished during its lifetime while the sensitivity to sunlight increased or that a small percentage of vampires could indeed fly or at least hover very convincingly. The research was still under peer review. Part of her wanted to raise her hand to see if anyone had ideas to remedy the pesky aversion to alliums so that she could eat garlic again.

"This is an excellent start." Eva surveyed the packed board of ideas. Mina had barely kept up with her own note-taking. Several items had been struck, with a select few factors circled for extra study. "But what do you think, Miss Park? What did we miss, from the vampire perspective?"

The attention of the room snapped squarely to Mina. She blinked at the crowded whiteboard, the blue ink mushing into unintelligible scribbles. "Um. I—" Mina stammered.

"Any idea helps us right now. How would you differentiate blood potency as a vampire?"

Mina thought back to the coppery taste of the blood she'd had for breakfast. The sweet richness of Javier's blood even earlier. The tart funkiness of the cow's blood.

"I would taste it," Mina said, the words sounding more confident than she expected.

"How so? Can you describe it?" Eva's hands fiddled with the cap of the marker as she looked intently at Mina.

"It tastes... full. It coats my tongue, and it almost tingles."

Some of the expressions around the room looked confused —others were openly dismissive.

"Sorry, that probably sounds stupid," Mina mumbled.

"No. It doesn't. That's not an ability I've heard of before, but I have no doubt it could be possible. I'll have to investigate how we could use it for our research, but the concept is intriguing. I appreciate your contribution," Eva said sincerely, adding a note to the collection on the board.

Mina sank into her chair, a small warmth tickling at her chest as she suppressed a smile. The word "taste" in Eva's loose scrawl sat on the board with the ideas from the rest of the educated researchers—a small way she'd actually helped.

"For our initial trials," Eva continued, "I would like to split into groups for each of the traits to be measured so we can cross-validate results once we arrive at the most effective way to measure the energy response derived from a dose of human blood. I can't tell you how thrilled I am at our collaboration."

As the groups filed out with their leaders, Mina could feel the excitement in the tenor of the side conversations. She had expected Eva to know her science, but she hadn't expected her to be so proficient at steering a team like this. Her leadership style was very different from Lady Zhang's but played to her strengths and still accomplished her goals.

Mina stood, collecting the materials into her new briefcase, letting her fingers linger over the supple leather buckle. She was actually participating in meaningful work—something that might benefit society at large in addition to the accolades from Lian. How the hell had she stumbled into something so satisfying?

Zhang Manor was quiet when Mina returned early in the evening. Yuxi would be getting ready for the Singh party, but Mina had little interest in socializing, even if she was technically invited. When she reached the top of the stairs, she spied the door to Lian's office, and another mischievous thought crossed her mind.

Mina took a step into the room, and the smell of ancient paper and leather greeted her nose. She flicked on the task lighting and moved into the space, feeling the gentle brush of the mercerized wool against her legs. Was this how Lian felt when she came into this room after a day at the office? Content. Dominant.

Mina's fingers trailed over the delicately carved wooden frame of the visitors' chairs, recounting the reprimands she'd endured there. Tonight, her legs carried her farther, to the uncharted territory of the other side of the desk. The tall-backed chair stood like a leather throne. The shelves beyond held a veritable museum of vases dating back to the Yuan dynasty, each with a unique motif and shape. Mina traced them with her eyes, finding her favorites like old friends.

With a shiver of thrill, Mina pulled back Lian's chair and tentatively sat down, laying her briefcase upon the barren desk as though it were hers. A lingering waft of jasmine perfume enfolded her, and a smile played on her lips. The heady feeling of power radiated from this place—wearing Lian's clothes, sitting in Lian's chair. Mina knew it had taken the woman tireless centuries of dedication to gain this level of preeminence. If the reward was feeling this level of satisfaction and control, though, it was almost understandable. Enviable, even.

"What are you...?" Yuxi pushed through the door, a confused expression quickly turning to a twisted cynicism. "Someone is certainly enjoying pretending to be Mommy."

"I was not." Mina jumped up from the seat. "I was just..." Her heart fluttered in her chest. This wasn't something she could actually get in trouble for, right? She hadn't really done anything wrong.

"Relax." Yuxi traipsed into the room, looking at the decor with disdain. "She could update things once in a while though, couldn't she? I've been staring at these ugly vases for a century now." The woman wore a knee-length qipao, under which a pleated pink skirt peeked through the daring side slits. Peonies danced along the side of the bodice, accented with gilt thread.

If Mina had to deal with Yuxi for the week, it probably wouldn't hurt to at least start off on a friendly note.

"You look nice. Heading to the Singhs' soon?"

"Oh." Yuxi looked down at her outfit as though it barely met her criteria for acceptable evening wear. "Soon. Can't be showing up too early."

"Naturally." Speaking to Yuxi without bickering was strange. Borderline sisterly.

"So, Mina," she started, a pinched smile on her face as she withdrew a small square of paper from her pocket and offered it. "A boy stopped by the manor earlier—the same one I saw you with at the party."

Mina's stomach plummeted as she accepted the note. Numb hands unfolded it to reveal an address. *Javier can't be this stupid.*

"What did he want?" she asked, her voice sounding distant.

"He wanted to see you, of course." Yuxi wrinkled her nose. "You know, it's not a bad thing to keep human companions— most of us do at one point or another. Certainly, Lady Zhang entertains her own playthings while she's abroad."

"What?" Mina spluttered, her attention drawn away from the paper. "No, she doesn't. Why would she do that?"

"For fun, you silly mouse. You think you're the only sad

little girl to catch her eye?" Yuxi rolled her eyes, a malevolent gleam shining through.

Mina thought of the way Lian always brushed away her tears like they were a treasured gift. The thought of her doing that with another woman—Mina vehemently shoved the thought down. *You're not special in her world. Why haven't you accepted that by now?*

"Regardless of how open she is with her dalliances," Yuxi continued. "She'd take objection if one of yours is caught sniffing around the manor. A little piece of advice, sister to sister." Yuxi leaned over the desk, lowering her voice to a silken purr. "You might want to make sure he doesn't come poking around again. If you care about his life, at least." Yuxi's eyes flicked down to the address and back up again.

"Anyway, I'm off now. Enjoy the rest of your evening. I told the guards to focus on the front entrance tonight, so if someone were to slip out the back... well, I'd consider it sisterly discretion."

Yuxi flounced off with a smile, her pleated skirt swaying in her wake.

Mina found herself rooted in place, contrition and self-preservation waging a war inside her head. What had Javier been thinking, coming to Zhang Manor? As if attacking him hadn't been enough of a deterrent. If he came back while Lian was home—Mina couldn't face that thought.

Mina tore down the hallway, yanking off the suit jacket as she went. She was going to change into something less mafia-boss, drive to this absurd address on the far side of town, and tell this human to back the hell off.

18

J avier sat in front of a clandestine laptop at his dining table, slurping sesame noodles out of a paper carton. One sprang up faster than expected, flinging oily droplets onto the monitor. Javier scrubbed at the mess with his sleeve, effectively smearing the small drops into swirls of rainbow refraction. Fantastic.

The Mid-Autumn Festival turned out to be a bigger holiday than he'd realized, giving him the day off work. Since Javier had nothing better to do, he convinced Arvind to let him take some work home. His fastidious manager bent the rules just this once so that he could chip away at the hefty backlog left by the last deficient IT employee.

Eva had blown him off at the last minute, saying she was caught up with some new findings in her research, though she encouraged him to still go and enjoy the lanterns. Whatever. Javier had seen a few on his way to the noodle shop. That was good enough. He wasn't really feeling celebratory anyway.

A timid knock on his door drew his attention away from

the screen. Javier pushed his chair back and stood reluctantly, wary of the contraband electronics strewn over his table. He cracked the door just wide enough to show his body and the kitchen.

Wenshi was crouched on the other side.

"Oh, I wasn't sure if you were going to answer." She stood, clutching a red tin in her hand, stylized golden characters embellishing the top. "Zhōngqiū jié kuàilè," she said with a small smile, wishing him a happy Mid-Autumn Festival.

"Same to you," Javier replied neutrally, accepting the offered tin, still regretting the ill-fated warehouse adventure he'd weathered on her behalf.

"They are mooncakes! These are my favorite fillings." Wenshi pushed the bridge of her acrylic frames up. "I wanted to say thank you again for your help the other night... and I'm sorry I put you in that position."

"Don't mention it," Javier said with a tight smile. What he'd seen at the Federov warehouse still ached like an abscess he didn't know how to excise. He'd gone to the police the next day, but once they looked up the registration on the building, they shook their heads at him. Apparently, logging a complaint was the best they could do against a vampire-run establishment. Javier was sure they'd shredded it the second he left the station.

"Anyway, I booked my flight to go home next week. Maybe we can get dinner one more time before I leave," Wenshi offered, cutting through his moodiness.

"Sure. I'm glad you're getting out. I plan to do the same thing soon."

Wenshi departed down the corridor, her curly hair bouncing with each step. For the short time Javier had been in this city, she'd been a part of the experience. Living in this building wouldn't be the same without corralling Maomao back to her apartment or running into her on the metro. Still, it was good she was leaving, and if he was smart, he would do the same soon. Shanghai simply wasn't a long-term option.

Javier shut the door and pried the lid off the festive container. He unwrapped one of the four palm-sized treats from the box. Intricate designs were pressed into their butter-yellow tops. After a quick sniff, he took a bite. The inside surprised him, dense with a sweet paste of nuts and another aromatic ingredient. *Orange peel? Melon?* He made it through about half of the treat before his laden stomach insisted he set the rest aside for later.

Reconsidering the laptop awaiting him on the table, Javier rolled his neck, stiff from staring at the screen all day. His body had clearly forgotten its native hunch and would require some readjustment when he returned to his actual profession. When he pulled out his kitchen chair to resume work, another set of knocks disturbed his quiet.

What can Wenshi possibly want now? Javier went back to the door, opening it with a bit of annoyance.

"What is—"

The woman on the other side of her door was not Wenshi at all. She was several inches taller, with long straight hair. Her eyes glistened with a fiery intensity that both thrilled and frightened him. Javier hadn't expected to ever see her again.

"Mina?"

"Invite me in. We need to talk." Her voice was far more commanding than he remembered, and in her outfit of all black, she'd taken on an edge that seemed incongruous with the timid, emotional wreck he remembered. Then again, her attack clearly proved his impressions of a benign woman weren't entirely accurate. Javier rubbed his wrist, assessing her.

"Why should I? You weren't exactly the most gracious dance partner."

Mina lowered her chin half an inch.

"This isn't funny, Javier. You came to Zhang Manor looking for me. Do you know how dangerous that is?" Mina held a piece of paper up between two fingers, and Javier plucked it from her hand like snatching something from a crocodile's mouth. The written address was his, but not in his handwriting.

"Um, no, I didn't," he said flatly. "Don't get me wrong. I enjoyed hanging out with you at the party until you got hangry." Javier lifted his wrist for her to see the remnants of the violence she'd inflicted. It was satisfying to see her eyes widen a fraction in surprise.

"If it wasn't you, then who...?" Mina sighed. "Will you please invite me in? I won't attack you again. You have my word."

Isn't there an aphorism about vampires keeping their promises? No, that didn't sound right.

"Look, I want to believe that when you bit me, it was an accident. But since that night, I've seen some truly terrifying ways your kind treats humans."

Mina's expression shifted from shame to outrage to something else entirely. "What did you see?"

Javier's throat tightened at the vivid memory of the warehouse. Did he even want to relay the events for someone who might view them as torture porn?

He settled on "I saw enough."

Mina glanced over her shoulder as a neighbor lugged a bag

of groceries past her, and she waited for them to pass before continuing, "There are vampires who take advantage of power disparity in Shanghai—I won't deny it. But I assure you, I am not one of them. Now, please don't make me ask a third time."

Javier considered the person standing on the other side of his door. Did he believe her? He'd promised Eva he wouldn't go looking for her—*knew* he was taking a real risk even being this close. Yet something inside him couldn't stomach the thought of turning her away. He felt a connection between them, and he needed to see if it was real.

"Fine. But give me a second." Javier went back to his takeout and cleaned the food off one of the chopsticks. Never mind the computer—verboten electronics were the least of his worries at present.

"All right, come in," he said, clutching the utensil tightly in his fist.

Mina stepped over the threshold, polished leather boots gleaming in the poorly lit space.

Alone in my apartment with a vampire. This is going to go great.

"Is that supposed to be a wooden stake?" she asked, an incredulous quirk to her brow.

"In case you decide to get bitey. Again."

"You know bamboo is technically a grass, right?"

"Hey, if you want to take your chances, be my guest."

Javier looked down at the slim piece of splintered wood—*grass*—in his hand. Who was he kidding? He tossed it back into his leftover container.

"Well, welcome to my apartment. Forgive me, I wasn't expecting company. I can offer you sesame noodles, moon-cakes, and..." Javier went to his fridge and opened the door.

"White wine." The waft of chill air was a balm on his suddenly flushed skin.

"I'm fine." Mina took a leisurely lap around his apartment, her eyes scouring his sparse belongings. He hadn't bothered decorating, so besides a few books on the coffee table a few dirty dishes in the sink, the room still just contained the dining table and solitary couch it had come with.

Maybe Mina wasn't thirsty, but he sure as hell needed a drink if he was really going to entertain Miss Vampire. Javier pulled the green glass bottle out, rattling the now-empty metal fridge rack, and set about cutting the foil cap. Hoping to goad her into drinking with him, he said, "Don't tell me vampires only drink reds."

"No, smart-ass. We drink white wine." Mina watched him with her warm brown eyes, back straight, expression unreadable.

"Good. Here." He handed Mina a tumbler, which she took with obvious disdain. Their fingers brushed for a brief second, and Javier ignored the residual tingling from the skin contact.

"Sorry, our fine crystal stemware is currently being polished by servants in the annex, so you'll have to make do with this dross." Javier took a sip of his wine, relishing the tang of the lemon notes that gave way to a muted stone fruit flavor: the closest he could find to something that tasted like home.

Mina sneered at him before taking a sip herself. He enjoyed the dramatic shock that crossed her face. "This is actually quite good." She considered her glass again.

Javier inclined his head, holding his commentary on her assumptions about his taste in wine. "So. Someone gave you my address to get you out of the house tonight. Who?"

"My sister, Yuxi. The one I couldn't find at the party." She took a seat on his shapeless brown couch, after moving the polyester pillow to the side. "It's possible she hoped I would attack you again, but after reconsidering an earlier conversation, I'm guessing she wants the house to herself to... entertain. Lady Zhang is away on business, you see."

Javier nodded though he had no idea what she was talking about. He sat back down at the kitchen table, keeping a healthy distance between them.

"I am glad to see you're all right after the party," Mina continued. "Dr. Robles said you were—I trust she passed on my apology."

Javier's jaw dropped. "Um, no, she didn't." How dare Eva keep this secret from him—there would be serious words with his duplicitous sister later. "Do you see her as a patient?"

Mina smiled into her glass. "I'm actually working with her now. House Zhang financed some of her research, and I guess I'm somewhat of a custodian of that investment." She said this with a level of self-importance that made Javier want to roll his eyes. *You sit around a table and listen to other people make decisions about money you didn't earn. Good for you.*

"I wanted to come see you after that night... but Eva said it wasn't a good idea. And my position in my house doesn't always afford me the liberty to do the things I want."

Javier did roll his eyes at that pretentious statement. "It's fine. Eva patched me up good as new. Probably better you didn't come."

Mina clutched her glass with both hands, her shoulders dropping at his brusqueness. If this wasn't genuine remorse, she was doing a damn good job faking it.

Maybe you should ease up on her. You didn't invite the

woman in just to give her a hard time. Javier decided to steer the conversation into more neutral territory.

"So, tell me. How did you end up here, a vampire of Shanghai?" He grabbed the wine bottle and topped off both their glasses.

Mina eyed him skeptically before taking a large gulp. "I suppose the short answer is that I have terrible taste in women."

Javier refrained from verbalizing the first follow-up question that came to mind: *How's your taste in men? Existent?* "I have time for the longer answer," he said instead, settling back into his creaky wooden seat, hoping at some point she would drop her prim facade and give him an honest toehold into her personality.

"All right then." Mina readjusted on the couch, trying to tame its lumpiness with her small fists. "My family moved from Korea to the states when I was two—my parents, my grandparents, and me all living in a two-bedroom apartment. My mom hated it and divorced my dad by the time I entered kindergarten."

"You really are giving me the long answer, aren't you?"

"Do you want to hear this or not?" Mina shot back, her eyes gleaming with warning.

"No, I do," Javier said more softly. He wouldn't have guessed she was a first-generation American.

"I was basically raised by my grandparents until I was sixteen, when Grandpa died. My grandma is kind of traditional and insisted that Grandpa be buried in the homeland. Dad packed up the house at her behest and said we were moving back. I refused."

"So, you've always been obstinate?" *Why are you needling her when she's actually opening up?*

"Yes, I've always been obstinate." Mina glared at him. "But mostly, I thought it was smart to stick around to apply for US citizenship." She sighed, taking another long gulp of wine. "They actually left me, in the end. They prepaid rent on a studio apartment and gave me an envelope of cash for emergencies. I was just a teenager. In between finishing high school, working full time, and navigating a ridiculous bureaucracy... I met Lian." Mina looked distantly out the window as she said, "I begged her to turn me into a vampire."

Javier choked on his wine. "You *asked* to be a vampire?"

Mina's expression hardened, her warm eyes a little darker. "Yes, I did. There was a time when I thought this would be the place that finally felt like home. I never fit in, growing up—I was always too Korean for the kids at school and always too American for my family in Korea. I thought I'd have a chance to make Shanghai a place of my own. And Lian... Lian was everything to me." Mina killed her glass of wine. "That was before I knew better. I tried to leave this place a few months ago... but you see how that worked out." She hoisted her empty glass in a sardonic cheers.

"Damn. That's kind of heavy," Javier said, trying to strike the right balance of nonjudgmental empathy. He could relate to feeling exceptionally American anytime he visited his relatives in Mexico, but he'd always felt at home in California around his family and with the land itself. Mina's experience was bound to be different, torn between two countries from the start. As far as her failed relationship with a woman who'd groomed her as a teenager... Yeah, he wasn't touching that one with a garlic-coated crucifix.

Mina recovered. "Enough about me—it's your turn. How did you end up a *human* of Shanghai?" This time Mina helped herself to more wine in the kitchen and refreshed him as well. Javier wished he had more than a single bottle on hand, at the rate she was going.

"Well. My past isn't nearly as exciting as yours. I came here to look for my sister. My application request finally got accepted this summer, right after I got laid off. But now that I found her, I need to get back home and find a new job—one in my actual field of work—and help Mamá figure out what to do with the vineyard."

Mina looked down at the translucent yellow liquid in her tumbler with a frown. "Your family owns a vineyard?"

"Yes. Not the one that made this. Same region, though," Javier said smugly. "Anyway, I'll probably stick around a few more weeks. Enjoy this palace of an apartment a little while longer." He gestured to the barren space with its empty walls. "And then it's back to California."

Mina's eyelashes batted a few times, her frown deepening. Was that a hint of sadness?

"It's nice you got to reconnect with your sister. Watching her work over the last week has really been something. She's so smart, and the way her team respects her is incredible." Mina's face took on a more relaxed expression talking about the work. It made her almost look like a human being.

"She always talked about being a veterinarian growing up, and I guess in a way she ended up pursuing that dream." Javier chuckled.

Mina did not look amused. "We are not animals."

"You *bite* like a poorly behaved animal," Javier said. When he saw the way his words smothered the spark in Mina's eyes, regret doused any triumph he'd felt at calling out her transgression. She hunched into the couch like she wanted to disappear altogether.

"Hey, that was harsh. Let me—"

"No. You're right," she said, her voice flatly somber. "I am a poorly behaved animal. Speaking of which, I should probably get back before someone realizes I'm gone." She stood stiffly. "Thank you for the wine. I won't be bothering you again." Her black boots clacked on the hardwood as purposeful strides took her toward the door.

"Mina, wait." Javier grabbed her arm as she passed.

Their eyes locked, and for a split second, he felt like he could see her soul, raw and vulnerable behind the layers of shielding she kept up. It was the same sense he'd felt when she bit him. He wanted to help her with an ache deep in his chest, certain that she needed him in some way.

As Javier raised his hand, holding it poised by her cheek, an obnoxious eight-bit trill sounded. Mina pulled away from him as he looked at the warning message displayed on his computer: "PC has encountered a fatal error with network connectivity. Reattempt connection?"

The door opening echoed through his living room.

"Hang on a sec, please," Javier said, jogging over to Mina. She already had one foot in the hallway. "I'm wondering if you can at least answer a question for me since you're here and all. Why doesn't this city allow mobile electronics?"

Mina considered him, her defenses firmly back in place. "Lian thinks they promote laziness and moral decay. She can be a bit Confucian."

"But it's also true that you interact poorly with them, right? Come back in for just one minute, please." Javier picked up the laptop and walked to the far end of the room with it.

Mina's chest heaved with an irritated sigh before she stepped back into the room. "I guess so. There aren't many electronics to break around here, but when I was in Singapore, I fried a few payment kiosks before I learned to avoid them."

Javier reset the network card on the PC then pulled up a diagnostic terminal.

"I see." He took a step closer to Mina then another, watching the health metrics of the computer as they degraded in real time. Halfway across the room, he got the same warning message about the network connectivity. Bizarre.

"Hey, Mina. You said your jailer is out of town for the week, yeah?"

Mina's gaze darkened. "Lady Zhang is away, yes."

"Good. Can you come back tomorrow? I'll have more wine."

"And why would I do that?"

"I want to try something. Get to the bottom of this electronics flakiness. Plus, I enjoyed talking to you. There's actually a person underneath all of that vampire posturing, believe it or not, and I kind of want a chance to make it up to her for being a dillweed tonight."

One second, Mina was standing by the doorway, and the next, her face was inches from his. The vampire speed unnerved him, but Javier held still as she took some unspoken measure of his intentions. Small puffs of breath from her nostrils curled around his cheeks as the hair on the back of his neck stood up. Javier stood silently—no fear, no guile, just an honest guy wanting one more night with the woman before him.

"Fine."

As soon as the words hit his eardrums, Mina vanished, leaving his door ajar. Javier padded over and glanced down the empty hallway before closing the door with a sad sigh. He had no idea what Mina's visit meant, but his engineer brain had already kicked into gear around solving the technical problem. The sticky emotional stuff could wait.

He shook off the wine haze as he sat down in front of the laptop once more. He focused on the data path of a wireless signal: the antenna modulating at time-multiplexed frequencies, digital data across copper traces, then to the CPU, where it became human-readable. Somewhere in that chain, Mina broke the system. He had a day to figure out how to debug it.

A smile tickled at his lips. God, he hoped she came back.

19

Mina sneaked in through the back gate of Zhang Manor, hugging the shadows. She belatedly wondered if Yuxi's earlier kindness was a ploy to get her into deeper trouble. This way, Mina's involvement with Javier wasn't just an accident caused by hunger—it was an intentional wrong committed behind Lian's back. But once Mina slipped through the back door without issue, her suspicions eased.

A hearty laugh—a *male* laugh—drew her attention from the sitting room. Mina didn't dare disturb her sister, but morbid curiosity compelled her to tiptoe past the entrance to the room. Actually, *two* devastatingly handsome men were entwined with Yuxi on the couch. One rubbed her shoulders and kissed her neck while the other sipped from a stemmed glass of deep burgundy, moving his hands toward—*Oh. All right, then.* Yuxi had been telling the truth about her own trysts, after all.

Mina took the stairs up to her room as quietly as she could.

From Lian's cold promises earlier this evening, to the scientific inquiry into blood potency, to seeing Javier again, this night wasn't one she would soon forget. And he wanted to see her the next day even after hearing the full truth about her inscrutable reasons for becoming a vampire.

A quiet knock on her door came as she stepped into her slippers.

"Yes?" she responded warily, ready to flop on her bed for the day.

Instead, a servant entered the room with an envelope on a lacquer tray. The front was inscribed with the word "Älskling" in August's slanted scrawl. Mina impatiently broke the fussy wax seal on the back and unfolded the small note.

"He won't eat. Please help. —AV"

She rolled her eyes at the epistolary dramatics before grabbing the jacket she'd just removed.

"Arrange a car to the Vasa residence."

WHEN THE ELEVATOR doors opened on the penthouse level, August was waiting for her in a dressing gown, wringing his hands as he paced.

"Thank you for coming, my dear. I thought surely he would turn about after a day or two, but the boy has gone mad with hunger." The man's skin hung sallow and loose, angry claw marks peeking out beneath the cuff of his sleeve as he fumbled with a cigarette. "He's in his room. I would join you, but I think my presence will only antagonize him further."

"What did you do to him?" Mina snarled.

Dmitri should have been feeding several times a day in his vampire infancy, and the fact that Vasa had waited this long to seek help only made her angrier.

"I know you've never held me in high regard," August said around the cigarette in his mouth, "but I assure you I am far more generous with my fledglings than that mother of yours. The boy is being petty, is all."

"Careful, Vasa," Mina threatened with the barest flash of fang. Something about him always brought out her temper in droves.

"By all means, älskling, intimidate me with your considerable menace. *After* you've talked to Dmitri."

Mina shot him one last glare before stalking down the darkened hallways of the Vasa abode. Several of the paintings had been removed from their mounts and were leaning against the walls. *Strange time to redecorate.*

When she reached Dmitri's door, Mina gave the briefest knock before pushing through. If he was in a rage, then he might be nonverbal at this point. She needed to reach the humanity inside him before he mauled her like he had August.

"I told you to stay out of my room!" Dmitri bellowed, and Mina ducked as a brass candelabrum crashed above her head. The entire room was ripped to shreds—the furniture toppled, the curtains torn from their rod, and feathers from disemboweled bedding dusting the floor.

"Dima, it's me! It's Mina!"

A lump of a figure emerged from the shadows against the far wall, its torso bare. Bloodshot eyes showed in the underlighting of an upturned lamp. Mina widened her stance in case Dmitri charged her. She knew she wasn't a strong vampire, but she could sure as hell take down a baby fledgling. Honestly, why hadn't August just force-fed him by now? Lian would not have tolerated anything close to this level of outburst. Maybe Vasa was being *too* soft.

"Mina?" Dmitri said, his fangs retreating into his gums as he took a few shaky steps toward her.

"Yes, it's me." She gave a supportive smile, encouraged that he recognized her.

Dmitri ran to her and caught her in a crushing embrace, his lithe body wracked with sobs.

"Hey, everything is going to be all right." Mina stroked his hair, trying not to shiver from the coldness of his unclothed skin. "Did he hurt you?" She saw no visible injuries, but that didn't mean they weren't there.

"No, it's so much worse than that," Dmitri whimpered. "Oh, Mina. You were right about everything."

"Dima, you're scaring me. What happened?" Mina grabbed his shoulders to look him in the eyes. The skin was puffy from days of crying.

"He says we're moving to Argentina, and he won't even *listen* to me when I try to tell him that my life is here, my friends are here, and Shanghai Ballet is the company I was going to join." The boy collapsed into a waterlogged mess on her shoulder again as Mina blinked in confusion. Dmitri was upset because they were moving? Oh, what youthful melancholy. Mina rubbed his back in gentle circles, relieved the situation wasn't nearly as dire as it first presented.

"Why don't we sit down and talk about this?"

Dmitri looked sheepishly around his room. "Sorry, I might have gotten carried away." He righted the upturned chairs, poking at one that had developed a dangerous wobble. In the end, he squatted on the floor while gesturing for her to take the single mechanically stable seat.

"You know that it gets difficult to regulate your emotions when you don't eat, along with a great many other things," Mina said, feeling infinitely wise in her seniority. "You're a dancer, though—you know the importance of fueling yourself. Blood isn't an optional part of your diet now."

Dmitri's brows furrowed. "I *know* that," he admitted. "I just couldn't stand the thought of drinking blood from *him*. As though everything is fine."

"This won't be the last time he makes a decision about your life that you disagree with. It's part of the deal. When I warned you about this, you said you could handle it."

Dmitri hugged his knees to his chest. "I just didn't think it would be about something this big. I never had a problem with his direction in the studio. He's always had my best interest in mind. But now... he's so *callous*."

"Did he tell you why you're moving to Argentina?" she asked, trying to hide the sadness in her voice. Having a friend the last few years had been a lifesaver. August even seemed to ballast Lian's moods at times. If the pair left, they would leave a void in Mina's Shanghai.

"I guess House Vasa is taking over Buenos Aires, but I'm not supposed to tell anyone that."

Mina swallowed. Hong Kong for the Zhangs, Buenos Aires for the Vasas—what other places would fall to vampire control next? Would the Singhs claim New Delhi? Or the Kòrúmas vie for Lagos? Mina would need to scour the office for gossip along those lines later. Right now, she needed to focus on helping her friend.

"Dima, you know you have a lot of life to live now, right?

You're going to make your home in many different places over the course of your lifetime. Do you even like Shanghai? I imagine Spanish would be easier to learn than Mandarin for you."

"But you're here." His voice was halfway between a plea and despair.

Mina's chest tightened. "I promise I'll come visit you. Besides, you have a lot to focus on in the next few years: growing into a strong vampire, building your relationship with August and with your family... I'll be around. Don't worry."

Dmitri looked so desolate that Mina could hardly stand it. With a frown, she forced her fingers into claws before raking them at her wrist, opening several slim gashes which instantly welled red. The rush of pain was unexpectedly grounding.

"How clumsy of me. You better get it before it stains your carpet..." A swollen rivulet trailed along the bottom of her arm. Dmitri moved so fast she almost missed it, sitting on the carpet one minute to latching onto her the next. Mina winced as he buried his fangs into her flesh. He could have been a little gentler. *Was this how Javier felt when I attacked him?*

"You taste different than August," he complained between swallows.

"Well, I should hope so."

Mina let him drink his fill, which was less than she would have thought. She hoped it would tide him over until he came to his senses over feeding from August.

Dmitri propped himself against the edge of his bed, his eyes drooping in post-meal torpor. Mina would bet anything he would be asleep in five minutes.

"Rest now." She gripped her wrist tightly to quell the

bleeding. It would take an hour or so to mend itself. "I'm going to go talk to August about a few things."

"Do you have to? We could snuggle..." Dmitri said hopefully.

"Tempting—maybe later."

Mina stood and stepped over his outstretched legs and the detritus of his tantrum on her way out. She could empathize with Dmitri's situation—accepting that someone else had the power to puppeteer your life wasn't easy. But in this case, his hysterical reaction was way out of proportion. Honestly, if he knew half of the things Lian had imposed on her in the early days of her vampire transition, he might not act so spoiled.

August awaited her in the hallway, legs crossed at the ankle as he leaned against the wall.

"I take it you were successful?"

Mina held up her bleeding wrist sarcastically. "If this is what you mean by successful, then yes."

"You have my gratitude," August acknowledged, pushing away from the wall. "Though I would suggest you be more discerning about whom you offer your vein to in the future. Accompany me to my study? I promise to be a gentleman," he said with a sly wink.

"What the hell did you expect me to do?" Mina grumbled under her breath, reluctantly following him to his office anyway.

Tall bookshelves lined the end of the room, bowing under the weight of their academic and literary tomes. Two wingback chairs sat before a barren fireplace. A phonograph quietly played Satie, one of the *Gnossiennes*. *If there were ever music to sulk by.*

August took a seat on a buttercup-yellow sofa and withdrew a filigree cigarette case from his pocket, delicate fingers opening the clamshell and extending it toward her. Did she dare partake in the opium-laced tobacco? As someone who had experienced the Opium Wars firsthand, Lian would kill her. But Lian wasn't here, and with all of Mina's other offenses of the evening, adding one more surely wouldn't make a difference.

When she reached for one, August caught her wrist in his hand and tilted it as he studied the injury. Vasa ran his thumb over the ragged skin, instantly knitting it back together without so much as a scar. Mina narrowed her eyes as she snatched one of the black cigarettes from the case despite his unsolicited advances. She lifted the emerald lighter off the coffee table and watched as the flame took hold of the end, bringing the tightly packed tobacco to a smolder. Mina sat back with a satisfactory inhale, the background tension dampening almost instantly: the stress of the compounding secrets, the ever-present threat of Lian's mercurial wrath and affection, along with the shifting geopolitical landscape. She sank into the chair with the weight of it all.

"You seem pensive," August observed neutrally, crossing one leg over the other at the knee. "Anything you want to get off your mind?"

"I... Not with you."

"Always so salty."

"August?"

"Yes?"

"Do you think Lian—Lady Zhang—wants vampires to take over the world?" It wasn't the most eloquent question, but she let it stand, curious if he would answer.

August snorted a laugh, ashing his cigarette before propping it on a concave rest. "I think *Lady Zhang* wants to take over the world but will settle for a vampire sovereignty."

"Why? Is it just her obsession with control?" Mina took a deep drag on her cigarette, realizing it was loosening her tongue in perhaps dangerous ways. But what was August Vasa going to do about it, anyway? She was here as a favor, and Mina trusted his ridiculous gentlemanly code of conduct to keep her confidence.

August quirked an eyebrow. "If you want to know my opinion, I think she's troubled by humanity's unwitting tendency for self-destruction and how their unchecked technological advances have made that destruction even easier, extending to the very planet they feed from. Her family is the largest of any of ours, and Lady Zhang views it as her responsibility to provide for them when our food supply is on the verge of collapse. This is her way of intercepting that fate."

"And she honestly thinks she can control them? The humans?"

"She thinks it's worth a try. You know how persuasive she can be, how cunning she is at getting her way. And despite her flaws, I do believe she is the best chance humankind has at making it to the dawn of the next century."

Mina pondered this. She'd never known Lian to fail at anything she attempted, yet Mina knew how Lian's drive for domination could harden her—as if Lian's entire worldview could be reduced to "things under her control" and "things *not yet* under her control."

"I worry about her, August." The unprompted confession left a quiver in her voice. "Her anger is *terrifying*, and yet her scraps of affection are so addictive. I feel like I'm being torn apart by an amused predator, and the worst part is never knowing if she... loves me or despises me."

"Oh, Mina," August said with a genuine sympathy that would've infuriated her on any other occasion. "My sister doesn't despise you. On the contrary, I think you are quite dear to her. This makes her act irrationally sometimes, scared of what it means to indulge her affection for you—the risk and vulnerability that emotion requires. If anything, she despises *that* she loves you."

Mina remained silent, her thoughts muddied past where she trusted herself to speak intelligently on this topic. She'd already overshared, in any case.

August went to a bar cart against the wall and grabbed a bottle of aquavit along with two exceedingly small glasses. He filled both and handed one to Mina. After an obligatory "Skål," he drained his glass without pretense. Mina took a sip of her own, the herbaceous spirits slithering down her throat with a deft burn.

"Your mother comes from a different time, filled with deeper injustices than you or I will ever know. It forged her into something... Well, *calculated* is a mild way to put it. She doesn't believe she can have something if she doesn't possess it in its entirety." August poured himself a second glass of aquavit. "Never forget your own strength, even when she aims to disillusion you from it. And... if ever she truly oversteps, please come to me. Lian isn't immune to reason from the right person."

Mina furrowed her brows, trying to make sense of August's cryptic speech. "No, I... I..." *What was I going to say again?*

"Hey, August?"

"Hej, älskling," he said with his amused smirk.

"Can I stay here a few nights? To make sure Dmitri eats."

Mina didn't like the idea of walking in on Yuxi with her conquests again, and staying with the Vasas would make it that much easier to sneak back to Javier's the following day. Not to mention, Dmitri could genuinely use her support, despite his overblown reaction.

"I would like that very much."

Mina's mind swam with the combination of stiff spirits and opium. When she blinked, August had vanished. The lights were dimmed, and a soft blanket was draped over her. Mina settled into the curve of the seat and shut her eyes once more. For right now, she was safe, and that was enough.

20

The next evening, Mina rifled through the Vasas' kitchen before the others were awake. Undercabinet lighting gave just enough illumination to read the names on the bottles she pulled out of the floor-to-ceiling wine cooler. She set the one with the fanciest French label on the marble counter before going to the fridge to find a suitable snack to bring. It only felt polite, not showing up empty-handed two nights in a row.

Something about being around the human felt like being fully alive and awake in a way she hadn't felt in a long time in this city. Like things were possible. What things, she didn't know. Going back for a second night might clarify exactly what his allure was. Maybe she could scratch the itch, figure out what this human's game was, then, satisfied with that knowledge, go back to her normal Shanghai existence. That was the hope, anyway.

The cavernous refrigerator was packed with an astounding quantity of cheese. Mina sniffed her way through half of the cellophane-wrapped bricks before picking a semisoft Manchego. Wine and cheese were customary offerings, she posited. Mina couldn't remember the last time she'd attended a BYOB event.

"Pray tell, älskling, what in the world are you doing up so early?" August asked blearily, cinching the belt of his paisley robe. He swiped a Moka pot off the counter and scuffled his way to the sink of the expansive kitchen island, before unscrewing the top and filling the base with water.

"I have a previous engagement to attend to. I'll be back in a few hours," Mina replied.

August's eyebrows shot up when he caught sight of the bottle underneath her arm.

"Good God, girl. Are you trying to rob me? Do you know how expensive that is?"

"Put it on my tab." Mina waved him off. As if he didn't have an entire cellar full of dusty bottles besides what was in the kitchen.

Vasa caught her by the arm as she tried to pass. "Tell me where this appointment is that requires you to bring your own libations. Is it something your mother would approve of?"

Her nostrils twitched as she wrenched her arm out of August's grasp. "What does it matter? Are you going to tell on me?" She meant her words to be cutting, but even she could hear the hint of fear in her voice at the unspoken threat of Lian.

"No, my dear." August pinched the bridge of his nose. "I simply wish to know. Seeing as you won't tell me, I insist on you being back by midnight."

Mina blinked in disbelief. "You're giving me a curfew? Who exactly do you think you are?"

August looked unperturbed. "My house, my rules. Timeboxing your outing minimizes the trouble you're liable to get into while under my care. Otherwise, you're welcome to return to Zhang Manor."

Under his *care*? Mina glared her disagreement.

A waft of espresso floated through the kitchen as August assembled his coffee gadget with oily, deeply roasted beans.

With a frustrated sigh, Mina muttered, "Fine," before tromping out of the kitchen. What the fuck did August care what kind of "trouble" she got into? It wasn't like there would be any consequences for him if it ever got back to Lian that Mina had spent multiple nights cavorting with a human. *I, on the other hand...* That wasn't a scenario she wanted to follow to its logical conclusion.

"At least decant that wine before you drink it!" August called after her.

HER STOMACH WAS full of butterflies by the time the taxi arrived in front of Javier's apartment. She hadn't felt like this the night before. Why were nerves kicking in now? Visiting him wasn't any more dangerous than it had been the night before—probably less, in fact, since she was outside the purview of Zhang guards.

Standing in front of Javier's dingy apartment door, the sticker numbers peeling from their surfaces, Mina hesitated. What was she really doing here? She was fulfilling his request, sure, but the part of her that *wanted* to be here was what scared her more than anything else. What if two nights weren't enough? What if she wanted more?

Those were questions she would figure out some other time, when she wasn't standing dumbly in a squalid hallway.

Mina knocked solidly three times. She could hear Javier spring from a seat, hustle to the door, then take several deep breaths before the knob finally twisted. At least she wasn't the only one who needed some self-assurance.

"I wasn't sure you'd come," Javier said, genuine relief relaxing his face.

After a few seconds standing in the door, Mina questioned, "Are you going to invite me in?"

"Is that really a vampire rule?"

"Yes," Mina said, getting impatient with the pretense. In theory, the restriction applied to all human dwellings and would make her violently ill if contravened. In this case, she didn't honestly know if it would kick in, since Javier was only a temporary inhabitant of a city-owned building. *Better not to test it, though.*

"Uh, sure. Please come in, then. I'm excited to get started."

Mina stepped across the threshold, taking in the veritable nerd nest that his apartment had become. Multicolored wires wriggled over furniture and across flooring to blinking gizmos set up sporadically throughout the living room. It looked like the lair of an unhinged anarchist who was tight on rent.

"I didn't even know Shanghai had this much electronic equipment. You're not trying to ensnare me in some force field, are you?" Mina set the bottle of wine on the Formica counter of the kitchenette.

Javier chuckled a thin laugh, scratching behind an ear. "No, no force fields. That's an FM radio, that's a Wi-Fi router, that's a Bluetooth receiver, and yeah... Basically, one of every-thing with an antenna."

"So, what exactly is your plan here?"

"Well..." Javier went to his laptop and spun it around so that she could see. Mina looked from a safe distance though the monitor burned her retinas. "I've paired—and otherwise wirelessly connected—everything to this laptop. It took some doing to find raw signal strength values for all of them, but with some less-than-expert hacking, I got there."

"What do you mean by 'signal strength value'?" Mina said, her nose instinctively sniffing at the faintly acrid scent in the air. Was that normal?

"It's a power measurement at the receiving radio, which indicates the attenuation of the wireless signal... but technical details aside, it's a way to measure how much you affect the system. I want to run a few different scenarios to see if it's more your proximity to the electronics or your interference with the signal propagation itself."

Mina knew he was trying to dumb it down, but in the end, Javier and Eva were both way smarter than she would ever be.

"Do I need to do anything specific for these tests?"

"Nope! I'll tell you where to stand and then take some measurements."

"Great. Sounds like something I can do with a glass of wine." Mina was starting to regret her decision to become a lab rat for these mad-scientist experiments.

"Right, of course." Javier shook his head and went to the kitchen and dug through the drawers for a corkscrew. "Do you want to drink what you brought—Oh my God. Mina. This is a 1982 Château Montclair Bordeaux. We can't just *drink* this!" Javier grabbed the bottle, his fingers caressing the dry parchment label as though it were a precious museum piece.

"Why not?" Mina grabbed the corkscrew off the counter. "Wine is made to drink, yes?" She took the bottle from him and started carving the foil off the top, enjoying the small pained gasp Javier let out as she twisted the metal curlicue into the cork. "Do you have a decanter?"

"Mina, I don't even have wineglasses. You think I'm hiding a decanter somewhere?"

She shrugged, glugging the ruby liquid into two water-spotted glasses on the counter.

"To your health," Mina said, more snidely than she meant and took a sip. It hit her palate like a freight train, and she set it back down on the counter with a grimace. "Sorry, I thought it would be better..."

Javier looked at her with an aggrieved expression to rival one of August's. "A wine like this—you can't just guzzle it. You have to give it time to *breathe* first." He swirled the glass in his hand a few times, holding it up to the fluorescent light before inhaling deeply over the rim of the glass. Javier took an appreciative sip, clicking his tongue a few times. "Yes, that will open up beautifully."

Mina quirked a brow at his antics. Was all this ceremony necessary?

"Sorry," Javier said sheepishly, picking up on her expression. "You brought out my inner wine snob." He set the glass down, pinning her with an odd smile. "Thank you for bringing it, though. That's a truly exceptional vintage. An unexpected and wildly generous gift."

Mina swallowed, his candor making her think better of the gesture. She hadn't done anything particularly thoughtful besides raiding Vasa's stores.

"Don't mention it. Maybe we can do this testing thing then sit for a minute to enjoy it, yes?"

"Right, yes. Good idea." Javier hopped back to his laptop and clicked a rapid sequence of keys that brought up a blinking terminal. It looked more nefarious than Mina hoped it actually was.

"So, I would like you to start by standing on the far tape mark by the door."

Mina traced Javier's finger to a blue X of masking tape.

"Here?" she asked, stepping onto the designated spot.

"Perfect, yes."

The next hour passed with little banter between them, Javier asking her to stand on various dots of tape around the room while arranging gadgets around her. He periodically checked his laptop and jotted down numbers in a small notebook, his careful concentration surprising her. Mina's gregarious admirer had a serious side, after all, and it left her with plenty of time to observe him.

She liked that he wasn't too tall—only an inch or two taller than her in block heels. Lian always looked down at her, but with Javier, it felt like they were on an even level. He was open with his expressions, and Mina didn't have to second-guess what his intentions might be. After so many years of playing political games with scheming vampires, that was remarkably refreshing. His amber-brown eyes were soft, just as soft as his hair looked. Mina guessed he was overdue for a haircut, the way he kept smoothing it back. His mannerisms, his appearance—it was all so frustratingly endearing.

"You seem excited," Mina finally interjected when Javier had been flipping through the pages of collected data in his notebook for several minutes straight, grinning like a madman.

"Sorry, yeah. I think I can conclusively say you have an impact on electronic equipment."

"I could have told you that," Mina said, keeping her taunt playful.

"But it's *how* you impact them. It's specifically your distance to the radios themselves and not just being in the signal waves."

"And what exactly does that mean?"

"Well." Javier looked up, the smile on his face joyously uninhibited. "I have a theory. You can't tell anyone until I confirm some things at the library, but..."

"Oh, just spit it out already."

"I think it's the silver that's used in traces around these radio chips."

Mina blinked at him.

"You know," he continued, "like how the old silver-backed mirrors don't show your reflections or how daguerreotype photography was blurry for vampires. It's the silver in those technologies that's the root of your influence. This is the latest iteration of that technological incompatibility."

Mina tried to process that conclusion, something about Javier's self-satisfied smile infecting her with its joviality.

"That's very astute of you, Professor Robles. Do you think this is something people know about?"

"Maybe. Probably. I mean, it wasn't hard to test, obviously. Just takes the right annoyingly inquisitive engineer paired with a patient vampire." He grinned at her. "I know this was a little silly. I just had to know why the heck they took my toothbrush at immigration. Hazard of the profession."

"You mean you're not a janitor back home?"

Javier threw a crumpled-up ball of paper at her.

"No, Madame Vampire, I am not. At least, not unless my mom tells me to clean the tasting room." He jumped up and grabbed the two glasses of wine from the kitchen and handed one to Mina.

"I think this deserves a proper toast."

"A toast to science?"

"Hmm." Javier's eyes rolled to the side as he pondered, chewing his lower lip pensively. Mina wondered what it would feel like to press her own against his. It had been so long since she'd kissed anyone other than Lian. *How different would it be?*

"Why don't we toast to Shanghai?"

Mina scowled at the suggestion. "Why? It's just a city."

"It's the city I met you in. Even its bizarre rules about electronics gave me a chance to spend one more evening with you, so yes. Let's toast to Shanghai." He held up his glass expectantly, and Mina's breath caught for a moment as the depth of his words hit her. Javier was falling for her just as much as she was falling for him. Was she really going to let this happen?

They clinked glasses, Mina's eyes not leaving his. Maybe she could indulge a little bit. They deserved this, right?

"To Shanghai, then."

She took a small sip, and the oaken cherry notes of the wine left a tingling sensation on Mina's tongue, awakening an appetite for another taste entirely.

Mina snaked a hand up to Javier's face, her thumb stroking his jawline with a hint of rough hair starting to emerge. Yes, she decided, kissing him would definitely feel different from kissing Lian.

Her eyes softened as she tilted her head to the side, starting to close the distance between them. Javier licked his lips nervously.

Buzzz, an obnoxious doorbell sounded through the apartment.

Javier glanced over at the door peevishly. "It can wait." His hand met her waist, but the jarring noise had already put her on the defensive.

Buzzzzz.

"Dammit," Javier said as he went to the door and threw it open. "What? Oh, Wenshi. Hi. Yeah, I can do it tomorrow. That's fine."

Mina could hear the faint responses of another woman on the other side of the door, and a knot formed in her stomach. Perhaps Javier already had a special someone—a someone who wouldn't appreciate sharing. And she had Lian, a certainly less charitable partner.

What the hell am I doing here? she thought with an astounding clarity, as if she'd been doused with a glass of cold water. She had no future here. No fun was worth the potential consequences of being discovered.

Mina set her glass of wine on the table. "I should go now. It's getting late."

"Are you sure? Will I see you again?" Javier shut the door with a crestfallen expression that broke Mina's heart.

How had she let this get so far?

"No, I don't think so," she said softly.

The ensuing grief at the realization that this was over constricted her chest. In an impulsive rush, she threw her arms around him, wanting to be close to him just once. She threaded her fingers through his chestnut-brown hair, his skin like fire against hers. A faint smell of soap met her nose along with an earthy smell, and beyond that... Mina nuzzled against his neck, preternaturally drawn to a certain spot that smelled divine. Her tongue came out to lick the skin, salty and smooth. Javier moaned beneath her touch. Her fingers twined in his hair, and she tugged, exposing even more of his delicate skin.

Her jaw hinged open, fangs fully descended, and Mina paused with the points poised over his throbbing artery. How easy it would be to slip them into the soft tissue, bringing his sweet blood to the surface for a small taste—

What the fuck *am I doing?*

She tore herself away from him and pressed herself flat against the opposite wall of the apartment, her chest heaving with the temptation to return to her meal. Mina drooped her head, letting her hair hide her reddened eyes as she willed her monstrous facade to retreat. This was what Eva had warned her about. She wasn't hungry, but she craved him regardless. *Needed* him.

I'm not doing this to him again.

Mina pushed speed into her legs as she raced out of the apartment and down the hallway to the elevator. She stood there mashing the button, waiting for the carriage to ascend to her floor.

"Mina, wait!"

She ignored him, waiting for the doors to open. She stepped in without looking back, pressing the button that would close the doors and letting out a choked sigh when they did so before he reached her.

Mina buried her hands in her face as the elevator plummeted to the ground floor. That had been too close. What foolishness it had been to think she could permit herself something so tender. *You are a monster. How long will it take before you accept that?*

She couldn't be trusted—couldn't trust herself—and she needed to stop pretending otherwise.

~

MINA MADE it back to the Vasa penthouse well before curfew, and she slinked down the hallway, hoping to make it to her room so she could contemplate the full extent of her fuckups and lament that she hadn't even gotten her kiss, for the danger she'd put Javier in.

"Älskling?" The voice called from August's study, grating on her frazzled nerves like Yuxi's bad erhu music.

She returned to the precipice of his study, her crabbiness demanding that she make it known. "Is there a reason you always find the worst moments to insert yourself?"

August nodded amiably from his couch, closing the cover of a report and laying it on the table. "It's a trait I've always had a knack for. But you, my dear, have had an excess of 'worst moments' as of late, wouldn't you agree?" The man took a debonair sip of brown liquid from a snifter glass. "Now, care to tell me the reason for your dour mood on this particular occasion?"

Damn this man to hell.

"The evening didn't go as I'd planned," Mina admitted, horrified that the urge to cry was gurgling up. *Don't you dare.*

"Ahhh, your appointment," August said, holding up his hands dramatically. "If I didn't know any better, from your stroppy expression, I'd say this *appointment* might have had a romantic element to it."

Mina glared at him, knowing how little she was doing to

hide her indiscretions. He could tell Lian, or he could punish her himself. She didn't care anymore.

"So what if it did? It was irresponsible and selfish. But maybe if you beat me, it will help the message sink in." She almost wanted him to, wanted to face some external repercussions so that she could stop pummeling herself emotionally.

"Spare me the glib sarcasm, darling. Honestly." August stood and adjusted his rolled shirt cuffs. "And I thought Dmitri was melodramatic."

Mina's mood only darkened at the comparison to Dmitri's histrionics. She could have killed someone tonight—this was *different*.

"May I be dismissed now, Lord Vasa?" she ground out, an excessively formal clip to her tone.

"No one is holding you against your will. I was only going to suggest that you might like to review Dr. Robles's latest report. It arrived by courier earlier this evening." He gestured toward a thick folder lying on the coffee table.

Mina's curiosity betrayed her, and she snatched it disdainfully. "I will peruse it at my convenience."

"Suit yourself." August shrugged. "By the way, Dmitri and I are watching *Dracula* in the solarium later, and you are most welcome to join. The boy has come around since you talked to him yesterday."

That was good to hear about Dmitri, but—

"*Dracula*? Isn't that a bit much, even for you?"

"It's one of my favorites," August said with a smirk. "Bela Lugosi is a *dream*, if I do say so myself."

Mina rolled her eyes before trudging to her borrowed bedroom. Beyond all reason, the man was actually starting to ingratiate himself to her. Just *maybe* he wasn't quite the monster she'd painted in her mind.

~

AFTER A HOT SHOWER, she felt more balanced about the evening. With her hair twisted up in a towel, she hopped on top of the buoyant mattress in the guest room. Everything in Vasa's apartment felt grandiose in a trying-too-hard kind of way, but at the moment, Mina was enjoying the extra plush bathrobe too much to bother being offended by the decadence. A glass of wine awaited her on the nightstand with a simple note from Dmitri: "Please come watch with us."

The Vasas were making it exceptionally hard to stay grumpy.

Mina took a healthy gulp of the liquid, catching herself thinking about the smell of it for once. It was smoother than the wine they'd had earlier, but also far less complex. She let herself sink into the pillows, wondering what it would be like to visit Javier's family vineyard in California. A smile came to her face as she imagined the crisp air, the rustle of leaves, and a gentle smile on Javier's face, cheeks kissed with sun.

That was a dream for a different Mina, she decided, shutting the image out of her mind, one that hadn't been condemned to an eternity in the possession of Lian Zhang. Daring to hope for something more was the thing that kept getting her into such messes, and the time had come to face reality.

With a sigh, she flipped open Eva's report, letting her eyes skim the language. The dense technical jargon was beyond her current aptitude, but she forced herself through it anyway. It seemed like a number of tests were proving challenging in unpredicted ways. Of the five factors they'd picked for study, only two showed measurable responses to the consumption of blood of different potencies, but even those might not produce statistically significant results for the quantities they wanted to test. By now, Mina knew that the denser Eva's scientific prose became, the less promising the results.

She cast the report to the side, taking another sip of wine and shutting her eyes for a moment as she held it in her mouth. Maybe she could stay here for a little while longer.

Mina swallowed, the epiphany dawning on her with a jolt. "Measurable vampire influence" was exactly what she'd spent hours testing with Javier earlier that night. If she'd only had some blood with her, she could have seen whether consuming it altered her effects on his equipment.

With a sinking realization, Mina knew she was going to have to bother Javier one more time to test the theory. *Not* because of any attraction—purely for science. Lian would still be away for three more nights—she had enough time. Somehow, she would have to figure out how to control her urges around him to prevent an accident. Mina had made it through two nights of successfully not biting Javier, despite the close call. Reminded of the blatant dangers, she could double down on her self-discipline and somehow manage not to attack him. That would have to be enough. This idea was too big to throw away just because a fledgling vampire couldn't keep her shit together. It could be the breakthrough Eva's research needed.

Full of an exuberant energy, she flipped the towel off her head. After running a brush through her hair, she shuffled her slippered feet through the quiet house and out to the lunarium. The horizon was starting to lighten, a tinge of orange warming the skyline. This really was the penthouse's best feature—she would sorely miss her evenings with Dmitri out here once the Vasas left.

An antique film projector cast images of a tuxedo-clad man onto a white wall, and Dmitri and August were snuggled underneath a blanket on the couch. Mina was glad to see them reconciled for the moment. They were going to have a lot to work through in the next few months, but sometimes, a moment of peace was a pleasant reminder of what was to be gained.

"Mina!" Dmitri cried. "See? I told you she would come." Dmitri bopped August on the shoulder before scooching over to make room for her on the couch. "I made him save some of the popcorn for you. We even put butter on it because you're here."

Dmitri offered her a bowl of fluffy kernels as she nestled into the cushion and tucked her feet underneath herself. It was all so ridiculously domestic that Mina didn't know if she wanted to laugh or cry from the sheer normalcy of it all. She settled for a quiet sniffle as she dug in the popcorn bowl for the perfect morsel.

"You know, I don't think I've actually seen this version. Just the remake."

August gasped dramatically. "You can't be serious."

"Yup, I'm serious," Mina said with a laugh.

"This is completely unacceptable. We're starting it over from the beginning! Älskling, prepare yourself for a cinematic feast."

Mina and Dmitri both gave each other a knowing look before bursting into giggles as August got up to futz with the whirring mechanics of the celluloid film reel on the large contraption behind the couch.

Javier did have one thing right—the city was spectacular in the meetings and moments it allowed between people, the genuine connections. Mina couldn't even fathom what her life would have been like had she not come here, despite the unpleasantries that came with it. She would take this moment for what it was, a respite from the quagmire of self-loathing and doubt she normally lived in. For right now, she could just be.

21

Javier jabbed his fork at the tender caramelized pork-belly chunks on his plate, twisting his utensil to separate the layers of shatteringly crisp crackling, blubbery fat and juicy meat. Eva had clearly spent hours on the meal, but he just wasn't hungry. After Mina left the other night, he had started piecing together all the things Eva had been keeping from him. His sister had been in regular contact with Mina and hadn't bothered to mention it, which irritated him in the same way Eva's unexplained disappearance did. She kept secrets from him as though he were a little boy that couldn't handle the truth, which was really beginning to grate.

"Is it too salty for you?" she asked.

"The meat is fine."

Eva took a sip of her beer with a reserved sigh. The weather had finally turned from the oppressively humid summer heat to a more temperate coastal fall. With the windows open in her apartment, a gust of wind tugged at the wisps of wavy hair framing her face. Javier stared at her, still baffled by how different this woman was from the sister he remembered. Not only her face and body had matured—she had an entire life that didn't include him or anyone else from her upbringing.

"So, how's your research going? I remember you saying you had a new team to work with," he said, shoving his annoyance down.

Eva's eyes lit up as though grateful for the excuse to forgo the banal dinner conversation and talk about the things that interested her.

"Yeah, and the team is great. They're really starting to collaborate, you know? It's just been slow—slower than I would have liked. I thought once we were fully funded and once we had the right people, it was inevitable that we'd start finding answers. I *know* there's a way to measure blood potency, but for all the interesting ideas we've come up with, nothing has clicked yet." She gave him a wistful smile. "The science will get there. The test subjects, on the other hand... Just be glad you'll never have to work this closely with vampires. They are truly an arrogant, entitled bunch, let me tell you."

Javier snorted. "Yeah, I could see that." He pegged Eva with his gaze, a malicious thought occurring to him. Did he dare say what was really on his mind? Oh hell, what did he have to lose?

"Actually, though, when Mina and I were running a little experiment of our own, she was surprisingly cooperative." He took a sip of his beer, a mix of guilt and satisfaction burning in his chest at the way his sister's expression morphed into furious indignation. *See? It doesn't feel good when people keep secrets from you, does it?*

"Javier," Eva said sternly, her voice taking on the tenor of their mother's. "You promised you wouldn't go looking for her. What the *hell* were you thinking?"

"I didn't. She found me. Showed up on my doorstep, in fact."

Eva's nostrils flared. "Your fascination with her, I can almost forgive. She's alluring and sexy in ways only vampires can be. But *Mina*? At least *she* should understand the dangers. Where did she bite you this time?"

Javier narrowed his eyes at his sister. "She didn't *bite me*. They aren't feral animals." At that, he felt like some amends had been made for his gaffe calling Mina a misbehaved animal. Javier also felt no need to tell his sister about the near slip-up preceded by their almost kiss. He still felt robbed on that account.

"You have absolutely no idea what you're playing with here."

"Oh really? Enlighten me then, Doctor. What is so wrong with me seeing Mina?"

"You really have no idea." Eva shook her head with a sad smile. "Besides the incredible stupidity of messing with a fledgling of Lian Zhang..." She stood from the table and went to stare pensively out the open window. "Our blood is different, Javier. *Our* blood. Robles blood. I wasn't sure if it was just me, but after she attacked you... The proof is there."

"What are you talking about, Eva? What do you mean, our blood is different? How?" Javier felt his palms sweating with uncertainty. Why was it that since moving to Shanghai, he was always the person with the least amount of information in the room?

Eva scrubbed at her face with her hands, her cheeks blotchy and red.

"You know I study blood potency, yes?"

"Yup." *It's all you ever talk about.*

"During my residency, a vampire came to the clinic in critical condition, his brain stem ravaged by a terminal disease. I thought he would die, and so I did the stupidest thing I could have and opened my wrist for him. His recovery was miraculous, the illness receding to a manageable condition. Since then, I have been tracking donor blood, trying to find anyone else in this city that even comes close to my—*our*—potency. None have."

"So we have potent blood. What difference does that make?"

"I prayed it was a fluke, Mina feeding from you at that party. When she came to me in my office, I had to test it. In an exam room, I pricked my finger, just enough scent of blood in the air to bring back the memory of you. Her fangs were out instantly. To think she's been around you again and resisted her urge to feed... Well, it's miraculously lucky, is what it is."

Javier pushed aside the insultingly unethical way his sister had manipulated Mina during a vulnerable moment. He could come back to that later. Right now, he needed more information, a niggling sensation in the back of his brain telling him there was more to this story than his sister was even letting on now.

"Why, Effie? *Why* is our blood so special?"

Eva covered her mouth with her hand, fingers clawing at the skin. Her face appeared haunted. "I don't know how to say this." Her voice was a mere whisper.

Javier stood from the table, going to her side and putting a hand on her shoulder. The anxiety of waiting for her revelation had him on edge. "Effie, you can tell me. I'm your brother. There's nothing you need to hide from me."

Eva's eyes flitted back and forth across the city skyline, a persistent tremor afflicting her chin. "Do you remember that night you saw me in the barn? The night before I left the vineyard."

Javier would never forget that night, Eva's fervent prayers over an altar while the full moon shone overhead. The candles, the rosary, and the dried branches, along with all manner of paraphernalia he couldn't discern.

"Yes, but—"

Eva hushed him. "Before Dad died—before I killed him," Eva said, her voice breaking over the confession, "he was teaching me... magic. The rites of our ancestors. I know it sounds crazy. I didn't believe it either, at first." Eva looked at him, her eyes glistening with an earnestness that stole all words from his mouth. "I just wanted to make it rain. We needed it so badly. But instead, I brought lightning. The wrath of the gods toward a daughter attempting brujería beyond her skill. He died within minutes. His last words..." Eva's face contorted as water spilled down her reddened cheeks. "He told me he forgave me, that it wasn't my fault, and said not to tell Mamá."

"Eva," Javier started, tears threatening to spill from his own eyes. Hearing her speak of their father's death churned up a silty layer of emotions he thought he had laid to rest a long while ago. Eva *couldn't* be responsible for their father's death— *especially* not via some alleged magic spell.

"No, Javier. You don't need to say anything. I have done my best to accept the past, and I hope you understand why I couldn't stay there any longer. Mom never knew about any of the brujería—the ocultismo. I mean, she knew he was sharing his heritage, but her Catholicism wouldn't let her acknowledge it as anything more than folk traditions. The reality is we are descendants of a long tradition of magicians. Dad would have shared this with you, too, once you were old enough to understand. But I took that from both of you."

Eva took a deep, shaky breath, miraculously finding composure in the wreckage of the family history she'd laid bare, while Javier was having an impossible time maintaining his. Not only had Eva upended everything he'd known about her and their father, but the revelation raised a multitude of other questions about his own identity in a way that short-circuited his brain.

"I'm sorry, Eva. I'm having a tough time understanding all this. Maybe I better go. Sleep on it."

Eva nodded sadly. "I want to give you something before you leave." She went into her bedroom, her long skirt floating around her ankles as she retreated, leaving Javier standing numbly in her kitchen. He wiped the excessive moisture from his eyes with the back of his rolled-up shirt sleeve.

When Eva came back, she was holding a leather notebook between both hands. The cover swelled with the pages, textured from use and stuffed with miscellaneous materials. Javier instantly felt an ineffable tugging connection to the volume.

"It was Dad's. I couldn't bring myself to throw it away, but I also haven't opened it since I left. If it brings you any solace in his memory, please take it."

Javier reached for the book with shaky hands, a renewed fountain of tears dashing all hope of leaving with any shred of machismo intact. As he touched the faded leather, a manic heat pulsed in his fingers at what secrets it might contain. He hugged his sister fiercely, his voice failing him entirely in the face of the significance of what Eva had offered him. The family history he didn't know he had.

"Thank you, Effie," he choked out.

"Javier?" she called after him as he walked to the door.

He paused, not turning around.

"If you do see Mina again, please be careful. Your blood will call to her in ways neither of you will be able to control."

Javier clenched his jaw. He understood the warning came from a place of concern, but with all due respect, he wasn't sure his sister knew anything about him or Mina or anything else right now.

THE RIDE HOME did nothing to ease the whirring thrum of disorienting emotions that had taken up residence in Javier's mind. The leather notebook sat on his lap, still emanating an uncomfortable warmth that made him question whether the stress was causing a psychosomatic reaction or whether, despite all logic, Eva's outlandish claims about their father's legacy were true.

Javier waited to open the book until he was in his apartment. He set it on his kitchen table, pacing the length of the space twice before finally sitting before it, his leg bouncing underneath the table in agitation. He reached for the cover—

No, wait. This calls for some ceremony. Something. A drink?

He jumped back up and went to the kitchen. The bottle of wine Mina had brought still sat on the counter, only a half measure gone from the top. Already it had sat recorked for two days—a damnable shame. He had just been hoping she might come back to finish it with him. Javier sighed. Who was he kidding with that fantasy? No sense in letting the rest of the bottle go to waste.

After pouring himself a hefty glass of the Bordeaux, he returned to the table, bringing the rest of the bottle with him. Javier took a bracing gulp, letting the bite of the tannins and the burn at the back of his throat ground him in the moment. In his apartment in Shanghai, about to connect with a portion of his dad he hadn't known existed.

He slipped the worn elastic band over the rounded corners of the book, flipping the cover open with an unwarranted hesitance. His hand went to his mouth as he saw his dad's name written in a looping scrawl. With his fingers, he traced the indentation the ballpoint had left, knowing his father had inscribed it sitting before this notebook. The specter of Pedro's presence lingered, regardless of any alleged mysticism.

Javier turned each of the yellowing pages reverently, ingesting the cursive text with a solemn silence. The book was filled with a stream-of-consciousness ease to the writing. Task lists were combined with notes on weather and the condition of the grapes. Sketches of wild herbs with lush descriptions of their smells accompanied passages that detailed rituals and incantations.

Javier didn't know what to make of the compendium. While scribbled notes in the margins gave a loose impression of what Pedro had been working on and the questions he had along the way, nothing in the book's pages addressed the *why* that Javier so desperately wanted to know.

Javier leaned back in his chair, surprised to find the glass of wine already empty. He refilled it as he thought, taking comfort in the gentle glugging sound as the wine passed through the slender neck. Pedro had always been a patient teacher, preferring to guide and let them experience their mistakes as opposed to correcting them in advance. It was difficult to reconcile that image of his father—almost mythical in the memories of his childhood—with a flesh and blood human who sat in front of this book and chose to make these notes. For himself? For Eva? Javier would never know.

His finger tapped the edge of the table as his brain churned on a way to make sense of the new information. Obviously, Eva's own recollection of the man was tainted by the trauma of his passing and the warping effects of time. She had been the only one there when their father's accident occurred. A freak accident—an unseasonable lightning strike in the Sierra Nevadas. It was tragic, but perhaps reasonable, for Eva to have assumed the blame herself. Perhaps her own mind had conjured the elaborate story as a way to ease some of that guilt. If magical elements were at play, perhaps that made her grief bearable by way of an explanation. It was hard to accept the randomness of loss. That, Javier knew as well as anyone.

But that didn't explain the straight-up sequences of magical rituals in this text. Perhaps their father had been passing something down to Eva, a cultural respect for traditions and stewardship for the land on which they lived. Javier could appreciate that, and he certainly would've loved sharing the spiritual beliefs of their heritage. That was a priceless gift his father had given Eva that he'd been too young for at the time.

But to think that an actual magical ability was connected with performing the rituals and saying these specific words was too much. He wouldn't begrudge Eva her accounts of the past, but no way could any of this be real. There was nothing wrong with praying for the rain, but believing you could actually make it rain was a step too far.

Javier shut the book with a sigh. Enough for one night. Not to mention, he was down to the sediment-laden dregs of the wine bottle and starting to feel it. He should have eaten more of Eva's pork when he had the chance. It would've been delicious were it not for the bitter emotions of bygone relationships he couldn't get away from lately.

As he stood from the table, a knock sounded at his door.

If that was Eva wanting to talk more, he really wasn't in the mood for any further reminiscing.

He went to the door, preparing his gentle but firm message that they could talk another time. But the person on the other side wasn't Eva.

It was Mina.

Again.

Javier stared at her in confusion. Her long, glossy hair contrasted starkly with her white buttoned blouse. The expression on her face was intent, keen with some unknown motivation.

"You said you weren't coming back," Javier said flatly.

"There's something else we need to test. Please tell me you still have all your equipment. Can I come in?"

Javier swallowed the lump in his throat. Did he have the wherewithal for this right now? Not in the slightest. He opened his mouth to say so.

"Sure, why not?" Javier retreated from the door, resignation settling in his shoulders. "It'll take a few minutes to set everything up again." After sweeping his dad's notebook into his bag, he went to the box in the corner, which contained all the equipment he'd been planning on returning to the bank tomorrow. Javier fished out a minimal setup with the electronics he'd determined in the last session to be the most sensitive to her presence. Maybe this would help take his mind off more existential questions. Plus, something about this woman negated his ability to say no.

"Care to tell me what it is we're testing?" he ventured.

"Not yet. Not unless it makes a difference."

"Of course. Why bother to tell the human assistant unless it concerns him?" Javier's lips pressed into a tight frown as he recalled the measurement script on the laptop and placed the wireless radio on a stool on the other side of the room.

"Is everything all right?" Mina asked hesitantly. "You seem... different tonight."

Javier ran a hand through his hair. "Does it ever occur to you that maybe other people have their own lives and own shit to deal with? And that maybe stopping by unannounced isn't always the most convenient?"

Javier glared at her, expecting to see some reaction—anger, regret, anything. Instead, she blinked at him, looking more withdrawn than ever. Right. How could the plights of the commoners possibly register with royalty?

Calm the hell down already. She's not the one who unearthed the trauma of your past.

"Look, I'm sorry. It's just—I can't even describe to you the level of exhausting this day has been."

Mina gave a slight nod of acknowledgment and nothing more.

"Anyway, I'm set up for the test again, if you want to stand by the radio."

Mina went to stand by where the blue tape mark had been. "Are the readings the same as the other night?"

"More or less."

"Could you check?"

Javier gave her a tight smile before fishing his own notebook out of his messenger bag.

"Yes, it looks like you reduce the signal strength by about half at that range."

"All right. I want to increase the distance until my impact is barely noticeable. Can you tell me when that is?"

"I guess."

Javier looked at the clock. Mina had about thirty minutes of his patience left, he decided.

Mina took slow steps away from the transmitter, her black boots clunking on the floor as she did.

"All right, that's the spot. You maybe have a three-to-five decibel impact at this range, which isn't much."

Mina nodded her approval, a nervous frown on her face.

"Okay, then. I want you to tell me if you notice a change." She withdrew a glass vial from her pocket, pulled the cork, and downed the contents before Javier could react. Mina's shoulders relaxed as a slight smile came to her face, eyes closed, like consuming the blood had been a thoroughly enjoyable activity.

Javier's head twitched with a certain ick factor. "Was that what I think it was?"

"Yes," she said plainly, a challenge in her gaze. "Now what does your computer show?"

"The same readings it had a second ago. Can you tell me what all of this is about now?"

Mina's shoulders slumped as she replaced the cork in the vial, looking more dejected than he knew what to do with. That's when he noticed something odd. The numbers were actually changing.

"Hang on a sec. It looks like you're up to ten dB attenuation now. That's kind of bizarre."

A grin spread across Mina's face. "Are you sure? Can I see?"

"I mean, yeah, the numbers are right there. It'd be kind of hard for you to see as the test subject, though."

"Javier, do you know what this means?" Her eyes sparkled with intensity.

"No, because you haven't told me."

"We may have cracked the code on Eva's research. She's been looking for a way to measure exactly this—how a sip of blood could register in the external world." Mina clasped her hands in front of her. "Damn, I wish I'd brought another sample. I mean, Eva can test this on her own, of course. I just wanted to make sure it's real before I tell her, you know? I'm new to this whole scientific hypothesis thing." She looked beside herself with self-satisfaction.

A chill prickled all the way down Javier's spine.

Blood potency.

Javier looked down at his wrist, at the slithering blue lines beneath the skin. Maybe they could kill two birds with one stone: Mina could test her electronics theory while Javier could figure out if Eva's claims about Robles blood had any merit.

"Give me that vial." He held out a hand toward Mina.

"What for?"

"I'll tell you if it makes a difference," he replied snidely.

She handed it to him reluctantly. "You're being really cagey tonight."

Javier ignored her as he rinsed the vial out in the sink, trying not to think about the person the pink-tinged liquid had come from as it washed down the stainless-steel basin. He grabbed a paring knife off his drying rack. It was dull as shit but the sharpest thing he owned at the moment. With a short inhale, he pressed the point to his skin over the largest winding blue vein of his wrist and bore down, dragging the blade an inch or so until the welling liquid dripped down his fingers. He watched it for a second, mesmerized by the way the droplets hit the wet sink below. The deep crimson turned to a translucent red Rorschach test, the pain secondary to the vortex of unknowns needling his psyche.

"What the *fuck* are you doing?"

When Javier looked over at Mina, ready to dismiss her concern, he saw what she had become. Her hands gripped the back of a chair with enough strength to warp the back, long claws piercing into the brown vinyl. She drew in ragged breaths, and although her hair hid her face, Javier was sure he would spy two white elongated canines protruding from her mouth.

"Can you keep it together or not? I need to test this." Javier grabbed the vial, holding it under the stream of dripping blood. They had to use the same quantity for this to be even remotely scientific.

Mina nodded between labored breaths, keeping her eyes trained away from him. For an unknown reason, Javier felt confident that he could trust her response.

It took a minute to fill up the glass tube, and by the time Javier wrapped a kitchen towel around his wrist and offered it to Mina, her hands were shaking with barely restrained blood-lust. Mina snatched the vial, still refusing to make eye contact.

"I'm sorry this is hard for you. Just give me one more minute, all right?"

"Hurry."

A flash of doubt clouded Javier's mind. What if Mina did

lose control? Would the creature inside her finish the job it had started? Javier swallowed as he went back to the laptop, admitting this might not have been his smartest move.

"Okay, you can drink it now."

He watched Mina raise the vial slowly to her lips before knocking the liquid back. A gasp escaped her as she did so, her head rolling back with an expression of extremes. Extreme agony, exquisite pleasure? Javier couldn't tell which. He didn't have time to analyze. He needed to watch the numbers. Over several seconds, they shifted from a moderately good signal to a weak signal to complete connection loss. He relaunched the application to be sure nothing was wrong with the laptop. No, it hadn't been lying. His blood had been potent enough to boost the effects of her signal suppression so much that the radio wasn't even detectable anymore.

"Mina, you won't believe it—Mina?"

She was hunched over the chair, panting in painful gasps. Javier took a tentative step toward her, gripping the towel around his wrist tightly.

"Don't come any closer. Please. This is hard enough as it is. Your blood... This is... I can't even describe to you how good it is. It's everything I can do to not pin you down and drink the rest," she said through gritted teeth.

Javier stilled as Mina slowly recovered herself. Several minutes ticked by on the clock before she was able to look up, her blood-red eyes surreal and gothically eerie.

Well, Javier guessed that answered that question. Eva was right about there being some link in the effect of their blood on vampires. The cause of that link, Javier could investigate another time.

"Are you all right now?"

"As all right as I can be. Do you have a death wish I need to know about?"

"No," Javier said, irritated. "Do you?"

"Of course not." Mina's claws had finally receded, and her eyes were dimming to their natural brown.

"Then why do you keep coming here? It sure as hell seems like it's something you're decidedly not supposed to be doing. And yet here you are."

"I just wanted to run the one test. That was it. Then you decided to go rogue and slit your wrists in front of a vampire. What the hell was that?"

"Right, it's about the science. In that case…" Javier flipped through his own notebook, finding the pages of readings from their last session and tearing them along the binding, their ragged edges uneven to the point of cutting off numbers. "You better take these. I'll warn you, though: Eva doesn't like the idea of us hanging out, so maybe tell her you got them from a different Javier."

Mina glared at him like he'd done something wrong, ignoring the ruled pages he shook at her. Javier glared right back.

The wine had uncorked his thoughts, freeing them of the inhibitions of polite conversation, and he was done being the nice farm boy that got walked all over. Something fundamental in his universe had shifted tonight in a way that would never fit neatly into the mental box he had for his worldview, shifting the ground rules for engagement right along with it.

"Mina? Why did you come here tonight? You could have gone straight to Eva with that idea. I'm sure she has droves of scientists frothing at the mouth for the chance to run this kind of experiment. Instead, you came here. Why?"

Mina looked at him, her eyes clouded with uncertainty.

"I... You... I—" She stumbled over the syllables before shutting her mouth for several seconds and regrouping. "I've enjoyed our time together," she finally ground out.

"Great, thanks. You really know how to flatter a guy." Javier shook his head, dropping the loose pages to float back down to the tabletop. "So, what's next for us, then? When will I see you again?"

The glisten in her eyes spoke of a barely suppressed anger. He couldn't care less.

"I don't know," she finally admitted, sotto voce. "Lian is back tomorrow. She travels often, though. I might be able to come back as soon as next month, even."

Javier's heart plummeted down through his stomach, and he turned away from her so that she couldn't see the furious hurt on his face.

"That's not how it works, Mina. You don't get to pop in and out of people's lives as it's convenient for you, and you don't get to assume I'm okay being your side piece."

He could hear her shifting stance, but she didn't move to approach him.

"Maybe if she..." Mina started. "If I had the freedom..." A frustrated sigh. "You don't understand the absolute obedience she demands. Every bright spot in my life feels like a stolen, illicit moment. I'm sorry this is not what you prefer, but it's what I have to offer."

So she was going to be stubborn about this. He could play that game too.

"Don't pretend like you're totally under her control. You came here tonight, didn't you? Make the active decision to defy her or don't, but don't pretend like that's not a choice you have."

Mina slammed the feet of the chair down on the floor, and Javier winced for the sake of his downstairs neighbors.

"I am a vampire, and I am subject to the demands of my vampire creator. I don't get to opt out now." Mina hung her head as she loosened her grip on the chair. "I'm trapped in this for an eternity. There's nothing I can do about that."

"Bullshit. The person I danced with at that party wasn't a mindless thrall of Lian. She was a vibrant and fierce woman who challenged me and made me laugh. Admit you want this as much as I do."

"Of course I do! What do you think I've been saying this entire time?" Mina opened her mouth and shut it again, her brows drawing together as her eyes darted around the apartment. "I don't know what you want from me."

Why was this so hard for her to get? He wasn't asking for the moon and the stars. He just wanted to know when he could see her again.

"I want to take you to dinner. I want you to show me the sights. I want a chance to get to know you." Javier gave an exasperated sigh, running a hand through his hair. "I want you to give me a reason to stay in Shanghai."

Mina inhaled sharply, holding his gaze for a single moment where he felt like she, too, was envisioning what that future might look like—a future together. And then, just like that, her eyes shut tightly as her fists clenched at her sides, extinguishing his hope that she might choose him over the obstacles she faced.

"I can't give you that." Her voice was barely above a whisper.

His chin starting to tremble, Javier turned away so she wouldn't see the gathering moisture in his eyes. "Then I guess you're not the person I thought you were," he said, his voice cracking like a ten-year-old boy. "I think you'd better leave."

Javier listened intently as the second hand of the clock ticked into the silence. For a moment, Mina just stood there—a moment long enough that he thought she would come around and tell him they could work through this. Eventually, though, he heard the sound of Mina's boots carrying her to the door, the mild squeak of the hinge, then the decisive *thud* of it shutting on his hopes of having something more with her.

Javier spun around, staring at the empty spot where she had stood only seconds before. He wanted to run after her, wanted to beg her to reconsider. With a dire certainty, he felt that something special was walking away from him that he would never find again. Letting her go felt like letting a small part of himself die. Yet if Mina wasn't willing to fight for her own happiness, let alone his, then they would never have a future, no matter how much he wanted it.

Javier snapped the screen of the laptop down hard before grabbing the empty wine bottle and tossing it in the trash.

22

Mina brushed tears from her face as she clomped toward the elevator. She needed to be out of this apartment building immediately, away from that man whose words tasted as sinfully sweet as his blood. Mina knew they would never—*could* never—have the kind of moments Javier wanted in Shanghai. It was honestly funny to think of herself on a date with a boy, taking bad tourist pictures at the scenic Yuyuan Garden or going on a hunt for the best sheng jian bao in the city. Mina forced a laugh out of her throat, but it came out strained and hollow in the emptiness of the hallways.

She waited impatiently as the elevator light slowly ticked up the floors, noticing for the first time how grungy the carpet was and how several of the sconce bulbs were burnt out. What was she doing here in the first place? How had she thought for a second that indulging herself in this charade was a good idea?

The elevator chimed its arrival, and Mina edged closer to the doors before they opened. It wasn't empty.

A slick-haired vampire smirked at her from inside, flanked by a bored-looking Yuxi and a hulking mass of a vampire Mina guessed was the muscle. She reeled back, instinctively knowing this could mean nothing good.

"See, I told you she would be there," Yuxi said irritably, examining her nails.

Mikhail stepped out of the elevator with his guard hovering in the background.

"So you did. I never would have believed it had I not seen it with my own eyes—the righteous Princess Mina slumming with the dregs of the human feeders." Both Mikhail and Yuxi watched her like cats tracking a mouse as Mina inched backward down the hallway in the direction away from Javier's apartment. There had to be stairs farther down, right? Maybe she could make it if she put enough distance between them before she bolted.

Mina turned to run but caught sight of a second guard looming at the far end.

Shit. She was going to have to talk her way out of this.

"Mikhail," she said, putting a hand out between herself and the man approaching with a confident swagger. "Think carefully about what you're doing. When Lian finds out—"

"You know, I find it hypocritical how you hide behind her when it comes to dealing with me, and yet the second she's gone, you're dining out with a human of your own."

"I was not—"

"Naughty little fledgling—I see that freshly fed flush to your cheeks. How did it taste, hmm? So much better than that drivel the city provides, no?"

Mina opened and closed her mouth, unable to come up with a convincing lie.

"That's what I thought. Now, you and I are going to go back to my place and have that chat I promised you." Mikhail yanked the silk pocket square from his suit jacket before retrieving a gleaming pair of handcuffs from his pants pocket, careful not to touch the silver with his bare skin. "Are you going to be a good girl, or do I need to restrain you?"

Her body was screaming *flight*, but instead, Mina rushed Mikhail, landing a solid jab to his nose before careening past him toward the open elevator. But something impeded her ankles after only a few strides, sending her crashing to the floor, fingertips shy of the metal door track.

A crushing knee came down on her spine, squashing the breath from her lungs as her hands were wrenched behind her back. The sizzle of silver against her skin was unmistakable, and Mina bit back a curdled scream as her face was ground into the grubby carpet. She could envision the blisters already forming under the caustic touch of the cuffs.

Yuxi's nude patent leather pumps stepped toward her before the woman crouched to whisper in her ear, "Stop embarrassing yourself, little mouse. As long as you cooperate, it will all be over soon."

"I've had enough of your sisterly advice," Mina spat, realizing she'd walked right into Yuxi's trap. She almost deserved whatever punishment was coming for being such a trusting fool.

The pressure on her back vanished before she was hauled up by a death grip on her upper arms, jostling the handcuffs to leave their burning imprint on new sections of skin. Mina tried her damnedest to block out the excruciating pain as a bead of sweat welled at her temple.

"Mina?" a distant voice called.

No.

Javier stood with one foot outside of his doorway, the knot of a trash bag clutched in his hand.

"Go back inside your apartment. *Now.*"

Mina watched for a glacial second as he surveyed the scene, hastily dismissed any sense of self-preservation, and started with a confident stride down the hallway. *Fucking moron.*

The expression on Mikhail's face shifted to cruel delight, made more demonic by the trickle of blood leaking from his nose. Mina's stomach dropped.

"Once again, your valiant hero comes to your rescue," Mikhail taunted. "I would have settled for just you, but I wouldn't mind teaching him a lesson as well."

"Your quarrel is with me, Mikhail. He means nothing. Let's just go."

Mikhail gave a deep chuckle. "Don't tell me you actually like this one. This night just became much more entertaining."

"Let the woman go," Javier said with all the bravado of a knight in shining armor while wearing jeans and a T-shirt.

Mina bit the inside of her cheek as she watched the second of Mikhail's guards pummel Javier in the gut before forcing him into the elevator. Javier didn't seem weak by human standards, but he didn't stand a chance against vampire strength. Mina's own henchman shoved her in behind, her body pressed so close to Javier's that she could hear the rapid thud of his heartbeat.

I told you to stay inside. Why couldn't you have listened? she wanted to say. Clutching at his stomach, Javier glanced around the elevator car, and Mina could finally see the calculations catching up in his mind: five vampires and one human—not great odds.

"Still think she's worth saving, human?" Mikhail blotted tenderly at his nose with the handkerchief.

Javier wisely stayed silent.

Mina and Javier were hustled out a side entrance and stuffed into a stretch limousine. The cocky Federov fuck even did his kidnapping in luxury. It did give Mina a flicker of a smile to see Javier donkey kick one of the guards in the balls, but he paid for it with three decisive head bashes against the side of the car. By that point, Mina was sure the silver cuffs had started to eat through the tendons in her wrist as she struggled to wiggle her fingers beyond the involuntary twitches that had set in. Her heart ached that Javier had been dragged into yet another mess due to her carelessness. She could do nothing about it now.

INSIDE THE LIMOUSINE, a heavy canvas bag was put over Mina's head, reducing her world to the sizzle of the silver cuffs and the lull of the car as they drove toward whatever doom Mikhail had planned for them. The hood sucked into her nostrils and mouth with each terrible inhale. She could tune out the Russian banter between Mikhail and the guards, but the periodic groans elicited from Javier as the guard continued to jab him in the ribs made her cringe each time. She had to concentrate if she was going to get him out of this. The fragility of human existence had never been so starkly pressing as it was now.

Mina judged the drive to be somewhere on the order of

fifteen minutes before the car came to a halt. The sound of the opening doors preceded rough hands dragging her backward. Scrambling to keep her feet underneath herself, she let the hands steer her, trying to minimize the chafing of the cuffs against her achingly raw wrists. Hearing Javier's wheezing nearby was a small comfort—they weren't being split up yet. That was enough to give her hope.

Together, they were marched into a cavernous building and through several sets of doors. After a backward shove something immovable met her calves, dropping her inelegantly onto the metal seat behind her. Mina clutched feebly at the slats of the back, steadying herself.

The bag was wrenched off her head, the harsh overhead lighting saturating her vision before the empty warehouse slowly came into focus. Javier's wrists had also been bound and were hoisted above his head by a hook dangling from a chain. The toes of his white socks brushed the cement floor as he sought to alleviate the pressure on his wrists, hanging a centimeter too high. The Federov guard landed a few more punches against his ribs, clearly still retaliating for the assault on his testicles. Javier took them with more stoicism than Mina thought strictly wise. They wanted a reaction, and they would keep hitting until they got it.

"Minka," Mikhail said, rounding on her. The pearly whites of his teeth shone threateningly above her.

Mina glared in defiance.

"Not talking to me now? Are you upset that I am damaging your toy?" Mikhail crouched in front of her, hands settling on her thighs, fingers squeezing to make their presence known. With a smirk, the greasy vampire let a hand wander up to her collarbone, stroking it lightly with his fingers like a musician inspecting an instrument to be played.

"Don't you fucking touch her," Javier growled.

"Gag him," Mikhail ordered calmly, maintaining his focus squarely on Mina as he undid the top two buttons of her white blouse, parting the neckline to reveal a generous amount of cleavage. "I never understood why you dress like an orthodox babushka. You have a beautiful body—you should show it off."

"Is that why I'm here, Mikhail? So you can enjoy my body?" Mina infused her tone with enough seduction to draw the man closer—then slammed her head into the tender cartilage of his already-bruised nose. Mikhail drew back, his mouth twisting into a snarl, then slapped her hard across the cheek. It landed with far more force than Lian's usual strikes, which always carried a dose of restrained, instructive pain. This was brute force. Mina could hear muffled protests from Javier as she breathed through the throbbing along her cheekbone.

Mikhail came to her side, wrenching down her blouse to expose her left shoulder and, thankfully, nothing more.

"You realize this is exactly why you're here, don't you? You have no concept of how to treat your betters. Your sister obviously agrees, or she wouldn't have approached me with this unique window of opportunity to teach you—along with that cunt creator of yours—a lesson about messing with the Federovs."

Mina clenched her jaw. She should have seen this coming. Yuxi had planted the idea she needed to seek out Javier outside of the protection of Zhang House guards and with Lady Zhang conveniently out of town. She should have known scheming was afoot when Yuxi professed anything other than hostile rivalry toward her. Mina didn't know what she blamed herself for more: that she had believed Yuxi capable of sisterly intentions or that she had taken the bait and returned to Javier on three separate occasions. She could feel the woman's presence behind her, lingering like a vulture about to come in and pick at the scraps after someone else's dirty work.

Mikhail spoke to one of the guards, who stoked a brazier of coals. Next, he shrugged out of his suit jacket, still eyeing Mina like a hawk.

"Yuxi, make yourself useful and hold this," he said before tossing it her way. Mina could hear the click of heels as the polished woman sidestepped the garment, allowing it to crumple to the ground. Mikhail merely grinned as he rolled up his shirt sleeves.

"All right, Minka, this will only hurt for a minute, but I need you to stay still." Mikhail sidled up to her, wedging one leg between her knees and hugging her head to his stomach. Her chin brushed his belt buckle, and Mina revolted at the uncomfortable nearness—the smell of his body and the hyper-masculine cologne he doused it in. She thrashed as his hand closed around the upper arm of her exposed shoulder.

"Fuck you, Mikhail," Mina spat, squirming against the stomach that squished beneath her accosted cheek.

"Careful, darling, or your gyrations might arouse a different monster. Don't tempt me into finding other uses for that filthy mouth of yours." Mikhail's voice was dark with sinister intentions. Mina could hear Javier struggling against his bonds, the sound of jangling chains ricocheting throughout the empty space.

"I think your human pet is jealous," Mikhail said with a laugh. He raised his voice toward Javier. "Don't worry— vampiress blow jobs are dicey on the best of days. When they're angry..." He gave a deranged chuckle. "I leave that for braver men than me."

Mina listened as the guard withdrew something from the coals, metal glowing a vibrant orange at the end of a long stick. With a nod from Mikhail, the man walked to the back of her.

"Mikhail, even I know you're not this stupid. Lian will—" Mina's speech dissolved into a piercing scream, sounding distant even to her own ears as her entire world narrowed to the scalding heat of the brand against her shoulder. The initial distinct pain of singed flesh suffused deep into her muscle as it radiated an agony so terrifying that she could hardly bear it. When the metal was finally removed, she could feel bits of her skin peeling away with it. Her face was damp from tears and sweat when Mikhail finally released her. Mina inhaled in shuddering breaths against the nausea as the burn continued to pulse through her in unrelenting waves.

Mikhail stroked the hair away from her face. "See? I told you it would be over soon."

Javier was doing his best to make his outrage known via strangled shouts through the gag.

"Pipe down. You'll get your turn next," Mikhail berated him.

That pulled Mina out of her trauma-induced trance. Her eyes snapped up to meet Mikhail's, staring sadistically down at her.

"You accomplished your goal, Mikhail. Let us go before you give House Zhang any more reason to start an all-out war." Her voice came out hoarse and far less menacing than she wanted.

Mikhail strolled easily behind her, shifting her shoulder to admire the work before brushing his fingers over the charred pattern. Mina gasped at the renewed pain.

"It never gets old, seeing my heraldic seal on the fair flesh of maidens, knowing the ownership it conveys. Lian took something of mine away, and now I've claimed something of hers for myself."

"No one fucking owns me. Mutilating me in *no way* gives you any power, Mikhail. In fact, I think you'll find this display of yours will backfire superbly," Mina said through gritted teeth.

"Well now, we both know that first part isn't true. In any case, I think it's time we move on to your boy. I'm curious how long he will scream for you before he passes out. Care to wager? I give him five minutes. Maximum."

Yuxi gave a melodramatic sigh, finally stepping around to where Mina could see her.

"I know you like to play with your food, but some of us have better things to do with our time. Finish Mina already so we can be done with this."

Mikhail put his hands in his pockets, considering the prissy woman with a lazy smile.

"You know, I think I've changed my mind about that part. I much prefer the thought of her living, knowing she carries my mark."

"That's not what we agreed to." Yuxi's voice lowered, dropping all its flirtatious charm.

"You want her dead? Do it yourself." Mikhail strode away, making a beeline for Javier. The pain of the brand and even the silver shackles around her wrists muted as Mina watched Mikhail approach him, an icy dread kicking her brain into overdrive. He'd made a critical error thinking her too broken to fight, leaving her bound, but not chained, to the chair. She could work with that, but the timing needed to be precise. She would only get one shot at a break.

Mikhail issued a few sharp commands in Russian, followed by what sounded like another joke at Javier's expense.

"I want to show you one of my favorite ways to punish serfs," the man said with a wistful sigh. "Those were the days. Vampires ruled with dominion and respect, claiming their due. This city breeds nothing but weakness in our kind, creating vampires that can't even hunt. It's despicable." He spun Javier to face away, bunched the T-shirt in his fists, and tore it down the middle, exposing Javier's back. Mina was transfixed by his lightly bronzed skin already mottled with purple bruising that wrapped around his torso. He was so human. So vulnerable.

Like hell am I letting Mikhail touch my human.

The thought came so fast that Mina could hardly process it. Her human? When had she ever thought that way before? She refocused as a long whip was handed to Mikhail, who let the tail drop to the ground. It consisted of two sections of rawhide linked by a metal ring. Mina eyed the end warily, which looked like a whole different kind of hellish material. Mikhail adjusted his grip a few times as if a sportsman rekindling a familiarity with his equipment.

"Back then, I could kill a man with a knout in under fifty lashes. Let's see if I haven't lost my touch." Taking a few steps back, he hefted the whip behind himself and brought his arm around in a circular motion, the tip tearing a vicious line of crimson across Javier's flesh. Mina could see every muscle along his back and arms tense as a wail tore through him, restrained only by the gag.

You did this to him, you stupid, selfish child.

Mina's face twitched. She didn't have time for self-deprecation right now. Mikhail was already enjoying himself far too much, oblivious to the rest of the room. Yuxi had stalked off, uninterested in Mikhail's barbarous games.

The second time the whip came down, Javier's body went completely limp, another throaty scream echoing through the room. The guards chuckled with each other, pointing as if analyzing the technical prowess of Mikhail's torture.

The scent of Javier's blood hit her nose, and it collapsed the entirety of her priorities into preventing the waste of another precious drop. Mina's arms tensed as she started winding one of the cuffs around her wrist, straining the delicate links between them. If she could get the softer silver to fatigue even a little, she knew she could wrench them apart with the fury building within her to an inevitable pressure release. She had to ignore the pain of the metal biting into her wrists a little longer as tension built in the coiled links.

As the third strike fell on Javier's back, Mina yanked as hard as she could against the deformed restraints behind her, feeling a small pop as they separated. With a fang-filled smirk, she launched herself at the first of the two guards, clinging to his back as she clawed at his face, layers of skin peeling back after the silver bubbled it enough to slough. Her fingers met the soft orbs of his eyeballs, and she dug in. He went down with less fight than she expected.

The second goon grabbed her around the middle, dragging her away from his fallen comrade. Mikhail had finally turned around, raising a single eyebrow as if mildly irritated by the interruption.

His complacency would be his downfall.

Restrained in the bodyguard's arms, Mina twisted belly-to-belly with the man. She hooked her fangs around his trachea before giving a yank that brought blood and viscera spraying onto her face. The triumph only bolstered her strength. As the hole in the guard's throat gurgled, she kicked out savagely at his kneecap, his hulking weight only helping to snap it backward at an impossible angle.

Mikhail simply stood and watched her spar with the guards, giving an appreciative slow clap as she turned to face him.

"Well done, Minka. You have some teeth, after all."

With a battle cry, Mina rushed him only to find Mikhail had stepped aside and given her enough of a shove to bring her crashing to the ground. In a flash, he was on top of her as her limbs scrambled for leverage. Despite her flailing, Mikhail wouldn't let her gain any. He grabbed a fistful of her hair and banged her head against the concrete once before pinning it there. Mina could feel his breath on her ear as he leaned in and licked the blood from her jawline.

"It's too bad your tastes are so provincial. I might have had fun with you if you had more refinement."

Mina poured one last burst of strength into an elbow, aimed back toward the nose she'd already smashed twice over. It landed on its mark, sending Mikhail howling backward. Mina scrambled to her feet, her eyes scanning the room for a weapon—anything that would give her an edge in the over-matched contest.

The brazier.

With not a millisecond to lose, Mina sprinted toward the rusty metal dish of embers, and grabbed hold of the lip. Despite the smell of burning flesh, Mina barely felt a tickle against her palms, the nerves long since charred through by the silver bracelets Mikhail had gifted her. With a strenuous heft, she lofted the entire bucket over Mikhail's head, who looked up just in time to see a fiery rain of coals coming for him. He moved, but not quickly enough to avoid the scarring nuggets of heat, nor the steel plate that Mina brought crashing down over his head. It knocked him out cold, and Mina reveled in the bitter satisfaction she felt leaving the embers atop him to bore their way into him.

She ran to Javier, hugging his torso and lifting him enough to free his bound wrists from their captive hook. They both crashed to the floor in a heap of bloody, sweaty mess. Mina tore the gag from his mouth and the ropes from his wrists, stroking his face with her decrepit hand.

"I'm so sorry—"

"We can exchange apologies later. Right now, we need to get out of here." Javier took stock of Mina with a grim, haunted look in his eyes. "Your hands..." Javier said, lifting one of the blackened appendages, a scored ring of bloody white encircling her wrist.

His lips pressed into a determined line before he went to Mikhail's body and dug through his pockets then finally found the key on a chain around his neck. Mina stood, watching the way Javier tried not to wince from the three ragged lines of red that marred his back. Even as severe as her injuries were, he would take ten times as long to heal from Mikhail's damage, and the overwhelming urge to kill the man possessed her so strongly that she started striding toward the limp body.

"Whoa, it's over now," Javier said gently, blocking the view of Mikhail as he unlocked the cuffs from her wrists. Mina had to admit having them off felt better. "I think I can figure the way out once I get my bearings. I've been here before, and I paid attention to the turns as they brought us in."

He had? She'd ask for that story later. "I'll follow your lead."

Javier gripped her hand tightly, ignoring the ruined flesh, and pulled her to the door of the warehouse. With a girlish smile, Mina thought, *We're holding hands.*

As they navigated the corridors, the battle rush faded from Mina's nervous system. Her feet grew sluggish beneath her as they made it out the last door to where the limousine still sat, keys inside.

"Do you want to drive?" Javier asked, hesitating behind the vehicle.

"Hmm?" Mina asked, overcome with exhaustion as the muggy chill in the air veiled her hair in a fine condensation. "No. I don't know how."

"Oh." Javier frowned at her like that was the most disturbing revelation of the night. "All right, then you're going to have to tell me where to go. I don't think going back to my place is such a good idea right now. I suppose we could try Eva."

"Right," Mina said, considering. Like hell was she showing up at the Vasas' to endure all their questions. Eva would likely be even worse. But Zhang Manor might be an option. Lian was still away, and Mina didn't think Yuxi would dare attack twice in one night. "Okay, we're going back to mine. Get in."

Mina went to the passenger-side door and hooked her fingers beneath the handle, but as she pulled, they slipped free. Frustrated, she pawed at the door again. The handle wouldn't budge, the dexterity completely gone from her digits.

"Here, let me." Javier stepped in from behind her, opening

the door with a quiet kindness. Mina looked at him, his shirt-less body shivering in the early dawn air.

How were they both still alive?

She settled into the seat, hissing as the leather grabbed at the branded skin. Javier had an equally uncomfortable time trying to find a position that kept a gap between the material and his raw back.

They rode to Zhang Manor in grave silence, save for Mina's sparse directions.

23

Javier drove the limousine through the empty streets of Shanghai, his mind crackling with white noise from the overload of this evening. This day? How long ago had it been since he sat down to dinner with Eva? It might as well have been an eternity.

He glanced over at Mina, whose expression had gone entirely blank since entering the car. In the warehouse, the noises she'd made and her complete obliviousness to the pain had been animalistic and terrifying. Yet here they were, both alive because she'd found something within her to make it so.

"Are you sure this is right?" Javier asked as they drove up to an ominous wrought-iron gate guarded by two stone lions that looked as though they might easily leap off their pedestals and consume him whole for daring to beg entry to their sacred abode.

Mina merely nodded as she picked at the dead flesh around her wrists. The gates opened soundlessly before them, and Javier slow-rolled the car through. At the end of a lengthy driveway, he could barely make out the silhouette of a grand fortress. The symmetrical castle was ringed in an impervious wall topped with an elegantly sloping roofline, all washed in the early glow of the approaching dawn.

Javier put the car into park on a gravel pad outside another impressive gate, this one designed for people. He looked at Mina again, who still stared mutely at her lap.

"Are you all right? We can find somewhere else to go."

"I'm fine. Just, the door..."

"Right. Of course." Javier unlatched his seat belt, hurrying to open Mina's side. She exited like a ghost, moving calmly toward a fate over which she had no control. For a second, Javier questioned whether he should follow. From the architecture to the landscaping to the statuary, everything gave the impression that his presence was an unforgivable offense. Mina was safe now, so maybe he could just leave. Yet as he watched Mina push through the gate and disappear through the circular opening in the wall, he felt his heart tug in her direction. His feet unwillingly followed.

As they walked through three separate courtyards divided by progressively more ornate walls, the winding flagstones took them through topiaries and other ornamentation maintained with such exacting precision that Javier felt the gardeners must have personally arranged every leaf. The elongated shadows of the foliage stretched in the sideways-cast light, spilling over the walkway like claws ready to ensnare him. Javier stepped carefully, staying as close to Mina as he thought permissible.

She gave him one last look before the grand doorway to the primary residence, her eyes filled with a mix of sorrow and despair, allowing him entry into the part of her life that garnered those emotions. With just a look, he understood that much, and he gave her a small smile of encouragement.

With a slow blink, Mina pushed through the door, becoming yet another person on the other side. She barked orders with steely authority at the servants bustling around the main level, none of whom dared more than a single glance at him before scurrying off to do Mina's bidding. How did she live in a world where she arrived home, caked head-to-toe with dried blood, and no one gave her anything but a "yes, ma'am"?

The open foyer was expansive, every element conveying a sense of power and tradition. A grand staircase led up to a second level of closed doors. Every piece of gorgeous wood-work was polished to a high shine, textiles plush and vibrant, tasteful artwork hanging at even intervals. It all gave Javier the creeps, like he was in a desolate museum after hours.

"Come on, let's go in here. The light will be better so I can look at your... what Mikhail, that is..." Mina said, her voice struggling as she led him to a formal sitting room off the main entrance.

"Are they bringing something to wash with? I think we really need to look at those hands first."

"I don't know." Mina's brows drew together. "I told them to bring supplies."

Okay, so this experience was as new to Mina as it was to him. Despite the prickly vampire exterior, she was just a city girl making the best of a whole hell of a lot of mess.

"Let's just sit for a minute, yeah? But uh, that couch looks like the kind my grandparents covered with plastic. So, here." Javier grabbed two olive-green pillows off the couch and plopped them next to the coffee table. "This work?" He squatted onto one of the pillows, crossing his legs in front of him, hoping she would follow suit.

Mina looked down at the front of her shirt as if realizing for the first time that it had originally been white, and not the rusty red it had become. He would need to keep her away from mirrors until he could clean some of the carnage off her face. Mina sank onto the pillow, eyes staring absently at a place on the ground behind him.

The servants returned carrying a tray with bandage rolls, cloths, and a steaming bowl of water. There was also a tall glass of crimson liquid. Thank God for all of it.

"Xiè xiè nǐ," Javier tried with a polite smile, and the young woman started so much that she almost toppled the entire tray. She fiercely ignored his gaze as she hastened out of the room.

"Drink this." Javier handed the glass to Mina.

She drained it in one continuous gulp before setting it back on the tray empty.

Good.

Next, he grabbed the soft cloth and dipped it in the bowl of tepid water. He reached cautiously for one of Mina's hands, which she gave without resistance, registering hardly above a coma patient in terms of reactivity. Javier dabbed at the skin, aiming to clean the worst of the blood so that he could see the true damage. Her palms were both charred to a crisp, the rings around her wrists deep enough to expose bone, surrounded by an array of ruptured blisters. After sniffing a small dish of what he decided was a medicinal salve, Javier applied it with its bamboo spatula. As careful as he was, he couldn't imagine how much it hurt to have wounds that deep. Mina didn't flinch once as he tended to them and wrapped them in the pristine white bandages.

Finished with the wrists, he took one look at the murky water with a grim sigh. He couldn't wash her face with that, and he didn't even know where to start with the brand.

Javier stood with the bowl, intending to find a servant to play charades with to get a fresh one. Instead, the same jumpy girl returned with another already in hand. She set it on the table before taking the used one from him. Javier didn't repeat his thanks.

He sat back down in front of Mina, hiding his wince when the skin tugged around his own deep lacerations. Javier didn't even want to know what kind of mess awaited him back there.

He moistened a clean cloth before raising it to Mina's face. Finally, she flinched. He hadn't even touched her yet. Javier's gaze lingered on the purple bruise blooming across her cheek, a grim thought circling: *Is she used to this kind of abuse?*

"I just want to wash some of the blood off. Is that okay?"

Avoiding his gaze, Mina nodded with a somber reverence. Javier moved slowly, being even gentler than when he'd cleaned her wrists and hands. Mina tolerated it though she radiated tension at the smallest touch. He longed to ask her why, to understand the reason for her reticence. Yet he knew he probably couldn't truly comprehend her particular emotional scars, and it would be cruel to even ask for an explanation. When he was done, some of her skin was still smeared with an unnatural pink, but the improvement was substantial. A shower should take care of the rest.

"Much better, right?" he asked encouragingly. Mina gave him a small smile back, tenuous and brittle. But it was something.

"Let me see your back," she said, her voice croaking.

With a suppressed sigh, Javier turned around, resigning

himself to confronting the reality of his injuries. The intense pain of the whip had been unreal, like someone drawing death itself against his skin in small enough slivers to prolong the experience. Certainly, he would carry the scars of that Russian bastard's casual violence for the rest of his life. Maybe he should have let Mina kill Mikhail back in the warehouse, come to think of it—for what he'd done to them, for what he'd done to countless others.

Mina's fingers, slender and icy, alighted on his shoulders, and an intense shudder wracked his body at her touch. That surprise was nothing compared to what he felt when her hot tongue touched the flesh of his back, licking at the blood dried around the injuries. His eyes flew open with deeply conflicted thoughts.

"Mina, is this really the time to—"

"Hush."

She continued her lapping along the lines of fire that criss-crossed his skin, leaving a tingling cool in the wake of her mouth. Mina kissed and licked her way to the base of his spine, where the trail ended. Javier was in his own special kind of comatose state by the time she'd finished.

"I think I healed you." Uncertainty clouded her voice.

"You can do that?" Javier reached behind his back to feel the skin. Sure enough, where he expected to find ruptured ridges was nothing but uninterrupted landscape. "Mina, that's incredible."

"But it left scars. Other vampires don't leave scars."

Javier turned to face her again with a wry smirk.

"Haven't you heard? Chicks dig scars."

"Not when they're the ones that caused them," Mina objected with a huff.

"You did no such thing," Javier said firmly. "Besides, admit you think I look like a suave bad boy now."

Mina gave him a deadpan stare for several long seconds, and Javier hoped his attempts at breaking the tension hadn't gone too far.

Suddenly, her lips crashed into his, urgent and coppery. Javier relaxed into the kiss and its developing tenderness—a moment of relief at being alive and at still having each other. He didn't question it or ask for any more than Mina freely offered. When she slowly pulled away, she left a smile on his face that made the entire experience of the evening worth that one precious moment. She wanted this as much as he did, if not more.

"I'm sorry." Mina pulled back, her gaze clouded once more with self-doubt.

"You have nothing to be sorry for, Mina." Javier swallowed, wishing she could glimpse herself through his eyes. "You saved my life tonight. You know that, right?"

Mina shrugged. "I had to."

"You didn't have to. You were courageous and strong, and you got me out of there. From the bottom of my heart, thank you."

Mina only lowered her head another fraction of an inch, her eyes unfocused.

As much as the kiss had clarified something for him, it had clearly had a tumultuous effect on her already volatile mental state. Mina wasn't even remotely receptive to anything resembling thanks or praise, despite being the sole reason he lived. One day, he would get through to her, but that level of psychological reparation couldn't be reached in a single night, especially not one as fraught as this.

Javier leaned over and snagged a throw from the arm of the couch. He lay on the floor, arranging the pillow and flapping out the blanket.

"Could we maybe just lie here for a moment? Together?"

For another second, he thought he'd pressed for too much, but Mina finally crawled over to the space beside him. She tucked her body into his, the curve of their forms fitting neatly together. Javier wrapped an arm around her torso protectively, settling into the pillow. Her hair smelled of sunshine or perhaps orange blossom. Whatever it was, it suited her. With that thought, his eyes shut, his mind dragged down into an inescapable, absolute slumber.

MINA'S EYES snapped open with a plunging sense of dread. She'd fallen asleep—they'd fallen asleep *together*, right here in the middle of the fucking sitting room. Heart racing, she untangled herself from the blanket. It was already midday—she needed to get Javier out of here *now*, before—

A chilling fear squeezed at her chest as her eyes settled on the outline of the woman looming at the room's entrance. Lian rested against the cased opening with her arms folded over her chest. Her black suit was flawless, her eyes gleaming crimson in the dim light. Seeing Mina awake, Lady Zhang took two casual steps into the room, her spiked heels clicking against the hardwood, her gaze as venomous as ever. Mina spread her arms defensively, shielding the sleeping Javier.

"Please let me explain," Mina begged, trying to buy time as her mind raced with any way to piece together a cohesive narrative from this disaster of a visual.

"Explain? I find you lying with a shirtless man in *my* house, and you want a chance to *explain*?" Lady Zhang's words brimmed with an unbridled fury that had Mina trembling from head to toe. She might have been able to save Javier from Mikhail, but Lady Zhang was a different monster altogether.

"Please—" Mina tried once more, but Lian moved too quickly for her to finish her appeal.

With a vicious yank, Mina was airborne for a nauseating second before she crashed into the wall at the opposite end of the room. From the ground, she pushed herself up in time to watch Lian's claws wrap around Javier's throat. Panic registered in his face, awakened as he was lifted off the ground by his neck. His feet kicked wildly beneath him, his fingers scrabbling at the tapered fingers crushing his windpipe. Points of blood welled where talons dug into his tender skin.

Mina stumbled across the room and prostrated herself at the woman's feet, grinding her forehead into the carpet.

"Please, my lady. Mistress Zhang. Please punish me for my mistakes and spare his life." Mina felt hot tears drip out of her eyes as noises of suffocation continued to emanate from the thrashing body above her. Mina couldn't let this happen, not after everything they'd already survived.

"Please, Lian." Mina's voice was the barest of whispers. "If you ever loved me, let him go. I beg of you."

"*If I ever loved you?*" Lian seethed with a tempestuous fury. "Spare me your sentimental notions, you blathering child. I have given you my *entire world*. Does that mean *nothing* to you?"

Javier's jerking motions were slowing, and Mina pressed her eyes shut as she reckoned with her abject failure to protect him.

"I am entirely undeserving of your generosity, my lady," Mina said, her words miserably sincere. "Had the Federovs not attacked tonight..." Mina trailed off, already sensing the uselessness of her excuses.

Mina started as Javier's body crumpled to the floor beside her. He gasped as he drew his knees underneath himself. A hope rose within Mina that she almost didn't dare acknowledge.

"Thank you, my—"

A hand closed around her arm and yanked her roughly to her feet. Mina suppressed a strained gasp, trying not to recoil. Lian tore at the collar of her shirt to expose her shoulder.

The brand.

"What. Happened." The words were a barely restrained tidal wave of anger.

"I was ambushed. Mikhail and Yuxi—"

"You allowed a Federov to *mark* you?"

Mina's eyes flicked up to the vicious intensity of her creator's face before dropping back down in submissive surrender. She knew she had no defense that Lian would find acceptable, despite the fact that in no way had she *allowed* any of this to happen.

"My deepest apologies, Lady Zhang. I understand the shame I have brought to your house."

Lian's breaths heaved with the weight of her growing rage, and Mina winced from the hand tightening against her arm, feeling her bones creak beneath its pressure. With a feral growl, Lian threw her onto the sofa with such force that she barely managed to keep herself from toppling over the back.

Mina turned around warily. Lian had disappeared. Javier remained on the floor, his eyes shut but his rib cage visibly moving again—alive. As long as Mina could keep Lian's ire focused on her, he had a chance at staying that way.

Lian was back in a blink, standing before the sofa with a ceremonial dagger from the display in her office, the shine on the blade matching the murderous gleam in the woman's eyes. Mina gasped as Lian forced her face down onto the upholstery and tore the shirt from her back. The point of the steel slid ruthlessly beneath the tender skin of the brand, and Mina sank her teeth into the cushion to muffle her screams.

She tried to convince herself Lian was doing her a favor, saving her from the permanent reminder of Mikhail. Yet it was everything she could do to not beg Lian to stop as the blade continued its unrelenting, surgical sawing.

"What the hell are you doing?" Javier yelled in English, sounding so dissonant in this place, in front of Lian, as he stood defiantly in the middle of the living room. Lian left her task long enough to bash him upside the head with the blade's pommel before returning to her butchery of Mina's shoulder. His form crumpled like a lifeless marionette. Mina kept blurry eyes trained on Javier, willing him to stay down. Thankfully, he did. She watched the rhythm of his breath, trying to match hers to the cadence, ignoring the agony of Lian carving the remainder of Mikhail's handiwork from her shoulder. When Lian finally peeled the flap of her skin away, Mina shivered at the touch of cold air on the palm-sized patch of flayed flesh.

At least it was over.

With a weary resignation, Mina sat up, hugging her arms around her bare stomach. "Thank you, my lady. I am grateful—"

"We're not finished yet." A deathly stillness suffused the chilly air. "Turn around and grab the back of the couch."

Mina opened her mouth, her mind a muddle of delirious pain and confusion. In horror, she watched as Lian unfastened her belt. The gold buckle tinkled as the woman slipped the supple leather from her hips and folded it into an oblong loop clutched tightly at her side.

"Do not make me repeat myself."

Mina swallowed and gave one last glance at Javier before resigning herself to her fate, her punishment, her lesson. She did as she was told, kneeling on the cushion with her bandaged hands on the back of the sofa. Her fingers dug into the plush fabric as she braced for the sting of the leather.

It fell in a blistering crescendo of blows, each lash designed to maximize the pain of the previous. They landed with both a savage precision and an unpredictability that kept it difficult to anticipate the pain. And when the length of the leather caught the edge of her open skin, Mina's choked sobs became undignified howls. The remorseless onslaught continued well past the point where Lian would have normally stopped.

When it finally did, Mina sank back onto her knees, her hands still holding fast to the couch's back. Her whole body was wracked by a tremor so fierce that she wasn't sure if she could even walk on her own. The emotional confession at Javier's, the kidnap and torture at the warehouse, followed by a savage battle for her life—and now this. Mina had nothing left to fight with, and still, she had to face Lian.

Just as she let her hands slip from their strongholds, confident it was really over, the leather of the belt looped around her neck. It wrenched backward, drawing tight like a noose. As Mina's fingers sought purchase at the slick edges of the belt, she could feel cool breath against her cheek as the woman choked her for several endless seconds.

Lian finally spoke. "If you ever see him again, I will kill him." Her words were an acerbic promise. "What I do to you will be *much worse*."

Lian relinquished the belt, and Mina plummeted to the ground, coughing in ragged spurts as she clawed the leather from around her neck, the terrifying memory of the serpent collar at the forefront of her mind. Unchecked sobs wracked her body as she clambered away from Lian, desperate to get away from the unforgiving predator that still pursued her.

The woman's hand twined in Mina's hair, dragging her from the room as her feet stumbled uselessly beneath her. She willed her battered body to fight, to move, to *do* something—but nothing obeyed. Lian hauled her down the basement stairs, each step thudding into her bones, every impact a fresh bruise.

Lian opened a small and ancient door, an earthy mustiness of the space filling Mina with an interminable sense of dread. Lian kicked the heavy lid off the coffin, and it fell to the side with a dull thud before Mina was tossed into its cloying embrace.

Mina scrambled out of the box, pressing herself against the far side of the room. "Please, my lady. Anything but that. I'll do *anything*."

"You will get in that coffin of your own accord, or you will share the confines with his corpse." Her voice was as cold as death itself.

Lian waited expectantly, her towering form demanding compliance, her threats as sinister as ever.

Barely able to get her shuddering limbs to cooperate, Mina climbed into the coffin, doing her best to compartmentalize the growing claustrophobia as she settled her shoulders between the wooden boards. Her back stung fiercely where the raw skin made contact with the base. She ignored it for the sake of Javier and the hope that he might survive this still.

The lid of the coffin slid over her without so much as a parting word or look from Lian. Mina sobbed as iron nails were beaten into the planks above her. The rasp of heavy chains sounded next, interminably entombing her for however long Lian intended. The thick wood muffled the outside world to a bare whisper of Lian's heels clicking their exit before the door to the room was slammed shut.

Then she heard nothing but devastating silence.

Mina held her breath as long as she could before her lungs demanded a ragged breath, the sound of rushing air deafening in her ears. She gagged on the moldy-wood smell. Her fingers found the grooves they'd carved during previous interments, and Mina raked the slots once more, trying to find comfort in the sensation.

Amidst the deafening silence, a voice materialized within her mind. A familiar voice. One that sometimes sounded like Lian, sometimes sounded like her mother, but most often sounded like her own—as it did now.

You know why you're in here, don't you?

Wood splinters compacted under her nails as she gouged at the wood. Her lungs refused to draw more than minuscule gulps of rank air.

Yes, Mina knew why she was in here. She'd dared to hope— dared to hope for a happiness she didn't deserve.

Even if she lets him live, you know he'll never want to see you again. He'll be on a plane home long before you even get out of this box.

Mina's eyes squeezed shut, and she pounded her fist against the lid of the coffin. Pain radiated down her hand, setting off a cascade of aches from the myriad injuries. Her feet kicked, finding the rigid boundaries of her confinement. The iron-wood had never yielded against her flailing in the past—it certainly wouldn't now with her strength so thoroughly depleted. Mina railed against the casket all the same.

Maybe she'll even bury you underground for a year or two. I'm not sure if she'll ever forgive you for a fuckup this big. Just when you were starting to regain her affection, too.

"Stop it!" she screamed into the void. An inconsolable sob wracked her body, and Mina curled onto her side, wedging her knees up against the wooden frame. Her back pressed against the other side, the sting astonishing in its all-consuming hurt.

She needed something to drown out the voice. Something pure. A child's song her grandmother used to sing to her. Mina forced a hum through her throat, letting the melody occupy the space around her. She imagined the woman's knobby fingers stroking her hair. "Gwaenchanha," Grandmother would say. *It's all right. Everything will be all right.*

Mina wouldn't let the darkness swallow her this time.

She couldn't.

Not again.

24

The car came to a momentary stop before ejecting Javier outside his apartment building. He landed on the pavement with a broken *thump*. His head ached, his ribs ached, his whole body ached. But more than his physical pain, his soul anguished for Mina, for the hideous assault she'd endured because of his ignorance. *He'd* followed her into Zhang Manor. *He'd* insisted they lie down together. Mina had been trying to tell him the entire night about the realities of her world while he dismissed her explanations for excuses.

With something between a groan and a whine, he pressed the concrete away from his chest, crouching on his toes for a steadying second before rising to his feet. The black car he'd been dumped from was long gone. Javier supposed he should be grateful to be alive twice over, but all he felt was a growing rage at the price Mina had paid.

As he hobbled to the front entrance of his apartment building, afternoon commuters clutching their bags cut a wide berth around his shirtless, shoeless, filthy form. *Yeah, everybody avoid the zombie and pretend like nothing's wrong.* At least Mr. Eyebrows showed shocked concern when he stumbled in. The man's Mandarin was way too quick for Javier to interpret and only caused a jarring spike in his excruciating headache. Javier waved him off as he vomited in a trash can, the nausea coming suddenly and uncontrollably.

"Sorry about that. I'll clean it up later. Just after I..."

What did he even do now? Did he dare go back to his apartment now that he'd attracted the negative attention of two separate vampire clans? His things were there, but was any of it valuable enough to risk walking into a trap for?

His dad's notebook.

A pang of worried guilt chased his staggering steps to the elevator. Mr. Eyebrows shouted down the hallway at him, but Javier was beyond listening. When the doors dinged open on his floor approximately an eon later, Javier's stomach plummeted at seeing his door still ajar, the black trash bag from the previous night sitting to the side, where he'd left it.

He swung his apartment door inward with a hefty degree of caution. A quiet emptiness greeted him, absent lurking vampires, best he could tell. Yet from the carnage, they had clearly been there: each piece of furniture was toppled, electronics eviscerated, and shreds of his clothing festooning the works. There was no method to the destruction. They'd meant to intimidate. Heart pounding in his chest, he waded into the mess and rummaged through the debris until he found his dad's notebook.

The antique leather volume was squashed under a motherboard, pages crumpled beneath its open binding. He choked down tears as shaking hands smoothed out the creases bisecting his father's preciously preserved handwriting before his anger flared to new levels. Whoever did this—the Federovs, the Zhangs—he didn't give a damn. They would both pay for this.

He needed a plan. Something smart. Something smarter than he was capable of in his current state, which required him to at least buy some time. Maybe even consult with smarter people. Yes, now he was getting somewhere.

First, Javier collected all the electronic detritus in the cardboard box. He would call in a personal day and sort things out with Arvind tomorrow. Next, he dragged his suitcase out from under the bed and stuffed it with clothes from his closet, the books on his nightstand, and his toiletries, toothbrush included. Groceries were packed into a few sturdy plastic bags. And that was the grand total of his possessions in Shanghai.

After sticking his head out into the hallway to make sure the coast was clear, he hauled his belongings to Wenshi's old apartment. Javier hip checked the door, which gave without protest. That broken latch was definitely getting fixed. Light filtered in through gauzy curtains, illuminating a stirring of dust. A faint waft of cat urine stung his sinuses—with any luck, it would work as a natural vampire repellant. Javier barricaded the door with his belongings and propped himself against the wall. His head tipped back with a clunk.

Maybe he could stand here for a second and give his eyelids a rest... The second round of nausea hit without warning. He barely made it to the sink before his stomach heaved up slimy yellow bile. The back of his shaky hand wiped the spittle from his mouth as he leaned his elbows on the edge of the counter.

No, he didn't have time for rest, not while Mina was trapped in that monster's lair.

Fragments of memory crowded his mind—waking up to an inescapable vice around his neck, crimson eyes boring into him like lasers, Mina's frantic pleas in Mandarin, the shriek of her smothered screams as the brand was carved from her back, and then—after all that unrelenting horror—the sound of a leather belt slapping against skin over and over again before she was dragged away. His head had been too dizzy to coordinate his sluggish limbs—absolutely useless while Mina suffered.

Another bout of puke liberated itself from his body, and he rinsed the bitterness out of his mouth with a cupped hand of water. Every time he stopped moving, it felt like his ribs were grinding up his lungs.

His body was in no shape to fight this battle right now, but he could still work on a plan. Javier pushed away from the sink, unwilling to give into the collapse his body was chasing. He tugged on a shirt, ignoring the agony in his shoulders, and donned uncomfortable oxfords, his last pair of shoes. Javier grabbed the notes from his and Mina's experiments along with his dad's notebook and loaded them into his messenger bag. Despite the approaching evening, he was sure his sister would still be at the office. She knew these creatures—she knew this landscape. She would know what to do. Christ, how Javier hoped she would know what to do.

"I TOLD you I'm not leaving until I see Dr. Robles!" Javier shouted at the security guard team trying to corral him out of the Sanguis Institute. He didn't have time for their bullshit. He darted to the side, and one tackled him around the middle. Javier went down with a loud groan and a variety of cursing that his mother would smack him for. The guards hauled him up as he let out a frustrated growl, struggling to wrench his arms free. He'd had enough of beefed-up guys shoving him around for an entire lifetime.

"Wait until I tell her about the way you've treated her *injured* brother. Think you'll still have these jobs tomorrow?" he spat.

The security guys paused, exchanging questioning glances.

"She was saying at dinner last night how budget cuts were going to force some staff reductions. She'll probably even thank me for making it easy to decide who goes."

That line hit the mark. One of the security guards let go of him entirely, while the other stopped marching him to the door. It was a good thing they didn't realize how unsympathetic Eva would be toward his injuries. After all, she'd warned him not to tangle with vampires.

"Let me see my sister, and I don't need to mention our misunderstanding. Sound fair?" Javier pointedly asked the guard still holding him. After a surly second of consideration, he got a curt nod before he was released. Javier rolled his shoulders, trying to work out the fresh kinks overlaying the strain from being suspended by his wrists for a good half an hour last night.

When he arrived at her office with the dutiful escort from the front desk, he spied Eva's blond vampire boss through the glass door, August somebody. Just wonderful. When Javier's chaperone gestured him toward a chair to wait outside, he sneered. No, he wasn't going to wait like a good boy.

With the briefest of knocks on the glass door, he barged into the office.

"Eva, I need a word—well, a couple. I'll need a couple of words," he said with a definitive nod.

"Pardon my brother, Lord Vasa." Eva rose from her seat.

She looked like she'd been here for several days, her hair greasy and her lab coat rumpled. "Javier, are you drunk?" she questioned in biting accusation as she tried to steer him back out of the room. He shrugged her off.

"No, I'm not drunk. Concussed is more likely. But actually, this might concern you too, Lord Frostbite."

Eva looked mortified, but the Nordic vampire placed an elbow on his armrest with a bemused smirk.

"I detect a hint of sarcasm from that subtle American wit of yours. Out with it, then. What undoubtedly worthwhile endeavor prompted this interruption?"

"We need to save Mina from that demonic overlord of a woman!"

August scoffed. "Did you just refer to Lady Zhang—"

"We don't have time for your outrage at the gall of commoners these days. I was with Mina last night, and then that woman came home, and now Mina is..." His stomach lurched as the sound of her screams echoed in his mind. *Keep it down*, he commanded himself. "She's in trouble."

Eva opened her mouth, clearly trying to comprehend the catastrophic mess Javier had created. Before she could respond, August stood from his chair, all traces of humor wiped from his face.

"Mina was sneaking around to see *you*?"

Javier squared his shoulders, so sick of the intimidating posturing of vampires. God, if this prick weren't Eva's boss, he would be pummeling him into the ground right about now.

"Yes," Javier said, swallowing his anger.

"And what on earth possessed the two of you to... That *daft* girl," August muttered.

"It's taking me everything to not storm the gates of that

place and demand she be freed from that hell," Javier said, doing a reasonable job of keeping the tremble out of his voice. "But I swear to God, I will if you don't help me get her out."

"'Get her out'?" August asked in an acerbic tone, tugging at the cuffs of his shirt sleeves. "And where exactly do you think she would go?"

"I don't know." Javier balked. "Back to the States? I can help her find a place—"

"You think it's as simple as getting her an apartment and a night shift at a bakery? Who will feed her?"

Javier swallowed. "I hadn't thought that far. I mean, I'm sure we can figure it out. Your lot survived before corrupt blood banks funneled donations to your dinner tables, right?"

August snorted. "Yes, we survived by starving ourselves until bloodlust forced us to feed, usually with lethal consequences for our hapless victims. I know Mina can be an enchanting girl, but surely you possess some of your sister's intelligence. Use it."

A starburst of anger flared in his chest, and Javier's feet propelled him toward Vasa before he could think better of it. He intended to tackle the arrogant bastard, but instead, he found empty air where the prick had been standing and promptly crashed headfirst into the spinning office chair before landing on the floor. Pain lanced through his forearm, and Javier clutched it as he tried not to vomit again.

"Charming," August said drolly from the other side of the room. "Dr. Robles, do reach out to my office to reschedule for a more convenient time."

Javier stumbled up from the ground, sensing his window of opportunity closing.

"Damn you, listen to me!" The volume of his voice

stopped the blond git in his tracks. "This is the Federovs' fault. Not mine. Not Mina's. They ambushed us last night and took us to a warehouse where they tortured us. But that was *nothing* compared to what the Zhang woman did to Mina after finding us together."

Vasa eyed him with skepticism.

"You need proof? Here's your fucking proof." Javier wrestled his shirt off and turned his back to the pair. Eva's audible gasp might have given him some satisfaction, but the emotion it elicited was something closer to shame. After letting the weight of the silence settle, he put his shirt back on. "Now will you *please* at least check on Mina? She saved my life last night. The thought of her suffering... Please, will you help her?"

"I'll see what I can do," Lord Vasa said flatly before striding out of the office.

Eva's face was as pale as a vampire's. "Oh, Javier, what have you done?"

Alone with his sister, the last of his bluster dissolved. "I don't know, Effie," he said, tears already forming. "After I left your place, Mina showed up at my apartment. She wanted to test something that connects to your research, and I just couldn't refuse her. Here, give me a sec." Javier rummaged in his bag, retrieving the loose sheets of his notes; he extended them like a peace offering.

"The vampires' impact on wireless electronics is measurable and sensitive to blood consumption," he said, schooling his voice into something more authoritative. "After she drank the sample she brought..." Javier paused, steeling himself for the backlash he would get for this, "I had her drink some of mine. From a vial. No biting, I swear." Eva's look was one of outrage, but she stayed silent. "The effect on the measurement was undeniable. Mina thought it would help your research."

Eva scanned the pages, her brows knitting together as she worked through the experiment setup. Her curiosity was clearly piqued, but she fiercely clamped it back down as she lowered the paper and refocused on him.

"I'm sorry, Effie. I should have listened to you," Javier acknowledged miserably.

"Yes, you should have. I told you she was dangerous, that bad things would happen," Eva snapped before tempering herself. "But you're still my brother, and I need to check you out. These medical facilities aren't exactly designed to treat your injuries—a vampire would heal broken ribs and a concussion in a day—but let's start with some diagnostics so I can see how bad the damage is."

"Well, good for the flipping vampires," Javier grumbled, choking the emotion back down. He wanted to refuse treatment, wanted to insist they do something for Mina instead. But what more could he do? "All right," Javier said with resignation as he collected his bag.

"Javier? Did Mina heal the lacerations on your back?"

"Yeah. Why?"

"She shouldn't have been able to... Oh, it doesn't matter."

Yet another magical occurrence to confront. *Later*, he thought firmly.

That was all Eva said on the matter before leading him from her office to an exam room where she prodded him with the detached brutality only a medical professional could impart. Then she made him sit through three separate rounds of imaging. In the end, she ruled that he indeed had a concussion along with several broken ribs and possibly a bruised kidney. He would know when he tried to pee. Joy. No severe internal damage, at least. She made him lie down on the couch in her office so that she could monitor him for the next few hours. Javier grumpily acquiesced.

That was the last he remembered of the evening.

THE NEXT MORNING, Javier returned to his apartment only briefly to shower and grab the smashed equipment he'd borrowed from the bank before going into work. There, he had the unpleasant task of explaining what happened to the box of obliterated electronics, which Arvind had hesitated to even let him take in the first place.

"And then they just slipped from the railing," he finished. "At least I was able to rescue that cat, though."

"Surely," Arvind said, unimpressed. Javier was going to need to get better at the lying thing if he was going to keep doing it.

"Hey, but I thought more about the IT job offer, and I'm ready to take you up on it. I can even work late to make up for the time I missed yesterday."

Arvind considered him silently for a moment before his radio beeped with something in maintenance demanding his attention.

"I can trust you to show up for your shifts from now on?"

"Yes, absolutely. If my sister hadn't been so sick yesterday..."

"As you've said," Arvind said flatly. "You remember the code for the server room? There's a substantial backlog of tickets for you to deal with. Salvage what you can from the box

and get me a list of what needs replaced by the end of the day—
it will be coming from your salary. And no more working from
home."

"Yes, sir," Javier said, feeling thoroughly scolded. Arvind
huffed a sigh before returning the radio call and pacing away.

Javier hefted the box of cracked plastic and circuit boards,
ignoring the sharp stabbing from where it rested against his
broken ribs. He pushed his way into the stuffy air of the server
room. When the door clicked shut, a strange and profound
sense of security enveloped him, relieving a tension he hadn't
known he was carrying. No one could get to him here. He was
tucked away in a room where vampires wouldn't dare venture.
The time had come to start playing offense of his own.

With an annoyingly unshakable sense of duty to Arvind
and his neglected job, Javier worked through the banal IT
requests as quickly as possible, running his server checks and
maintenance in the background. The box of electronics could
wait until later. He was pretty sure it was all destined for the
recycling bin in any case.

After keeping his head down through lunch, he finally got
a chance to crack into the server he suspected might have the
kind of information he wanted: records of business listings,
including a database with their addresses and real estate hold-
ings. Javier ran a reverse query on the address of the warehouse,
doing his damnedest to remember SQL. Eventually, he got
names of three different business entities, none of which
directly linked to a "Mikhail," but all of which had tangential
Federov connections.

Yet a different server housed financial transactions associ-
ated with business customers. The data was encrypted, but it
seemed like Terry's laziness extended to password protection as

well. Javier gained root access with his first guess of "pass." Genius. With elevated permissions, he could decrypt the transaction sequences, dates, and amounts.

Javier spent the next several hours mining the database, jotting down abnormalities along with patterns in payment transactions. A vast amount of wealth was funneling through the Federov organizations from a plethora of sources. Was this deliberate misdirection of money, or were the Federovs supplying so much illegitimate ware that their GDP topped that of a small country? It might help if Javier knew anything about criminal accounting besides what was portrayed in movies.

When the server room door beeped its acceptance of an access code, Javier jumped so violently that he almost knocked the monitor off the table. Arvind poked his head through, and Javier's heart slowed from a thunderous thumping as he tried to keep the panic off his face.

"Hey, boss, what's up?"

"Javier, I'm about to lock the building for the day. I'm surprised you're still here."

"Sorry, yeah. Just trying to get caught up. Is it all right if I stay a little while longer?"

Arvind hesitated, appraising him with keen eyes. "I think it's best if you call it a night. The work will still be here tomorrow."

Javier looked back at his terminal, the green cursor on the black background blinking at him like a taunt. With another hour or two, he could... *Arvind is right. You need some sleep.* With a restrained sigh, Javier started closing out of windows.

"Sure thing. Let me pack up."

After clocking out, Javier walked out into the chill of the

autumn evening air prickling through his shirt. Rubbing the sleep from his eyes, he crossed the street, subconsciously registering headlights flashing on about a block away. Javier kept his head down and picked up his pace a notch. The inky sky, combined with a distinct lack of pedestrians, made him clutch his bag a little tighter.

His eyes darted toward the SUV as it pulled out and headed down the street toward him. Javier started jogging, aiming for the alley half a block down. The car pulled into the lane closest to the sidewalk as it approached. He moved at a dead sprint. He was feet from the alley when the car drove past, splashing a gutter full of wastewater onto his pants. Javier bent over, bracing himself on his knees as his ribs punished him for each gasping breath. He glanced over his shoulder to watch the car turn the corner, not feeling relief until it was out of sight.

Javier didn't look at a single person or car for the rest of his commute home. He even went in through a side door at the apartment complex to avoid well-meaning concern from Mr. Eyebrows.

By the time he got home, a bone-weary tiredness had suffused him, mind and body. He knew that he needed sleep, that his concussed brain needed it to function. Yet he couldn't stand the thought of a comfortable night's sleep when Mina was enduring God-knew-what kinds of torture.

You should have done more for her. Clenching his jaw, he replayed in his mind the soundtrack from the previous night: the sizzle of burning flesh, the crack of the whip, the popping tendons in Zhang's hand as she squeezed his throat. He'd been helpless to stop any of it.

He let his bag slump to the floor and toed off his shoes. In the kitchen, Javier poured a cool glass of water and drained the entire thing in one gulp. His stomach was empty, but nothing in his kitchen seemed remotely appetizing. Shutting the fridge door on a single bruised apple, he bargained with himself that he would eat something tomorrow.

Javier slid an end table in front of the door with its faulty latch, along with a few glass jars that might topple and clatter if it were forced open. Tomorrow, he should really try to leave work on time so that he could actually replace the worn strike plate.

Still repelled from bed by a restless energy, Javier dug his father's notebook out of his bag. The crumpled pages flared from the binding, straining the overstretched elastic band. He slipped it from the edge and opened to the title page, where his dad's nombre was etched in memoriam.

"What secrets do you hold?" he whispered into the silence, easing down into the rough-textured couch cushions.

Javier read through the entries of the notebook once more, not with the careful attention to detail he'd used going over bank ledgers, but with the leisure of someone reading a book before bed, letting the words wash through him like a story. He let himself feel the breezes his dad described and smell the scent of soil after the rain. Taste the first tart and piquant grapes off the sun-warmed trellises.

"Care for the rootstock over the vines. Deep growth yields the best fruit. The roots remember."

He read that passage over and over again. The detail came after a litany of descriptions of which scions grafted best to the rootstock his mother and father had cultivated. Something about that last line carried him into a somnolent dream.

The entire family gathered around the rickety farm table on the patio for a late summer dinner. Roasted corn salad over grilled flank steak. A full-bodied cabernet served with the slightest chill. His father's warm smile. Javier felt more at ease during that dream than he had in days—weeks, even.

When he woke in the early hours of the dawn, Javier felt decidedly more rested despite having fallen asleep on the couch. He bound his dad's notebook before shuffling to the kitchen to wet his parched mouth. In a sleepy haze, he wondered if he dared climb into bed for an extra hour's sleep. *Better not risk it.* He was on thin ice with Arvind already.

Out of habit, he opened the fridge once more in search of something for breakfast. The bruised apple still sat on its shelf, more shriveled than the night before. Javier brought it closer to his face to inspect. A small crack bisected the fruit from stem to blossom end, with a kinked shoot emerging from the split flesh —a pale-green whisper of a stem with two feeder leaves unfurling at its top.

Bizarre.

Javier grabbed his empty glass and balanced the apple on its rim before placing it by the window. He watched it for several minutes, catching the subtle way the translucent, fragile leaves tilted to intercept the direct force of the incoming light. He glanced over at the notebook once more. This was just a strange coincidence, right?

"The roots remember."

What the hell does that even mean?

25

August took a skeptical spoonful of shockingly purple ube ice cream and was pleasantly surprised by the starchy sweetness. He indulged in a second bite before setting the fluted dish aside, his stomach already unsettled from the seventeen preceding courses. Whether the nausea accompanying solid food was a natural phenomenon of vampire aging or yet another delightful symptom of the intensifying disease, August did not know. Either way, his diet was slowly devolving to blood, spirits, and espresso, which he sipped contemplatively now.

He'd been watching Lady Basundara flirt shamelessly with Lord Temuroğlu for the better part of three hours, with only lackluster new gossip to show for the effort. The restaurant's human waiters dutifully served them though August could sense the heaviness in their motions as they neared the end of their shifts, extended by nocturnal diners.

"I rather like the idea of summering in Anatolia. I hear the peninsula is lovely that time of year," Lady Basundara plied, batting her full eyelashes. The flawless beauty of her face was always a jarring juxtaposition to the bubbled skin of her neck—a mutilation, August ascertained, that was meant to strip her of her voice during her humanhood. After listening to her drone on for ages about the beauty of her Javanese court days, August nearly wished they'd made proper work of the maiming.

"Certainly, you should visit once you're settled in Bali," the man replied, stroking his dense beard of ebony.

Finally, an opportunity to intercept some meaningful conversation.

"That's right—I heard mention of your house's strategic success abroad. When do you announce your move?" August interjected with a polite smile. His dining companions did him the courtesy of tearing their eyes away from each other for all of five seconds to answer.

"Within a few months, I suspect," Basundara replied with a cunning smile. "Before the end of the year. Lady Zhang's intentions are becoming quite clear in Shanghai, and especially with the reduced Federov operations, remaining here is becoming... precarious. When do you leave for... Buenos Aires, was it?"

August gave her a nod, ignoring the derision in her voice. They would see the benefits of the South American stronghold when the time came. "Tomorrow evening. I'm curious to get your opinion on a matter, though. I am considering a different supply model for Buenos Aires, perhaps a permit-based direct-feeding system. Pending a breakthrough in the potency research, I think that might be the best way to address the nutritional shortcomings of stored blood. What are your plans for Bali?"

While Temuroğlu had seen the potential in his research and invested, Basundara had not.

"As you say, there are many factors to consider," the woman said. "Going back to the old ways has a certain appeal though some measures to prevent accidents will be necessary. We will likely land on a hybrid model after piloting a few methods."

August judged her response to be purposefully vague, her mention of the "old ways" not sitting particularly well. Alas, Lady Zhang would likely contain the vampire violence if it got too out of hand. The woman was obsessive about maintaining a certain image before the humans, if not especially concerned with their well-being.

"And Lord Temuroğlu? Not to pry, but I have overheard some rumblings of an Istanbul takeover. Were my sources incorrect?"

He had no sources, just an obvious guess. A failed grand vizier from the Ottoman Empire, Temuroğlu had always had barely veiled ambitions to retake the region. He hadn't made a new attempt in at least three hundred years, though, to August's knowledge.

The point of the man's bushy beard twitched. "Nominally, yes, House Temuroğlu will take Constantinople. My personal residence may well be someplace removed from the city center, however." A bald-faced lie.

"Certainly, it's worth considering all the options," August observed mildly. He knocked back the dregs of his espresso before standing. "I'm afraid I must take my leave. A few last-minute items to take care of before the flight, you understand."

The pair gave him cordial nods as he departed the private

dining room, already scooting their chairs nearer one another. Honestly, they were worse than teenagers.

By the time he made it past the effusive maître d' and out into the evening air, August's hands were shaking so badly that he dropped the first cigarette. The second one made it to his lips, where the dry parchment and earthy taste of the tobacco greeted him like a lover's kiss. The first inhale was heavenly relief, tamping down the headache enough that he could hear his own thoughts again.

He was on his third cigarette by the time he got home, yet the typical dulling effect had plateaued before actually mitigating the pain in any lasting way. He tossed his coat to the butler before striding down the hallway to his study. Most of the furniture of the penthouse had been covered in sturdy drop cloths, the shelves empty as the personal belongings preceded them to their new accommodations halfway across the world. August hadn't seen the apartment in person, but Johan— August's eldest fledgling—had deemed it acceptable, so that would have to do. There simply had not been enough time to steal away with the research progress, concluding business, and keeping tabs on the political movements of the rest of the houses, now that each was seceding from a Zhang-run Shanghai.

Reaching his study, August shut the door and considered locking it. No, not yet. He wasn't committed yet, only contemplating. Tension vibrated in his body as he crossed the room to his desk. He sat primly in the wooden chair behind it. His fingers wandered the carpentry of the ornamental carving along the drawer front before grasping the brass ring and sliding it out. A single box sat inside. He'd promised himself he would wait until it became essential for pain management, but the constant, pulsating pain at the base of his skull was making it impossible to not consider the option.

He lifted the lid apprehensively, revealing the sterilely packaged syringes and the glass bottle of rarified opium isolate. An addict's treasure trove and one he hadn't dared touch after spending the entirety of the eighties lost beneath the hazy seduction of heroin. August let the lid fall back down as he leaned back in his chair, lighting another cigarette instead. If that one didn't work, he would resort to the more extreme method. But perhaps he needed only a moment to relax for the pain to subside.

Gentle footsteps sounded in the hallway beyond his door. They hesitated before walking a few steps away then back again.

August slid the desk drawer of illicit substance shut, before calling out, "I can hear you skulking about. Either come in, or be on your way."

The timid boy finally pushed the door open a crack. "Am I interrupting?"

"Presently, no. I suppose you're hungry," he said, already undoing his cufflinks.

"No, it's not that. I ate earlier, remember?" Dmitri slipped through the doorway but stayed at the far edge of the room.

"That was barely a taste—certainly not enough for a growing fledgling." An odd thought occurred to August, a topic that needed to be broached gingerly. "I do hope you're not restricting again."

The boy had picked up the bad habit at the St. Petersburg academy despite August's best efforts to counteract the destructive messaging of some of the more aesthetically driven instructors.

"No," Dmitri said firmly—a bit *too* firmly, in August's opinion.

He made a mental note to pay closer attention to the boy's consumption. "Well then, how can I help you? You better have finished packing if you have time to pester me." August had meant it playfully, but from the way Dmitri's shoulders hunched, it hadn't landed that way.

The boy covered his hurt quickly, slipping into a more seductive demeanor. "Actually, I was hoping I could help *you*. You've been so tense lately. Perhaps there's something I can do to help you unwind."

August regarded the brunet as he padded across the carpet, wary of rebuffing him after the earlier misstep, but also definitely not in the mood for the energetic activities Dmitri no doubt had in mind. Cool fingers trailed across his shoulder as Dmitri moved behind him. When August opened his mouth to gently decline the affection, a pair of thumbs met the knots in his shoulders, eliciting an undignified moan instead.

"Don't start that if you don't mean it..."

He could almost hear the boy smirk as his physiologically informed fingers found just the right overlaps in sinew and muscle to knead. Miraculously, the headache began to lift after several minutes of dutiful, blissful massage. As he was beginning to relax, Dmitri's hands slipped lower to his biceps. The boy's tongue found the shell of his ear before hands tugged at the top button of his shirt.

But of course.

August caught Dmitri's wrist in his hand. "Not tonight, my dear."

Dmitri nipped at his ear, and August increased the pressure on his wrist to reinforce the boundary.

"Why not? You're always grumpy lately. Always tired." Dmitri pouted.

"I'm over three hundred years old. Surely that buys me the right to an evening of respite."

"You're a vampire—this should be your prime! Instead, you act like an old man."

August bristled at the accusation. Eventually, he would have to disclose the diagnosis causing the symptoms Dmitri ascribed to disposition alone. After the move, he'd told himself. For the time being, he deflected: "Yes, a vampire with a burdensome fledgling."

Regretting the sharp words as soon as they left his mouth, August watched as Dmitri's face became a mottled red before he spun on his heels and marched toward the door.

"Dmitri, wait..."

The boy ignored him, jogging toward the exit. August tossed the cigarette on the ashtray and pushed into his vampiric speed. His hand landed heavily against the wooden door as Dmitri tugged ineffectively at the knob.

"Let me go, August," he said, an angry quiver to his voice.

"Dmitri, look at me. I didn't mean that."

Dmitri folded his arms across his chest, stubbornly staring at the door. August inhaled the delicate smell of his sandalwood cologne, realizing for the first time how strained he'd let their relationship become.

"Mina told me you'd be different after the transformation. I didn't believe her, but she was right, in a way. You don't talk to me anymore. I don't even think you want me around anymore. Which is fine, I just... I don't understand why you offered to turn me, in that case. I hate that I depend on you so much when you're so clearly struggling."

Dmitri had always been sensitive. It had endeared him to August instantly, but he'd clearly neglected the emotional demands of those sensitivities, not to mention the reminder of Mina. August had given the Robles boy's accounts of her predicament a few days to settle, hoping that girl would emerge from the woodwork as she always seemed to. He would be lying to say he wasn't worried at present.

"You're right. I am struggling," August admitted softly. As Dmitri's shoulders gradually turned to face him, August used his hands to brace both sides of the boy, penning him in. "Managing this move, combined with maintaining momentum on the research, has taken its toll on me. Believe me when I say you are the singular bright spot in my life. I see now how unbalanced my priorities have been lately, in light of that fact. Please give me a chance to do better."

Dmitri's throat bobbed once before he answered. "I'm lucky to even have this opportunity, the opportunity to be with you and dance again. I shouldn't complain, but it's been hard seeing you shut me out, especially when we're leaving for an entirely new city tomorrow, and my supposed best friend can't be bothered to say goodbye to me."

Damn that girl for her propensity to run afoul of Lian's temper.

August cleared his throat, resigning himself to play peacekeeper one last time. "As a matter of fact, I'm due to pay my sister a visit before we depart. Perhaps I can inquire about what might have detained Mina."

"You would do that for me?"

"Of course. And when I get back, we can watch the sunrise in the solarium together one last time. Does that sound all right?"

Hazel eyes met his, full of a reserved kind of hopefulness, as Dmitri rose to his tiptoes and placed a chaste kiss against August's lips. The ancient vampire savored the taste of youthful intrigue. He wasn't afraid of death, save for the fact that he would be giving up these tender moments.

"See if you can't scare up a bottle of wine and some glasses, and I'll be back in a flash." The man finally withdrew his hands from the wall, unbarring the exit.

"Thank you, August."

As Dmitri left, August trudged back to his desk, rubbing his temples. There, he relit the unattended cigarette. It would have to suffice for the moment. Harder drugs would have to wait until he'd taken care of a few final problems.

OUTSIDE THE GATES of Zhang Manor, August ground his cigarette butt into the paw of the guardian lion. He'd been standing there for over fifteen minutes as the guards conferred about whether they should allow him entrance, unexpected as his presence was. His patience was reaching his limits.

As they finally parted the gates for him, he swept through without waiting for a formal invitation, trench coat flaring like a cape as his heels clicked against the flagstones. Anyone requiring such an elaborate entrance was compensating for something. Once he made it to the front door, a maid ushered him toward the staircase. As his hand met the banister, he took a deep breath of the varnish-laden air, seeing if the manor might give up the secret of where the missing Mina might be hiding. A tingling sensation suggested she was on the grounds, but August couldn't divine her location with further specificity.

With a cool rap of his knuckles against the solid door, August slid into the study steeped in artifacts from the dynasties of Lian's early years—the den of the dragon.

"Sister, I hope you've been well," August said in greeting, smoothing his waistcoat.

"Quite," Lian said offhandedly as she continued jotting notes with the nib of a fountain pen, her obsidian fringe obscuring the frames of her glasses. So, it was going to be one of those frosty visits.

She hadn't gestured for him to sit—another power play—so out of deference, he strolled to the cabinet where he knew she kept the whisky.

"May I?"

Lian inclined her head noncommittally, and August removed two crystal tumblers and considered the several fine bottles she kept. He took his time as he decided on the selection, settling in for a long game of chess, based on Lian's opening moves. After pouring a generous two fingers in each glass, August restoppered the bottle before approaching the desk.

"Come now, Lianna, set the work aside for a moment so we can have a proper toast," he said, setting a glass to the side of her papers as he pulled out a seat for himself, permission or no.

Lian finally looked at him, her expression coolly unreadable. While she didn't move the papers, she did fold her glasses with deliberate precision before setting them on the stack.

"To your health." August raised his glass, keeping his elbow respectfully raised.

"Who needs health when you have an empire?" Lian asked,

giving her own glass a casual jerk upward before downing half of its contents and clunking it back down on the leather desk surface. Christ, she was cocky. August would love her for it if it weren't so often at his own expense.

"Indeed," he remarked, taking a more restrained sip of his own beverage. "I must congratulate you on your impressive command of diplomacy in this country. I've heard nothing but praise from the way the Hong Kong transition was handled, and I have no doubt Beijing will shortly follow."

A small smile tugged at the corner of her lip as she sat back in her throne of a chair, bringing her glass with her.

"The pieces are finally locking into place, August, after all my decades—*centuries*—of strategy and negotiation." Her lustrous jade blouse gleamed in the warm glow of the lighting, her eyes ablaze with conquest. As long as he'd known her, Lian's ambitions had always exceeded all limits of his own imagination. Before she made them reality, that was.

"I still remember the night we met on the docks of Stockholm," August said, an unbidden chuckle rising to his lips as the memory dredged up his youthful naïveté. "Me, a young nobleman from an imploding lineage, and you, a deck-hand on a cargo ship calling to port, barely a knapsack to your name. Neither of us had any idea what was to come."

Lian's gaze focused on him, narrowing as the slight smile still held on her lips. After a lifetime together, the signals of her waning patience were as obvious to him as his own exasperation with her difficult moods.

"In any case, I wanted to congratulate you on achieving your dreams, before I leave for Argentina tomorrow. We have had quite a journey together." August took another, heartier sip, the smooth peat of the liquid giving way to fire in the back of his throat. He much preferred the refined taste of clear spirits, but that was neither here nor there in Zhang Manor.

"Are we feeling maudlin tonight, brother?" Lian jabbed as she emptied her glass then set it down on the table and slid it toward him with the tips of two extended fingers. August did his best to temper his glare as he swiped it off the desktop and went to refill it, giving her an even more generous pour to reduce the recurrence of her using him as her personal barkeep.

"On the contrary, sister. Merely remembering the legacy that comes before." August wet his lips as he reclaimed his seat, bracing himself to broach the next subject.

"Actually, there was a secondary reason for my visit." His fingers wandered the labyrinth of grooves cut in the crystal tumbler.

Lian arched an eyebrow as though she'd been waiting for this since his arrival. Typical.

"My boy would very much like to bid farewell to his friend before we depart, yet he hasn't been able to get a hold of Mina all week. You wouldn't perhaps allow me to talk to her to sort out the problem?"

Lian stilled to a glacial freeze. "That won't be possible."

"May I inquire as to why not?" August said with a playful smile, taking another drink from his glass as though he weren't about to be devoured whole.

"She's being disciplined."

"Ahhh, I see. Insubordinate fledglings is certainly a topic on which we could commiserate, however, seeing as this is the last time we will see each other for some time, I would be grateful if you would make an exception for a simple goodbye. For me, Lianna."

She considered him for a measured moment. "No."

"Surely, the girl's crimes can't be that serious," August chided, pushing past his internal warnings to stop pressing the woman.

"Drop the act, Vasa. You know exactly what the girl has been up to behind my back."

And there it was.

"Why, whatever do you—"

"Enough," Lian said, shoving her chair back as she stood to tower over her desk, fingers splayed against its surface. "This *boy* she's been cavorting with—she met him at *your* estate. *Attacked* him. You didn't think this pertinent to mention?"

August rolled his eyes dramatically. "Did I not? Must have slipped my mind."

Lian's sneer kicked into full tilt. "She is my fledgling, August. She is my responsibility, and—"

"Spare me your soliloquy on parenthood," August snapped. "I know exactly how you feel about that girl and how clouded your judgment is when it comes to her actions. You stifle her—*starve her*—and then use it as an excuse to punish her when the inevitable happens. I don't know how in your warped world that equates to love, but I will not sit here and endorse you torturing her for your own twisted enjoyment."

August locked eyes with Lian and frowned, feeling neither of them had expected that tirade. His oppositions to Lian were universally more subtle than whatever verbal landslide had escaped his mouth.

Lian stiffened to ramrod straight before delivering in a stark tone: "I am not interested in discussing this matter with you further, Vasa. She is my fledgling, and I will do with her as I wish."

August held the staring contest with her for a moment

longer, Lian's statuesque posture unwavering. There was no more ground to be gained with her tonight; she would either heed his message or not, but more words would not benefit the matter. It pained him to know he'd let down two defenseless fledglings tonight.

With a sigh, August stood, leaving the half-full glass of whisky on the desk. He let his hand rest on the back of the chair, taking a long look around her office, at the rigid order of the world she maintained.

"In all our time together, I don't think I've ever seen you care for a fledgling like you do Mina. You exploit them, dominate them, train them, and so forth. But genuine fondness? This is a first. I hope you realize it before you break her."

Lian's irises showed crimson in the office light, catching August off guard with how truly furious she'd become over a gentle observation.

"Your boy—he's a bit soft, isn't he?" Lian took a generous swallow of her drink.

"Careful," August said, his voice a notch lower with warning.

The woman cut him a sinister glare. "I wonder what will become of him after you're gone."

August's heart skipped a beat as a snarl settled on his face. She knew. That devil woman *knew* about his illness. For how long? Certainly, Dr. Robles would not have divulged his secrets, but perhaps another had pieced together their time in treatment rooms. Heat rose from beneath his collar, but August refused to give into her provocation.

He tugged at the bottom of his waistcoat. "If Lucrezia could see what you've become..."

The glass of whisky flew straight toward his face and

glanced off his temple as he failed to dodge it entirely. As it erupted against the wall behind with an explosive crash, a trickle of blood meandered through his hair.

"Speak that name again in my house, and I'll show you *exactly* what I've become."

August stood stunned for a moment longer, his mind awhirl with the implications of her escalating threats. The raven-haired creature staring back at him barely resembled his Lianna at all; he'd put faith in their shared history beyond its merit. He didn't have the forces to wage this war yet. However, if the shots fired across the bow were any indication, the time had come to start preparing for one.

"Let me be quite clear: your brutality against me is one matter." August dabbed at his temple and rubbed at the slippery blood coating his fingers. "But I will not tolerate threats against my family. I may be unwell, but I am not the defenseless boy you once met. Mind your house, and I'll mind mine."

Before she could respond, August strode out of the room with a flush of anger threatening to make the engagement one he couldn't walk away from. On his way out, he yanked his coat roughly from the arms of the maid, cursing the blasted kilometer-long walkway from perdition. He needed to cool off before he went back home to Dmitri to tell him of his failure.

Yet the more haunting notion was one of Mina, ensnared in Lian's sticky web. There had been a time when he hoped the headstrong young woman would remind his sister of her humanity. A decade later, Mina seemed to have become only an excuse for Lianna to unleash her worst, so terrified by the vulnerability of admitting she cared for another. August didn't know how to save either of them, and with a macabre lucidity, he didn't believe he would have time to figure it out.

Regardless, the visit had only reaffirmed his decision to move his family abroad. Lian's instability was reaching mythic proportions to rival Lucrezia herself, and the impending implosion of power would surely wreak insurmountable damage to those in her blast radius. August could at least make sure that Dmitri wasn't one of them, that his own family was securely extricated from Lian's authority.

26

In the dark, infinite chasm of the coffin, Mina strained her ears for any sign of life outside the confines of her reality. Nothing. Still nothing. The longer she remained, the harder it became to estimate the duration of her sentence. It felt like days, but it could have been weeks. Months? Mina shuddered at the thought.

The vampire within her urged her to slumber, to give into the stasis the darkness invited. Mina resisted it with the entirety of her fractured will, forcing her eyes open, though there was no light and nothing to see. She floated in an abstract abyss, anchored only by the rough grain of the wood, the troughs her fingernails had carved, and the ache of her spine against the rigid floor.

An unbidden memory entreated her, another in a sequence of recollections. She was on the balcony of Lian's Seattle apartment—Mina's home yet not her home. The misty rain dampened her clothes as she hugged her knees to her chest against the relentless western wind. Mina couldn't remember why Lian had locked her out there that night, but she remembered the stinging loneliness and shame of being trapped with her tears, her back pressed against the sliding glass barrier.

It was nearly dawn when Lian finally allowed her inside. With a teary sob, she stumbled into the embrace of the warm blanket Lian held out.

"I'm so sorry," she stuttered through chattering teeth with the conviction of her entire being. If she lost Lian, she had no one and nothing in the city to fall back on. Her entire life was predicated on keeping in the woman's good graces.

"I know, my love," Lian said and poured her a cup of tea. "Time to reflect always helps you see your errors more clearly."

Mina wordlessly agreed at the time, thankful for the mercy and determined to do better. Yet she now wondered what errors she had been meant to see. That she hadn't anticipated Lian's moods better? That she hadn't ensured her actions always carried the appropriate degree of submission? Those lessons, she had certainly learned in the years since, and still Lian made her feel like that vulnerable girl shut away on the balcony with all her wants singularly focused on forgiveness from the one woman who always found reasons to make her earn it.

When her ears detected a soft thumping in the distance, her first instinct was not to trust it. This wasn't the first time she'd heard—or hallucinated—steps, and the rush of hope followed by the crushing grief when she realized no one was coming was too much to bear. Better to ignore it altogether than reaccept her confinement.

The chains scraping over the top of her coffin, their heavy links knocking above her head, drew a stifled yelp at the deafening auditory intrusion. Mina's heart thudded loudly in her chest. Was she really being let out?

A crack of light pierced through the sliver of a gap before exploding her retinas like a blinding flash. Mina threw a hand over her eyes, fangs emerging as she hissed at the onslaught. Shakily, her hand felt for the edge of the coffin. It was real. The lid was off.

Mina clambered out of the box, her joints protesting from the sudden disturbance of their rigor mortis. She spilled out onto the floor and inhaled a breath of the musty earth. Oh, the joy of a smell after being locked in that box for so long. A small sound—half laugh and half sob—escaped as she pushed her torso from the ground, her eyes slowly adapting to the reintroduction of light.

At first, she could only make out the woman's silhouette in the doorway. Lian stood with her lean forearms crossed, scowling down at Mina's body. Instinctively, Mina hunched, drawing her limbs in as close as the stiffness would allow.

She wouldn't break the silence with an apology. She wouldn't do it this time.

They steeped in the quiet for what felt like several minutes though it could have been much longer, for as much as Mina's sense of time had slipped.

"Well?" Lian finally questioned, her voice softer than Mina expected. The softness was what broke her.

"I'm so sorry." As the rote words slipped from her lips, hoarse and hollow, Mina ground her palms into the sharp gravel at her own weakness, training her eyes on Lian's shoes as they approached. Now that Mina had delivered her cue, Lian could proceed with her part in this ceremony.

Why are you questioning this? Let her take care of you, and things will go back to normal.

Mina's brows furrowed. *But what if I don't want normal?*

Lian crouched before her fingertips came up to brush a lock of hair from Mina's face. The small tenderness made her lower lip tremble with emotion.

"Why do you force me to such extremes?" Lian asked, a look of genuine consternation on her own face as she surveyed Mina's back. "I never wanted this for you," the woman said softly, almost a confession.

Mina had no words—there were no words to describe how they had ended up here. Only raw and ragged shards of Mina's own identity, fractured between what Lian wanted her to be and what she was, knowing she could never fully reconcile the coexistence.

The woman slipped an arm around Mina's torso, helping her to her feet. Mina winced as her knees gave out, and Lian scooped her up in one deft move. The closeness was too much for Mina to stand, and she buried her face in the crook of Lian's neck, tears sliding down her cheeks as the woman carried her up the stairs.

The household was silent, and Mina kept her eyes shut, unwilling to face the room on the main level where her crimes had taken place, strangling the memory before it fully surfaced. Thankfully, they ascended to the second level, Lian proceeding directly to her own spa-like bath.

Shades of ivory and obsidian harmonized with glass and stone. A luxurious tub stood in the middle of the room, already filled with steaming water. Lian set Mina down on a bamboo stool before rolling up the sleeves of her jade blouse. Mina observed her numbly, knowing her role was to passively and humbly accept the forgiveness Lian would bestow upon her.

Through the windows overlooking the private back courtyard, Mina watched a chickadee bounce on the drooping branches of a golden rain tree, its blossoms long spent. Another bird landed on the same branch in the pale morning light, and a small smile pulled at Mina's cracked lips as they chirped at each other before flying away.

Lian's frowning face came into focus as the woman unwrapped the bandages around her hands with deft efficiency. So different from the hands that had placed them there. Warm, gentle hands of tanned skin. Try as she might, Mina couldn't remember the face that went with those hands. Even the name remained misplaced. *It's better that way.*

"These should have healed by now," Lian remarked, fingers tracing over the scaly scabs covering her wrists and palms. Mina shivered under the woman's touch, recoiling involuntarily. Lian froze at the movement, and Mina expected a blow to fall next for her insolence. It didn't come. Instead, Lian finished undressing her before helping her to the tub, settling Mina into the suds floating atop the surface. Aromas of lavender and jasmine perfumed the air as Mina relaxed into the marble embrace. A ghost of her time in the coffin emerged in the way the sides of the vessel confined her limbs, and Mina put her arms on the rim to push herself out, breath trapped in her lungs.

Instead, Lian placed a hand on her sternum, firm but not harsh.

"Relax, Mina. I have you now."

Mina shut her eyes, trying to envision the swirling mist entering her body, focusing on the steadying presence of Lian's palm. They stayed that way for several seconds until Mina's arms slipped from the edge of the tub and back into the water, where Lian wanted them.

"That's better," the woman said, letting one hand cup Mina's cheek.

Mina nuzzled into it, at first warmed by the affection, only to be immediately ashamed for giving into it. She didn't know how Lian always managed to make her feel so safe even after she'd taken everything else away—*especially* after she'd taken everything else away.

"Why do you do this to me?" Mina whispered, hugging her knees to her chest. She didn't know what she was asking and didn't expect an answer.

"I don't know," Lian replied softly before stroking her hair once. And with that, an accord had been reached—a wistful, confusing summation of their relationship. For some inexplicable reason, Lian's admission that even she didn't know put something at ease in Mina's mind. It could rest, knowing the lack of resolution had been named.

With a breathy exhalation, Lian resumed the task she'd set out to do, gathering bottles and a washcloth and finally setting the stool at the head of the bath. Mina became pliant under the woman's hands, letting Lian tip her head back and cradle her neck as she ran her fingers through the snarled and matted mess of her locks. As the crust dissolved, Mina could feel the glossy ends brush against her shoulder, and she smiled with the weightless feeling of being cared for.

Propped back up, Lian lathered the floral-scented shampoo in her hands before working it into Mina's scalp, the calming pressure points of her fingers sliding through Mina's hair with a reassuring presence. Lian bathed her, ritualizing each step of care. As she washed the sins and their punishment from Mina's skin, Mina enjoyed the closeness despite herself. Maybe she had earned this. Maybe it was okay to let it happen and worry about the rest tomorrow. The kindness was too rare to discard. She let herself appreciate it for what it was, even with the lurking epiphany of what it was not.

Lian didn't press her for any more demonstrations of remorse or compliance, for which Mina was grateful. After she had been rinsed, dried, and wrapped in a silk robe, Mina was carried to Lian's own bed and placed beneath the covers. As Lian went to the door and clicked off the lights, a spike of unwelcome panic hit Mina in the chest.

"You're not leaving, are you?"

Lian hesitated.

"You want me to stay?"

"Please."

The woman's expression was unreadable in the dim light, her hand resting on the doorframe.

"All right."

Instead of returning to the bed, Lian went to the sitting area and illuminated the reading light before collecting a book off the table. Mina hugged the pillow tightly to her cheek, watching Lian read, carefully turning the pages as she considered whatever knowledge they held—poetry, strategy, moral principles, it didn't matter. All that mattered was the constancy of Lian in her world, and that she was here—for now, if not forever.

27

In the bank server room, Javier banged on the enter key on the keyboard so emphatically that the hinge jammed, scrolling the terminal indefinitely with blank commands.

"Dammit," he said, trying to get short fingernails underneath it to pry the thing up. Eventually, Javier unplugged the keyboard and tossed it into the scrap box with a satisfactory clunk. The piece of junk had laggy keystroke recognition and impossibly spaced special characters. Hopefully, he could requisition something newer, quieter, *mechanical*. Oh yeah, that'd be the stuff.

He'd been deep in the annals of databases all day, trying to piece together the multitude of transactions aligning with Federov accounts. Most appeared with a set frequency, suggesting a long-standing payment for a regularly provided service. After nearly a week of trying to determine the pattern of where the transactions were originating, it finally occurred to Javier to look at the absence in the data. No transactions from Zhang-aligned accounts were ever present in these trans-actions, and traces of the Vasas were negligible. Could it be that they were the sole noncorrupt vampire houses in Shanghai? Surely not. But in that case, how else were they gaming the system so that they weren't dependent on Federov blood to supplement their city-allotted supply?

Another phenomenon he couldn't explain was that the payments from all sources had dwindled significantly in the previous months. Someone was making it difficult for the Federov operations to persist in Shanghai. *Who?* he wondered.

By the end of the day, Javier had amassed more questions than answers. After jotting down tallies of his discoveries in his notebook, Javier closed down all the open terminals. While at first he'd been moderately paranoid that his snooping would set off triggers for some other IT team, it seemed like he was the sole individual responsible for the oversight of those systems. Shanghai had apparently never had to deal with malicious attacks, ransomware, or even employee negligence. And maybe they hadn't, with the lack of electronics in the building. Secu-rity via hard access limitations—bold, but apparently effective enough.

Javier rubbed the weariness from his eyes as he packed his bag. He'd clocked in over fifty hours that week already, and it was only Thursday. Most had even been doing his actual job, saving the sleuthing for unpaid overtime, which in his mind, made his breach of access less morally objectionable. Arvind was effusively appreciative, in any case. In all honesty, being at the bank, staring at a screen, was the only time he could avoid the crushing feeling of failure for not helping Mina. As much as his brain tried to design a viable way to rescue her, even in his wildest fantasies, he fell short of doing anything but causing her more trouble. At least the work at the bank felt like it was accomplishing something. If he could expose Mikhail—expose the Zhang woman—for whatever unscrupulous deeds they were committing, maybe he could feel effective.

He left work and hopped on the metro to travel the few stations down to the Sanguis Institute. Eva had messaged that she had something important to show him, but she'd been cryptic about what. He could only hope that Eva or Vasa had made some headway in getting Mina out of that house.

For once, the guards at the medical office didn't give him any grief as he walked through the lobby and boarded the elevator. His hand rubbed at the frayed edge of his bag strap as the carriage glided to the upper floors.

When he reached Eva's office, two other lab-coated doctors buzzed around her conference table, the chrome-plated executive chairs all pushed to the side of the room. Racks of test tubes sat next to an intriguing contraption connected to what looked like an analog voltmeter. Very retro.

"Javier!" Eva beamed, a self-satisfied expression on her face. "I can't wait to show you what your notes have unlocked. Your hypothesis that vampire auras spike with blood consumption directly correlates with an impact on silver electrical components. We've built this device—an induction coil with fine gauge silver wire—that detects even trace amounts of blood consumption. Along with potency."

Eva rattled all that off without so much as a hello. Javier didn't know what to say. *Good for you? You're welcome?* He settled for a slight nod.

"We thought we'd arrange a demo for you. And don't worry, I added your name to the list of inventors on the patent application, since this all originated from your proof of concept."

Javier furrowed his brows. *What the hell is Eva rambling about?* He couldn't care less about his name on a patent for vampire medical devices.

"Um, cool?"

"Here, let me show you. We've determined the ideal amount of blood to cause a temporary effect that normalizes after only thirty seconds. Dr. Her will drink the first sample now at a fixed distance from the device."

One of Eva's doctors downed a vial of blood, and the needle on the analog meter jumped up. Javier couldn't help himself—he approached the equipment with a squint to read the tiny values along the arch. After peaking out and holding steady for a few seconds, the needle slowly went back down to a baseline reading.

"You see? Isn't this fantastic? You've sped up our initial measurements of blood potency by a hundredfold. And this isn't just a categorization or a qualitative measurement. It's a number that we can use for correlation with other test methods. Soon, I'll have enough pooled data that we can actually start working on an in vitro one—one that doesn't require a vampire. Of course, I'll need to get more samples from outside the hospital supplies to make sure we've captured the full population, and—"

Javier finally put a hand up, pausing his ecstatic sister. "Look, Eva, that's great and all, but I'm more concerned about what might have happened to the other researcher that helped with the breakthrough data. You know—Mina? The one who had this idea in the first place?"

Eva's look soured like Javier had broken her toy.

"I'm sorry, Javier. I haven't seen Miss Park, and my attempts to contact her have gone unanswered."

Javier's chin lowered as he processed this statement. Some attempt Eva had made, sending a note.

"In case I was unclear the other night, she was in worse shape than I was, and I—"

"Dr. Her, Dr. Gupta, would you excuse us for a moment?" Eva shot Javier a stern look as though he were literally airing dirty laundry in front of dinner guests. He gave her the courtesy of letting them shut the door before he exploded on her.

"What the hell is your problem, Eva? When I came here the other night, the main takeaway wasn't 'here's cool science.' It was 'Mina needs help!' Are you so blinded by your work that you can't even put it down for two seconds to help a fellow human being?"

Eva's eyes went wide with shock before narrowing in anger.

"Javier, your girlfriend is *not* a human being. She's a vampire. Their society operates on internal hierarchies and rules—ones that humans don't interfere with and live. But here's some good news for you: vampires are notoriously difficult to kill. Even though you undoubtedly pissed off Lady Zhang something fierce, Mina will live to bite another hapless boy at a party. Fear not."

Javier took a deep breath, trying to calm himself before he smashed her precious measurement device or something worse.

"How can you be such a... such a..."

"Such a bitch?" Eva said, anger clouding her own eyes. "Is that what you want to say? Since I left California, I've actually made something of myself. This work will change the way humans and vampires live together. It's revolutionary, and none of it would be here if it weren't for me. But because I didn't drop everything to assassinate my career for someone *you* got into trouble, you stand there and judge me?" Eva crowded into his space aggressively.

"I just asked you to help," Javier said bitterly. "What about your Lord Vasa, then? Did he try to help her? Or is he also exempt from giving a fuck about anyone but himself?" He gave a short, humorless laugh. "Based on what I've seen from others of his kind, maybe I should have tried offering him a blow job. What do you think? Is that how you landed this big office in—"

The slap landed smartly across his cheek, and Javier clenched his jaw as the sting dissipated. Eva's ferocious glare cut him down more than any physical blow ever could.

"Look, Effie, I didn't mean it like that."

"Fuck you."

Javier opened his mouth to apologize, but he shut it again with a resigned breath. There was no walking that one back. Nothing else to be gained here tonight. He'd managed to screw up his sister's happiness over her research success while making absolutely no progress on Mina. *Brilliant.*

"All right, Eva. I deserved that one. I'll just go."

Eva didn't stop him as he walked out of her office, only adding parting words: "I warned you about her, Javier. This was never going to end well."

HE SEETHED the entire walk to the metro. Sure, he'd said some uncalled-for things, but that didn't change the fact that Eva couldn't be bothered to do just one thing for him. He'd flown all the way here to find her, endured all kinds of vampire shenanigans in the process, let her unload her "magical" legacy BS, and here they were. Everything was so damn frustrating that he could just—

Javier threw a punch at a neon sign on springs on the sidewalk. It rattled his knuckles pretty good then got them even harder on the backswing. He contained the rest of his outbursts to muttered grumbling as he rubbed his knuckles on the ride back to his apartment. The metro car was empty that time of night, and Javier didn't know if he was glad for the quiet with his feelings or if the isolation only made him feel more alone and hopeless. God, he hated feeling like this. He was the one who fixed things, the one who showed up. Right now, incapable of either, he had nothing to do but pickle in his own self-resentment.

Back in his apartment, Javier pulled a cold takeaway container of congealed noodles out of the fridge. He pried some of the strands apart with a fork before taking a mushy bite. The wails of a screaming infant floated through his walls, completing the dining atmosphere.

On second thought, maybe he wasn't that hungry after all. He tossed the container onto the stove and got a glass of water instead.

His apple seedling sat proudly at the window, almost a foot in height already. The stem emerged from the shriveled apple vestige sunken to the bottom of the glass. Javier thought bitterly that, at the very least, he should get it some dirt and a pot. *Right? You're still capable of basic gardening, aren't you?*

Tomorrow. He would do that tomorrow.

He glared at his dad's notebook, sitting innocently on his coffee table. He'd read and reread every page for a week—could probably recite half of the passages by heart. Javier scoured the pages for anything that might help him with Mina, something that could unlock the superpower within him, the one Eva insisted was somehow his birthright.

Instead, he got vague recipes for "healing the ground" and "cleansing the home." He'd even procured the requisite earthen bowl, green candle, and salt for one of the spells. None of it seemed to do anything at all. It read like something between an experimental setup, holy scripture, and a fantasy novel—and the scientist within him screamed for him to stop pretending any of it was worthwhile.

Javier sat on the couch, the very spot Mina had sat only a few weeks earlier. "Give me something. Give me anything," he implored the book, placing his hand on the cover. It pulsed with warmth for him, like it so often did. *Great, more stress-induced phantom sensations.*

This was ridiculous. Not magic, just a way to feel spiritual. And that wasn't what he needed right now. He was accomplishing nothing, playing at being Merlin the Great while people needed his help—real people in real-world danger, not the kind that the jibber-jabber in this book could ever combat.

His thoughts floated to Mina once more. Being dragged away from him, leaving a trail of unctuous blood as she went. The vicious eyes of Lady Zhang as she held him, her hand closed around his throat. A white-hot rage flared within him. God, if she were here now, the things Javier would say to her. *Do* to her.

The acrid smell of smoke hit his nostrils a second before the fire alarm started blaring, not only in his apartment, but in the hallway as well.

"What the...?"

Light crackled in his kitchen, and Javier jumped up to find

a small inferno incinerating his container of noodles, the top disintegrated into a fiery mass of oily carbs. He grabbed a pot lid and slammed it over the flames, the hot air stinging his skin. His heart pounded wildly as he waited for the smoke to abate before lifting the lid. The flames were out on the blackened noodles and veggies, but a charred smell remained, saturating his apartment. Just wonderful.

How the hell had that happened? Had he turned the stove on...? Nope.

Javier swallowed as he turned back to the journal. There was no way he'd done this, that his anger toward the Zhang woman had translated into an actual physical fire. Vibe magic made even less sense than spellwork, and nothing in that book even mentioned fire.

People shouted in the hallway, evacuating the entire floor as Javier tossed the container into the sink and doused it with water. A loud banging on his door was accompanied by terse Mandarin that wasn't too difficult to interpret. The night just kept getting better.

His watery eyes tracked the smoke plumes curling against his ceiling. Was this the closest thing to magic he was ever going to get?

One building evacuation and two hours later, Javier reentered his apartment, carrying a slip with a hefty fine for starting a fire. He went straight to the apple seedling. It didn't matter that it was the middle of the night—he needed to *do* something he could control.

Together with a spoon and a glass of water, he marched with his small plant back out into the chill air of the Shanghai October. A wayward cricket chirped while a distant siren screamed into the night. Javier walked across the concrete courtyard to the edge of a park. Beyond the rows of uniform shrubs, a modest ring of ornamental plants held husks of spent blossoms. He pushed his way to the center, a small opening skyward that left just enough bare ground for a young tree.

He chipped at the compacted dirt with his spoon, but the handle bent under the force. Casting it aside, he used his fingers instead, clawing until the crust gave way to a loamy layer beneath the topsoil. Good. Javier worked the dirt with his fingers, turning it over in the hole before nestling the soggy bottom of his seedling into it and mounding the dirt around its stem.

"One day, I hope your roots will be strong enough to remember." Javier sat back on his heels, staring up to the starless sky. If nothing else, having dirt beneath his nails was clarifying. His father had planted every vine on their vineyard—planting a seedling was reconnecting with him just as much as reading any scribbled notes.

"If there is some magic in me," he whispered to the night, "don't let me burn the world down before I get a chance to understand it."

28

Mina tentatively padded downstairs the next evening, wondering which version of Lian she would get that night—the cold matriarch or the remorseful caretaker. Uncertainty knotted her stomach as she entered the dining room. While the same number of dishes as usual cluttered the table, only Lian sat on the far side with her usual newspaper and cup of tea. Mina lingered in the doorway, exhausted by the constant calculations of determining how and when her presence was acceptable in Lian's meticulously curated world.

She took Lian's lack of acknowledgment as a neutral sign to proceed and slipped to her usual chair at the round table. As she surveyed the glossy, steaming dishes of food and the full pitchers of blood, Mina kept her hands in her lap. Was she allowed? Was she even hungry? Despite whatever time she'd lost in the coffin, her appetite was unconcerned.

A newspaper rustled. A frown settled like a heavy yoke of judgment. Lian stood, and Mina tensed, keeping her eyes trained on her empty plate. As Lian made her languid approach, Mina held her breath, stilling herself like a creature being hunted.

A spoonful of vegetables landed on her plate, followed by a bowl of porridge with a baked egg. Lian poured blood into her glass before holding it before her. An offering. One she didn't want. One she had no choice but to accept.

"Thank you." Mina's fingers closed around the glass. She brought it to her lips and took a small sip, one that turned into a bigger gulp once her whetted palate remembered its requirements for sustenance.

Lian returned to her seat, satisfied.

"Where is Yuxi?" Mina asked, her tone even despite the whirring of worry in her head.

"Gone." Lian resumed her newspaper.

"Gone?" The spoonful of porridge was gummy in her mouth.

The woman snapped the newspaper together with a sigh, her ruby lips pursed. "Yes. She threatened the unity of this family. She conspired with a rival house and betrayed her sister. These are errors I cannot forgive."

A terrible premonition slackened Mina's fingers, and her spoon clattered to her plate as she lost her grip. "You killed her."

"No, you foolish girl. She has been banished from the city. Yuxi is still my fledgling, but she has no place in my home." Lian drained the rest of the tea from her cup, setting it in the saucer with a *clank*.

"Oh."

They had been sisters, entwined by shared circumstances.

That wasn't even the first time Yuxi had tried to kill her, yet Mina felt more remorseful than avenged at Yuxi's downfall.

"Finish your food and then get dressed. We have a meeting at the Sanguis Institute. A research update." The woman dabbed her mouth with a napkin before leaving the breakfast table without further comment.

A new kind of panic took root in Mina's stomach, unsettling the few bites of food she'd managed. During her time in the coffin, how much of the truth had Lian unturned? Did she know the extent of Mina's involvement with Javier? About the midnight research trysts? What exactly had Yuxi divulged before her exile?

Certain she was headed toward a summary execution, Mina dressed in somber office attire. With any luck, she would be able to throw herself in front of Lian's wrathful vengeance to save one or both of the Robles siblings.

THE EXPANSIVE CONFERENCE room was already surrounded by the most influential figures in Shanghai by the time they arrived: Lady Singh, Lord Temuroğlu, and even Lord Federov. Mina swallowed and stiffened her spine as the Russian vampire approached.

"Lady Zhang. Mina," he said with false warmth. Lian shook his hand, returning the danger-laced congeniality.

"On behalf of my family, I apologize for the liberties Mikhail took, and I assure you he'll be reflecting on his misdeeds in Siberia for the foreseeable future. Please let me know how we might reconcile after this unfortunate series of events."

Lord Federov addressed only Lian, sparing Mina a small pitying glance at the end of his spiel. A flare of irritation flickered in her chest as she took measure of the man's paunchy physique, his astringent cologne assaulting her nostrils.

"I'm glad you understand the gravity of the offense, Victor." Lian only smiled cooly. "In fact, I was hoping to stop by your office next week to discuss Zhang mineral rights in the Ural Mountains, presuming you're amenable."

Mina's face twisted into an open sneer at Lian capitalizing on Mikhail's transgressions to profit the family. Lord Federov looked equally irritated, but he gestured his assent and turned to leave with his business concluded, despite the arrears it left him in.

"Lord Federov," Mina called, her own voice a shock to her ears.

The Russian man turned with a look of perplexed annoyance.

"I hope Mikhail will carry scars of the burns for a long while," Mina said with a sweet smile, thinking of the patch of fresh skin on her own shoulder that tugged when she reached too far. "The next time I see that asshole, I will kill him. Do pass on the message."

Victor's eyes fluttered a confused blink before inclining his head to Lady Zhang. The woman's eyebrows flickered up in displeasure before she reached for Mina's wrist to shepherd her away.

Mina dodged, striding to the conference table and taking a seat before the flame in her chest sizzled out. She could feel the astonished ire in Lian's aura as the woman took a seat next to her. There would be words later on the topic of Mina's audacity, it promised. Mina didn't care. She wasn't ready to let the entirety of her suffering—of *Javier's* suffering—that night be reduced to renegotiated mining boundaries.

Dr. Robles entered the conference room with a squadron of doctors, each exchanging confident glances with one another as they distributed spiral-bound reports on their research. Mina opened her booklet and skimmed the text, the charts on blood potency drawing her attention. She traced the axes and the dual-curved trend line drawn overtop the histogram. If she was reading it correctly, the samples were now being reported in the thousands of donors.

Eva did it, she thought triumphantly. The electronics research had unlocked the measurement method she needed to get her benchmarks. A sentimental weight lifted from her chest. She hadn't begun to pay the price for her evenings with Javier, but knowing the risk they'd taken meant progress toward a better coexistence for vampires and humans was something positive salvaged from the wreckage, at least.

"Thank you all for gathering on such short notice—the recent progress made by the team warranted an update, which I am pleased to provide you with today." Eva smiled warmly from the front of the room with her hands clasped before her. "In short, we've achieved the first milestone of our research objectives: an in vitro test method for blood potency. Initial testing shows a potentially bimodal distribution of potencies among the population of Shanghai. The standard deviation on each of the Gaussian curves is quite large, however, with the most potent donors supplying nearly forty times the magical energy as the least potent donors." Eva looked proud and tired, like a new parent.

"Have you investigated the cause of this spread or the bimodality?" Lady Singh asked, hair bundled into a functional braid draped over one shoulder. She spun a black acrylic pen in her hand before jotting down notes in the margins of the report. "Are you suggesting specific environmental or natural factors that diverge into two distinct groups? Male and female, perhaps?" Mina tried to process the words, once again aware that her scientific vocabulary was limited amongst a crowd of intellectuals.

"The distinct peaks represent samples collected from the municipal supply and those from the hospital supply. We don't have enough data to suggest statistically significant populations —this is likely collection bias—but we will report our findings once we investigate the discrepancy. Determining factors that contribute to higher or lower potency is the entire motivation behind collecting this data, so perhaps this is our first clue to how it can be improved."

"Dr. Robles," Lian interjected, "have you considered the implications of releasing such incendiary and misleading numbers without an accompanying explanation or justification for your results?" The woman's arms were folded over her sage double-breasted blazer, the untouched research report still sitting on the table before her.

Eva's eyebrows flashed a degree of shock, but she recovered her composure quickly. "I'm not sure I understand your question, Lady Zhang. These preliminary results simply demonstrate the success of our testing method. We have no conclusions regarding causal variables for blood potency yet. A viable measurement system was essential to having enough data to—"

"I see," Lian said definitively, sending a chill through Mina. This wasn't a remark on Eva's work. This was the character assassination Mina had been waiting for. Lian let a dramatic pause hang in the air before continuing. "Dr. Robles, it is clear to me now that this research not only undermines the basis on which the blood donation system is predicated but furthermore includes rhetoric suggesting these so-called 'high potency' individuals are exceedingly rare. Disseminating this information would not only promote the collapse of the democratized blood donation system of the city, but additionally encourage our kind to acquire and hoard humans with higher-potency blood."

"Lady Zhang," Eva started, her tone incredulous yet placating, "surely you understand the stages in which the work is completed. These numbers will not be released externally."

"Of course they will," Lian snapped back. "Once a conspiracy like this takes root, it will fester and corrupt the city I have so strategically built. I cannot support this research any longer, and I would suggest the other investors consider carefully the ramifications of their continued support as well."

The tendons in Eva's neck pulled taut as she now openly glared at the woman publicly lambasting her work. The research was solid, and Lian was purposefully maligning the argument Eva was trying to present—that the facts so far suggested nothing besides having a way to measure this stuff, whatever it was. Judging from the murmurs and glances between the other vampires, as they sat back in their chairs, distancing themselves from the scientific information in the report, Lady Zhang's propaganda had landed.

"I admit I am surprised to hear you reverse course so suddenly on this work." Eva's gaze snapped to Mina's.

With a sickening fear of what she was about to say, Mina tried to imbue as much pathos into her eyes as she could. *Don't do this.*

"I assumed, since Miss Park's involvement in the development of the measurement method was so foundational—hers along with my brother's—that you saw the inherent value in gaining a deeper understanding of what sustains your kind."

All attention in the room focused on Mina, Lian's rolling toward her with carefully measured disdain. "Would you care to respond to that assertion, *pet?*"

Cold shame pooled in Mina's stomach at the impossible position Eva had put her in. She *couldn't* publicly refute Lian —that would only make the ordeal worse for everyone. With a last, regretful look, Mina closed the report before her. Scientific progress was no longer the objective. This was about survival now.

"Yes, it is true," Mina said calmly. "I was misled by the discourse of the early research proposal, which indicated the aim of this work was to understand and increase the donor potency as a whole. I now understand its dangerous potential for sowing division with the early numbers presented. I agree our support should be revoked, effective immediately. Dr. Robles's research implies a scarcity that doesn't exist. We have managed our population wisely and pooled the donated resources of this city to guarantee abundance in the blood supply for all. Lady Zhang is right. This research is not only a waste of time but a danger to the systems that sustain Shanghai as a whole."

The skin of Eva's neck had taken on a pink flush as she opened her mouth to respond. The other physicians in the room were equally aghast, comprehending the political reality their science had walked into. Lian held up a hand to silence her, smiling toward the other vampires in the room.

"My pet's ambitions so often exceed her intelligence and

discretion. Her influence in these matters will be limited in the future." Lian simpered. "I believe this meeting is over." She stood and walked out of the room, not waiting for Mina to follow. Slowly but surely, the other vampire benefactors stood as well, most looking discomfited by the machinations they recognized but didn't fully grasp. Yet none dared to go against Lian's edict to cease support for the work. Eva tried to individually entreat the departing vampires, but each rebuffed her kindly but resolutely.

Mina stood, intending to slip out with the rest of the crowd. That Dr. Robles's research had been derailed was unfortunate, but maybe she could revive the project under a different charter in a few years.

"Miss Park. A word." Eva grabbed her by the arm and wheeled her down the hallway to a private room, slamming the door behind her with a resounding echo. Mina could have resisted—likely should have—but part of her wanted to apologize, and the other part wanted to feel a proxy connection to Javier through Eva one last time. Afterward, she was unlikely to see either of them again.

"What the *hell* was that?" Eva spat.

"You put me in a position with no room to maneuver. What was I supposed to say?"

"You were supposed to tell the damn truth!" Eva shouted, taking Mina aback. "Look, you can play submissive pet in the bedroom all you like, but this is bigger than that. This is about the future of our species, and that woman is demolishing our chance at a better understanding—not to mention my life's work. I will not sit here and just take it."

Mina's pulse raced, her fangs itching in her gums. In this confined space, alone with a human, *she* was the apex predator.

Mina pressed forward into Eva's space, relishing the uptick in her heartbeat.

"You will, because if you don't, she will drive you from this city. If she doesn't just kill you outright. Lie low. Regroup. You'll survive this."

Mina forced her fangs to recede. She wasn't the monster here. Not today. With a last head shake, she turned to leave.

Straightening her lab coat, Eva called after her, "I have to know—are you aware of the fraud she's engineered in this city? The one she touts as democracy?"

"What?" Mina's voice was ice, her hand resting on the door knob.

Eva snorted. "That's almost sadder than if you had known. It makes sense now that I've put it together." The doctor's eyes traced the ceiling of the room. "We used the hospital's blood banks for initial testing, which are managed independently from the main supply chains. The lower measurements from the municipal blood banks aren't a fluke. She's diluting them. Christ, maybe she already has a way to measure and sort for more potent donors. That woman is unbelievable." Eva shook her head, shoving her hands in her pockets. "That's why she couldn't let this research go any further. It would uncover her scam."

Mina processed the information so deeply at odds with the principled woman she knew. When Lian spoke, it always came from a place of moral high ground, of believing the rest of the city, humans and vampires alike, weak of will and undeserving. Confronted with the likelihood that Lian was purposefully ousting vampires from the city she'd always considered her own, with a sinking realization, Mina knew it to be true.

"I would be careful who you share these theories with, Dr.

Robles," Mina warned. "I don't think I need to tell you how dangerous they could be if they landed on the wrong ears." Mina left the room and stormed through the office building.

Lian's manipulation of the city only validated Mina's lived reality—subtle commands, blurred boundaries, and a self reshaped so slowly that she couldn't remember where it had begun. It was time for Mina to start reclaiming the lost ground. It was time for someone to stand up to Lian.

THE CHAUFFEUR STOOD outside the car as Mina approached, opening the door for her expectantly. Lian sat on the far seat, glasses on, poring over the report provided in the meeting. Mina climbed into the back seat, and the car rocked gently as the door closed.

"You've embarrassed this house for the last time." Lian issued the proclamation sternly, not bothering to look up from her work. "From now on, the only time you leave the manor will be at my heel. Do you understand?"

Mina's nostrils flared, Eva's words ringing in her head— *"You can play submissive pet in the bedroom all you like."* Mina was done filling the role Lian had decided for her, that much was certain. She had spent so many years trying to get Lian to let her in, that when the leash slipped around her neck, she hadn't even noticed. In fact, Lian had made it feel like both an honor and a condition of belonging, and the implication of ownership had never even crossed Mina's mind until she was so thoroughly ensconced in this gilt cage that she had no way out.

Leaving Shanghai had been a sweet taste of freedom, but even as she prepared for the flight to Australia, Mina had known Lian was never going to let her go. Physical distance alone was not enough to break the bond between them; it required more mettle than that to split from the rotten core where a relationship had once been.

"You know the research is fine. You know the information is valid. The secret you're trying to suppress must be—"

"*Silence*," Lian bit out, slapping the report against her thigh as she pinned Mina with a fearsome gaze. "I will inform you when you have earned the privilege of using your voice again, pet."

The woman's reaction all but confirmed that ulterior motives were at play. The severity of the rebuke was meant to make Mina cower. She glared instead, wishing some clever rebuttal would come to her tongue. None did.

Lian frowned when she sensed Mina's defiance. "I thought I had relieved you of that recalcitrance by now. Perhaps a reminder of your place is in order."

The woman's words were as sharp as a dagger held against Mina's throat, daring her to lean forward. Suicide wasn't the point, though. Mina lowered her chin as her fingernails scrabbled at each other in her lap. What would it take to uncover Lian's plot? What would it take to free herself from this monster? It wouldn't happen through force alone. She would have to play into the woman's narcissism—her need to have the totality of her power reflected in those around her. Only then might Mina find the leverage to thwart her creator.

Satisfied her docile daughter was subdued, Lian returned to her report, scribbling annotations as she cross-referenced it with a secondary document. Mina dug at the skin of her cuticles until blood slicked her fingertips, and the coppery scent filled the car.

When they arrived home, Lian gave a curt "Follow me" as she exited the car. She marched up the stairs without looking back, sure her orders would be obeyed.

Clenching her jaw, Mina trailed the woman's footsteps to the second floor. Instead of going to her own suite or even Mina's room, Lian turned instead toward Yuxi's wing of the house. Or at least what used to be Yuxi's wing of the house. Mina followed, doing her best to not let creeping dread wear her down before she reached the actual trial.

Mina had never set foot inside the more spacious room Yuxi used as her own, and yet she had known there'd been a bed, a large vanity, and an even larger wardrobe. Now, the space was empty, devoid of even the belongings that designated it as Yuxi's. All that remained was a faint outline on the hardwood where a cream rug used to lie. A whiff of sweet plum perfume. Smudged paint where mirrors used to hang. Mina stepped into the room, coming to stand a few paces away from Lian. A severe expression adorned the woman's face as she surveyed Mina with her hands clasped behind her back.

Lian paced an unhurried circle around her charge as though taking measure of the discipline required. As the woman disappeared behind her, Mina could feel the specter of Lian's presence drifting over her consciousness. A shiver ran down her spine as a heavy hand settled on her shoulder. Fingers slipped to Mina's shirt collar, tugging it roughly into place. Hair was tucked behind her ear—not a gentle gesture but one of organization. Lian prodded Mina's chin up a centimeter with her knuckles, the woman's gaze never wavering from her project.

"Tell me what you see in this place."

Mina's eyes glanced around the barren room, fighting every instinct she had to pull away.

"I see emptiness."

"Very literal," Lian said with a sigh of disappointment. "What does the emptiness convey?"

Mina swallowed, sure a right answer didn't exist.

"Something that once had a place. Someone that is no longer here."

Lian inclined her head as though giving a concession to a well-intentioned but hopeless, pupil.

"When I look around this room, I see failure. For nearly a century, I have provided for Yuxi. Generously, as I do for all of my fledglings. She wanted for nothing. Had every comfort available. And yet..." Lian paused, a small, almost wistful smile tugging at her lips. "And yet I failed her." Lian continued to pace the perimeter of the room.

"Perhaps it was those very comforts that made Yuxi believe herself entitled to them, believe herself exempt from earning them. They fostered an independence that ultimately drove her from this family. These are things for which I take responsibility." Lian approached Mina once more, a seriousness having settled on her face. "I will not make the same mistakes with you."

Mina let her eyes drop to the woman's collarbone as she drew near, close enough that her imposing presence almost forced Mina back a step on its own.

"You will accompany me to Beijing tomorrow so that you might learn what acquiring these comforts entails. Don't bother packing—I will arrange your wardrobe."

Her declaration on the matter absolute, Lian moved around Mina toward the door, her heels rapping against the hardwood floor. The woman's assured control squeezed Mina's insides like a pressure cooker. She couldn't take it anymore.

"And if I refuse?" Mina said, fists vibrating tightly at her sides as she stared at the empty wall. Submitting to Lian at home was one thing, but performing it for others was another entirely. And Mina was certain that's what this trip would be— a showcase meant to make her feel small while reinforcing Lian's preeminence to those who needed the reminder.

An icy hand wrapped around her throat, and Mina froze. Lian purred in her ear, "Keep up this defiance, and I will make you forget what your voice ever sounded like." A thumb stroked Mina's windpipe—once, like a promise—then vanished.

As Lian's footfalls echoed their departure, Mina stood silently in the middle of the room, refusing to let her tears fall. The threat of the grotesque collar back at the forefront of her mind, Mina's resolve calcified. She would go to Beijing. She would continue pretending to be Lian's pet. She would bide her time until she could get away for good.

Vasa's offer to help her, should Lian truly become unbearable, was one she needed to consider. Mina didn't know whether he would truly be willing to stand up to his sister. It might be her only chance, knowing the dismal outcome of her solo escape attempt and the impossibly high risk of failing again.

Mina's shaky hand rubbed the unfettered skin of her neck. Whatever she did, she couldn't let the collar end up there.

29

Toward the end of his work shift, Javier received a distressed message from one of Eva's coworkers: the entirety of their research was being shut down, and Eva had retreated to her apartment, babbling about the meaning of life—or rather, the lack thereof. They suggested it might be best if Javier checked on her himself. While they were concerned for their boss's welfare, they all seemed somewhat afraid of her abnormal volatility. Apparently, she'd trashed two microscopes and one electron scanner before she was gently escorted from the building.

"Effie, open the door. It's me." Javier knocked insistently as the muffled sound of soulful fado music warbled into the hallway.

No answer.

"I will get the building manager if you make me." Javier pressed his ear to the door, listening for movements on the other side. When the door swung inward, he caught himself just before bashing into Eva.

"See? I'm fine. Now, leave me alone." Her untucked burgundy blouse matched the liquid in her smudged glass. Her eyes were red and puffy, her necklace clasp dangling against her sternum next to an obsidian pendant—that condor again.

Javier shoved aside the faded memory of the dinosaur bird who had squawked at him the night Eva disappeared. "Let's chat, hmm? You can tell me what happened, and I can make you some food."

Eva hiccupped, her eyes going watery. "There's nothing to talk about. It's all over now. All of it." She wandered away from the open door.

Javier took that as the most willing invitation he was probably going to receive and slipped in behind her.

As he shut the door, he scanned her apartment for carnage. Briefcase contents were spilled across her kitchen island, the documents stained with wine rings from the empty bottle that now rested on its side. The sleeve of a lab coat poked out from the lid of the trash can. Javier adjusted the volume dial to a reasonable level and shrugged out of his messenger bag, treading toward the kitchen to pull out something for her to eat. This much wine on an empty stomach was teenager-level arrogance.

"I'm a little confused, Eva. I thought you said your research was going well." Javier withdrew cold cuts from her fridge and unwrapped a loaf of bread, something quick to soak up the alcohol.

"Oh, yeah. Fantastically." Eva plopped into a white leather chair, the wine in her glass sloshing dangerously close to the rim. "So well, in fact, that I unwittingly uncovered Lady Zhang's scheme to starve out her rivals."

The mention of Mina's captor made his ears burn, but he

would save prodding Eva on that particular topic until she was more emotionally regulated. Eva had made it clear that Mina's well-being was decidedly secondary to her research progress. With that research under attack, it was doubtful Eva's self-pity had left room for the misery of others.

Eva drained the rest of her drink in three large swallows before letting the glass dangle precariously from slack fingers. "Open another bottle, will you?"

Javier raised an eyebrow, but a sloppy Eva was better than a belligerent Eva, which was certainly what she would become if he refused.

"Fine, you can have more sad-girl juice, but you're going to pair it with a sandwich," he said, setting the food on a plate alongside a glass of water.

Eva grumbled incoherently in return. Good, she was starting to mellow. Maybe she would cough up some actual details behind her theatrical wallowing.

"'Starve out her rivals,' huh? What exactly did you find? Is she dumping blood into Hangzhou Bay or something?" Javier pulled a bottle of an Argentinian red blend from an open cupboard and peeled the foil from the corked end. If nothing else, it might bait her to the meal on the counter.

"Ha, nope. That would be far too obvious for the illustrious Lady Zhang." Eva pushed herself off the chair and arced a wobbly line to the kitchen, where she rested her elbows on the granite and pushed her empty glass toward Javier. "She's meddled with the blood supply somehow, giving the other houses the crap blood while saving the good stuff for herself. I just wish I knew how she was doing it. She *must* have a magical way of telling the donors apart—one that Vasa doesn't know about."

Javier's hand stilled with the neck of the bottle poised above Eva's glass.

"Wait, are you serious? She tampered with the blood supply?"

Eva wiggled her glass expectantly. "That's what I said."

Javier set the bottle back down, the gears of his mind grinding through an unexpected mesh.

"Then the Federov black market... It's not just a cash grab. House Zhang thins the supply, but the demand stays the same. It was going to be filled one way or another. Jesus, Eva. How far were you able to trace this?"

Rolling her eyes, Eva snatched the bottle and filled the wineglass to an indecent halfway mark herself. At least she grabbed half of the sandwich too.

"She shut down my lab this afternoon. I only had time to verify the hunch with the few remaining samples of municipal blood on hand before Zhang security barged in and forcibly removed my entire team. I imagine they are destroying records as we speak, and there's nothing I can fucking do about it. And Vasa isn't even here!" Eva's body lurched with a hefty hiccup. "My work is over. My life is over."

Javier squinted at his miserable sister, half expecting her to upchuck right there in the kitchen. He felt for her, but she needed to get over this hang-up of tying her entire identity to lab work. Besides, if she got any more melodramatic, she would start rivaling their mother.

"You remade yourself once already. Do it again. Better yet —come home. This vampire city is bound to implode, hungry and politically fractured. You think it's going to go well for the humans trapped in the middle of warring clans of eternal overlords? Especially when the Zhang woman makes her move—

and it's gotta be soon now that she knows you are onto her—she'll impose total despotic rule over this city."

Eva snorted. "Pretty sure she's after the entire country at this point. But no, I'm not going back to California. Maybe my colleagues in Geneva or Barcelona have open research positions. Vampire physiology isn't a widespread field outside of Shanghai, but eventually it will need to be. They're not going away anytime soon."

"Eva, drop it!" Javier finally snapped. "You are a *human*. Be a *human* doctor. There are plenty of good places to practice in the US. Being around family would be good for you."

Eva glowered at him. "I told you. I'm not going back home. Not after—" Another hiccup, this one somber.

"You did not kill Dad, Eva. There is no such thing as magic. You needed a way to rationalize his death, and this is what your mind came up with. You had a spiritual connection with our heritage, and that's great, but that's as far as it went. You are pretty damn tenacious, but even you can't summon lightning bolts."

"Did you even look at that notebook?"

"Yes!"

"Then you're an idiot."

"Eva. We cannot do magic."

"Oh yeah?" Eva looked up, eyes suddenly clear with a challenge that sent shivers down to Javier's toes. She skirted the edge of the counter before settling in front of the glass of water. Eva closed her eyes, extending a hand over it. Her fingers twitched sporadically as she chanted under her breath. The language wasn't one Javier recognized.

Just as he was about to tell her to drop the act, he noticed a small but building opacity above the water. A cloud, white at first, faded to a dingy gray as it became laden with water. Javier squinted as he neared the glass, studying the roiling storm inside. Gathering static tugged at the hairs on his arms before a spark of lightning crackled its way down to the surface. Javier jerked back at the unexpected *pop*.

Eva dropped her hand, and the storm dissipated.

"Believe me now?"

"How did you—"

"The same way I killed Dad. I was always good with rain, but the droughts kept getting worse. I thought stronger magic was the answer. Building clouds is one thing, but controlling the lightning is near impossible. Dad tried to help contain the electrical storm, and it... it got him. That was my fault, and don't you dare tell me otherwise."

Javier stared at Eva, eyes wide. His brain churned to make sense of the spectacle he'd witnessed. A parlor trick, surely. Except he could find no logic for how she'd accomplished it... or for why she would want to trick him.

"Okay, say I believe you," he started hesitantly. "What does that even mean, that we have this capacity for magic?" Ever since the charred-noodle incident, Javier hadn't dared open the notebook again. He even tried to prevent himself from getting angry, fearing another fiery outburst. What if the next time it wasn't just leftovers that caught flame?

"It means whatever you want it to mean. None of it is the kind of magic from the fantasy books you read as a child, with wizards in Europe casting curses on each other. It's all earth magic, amplifying natural forces. Great for maintaining a vine-yard, assuming you don't accidentally kill someone. Not so great for anything else." Eva polished off her glass of wine, her eyes glazing over as she wandered back to her living room and flopped down on the couch.

Javier followed her, perching on the edge of a chair.

"You said you're good with rain... Do you know of anyone in our family who was good with fire?"

"No. Why?" She narrowed her eyes at him. "Are you making fun of me? Really fucking mature."

Javier heaved an exasperated sigh, feeling delusional for even bringing it up. Obviously, he couldn't just manifest fire. Later, he would figure out how Eva had performed her magic trick with the lightning bolts. In the meantime, he had a more pressing issue to consider.

"Eva, I think we should rescue your research."

His sister snorted. "Did you miss the part about Zhang guards locking down the building? I don't even know if they'll let me back in to work tomorrow."

"Please tell me you stored some of it on computers. The Sanguis Institute must perform regular backups, right?"

Eva's head lolled to the side.

"Wake up," Javier said sharply, reaching over to shake her arm.

"*What?*" She groaned.

"Do you have backup servers?"

"I don't know. Maybe?" Eva furrowed her brow. "Yeah, actually. It went down a few weeks ago. Huge pain."

"Great. Where are they?"

"No idea."

Javier's mind raced. Vampires didn't understand technology—even as they sought to destroy her records, the idea to wipe remote databases likely wouldn't occur to them until much later. If they could even figure out a way in. That gave him a chance. With her data, maybe they would have a shot at discrediting Lady Zhang once and for all. Maybe that could mean something for Mina and for the humans bleeding themselves dry to feed the vampires left hungry by the system that was supposed to nourish them.

"I'm going to go get your data." Javier stood with one last wary look at his sister. She would be fine. Hungover but fine. Out of pity, he pulled the blanket off the back of the couch and draped it over her—she didn't seem likely to make it to bed tonight.

"Leave it, Javier. Haven't you tangled with vampires enough to know it never works out? You're not being valiant, trying to rescue my work—you're being a moron."

"What happened to you, Eva?" Javier asked, his voice heavy with disgust. "We were raised by the same parents. Why won't you ever stand up for *people*? For what's right?"

"What do you think I was doing with my work?" she shot back at him, propping herself up on an uneasy elbow. "If we don't understand what sustains them, then we're fucked when starving vampires take to the streets to satisfy their hunger—*especially* with Lady Zhang cutting the blood that's already less potent than it once was. How is that not standing up for people? For our world?"

"What about the individuals in that world, though? Me? Mina? Our mother?"

"Enough with your fucking girlfriend." Eva flopped back down on the couch, her expression curdling. "She totally threw me under the bus today—arrogant, coddled princess that she is. She and Lady Zhang deserve each other. They really do. You never stood a chance, Javi."

Javier took a deep breath to prevent the verbal explosion

welling in his chest. How dare Eva make those assumptions—say those things. She was drunk, but he got the impression she would say the same thing sober. Christ, she could be a bitch sometimes.

"I'm going to get your research, and then I'm coming back, and then I'm getting you out of the city. *Then* I'm coming back for Mina."

"You're going to get yourself killed."

Maybe, Javier thought as he opened the door to her apartment. *But at least I'll die fighting for something.*

"Javier. Take my badge. It's on my coat," Eva said with slurred words. Her hand gestured vaguely toward the kitchen, where Javier once more noticed the white sleeve sticking out of the trash. He fished the clipped piece of plastic from the coat and wiped the tomato sauce from it before sticking it in his own pocket. As he was about to open his mouth for a departing statement—something undoubtedly wise and resonant—Javier noticed Eva was already gently snoring with her mouth open.

If this city could reduce his brilliant sister to this drooling mess, what chance did any of the rest of them have? Javier braced himself for the answer.

30

Mina's stomach lurched as the plane descended into Beijing. The lights of the sprawling metropolis stretched for dozens of kilometers in each direction below—a patchwork grid of modernity overlying the legacy of an empire. The flight had been a silent one. Since Lian's threat in Yuxi's room, their communication had devolved to short commands, which Mina obeyed either wordlessly or with a reverent "Yes, Lady Zhang." She was starting to feel like a toy with a broken mechanism, doomed to repeat the same tired phrase for the rest of her life. Mina reminded herself it was for show and not true submission. It couldn't be as long as she held onto that thought.

The plane came to a bumpy landing, and Mina covertly watched as Lian packed her briefcase with the pile of documents she'd annotated during the flight. Mina had spent the time staring at moonlit clouds. Even the small bag of personal items she'd packed had been taken from her. Lian meant to strip her of her agency—the same move she'd made after abducting Mina from Singapore. Mina refused to respond with frustrated anger this time. She would save her energy for when it would matter.

They arrived at the hotel shortly before dawn. The luxury establishment was lavish, with gold-accented imperial splendor. Lian strode through the lobby like she already owned the place, and every single person they encountered only vindicated that haughty attitude with their servile scraping. Mina kept her head down a cautious three paces behind Lian.

A palatial suite awaited them on the top floor. Despite the number of unnecessary rooms, only one contained a bed. Mina swallowed her fear, staking out which couch she might curl up on for the day as Lian issued sharp commands to the guard before the grand double doors shuttered both of them in. For the first time since leaving, Lian cast a glance Mina's way, almost as if disappointed she was still there. Mina kept her stance calm, her shoulders neutral, hands clasped before her.

"I will be attending meetings during the day. You will stay here and rest. I want you dressed for the evening by seven. Wear the black one in the wardrobe. Red lips. Hair up."

"Yes, Lady Zhang."

Lian left Mina alone in the room without another word. Her mouth dry, Mina went to the lacquered piece of furniture in the cavernous bedroom and pulled on the central gold tabs, releasing the magnetic clasp on the doors. Her fingers trailed over the lustrous row of hanging silk—formal yet sensuous garments. The kind that decorated a trophy.

Mina withdrew the hanger with the black brocade fabric. The qipao had an elegant standing collar with contrast piping and complex frog knots joining the fabric along the asymmetrical front seam. A turquoise phoenix took flight over the dangerously high slit of the left thigh, aiming for flower-laced branches on the opposite side. This wasn't a dress Mina would have chosen—this was a dress for a woman confident in her appearance. Someone like Yuxi. Mina hooked it back on the rod and shut the doors to the closet, trying not to let her thoughts run away with what the evening had in store. Probably just some corporate dinner where she should be seen and not heard. That, she could manage.

After splashing some water on her face, Mina slid under the edge of the thick duvet. Sunlight peeked in around the curtains, and she drew the covers over her head entirely. It didn't work. Lian had never specified her attire quite like this, and Mina worried over what it meant to the point of nausea. After ten minutes of empty retching, with nothing to offer the toilet but anxiety, Mina curled up on the couch. She drew the thin blanket up to her chin and pressed her face against the overstuffed accent pillow, her eyes finally drifting closed. When they opened, it was already well into the afternoon.

A long shower did nothing for her nerves but helped pass the time that stretched in the absence of direction. She applied the cosmetics that had already been laid out for her. Winged liner, strong brows, and the requested ruby lip. With her hair dried, she twisted it up into a single tidy bun, the only style she'd ever been able to accomplish on her own. The woman in the mirror looked polished. Docile. Almost peaceful. Mina looked away, refusing to let tears mess up the charcoal lines she'd finally gotten straight.

This *wasn't* submission—it was what she had to do to survive. The excuse felt hollower with each repetition.

She wiggled the black dress over her hips while avoiding her reflection in any of the gaudy mirrors. The bodice was fitted in a way that would strain when she sat. The only shoes were a patent leather platform—the kind that would require slow, measured steps to stay upright. Mina stepped into them and buckled the thin straps around her ankles.

The squeal of the opening door made her flinch, but Mina recovered her composure and stood straight for the forthcoming inspection. Maybe if she placated Lian, the evening wouldn't be as terrible as she'd imagined.

The woman strode over to her without acknowledgment. Lian considered Mina, gripping her chin and tilting her face left and right. Mina remained pliant and mute.

"Yes, I think he'll like you."

Ice plunged down Mina's spine, her worst fears realized. Her eyes flickered upward. Questioning. Hoping Lian wasn't serious. A smirk was her only response.

Lian slipped a hand inside her briefcase and drew out a slender box decorated in pale-blue rice paper and an intricate cyan knot.

"I shouldn't be rewarding you. And yet, when I saw this, I couldn't help but wonder how it would look."

The woman opened the lid, revealing a delicate wooden pick, the top adorned with a cluster of pale-pink flowers trailed by a cascade of teal gems and pearls. The intricate details of the petals and leaves mesmerized Mina, and without thinking, she raised a hand to touch it. As soon as she realized the audacity of the gesture, she let it drop to her side once more, along with a small head bow.

"It's all right, pet. You were meant to like it." Lian withdrew the ornament from its box and disappeared behind Mina.

The pick dug at her scalp as Lian threaded it into her thick hair, pulling the chignon even tighter.

"Lovely." Fingers ghosted down the nape of her neck.

When Mina turned her head, she could feel the motion of dangling gems. She hadn't expected a gift and hadn't expected to feel a tug at Lian's praise. Why did it still make her feel so treasured to be treated like a doll?

"Come along. We're already fashionably late."

Mina watched as Lian disappeared through the doorway, terrified of where following her would lead.

One foot in front of the other. That's all you need to focus on right now.

THE CAR CAME to a halt outside a traditional building, its facade splashed with vibrant red-and-gold paint. Resplendent flowing banners beckoned guests inside the Jade Teahouse. Lian exited the car efficiently in her black trousers, while Mina carefully slid her legs out, doing her best to limit the skin that the side slits exposed. Lian finally offered a hand to help her out, which Mina accepted gingerly, the woman's touch still electrifying.

"You're trembling," Lian noted, her sharp gaze unwavering.

Mina came up with no suitable response and settled for lowering her chin in apology, doing her best to calm the way her body seemed to hum with the tension of each breath. She couldn't stop thinking about the nebulous "him" Lian had referred to.

"You know I wouldn't put you in a position you couldn't handle, don't you?"

"Yes, Lady Zhang." The only correct response.

Lian's lips pressed together as she kept them standing there on the sidewalk. Pedestrians cut a wide berth around them as signposted by the bodyguards.

"I know you're having a difficult time with the limitations I've imposed on you, but I need you to be charming tonight. Show me I can trust you to have our family's best interest in mind. Show me the girl I met in Seattle, the one who would do anything to be mine." Lian's voice carried a nostalgic warmth as she cupped Mina's cheek with her hand, clouding Mina's mind with uncertainty. It was so easy to fall back into this beautiful trap, but now that Mina had felt its edges, she couldn't ignore the falseness of the illusion. She wasn't that girl anymore, and she didn't want to be. But Lian would never accept that.

"Yes, Lady Zhang," she acquiesced softly.

"Now, can you shed some of this melancholy? How about a smile?"

With extreme effort, Mina let her hands relax by her sides and forced a flicker of a grin.

"Good girl. You know this will only be as unpleasant as you let it."

Lian led them in through the front door into an emporium of entertainment. A large central room contained dozens of tables, each attended by an array of businessmen and the occasional businesswoman. Hostesses dazzled in costumes that matched the classical legacy of the architecture. Ribbons streamed behind them as they floated through the room in bright streaks of color, serving drinks from trays with generous smiles. A quartet of musicians played the erhu, gaohu, cello, and dizi, accompanying a single vocalist whose sonorous music wound through the backdrop of the lively conversations.

Lian blended in seamlessly as a member of the affluent

clientele, her dark suit in an angular cut with an elegant cream blouse underneath. Mina, however, fit neither with the staff in their costumes of dynasties past nor with the empowered group of individuals soliciting them. The waitresses kept cutting their eyes toward her attire in a questioning, leery sort of way that only heightened Mina's aberrant existence in this space.

They were escorted down a hallway, the carpet deadening the music of the main hall with each step. Mina jumped as a burst of laughter erupted from a closed door to her right, and Lian shot her a stern look. The hostess didn't stop until the very last room before inviting them through with a low bow.

"General Chu," Lian said with a reserved smile. "You remember my fledgling, don't you?"

Mina froze at the door, recalling the man in military garb from the night she'd decided to flee Zhang Manor. Tonight, his cheeks were already rosy from drink as he enjoyed the company of several young attendants. The pale-pink-and-yellow organza they wore only made Mina feel more severe in her stark black. A vampire among humans.

"Of course I remember." General Chu's eyes traced down the length of Mina's legs before coming to rest on her face, a lascivious look already in his eyes. As if on cue, the rest of the serving attendants vanished, leaving the three of them alone in the room. Lian unbuttoned her blazer and took the chair to the right of the general, gesturing for Mina to take a seat next to him on the far side of the couch.

This will be easier if you play along. Be the brooding sex object the world expects.

Her creator's possessiveness was one of the few traits Mina could rely on, and Mina was pretty sure Lian wouldn't offer her body to the man. At least, she hoped not. If all Mina had to do was be a testament to Lian's dominion for the night—docile, attractive, with an edge of danger—she could manage that. *No different than any other night,* she told herself.

Mina sank into the cushion next to the general. She could all but feel the arousal in his exhalation as he watched her.

"Shall I propose a toast?" Lian cut in. "To a successful day of opening meetings."

The general tore his eyes away from his prize. "Certainly, Lady Zhang," he said as if obliging her.

"Mina?" Lian raised an eyebrow as her eyes flicked down to the bottle of baijiu on the low table. Mina balked at the thought of serving the man. Lian was leaving no questions about the power dynamics in this room.

Mina shifted closer to the general to reach for the bottle and short-stemmed glasses on the central table. She recoiled at the smell of his stale breath but dutifully poured the clear liquor and distributed the beverages all the same. While Lian took hers perfunctorily, the general let his fingers linger on Mina's before she could pull them away. Her skin crawled with unease as she shifted to the edge of her cushion. That only encouraged him to spread his thighs wider, invading her space.

"To new alliances." Lian lifted her glass in toast.

Mina raised her glass briefly and took a pull of the strong alcohol. It burned a bitter trail down the back of her throat. Baijiu was a drink served to make a point, not to enjoy. Still, Mina was glad she wouldn't have to endure this ordeal sober.

"I am glad we were able to meet... informally this evening," Lian continued. "I know you have some remaining reservations about our kind and what we might offer. Perhaps a more intimate setting will allow you to experience that more fully." Lian finished her baijiu and returned the empty glass to the table. Mina refilled all three glasses without prompting.

"I admit I find your species fascinating, and I have been impressed by your policy proposals and funding schedules. There is something quite different about getting to see you up close, though."

The general brought his hand up to caress Mina's arm with the back of his fingers. Before they met her skin, Mina's hand closed around his wrist, holding it fast with inhuman strength. Maybe she could find a way to be charming while not letting this creep take advantage. She imbued a sultry suggestion into her voice as she asked, "Did I give you permission to touch me?"

"My apologies." The general licked his lips with lust. "Only I was overwhelmed by your beauty." Mina's eyes flicked to the gold of his wedding band and felt sorry for the woman tending his home.

"General, perhaps it might help to quell any remaining suspicions about our 'ravenous urges,' as you called them earlier, to witness the act of feeding firsthand. I assure you it can be quite pleasurable under the right circumstances."

The vein on the side of his neck pulsed wildly with excitement. "You would... I mean... is that...?"

"Not me. Mina."

Mina's eyes darted to Lian as images of a man in a tuxedo lying on the ground before her flashed through her mind. Her only other attempt at feeding directly from a human had been an utter fiasco. And yet even then, a part of her had *wanted* to taste him—couldn't bear the thought of not sinking her teeth into Javier's flesh. The thought of performing the same act on the man beside her was a thoroughly revolting contrast.

"My lady," Mina interjected. "Perhaps it might be better if someone more experienced demonstrated." She gave the general a placating smile—he was the one she needed to convince that this was a truly bad idea. "I'm only a fledgling. The risk of an accident..."

"If the girl is nervous, perhaps—"

"Nonsense. I have been raising fledglings for centuries, and I assure you Mina is entirely under my control. Nothing will happen that you do not enjoy."

The general equivocated, fondling the glass between his hands as he struggled with his curiosity, desire, and instincts.

"Lady Zhang, I'm not sure—"

"Let me prove it, then." Lian pinned Mina with her gaze, a hard edge to her mouth. "Mina, come."

Mina bowed her head, anger flaring in her chest. It was one thing to be Lian's pet in private. This public charade—in front of a human, no less—was a paramount humiliation. And Lian knew it. And that was the entire point of the exercise. To not only dangle the allure of her daughter, but to show Lian as a supreme empress among her kind.

Begrudgingly, Mina rose and tottered a few uneven steps to Lian's side.

"Kneel."

An embarrassed flush rose to her face as she sank to her knees on the plush carpet. She glared up at the woman with hatred while General Chu leaned forward on the edge of his seat, enraptured by the performance unfurling before him.

Lady Zhang made a slow show of unbuttoning her cuff, letting the anticipation grow to suffocating oppression as Mina waited, no longer able to lie to herself that this was anything but submission of the deepest order. Submission under duress but submission nonetheless.

"Show General Chu how gentle you can be, pet." Lian draped her wrist over the edge of the chair, angling so that the general would have an unobstructed view of the proceedings.

Brimming with loathing, Mina let her fangs descend to their full length. The general gave a sharp inhale as Mina brought her lips to Lian's wrist, setting the points of her teeth above their mark. Mina pierced the pale skin with a delicate pressure. The ancient power of Lian's blood coated her tongue like syrup, sweet and dense, even stronger than the baijiu.

After a few swallows, Lian twitched her wrist almost imperceptibly—Mina's signal to withdraw. She sat back on her heels, wiping her mouth with the back of her wrist, disgusted with herself for participating.

Lian's wounds knit back together, vanishing in a matter of seconds. "You see, General? Nothing to fear from this tame creature."

Mina's fingernails dug into the fleshy part of her palms, enmity welling in the pit of her stomach.

"Will it leave a mark?" the general asked tentatively.

"No. No one will ever know."

The general licked his lips.

"Could she..." He glanced down at his bouncing thigh. "Could it be on the neck?"

Lian's smile was wicked with triumph. "That can be arranged. Mina? Care to join us?" Lian asked as though Mina had a choice, relocating herself to the cushion beside General Chu. Sensual hands encouraged the man's shoulders to relax into the couch before slipping his tie from its knot. Lian undid the top two buttons of his shirt with leisurely assurance.

Mina didn't move, frozen in her spot. *I can't go through with this. I can't do this again to another—*

"Don't be nervous, child. I will help you." Lian's voice had acquired a severe edge not to be ignored.

It roused Mina from the carpet, her limbs operating on autopilot as her head buzzed with denial. She sat on the couch, her palms clammy against her thighs.

"I never imagined it would be this... civil," the general stated as though tickled by his own revelation.

Lian smiled, an edge of irritation to her expression that only Mina would catch. "Indeed. Our house prides itself on propriety and traditional values. Isn't that right, daughter?"

"Yes, Lady Zhang."

"Remarkable," the general said, openly wondering at Mina as though she were a specimen to catalog.

"Just here, I think." Lian tapped a spot a centimeter below the rapidly pulsating jugular. The tented bulge forming in the front of the man's slacks made it impossible to ignore the grotesque nature of the act she was unwillingly performing. Mina closed her eyes and leaned in despite herself. If she refused—if she compromised the Beijing deal again—the consequences would be extreme.

Heat rose from the general's neck, and with it wafted the smell of perspiration beneath his deodorant. She opened her mouth and set the top of her fangs against skin loose with age. Her tongue met the salty surface, bitter with his aftershave. Mina gagged once before she felt Lian's hand at the back of her head, holding her in place.

Just get this over with, and then you can leave.

Mina bit down in one solid action. The man gasped, his body twitching beneath her as his hand came up to grip her waist. The monster within her caught his wrist and rose to pin him against the couch as she drank deeply. His blood was thin, watery, and laced with the barest hint of alcohol. It made Mina's stomach churn as it spurted hot and fast into her mouth. Faster than she could keep up with. Blood ran down her chin and stained the white of the general's shirt, and yet she couldn't stop.

"That's enough, Mina," Lian's voice cut through the rapture as sharp nails dug into the back of her neck.

Coming back to her senses, Mina pulled away, a perverse confusion muddling her thoughts. Why had part of her enjoyed that? The general's face was pale but relaxed with a euphoric grin. At least she'd performed her role well. The thought brought acid to the back of her throat, and Mina scrambled off the couch.

"Excuse me a moment," she managed as she raced to the private bathroom. As soon as the door was shut, she dropped to her knees before the toilet and vomited violently, fresh blood staining the inside of the white porcelain bowl. Mina's trembling hand found the lever to flush the toilet, and she continued retching until her stomach had completely emptied its contents.

Shakily, she stood and went to the sink to rinse out her mouth. Mina sniffed her tears down as she dabbed at the smears of blood on her face and chin. The sight of the diminished, fearful expression reflected in the mirror haunted her. A wave of bone-deep exhaustion hit her, and she braced herself against the counter. When had this become her life? Reduced to a circus act to gain favors for Lian's political agenda.

Mina tossed the towel into the basin and took a deep breath. "I'm not doing this anymore," she spoke aloud. It was a promise. A promise she would likely break. A promise she would cling to anyway.

When she returned to the main room, the general was nowhere in sight. Lian leapt from her chair, beaming as she approached Mina.

"You were absolutely marvelous, my love." Lian placed an ardent kiss on her forehead, and Mina bit down hard on the inside of her cheek. "He was absolutely besotted with you." Lian heaved a self-satisfied sigh as she tilted Mina's head up. "Mmm, you missed a spot." The woman trailed her tongue along Mina's jawline.

Mina shoved her away without thinking but immediately shrank as Lian's demeanor shifted to subdued outrage.

"Please don't make me do that again," Mina whispered as Lian drew herself to her full height.

"Whyever not? I gave you an opportunity to be a cultural ambassador for our species and a benefit to our house. You should be *thanking me*."

Mina's breath stuck in her throat. Lian was too close, too dangerous to fight.

"Just let me go back to the hotel. I feel sick," she said, her voice wavering and weak.

"You will go nowhere. The night is young, and this is one of the finest establishments for entertainment in Beijing. You may have had your meal, but *I'm* still hungry."

Mina shivered.

"Enjoy yourself, but I'm not—"

A sharp slap snapped her head to the side, quick and corrective. Water collected in Mina's eyes as the sting abated. She glared at the clawed foot of a chair, trying desperately not to come apart.

"You know how I feel about those tears. Go ahead—let them fall." Lian traced a finger down Mina's hot face.

She ducked away, blinking fiercely to prevent the moisture from beading. Mina could withhold that singular satisfaction from Lian, if nothing else.

"No?" Lian snorted. "We'll see if we can't change that before the night is over."

31

dainty knock sounded from the main door, drawing Lian's attention after a final menacing glare in Mina's direction.

"Enter."

A woman burst through the door, carrying a tray, her effervescent grin beaming. Her gauzy outfit was in shades of pale greens and buttercup yellows, the fabric iridescent and ethereal.

"Lady Zhang! It's been so long since your last visit I was starting to think you found a different teahouse." The woman dipped into a graceful curtsy before setting the tray down. The bottle atop it contained an apricot-colored liquor, its label embellished with a string of ink-drawn blossoms.

"My precious Peach. You never fail to brighten my night," Lian murmured, cupping the woman's face with her hand. The same one that had slapped Mina only a moment before.

Resentment burned within her chest as she watched "Peach" shamelessly nuzzle into the affection.

"This simple girl is undeserving of my lady's flattery,"

Peach said, a mischievous smile on her smooth, round face. She was young, maybe not even twenty. "But I hope you don't mind that I enjoy it, nonetheless."

Lian's gaze snapped over to Mina.

"If you're just going to stand there, you might as well serve. I see you've brought your own refreshments, Peach."

Mina's face twisted into a scowl as Peach cast her a pitying gaze.

"Osmanthus wine is more attuned to my delicate palate." Peach's voice walked the jagged line between humility and flirtatiousness with expert aplomb, perfectly fitting the mold of Lian's ideal companion. Her skirts billowed around her as she took a seat in the chair previously occupied by Lian. Peach was effortless, and Mina hated her for it as she went to the table numbly, demoted to simple serving staff.

"Which would you prefer, my lady?" she asked, her voice hoarse from lingering stomach acid.

"Lady Zhang wouldn't dare drink something as feminine as osmanthus wine," Peach said with a tinkling giggle hidden behind her wide sleeve. Lian lavished a warm smile on her preferred daughter as Mina poured two glasses of the baijiu and one of the orange syrup. She didn't wait for a toast before downing her own and taking a seat opposite Peach, the baijiu burning as it puddled in her empty stomach. Mina poured another for herself and repeated the tipple.

If she had to wait out this disgusting display, she would endure it. At least her own performance was over even if she was still dressed in this costume, which seemed to grow tighter by the minute. The tapered points of the shoes pinched, and the hairpin tugged at her scalp. Beauty in discomfort was the sincerest of any, Lian had lectured her in their early days of navigating the dress codes of Shanghai. Mina had never disagreed more than right now.

"How long will your business keep you in Beijing this time?" Peach inquired.

"Only until the end of the week if things go according to plan. So far, it looks promising." Lian leaned back into the cushion of the couch, letting her rigid posture soften ever so slightly.

"It's only a matter of time before this city succumbs to your charisma." Peach set her nearly full glass back on the table and clapped her hands together excitedly. "What are you in the mood for tonight? I have been rehearsing a new dance, but I'll only show it to you if you promise not to correct my mistakes. Or I would love to sing one of your favorites." Peach glanced at Mina as if troubled by an afterthought. "Does she play any instruments? Yuxi's accompaniment was always so serene."

"No," Lian drawled, casting a scowl in Mina's direction. "In fact, this one doesn't possess much talent at all."

Mina opened her mouth to argue but shut it once she realized the futility. Tears prickled at her eyes once more, and she looked down at the phoenix embroidery on her dress to avoid letting it show. The bird only mocked her, a symbol of the regality she failed to measure up to.

"I just had an inspired idea," Peach said, her eyes growing wide with amusement. "What if I taught her a dance? Something simple, of course. Would that be okay with you, older sister? May I call you that?"

Mina choked on her sip of baijiu and opened her mouth to reply that in no way would she respond to that form of address, but Lian interjected.

"That sounds quite entertaining indeed. Very well. Let's see if you can turn her into something worth watching."

Mina's cheeks grew warm with the degrading prospect of being taught a dance by Peach. She'd already played her part, and now she just wanted to go home. What had she done to deserve this continued cruelty?

"You won't be disappointed!" Peach topped off Lian's glass before standing in the open space before the table. "Older sister, won't you join me?"

"My lady..." Mina started.

"Don't."

After downing the rest of her baijiu and thudding the empty glass back down on the table, Mina stood by her new younger sister, thoroughly dreading this dance lesson.

"Okay, so you start by placing your hands by your face like this, and then when the music starts—don't worry, we'll have a musician—you spin around and kneel down like this."

Peach performed a deft series of movements that had Mina lost after the very first pose. None of it was anything she could successfully accomplish.

"Hmm," Peach pondered from her kneeling position. "For the quality of the movement to really shine, you'll need a different dress. And shoes." After a short sigh, she spun to face Lady Zhang, clasping her hands in front of her chest. "Oh please, my lady, can I take her to our wardrobe mistress to find something more suitable? It would be so wonderful to have a sister to dance with."

Lian smiled at Mina, open amusement on her lips. "Yes, you may. She's looking a bit disheveled, at any rate."

Peach joined her hands in front of herself, dipping her head behind her sleeves in an exceptionally formal Chinese bow. "Your ladyship honors me."

Mina simply stood there, weary and disillusioned that she could ever live up to the version of the daughter that Lian clearly preferred—bright, obedient, and untainted by rebellious thoughts.

Not half a second later, Peach popped up from the floor, grabbed Mina's hand, and tugged her toward the door. "There's a midnight-blue gown I know will look absolutely lovely with her complexion."

Beleaguered, Mina allowed herself to be drawn from the room. At least it was time away from the woman intent on her destruction. Maybe when she got back, Lian would tire of this charade and let her return to the hotel. Mina could hope, in any case.

As soon as they exited the room, Mina jerked her hand away from Peach's.

"What the hell do you think you're doing?" she growled, fangs flashing.

Peach dropped her charming grace as she turned to Mina. "I'm doing my job." Her voice was a half octave lower than in front of Lian, tinted with a harder Beijing accent. "Which you've made impossible with your negative energy. I don't know what you did to piss her off so much, but I needed to get you out of there so I can fix the damage. Now, follow me."

Mina came around her with a flash of supernatural speed, bringing out her best intimidating-vampire impersonation. "Do you even know who I am?" she growled.

Peach sighed, her hand on her hip. There was that damnable pitying look again. "Yes, I know who you are. Do you know how many hours I've listened to her complain about your disappointments? Look, I don't envy your position, but... let's just get through this together, okay?"

The second Mina's terse expression wavered, Peach brushed past her, bustling off down the corridor. Mina glowered for a second longer before tromping off after her. Between the choice of being alone with Lian or playing dress-up with Peach, the second sounded like the better option.

The younger woman led her into the sterile service corridor. The mood lighting of the guest area gave way to harsh overhead illumination in the functional space, a maze complete with a disorienting stream of people carrying trays and instruments. Mina got only the occasional odd glance as she tried not to lose Peach in the chaos.

"Auntie! I need your help," Peach whined as she pushed into a room bursting with costume racks. Auntie was on a small stool with her legs spread wide, fixing a torn hem on the dress of the woman standing before her. Her hair was mottled with gray, and her knobby fingers pulled thread through fabric with impressive steadiness. "Please tell me the navy gown is here." Peach started digging through the racks of vibrant cloth with hasty hands.

"Aya! You know not to touch those. And who is this?" The woman side-eyed Mina. "Why is she dressed like a cheap prostitute?"

Mina's face burned with embarrassment as Peach shrugged.

"I didn't choose this," Mina stated, hands clenched beside her. Whatever sultry appeal the onyx qipao once held was now thoroughly spoiled by the truth laid bare of how Lian had dressed her.

"Good. Then you won't have an issue taking it off."

Mina blinked. "Right here?"

The costume mistress cut the thread on her mending and shooed the other girl away. Meanwhile, Peach held up a hanger with a triumphant "Ha! I knew it was in here."

Auntie tossed her scissors into a small basket overflowing with vibrant spools and stood from her stool, massaging her lower back. "Trust me, honey, we've seen it all before."

"Thank you, āyí! I need to go—Lady Zhang is in a *mood*." Peach handed the hanger to the older woman and bustled past Mina. "Give me at least ten minutes to calm her down before you come back. And maybe try to perk up a bit? This will be easier for both of us if you do. I need this job... so, yeah. All right."

Peach's earnestness deflated whatever righteous indignation Mina had mustered. She wasn't Mina's enemy—just a young woman trying to get through a shift. Hell, maybe she would even temper Lian or, at the very least, give her something different to fixate her attentions on. Mina gave a small nod as she started undoing the closures at her collar.

"Thank you!" Peach's bubbly voice trailed off as the metallic door clicked shut behind her.

Auntie clucked her tongue as she inspected the taffeta gown. "The beading needs some repair, so be gentle with her." Crystalline beadwork down the front of the gown glimmered like sapphires against a midnight sky. The loose skirt hung from a strapless bodice, covered with intricate, swirling embroidery. Mina wasn't an expert in historical fashion but wagered it was more an approximation prioritizing glamour over historical accuracy, although a stunning creation in its own right.

As soon as Mina had her original dress off, the woman was already throwing the fabric of the next garment over her head. Mina wriggled free when the gathers caught on the hairpin, irritated that the woman had risked its damage in her haste. Suddenly, tears pricked at her eyes once more as a zipper was done up at her side. Mina raised her hand to blot at them, but auntie swatted it away.

"You'll mess up your makeup. Here." She withdrew a handkerchief from the sleeve of her cardigan and lifted it to Mina's face. "Aya," she said grimly, noticing whatever mark Lian had left with her earlier reprimand. As Mina sniffled and looked away, auntie pressed the soft cotton corner to her waterline. "Nothing lasts forever, dear. Just take it one day at a time."

She was clearly unfamiliar with the nature of vampirism, but the kindness was touching nonetheless.

A gauzy shawl was slipped over Mina's shoulders before the woman tied an honorary ribbon around her hair. Catching sight of her reflection, Mina had to admit it was an improvement over the previous outfit. Her pale skin created the impression of stark beauty. Red lipstick had faded to a muted pink. Even the loose tendrils of hair framing her face somehow now worked.

Maybe she'll like this version of you more.

"I should be getting back. Thank you."

Before auntie could respond, a pair of girls burst into the room, talking in a dialect Mina didn't even recognize. One woman cradled a sleeve that had been splashed with an orange sauce, and the room was already moving onto the next wardrobe debacle as Mina stepped into a pair of silk slippers and disappeared from the room.

MINA WALKED SLOWLY on her way back, stopping to ask for directions a few times. Now that she properly looked the part of the service staff, her navigation of the place came more easily. Even if she was bumped out of the way or herded away from customers, the anonymity of the costume was a comfort. Part of her wished she could simply slip into a different room to entertain a different guest here tonight. *Alas, you have no talents. Now, stop dawdling.*

When Mina pushed her way back into Lian's room, her expression instantly darkened. Lian had shed her blazer and stood behind Peach with an arm wrapped around her chest. Peach smiled at her own reflection in the mirror as she caressed a pair of pendant earrings, the teardrop diamonds absurdly large. That gift made a mockery of the hairpin Mina had been given earlier. Likely, that was the point.

A large assortment of fussy food, a full tea service, and a vase of peonies had displaced the drinks from earlier, but the bottle still stood on a buffet to the side. Mina helped herself to some osmanthus wine—at least it gave her something to do while she was being ignored.

"You are too generous, Lady Zhang!" Peach giggled before placing a tender kiss on Lian's jawline. Mina turned away, gripping her glass a little too tightly.

"Mmm, I enjoy rewarding those who earn the recognition." Lian's voice was silken with desire, and Peach half shrieked and half giggled at whatever attention was lavished on her next.

"Not before I've shown you my dance!" she objected lightly. "Besides, you haven't had a chance to admire elder sister's new dress. Isn't she stunning?"

Mina looked up in time to catch Lian's cool appraisal.

"A bit Tang dynasty for my taste. The color does suit her, though."

Mina forced herself to put a smile on her lips though she couldn't bear to look at Lian again. It was so abundantly clear she was unwanted that it was difficult to breathe.

Suddenly, Peach was at her side, grabbing her hand and dragging her back to the front of the room. The small squeeze in her grip reassured Mina only slightly. This was still going to be a disaster, regardless of Peach's optimism.

"Yay, all right. So, let me show you the beginning of the dance once more, and we'll tack on a few eight counts from there."

For the next half hour, Peach drilled Mina. While the general footwork and arms weren't too difficult on their own, coordinating them together was a chore. Lian's comments about her finger position and head alignment weren't making it easier.

"Can't you see how poised Peach is when she spins? You must float." Mina tried not to let it fluster her, but by the time they finally set the mangled choreography to music, it was painfully obvious how far Mina's performance lagged behind Peach's both in tempo and skill.

With a sigh, Lian refilled her teacup. "While your patience has been commendable, Peach, I can think of better things for us to be doing than watching Mina flail, two beats behind. And

Mina? Perhaps it's best if you practice stillness before attempting movement again."

Mina shrank under the rebuke. Why had she let Peach embarrass her like this? Why hadn't she just gone back to the hotel when she'd been out of the room? She would not have been missed.

As Mina started to slink away, Lian snapped her fingers and pointed at a spot on the hardwood floor. "I was quite serious. Come here, pet." The icy amusement in her voice felt like a death knell.

Mina walked to the indicated position and, at an inclination of Lian's head, understood what was meant by the nonverbal command with an impossible sense of shame. Stiffly, Mina dropped to her knees, the midnight silk taffeta puddling around her, the costume only feeling more farcical.

"Come, now. Up on those knees. This is active practice, not an excuse to relax." Lian approached, teacup in hand.

Mina shifted, lifting herself off her heels. The gown's beading dug into her kneecaps like gravel.

"Long, graceful neck—yes, that's a good girl." She lifted Mina's chin, coaxing it higher, until her spine was achingly elongated. Then came the weight, settling like a crown of porcelain.

Mina stilled. Acrid disbelief rose in her throat. The teacup wobbled.

She froze, drawing only the smallest pulses of air, terrified of tipping it.

"Much better," Lian murmured. "You are exactly as you should be. Beautiful. Silent. Still."

Peach cast her a sympathetic look before her performer's mask was back in place.

"Lady Zhang, you must try these cakes. I had them flown in from Paris just for you." Peach popped one of the morsels into her mouth with a flirtatious smile.

Lian went to her and let Peach feed her a bite of cake before pulling the younger woman into her lap on the couch.

"You know you've only managed to whet my appetite," she said, licking her lips.

Peach simpered, unbuttoning Lian's blouse as the woman lavished kisses on her neck.

And just like that, Mina was abandoned. Spectator to a fantasy she'd never been able to make materialize—Lian's warmth and praise going instead to a different woman. Mina focused on her breathing and on the patterns in the carpet. Anything to distract from the abject erasure she was living.

Her attention was dragged back by a gasp from the courtesan as Lian struck her fangs into the soft tissue of her neck, too quickly to be enjoyable—a predator finally claiming her prize. Peach moaned, the erotic intonation laced with a hint of pain as her fingers clung to Lian's shoulder. Lian growled in response, continuing to drink.

Mina choked down the possessive jealousy that bubbled up. Once, she had been the girl Lian chose to drink from. Yuxi had warned her that Lian kept other playthings, but confrontation with the intimacy stung deeply all the same. After several minutes, Lian finally withdrew, leaving the younger woman a paler, more compliant version of the vivacious original.

"You were hungry tonight," she remarked, letting her head rest in the crook of Lian's neck while Lian stroked her hair.

"My precious Peach, you are simply too delectable."

Peach placed tired kisses along Lian's shoulder, shoving the woman's shirt down and revealing the sloping lines of Lady Zhang's tattoos.

"Let me see your beautiful artwork, won't you?"

Lian shrugged the rest of the way out of her blouse, leaving only the silk camisole underneath. The lithe lines of the woman's form were on full display. Locks of short hair fell across her full cheeks, her face flush from a fresh feeding.

"Happy?"

"You're always so secretive, but these painted brushstrokes tell a story. Like this one"—Peach trailed her hand over Lady Zhang's spine—"the White Tiger. Or this one." Her hand trailed to Lian's shoulder. "It's older. The lines are denser than your others. Perhaps a wilted—"

Peach gasped as Lian pinned her against the cushions.

"Don't mistake my affection for an invitation to presume."

For the first time that evening, Peach became flustered. Her face reddened ferociously as she backpedaled. "Please forgive this simple girl's insolence. It was a silly comment—one I had no place making."

"Hmm." Lian smiled languidly, letting the menace linger for several taut seconds before releasing Peach and relaxing back into the couch. "Then again, perhaps you've earned a story." She gave an exaggerated sigh. "I must be feeling indulgent tonight. Refill my glass, and I'll tell you."

"I am honored by my lady's mercy," Peach said with a meek bow as she went to the buffet to retrieve a glass, a slight wobble to her gait.

"This tattoo was my first, in fact," Lian started, a contemplative expression settling on her face. "I was a young human at the time—ambition my only concern in a court of dragons and snakes. It took an unyielding decade of diligence to rise to the rank of noble consort. The Ming dynasty was a time of both wretched squalor and unimaginable splendor. I managed the unprecedented privilege of climbing from one end of that spectrum to the other, perhaps embodying the proverbial lotus itself." She accepted the fresh glass of baijiu from Peach without acknowledgment, and the younger woman sank to a humble posture at her feet.

"But it wasn't enough to be near the top—I wanted to *be* the pinnacle. The emperor was an insipid man. Useless in court and even duller in bed. The empress, on the other hand..." Lian's fingers caressed the rim of her glass. "She was radiant, her unmatched beauty completely wasted on that lazy Mongol half-breed." Lian's chest fell with a wistful sigh. "It took months of subtle persuasion before the first stolen kiss in the gardens. Twice as long before I bedded her."

Lian glanced over at Mina, tilting her head as she sipped from the dainty glass. Mina kept her breathing even, her gaze level. Faltering wasn't an option.

"In hindsight, the throne room might not have been the most discreet location to consummate our affair," Lian said with a small chuckle. "But the shocked look on that pompous bastard's face, swaddled in his imperial yellow, when he found me with the empress bent over his heavens-ordained chair... That was worth the damned consequences." Lian shook her head with a smile. "I was brazen in those days, if nothing else. This tattoo preceded my exile—the wilted lotus. It was by the empress's good grace that it didn't end up on my face."

"Did you love her?" Peach rested her head on Lian's thigh.

"I find the concept of love trivializes most relationships, don't you?" She smoothed the sleeve of Peach's gown.

"That's such a thoughtful reflection, my lady."

"I did care for her, as I believe she did me. Of course she would have after I showed her what those relationships could *feel* like." Lian licked the edge of one pointed canine. "Tell me, Peach, would you like me to show you what I did to the empress that day?"

Peach met Lian's gaze with a shuddering breath, the perfect picture of barely restrained wanton lust. From Mina's vantage point, however, she caught the way Peach's fist tightened against her gown, looking more like apprehension than anticipation.

"I wouldn't dare refuse an offer as generous as that."

Lian set down her glass. She put her hands on her thighs and stood, never breaking eye contact with the entranced Peach. She went to the chair—the one directly across from Mina.

Knowing full well what Lian intended, Mina still prayed: *Please don't make me watch this.* Her eyes shut for half a second before a wobble from the teacup roused them once more. Reduced to balance, aching knees, and a tortured heart as she watched the woman she loved seduce another. The worst of it all was that it was a performance *meant* to hurt her.

"Come here."

Peach rose and crossed the room smoothly, her chest heaving with nervous breaths. Lian tipped her chin up and kissed her deeply once before spinning her around to face Mina. Uncertainty flashed in Peach's eyes as Lian's fingers coaxed her to bend over the back of the chair. Peach's arms braced her upper body against the cushion as Lian lifted her skirts, the rustle of taffeta the only sound between the three women.

Mina thought to protest, to draw Lian's attention to

herself once more. Yet she didn't. Was it that she couldn't guarantee it would help Peach any more than silence? Or did it make her feel better to know she wasn't the only one Lian manipulated into asking for suffering?

However, once Lian's fingers met their mark beneath the fabric, Peach's demeanor shifted entirely. The nervous reservation melted as Peach gasped a small "Oh." She moaned as her skirts rustled rhythmically, the diamonds from her earlobes swaying with Lian's penetrations. Lian reached down and grabbed a handful of the woman's hair to tilt her head back, making sure Mina could see the full range of the pleasure building on Peach's face.

Lian toyed with her until Peach was begging for release, her carefully constructed performance stripped to animalistic need. Mina watched it all, knowing all she had to do was remove the teacup from her head and walk out the door. It seemed so simple. And yet it wasn't because Lian had preordained that this was exactly where she would be and what she would experience. This unmitigated cruelty.

As the throes of Peach's orgasm waned, her brow beaded with sweat, Lian wiped her fingers on the back of her dress.

"Did you enjoy that?"

"Yes, my lady," Peach answered breathily.

"And how would you enjoy becoming my daughter?"

Peach's eyes opened wide though she carefully kept any tension from her body. Mina, on the other hand, felt the teacup wiggle precariously, nearly beyond caring.

"Lady Zhang," Peach said, awkwardly twisting her torso. "That would be an unimaginable honor."

The only right answer.

"I knew you would say that."

"But what about... what about Mina?"

Lian glanced her way. "What about her? She's disappointed me for the last time. I'll have her relegated to a lower clan soon enough."

A quiver started in her hands and spread to her torso with each ragged exhalation, a fundamental part of her world sliding out from under her. Lian could—*would*—replace her as simply as that, robbing Mina of what little security she still clung to in this world.

The teacup clattered to the ground as the dam burst on her tears, hot beads rolling off the point of her chin. After every-thing—everything she'd endured for the sake of Lian, for the sake of being crafted into something better—this is where it was ending? Discarded for the next accessible, amenable girl?

"See? I knew I'd find those tears eventually, pet."

A monstrous revulsion burned at her core. Mina would not accept one more insult, one more attack against her exis-tence. She placed one foot flat on the ground and ignored the protest of her stiff legs as she pushed herself up, her hand grasping the hairpin Lian had gifted her and pulling it free.

"I am not. Your fucking. *Pet*."

"What did you just say to me?" Lian's expression darkened like a growing storm.

"My name is Mina Park." The hairpin felt like iron in her hand. "And I am my own. Fucking. *Person*."

Lian gave one bitter laugh before she crossed the room in a blur. Her hand closed around Mina's throat just as Mina maneuvered the pin between their bodies. The impact with the hard stop of the wall, the momentum carrying Lian's body onto the wooden skewer, it all happened in a single, terrible instant. A tangle of emotions crossed Lian's face: vengeful fury turning to surprise... and finally to hurt. Lady Zhang took one step then two steps away. The woman's fingertips brushed the strands of jewels dangling from the hairpin protruding from her chest as the dark stain of crimson radiated outward on her silk camisole. Lian's eyes met Mina's, full of wonder and betrayal, before the dying woman collapsed to the floor.

Mina held up a trembling hand, the one that had plunged the stake into Lian's heart, with a horrific disbelief. She waited for Lian to stand back up. To demand Mina's life for this treason. Instead, the woman's willowy hands clutched futilely at the hairpin, unable to remove it. A small trickle of blood trailed from the corner of her mouth as her body convulsed with the spasms preceding death.

And gradually, Mina understood. There would be no more Lian.

Mina's legs gave out, and she crashed back to the floor. Peach fled the room. Mina couldn't bring herself to care.

"*Why?*" she whispered, her voice raw. "All I ever wanted from you was a home. A shred of kindness. I did *everything* to be the person you wanted." Mina's hands twined in Lian's camisole. "*Everything.*" Her head tipped forward to rest on Lian's stomach, her cheek nestling against the puddle of blood.

A strained whisper crossed Lian's lips: "I've always underestimated you, haven't I... my love." She rested a hand on Mina's head.

Mina nuzzled into it, allowing herself this last comfort. This last touch. Mina sobbed with her eyes squeezed shut, savoring the last moment of closeness she would have with this infuriating, extraordinary woman. It felt so wrong that she would exist beyond her life with Lian, it was difficult to even fathom the shape of it.

Time and pain ceased to exist as Mina stayed curled beside Lian's cooling body, ignoring the fact that the hand had slipped from her head and tumbled limply to the floor. She hugged Lian's body fiercely all the same. Considered taking the stake from Lian's heart and throwing herself on it. It seemed the most logical thing to do. How could she possibly go on in the absence of Lian's immutable guidance? The prospect was absurd.

As her fingers began to reach for the hairpin, Mina heard a smattering of quick steps. Coarse hands shook her shoulders. She shoved them away. The hands returned, more insistent.

"Honey, you need to get up."

"Leave," Mina growled, imbuing compulsion into her command as she glared at the elderly wardrobe mistress.

"Huh?" The woman withdrew confused.

"No, Mina. You don't need to do that. We're here to help you." Peach tugged at her arm. "She's gone, Mina. You need to get out of here. We'll do what we can to buy you time."

Mina sat up reluctantly, her eyes drifting to the lifeless form of her tormentor—her greatest love. Lian's head had rolled to the side, her eyes staring vacantly into the distance.

"What have I done?" Mina stared down at her shaking palms as sobs overwhelmed her body once more. Then, suddenly, she was in a warm embrace as Peach wrapped her arms around her.

"You did what you needed to. And I... *Thank you*, Mina. I wouldn't have been able to refuse her offer, even knowing she would do the same to me as she has to you." Peach sat back, wiping her own tears with a sleeve. She thrust a small bundle into Mina's hands. "Change into these. There's a car waiting in the back that will take you wherever you want to go. It needs to be now, though. Make this count."

Numbly, Mina rose to her feet, using every scrap of willpower to keep from returning to Lian. Not Lian. The corpse of Lian.

Just put one foot in front of the other.

After she'd put on the jeans and T-shirt and Peach had scrubbed the worst of the blood from her face, Mina was prodded down the back corridors of the building once more. The teahouse had quieted in the late hours of the evening, all but the closing workers vacated for the night. Feeling like nothing more than a husk of a person, she went where Peach told her to.

Peach shoved her into the car with one last squeeze of her hand. "Good luck, elder sister."

The driver had to repeat his question twice before Mina broke through the daze to answer.

"The airport. I'll be returning to Shanghai alone."

32

Javier's hands lingered on his father's journal one last time before packing it in his suitcase. Together with the hard drives and notes he'd absconded with from Eva's lab, half of the shabby soft-sided bag was already full. Getting past the Sanguis Institute security had been easy. All he had to do was play into the expectation that human underlings were capable of only a singular thought process. If he said he was there to collect and destroy electronic information, that must be true, especially if he had a badge and a jumpsuit backing the story.

Sitting back on his heels, he set about actually folding the pile of clothes that wouldn't fit in their original wadded form. Not all the T-shirts were going to make it, but he would at least need some of his clothes. The remaining balance of his bank account wouldn't support updating his wardrobe for quite some time. Javier bunched socks around spinning disk platters, pretending like the heaped belongings would magically compress beneath the lid. Maybe he could find one of those straps to keep his bag from exploding on the carousel.

After a long conversation with Eva, combined with the incentive of holding her research notes hostage, Javier had convinced her to come with him—not to stay in California, but just to get out of this politically reckless situation with the Zhang woman. Even Eva admitted that her career was effectively torpedoed, but with the stolen smatterings of her research, she could re-create much of her work if she was able to find funding elsewhere.

Deciding it was time for a packing break, Javier trundled a twenty-two-inch flat screen TV down to the front desk. When he'd asked Arvind if he could buy the spare equipment off the bank, in a rare act of dubious morality, the man said he could simply take it as a parting gift for all the late nights.

Setting his haul on the counter before Mr. Eyebrows, Javier relished the way the eyebrows danced for him one final time.

"I'm leaving tomorrow, so I just wanted to say thank you for your help and humor along the way."

The man gave him a skeptical nod, eyes fixed on the small television under his arm.

"This is for you, yup. To replace that antique you've been rocking." Javier gestured toward the tiny tube TV, currently color glitching a chess match into a purple-hued fever dream. "You were a good gatekeeper to this building—thank you."

Javier hooked up the power and the coax cable for the antenna. The chess match popped back up in its expected black and white, and Mr. Eyebrows clapped him on the back with a delighted chuckle. "Nǐ shì gè hǎo xiǎohuǒzi."

The phrase was unfamiliar, but Javier warmed under the presumed goodwill. He strolled out into the courtyard, kicking at the dried leaves that crackled underfoot. His apple tree still stood ensconced in its nest of industrial plantings, where he'd left it. The transplant had stalled its alarming growth, but a few fresh buds notched out just above the last set. Javier stroked the silky leaves with a smile. This small plant would be his lasting mark on this place even if his time here had accomplished nothing else—a striving sapling amongst a copse of manicured shrubs.

All right, enough with the sappy goodbyes. Back to your packing, already.

Javier rode the elevator back to his floor. As the doors opened, the sound of someone banging on a doorway echoed down the hall. As he stepped out, a panic gripped him as he realized it was the door to his old apartment a woman was banging on. Should he make a run for it? Javier looked more closely at the woman, her hair splayed wildly around her shoulders, disheveled in casual attire. Something about her was breathtakingly familiar. Did he dare hope...

"Mina?" he called hesitantly.

She looked up, her face blotchy with emotion. It *was* her. Javier's heart skipped a beat with unexpected joy and relief all balled together. In a blink, her body was crashing into his. For a second, he worried she meant to attack him, but he realized her arms clung to him as though he was the only thing grounding her to reality. He ignored the pain of his still-broken ribs being crushed beneath her embrace and hugged her fiercely in return.

"I'm so sorry," she sobbed into his shoulder.

"You don't know how glad I am to see you," Javier said softly, letting his head rest against hers. "I moved apartments in case those other bastards came back. Do you want to come inside?"

With a shuddering breath, Mina nodded. The back of her hand dragged across watery eyes, further smudging the dark rings of makeup. Those weren't the first tears she'd shed in the last twenty-four hours. Reserving his interrogation, he led her down to his new place.

As soon as the door shut, she was on him once more, her lips pressed firmly against his. Fervent hands glided up his chest and settled on his shoulders, drawing him closer. So grateful for her unexpected presence, Javier returned the kiss with a comfortable passion, letting his hands twine with her hair and settle around her waist. She was alive. She was *here*.

But when he expected her to pull back, she intensified the kiss instead, her hands venturing lower to the seat of his jeans. She pulled him into a suggestive hip thrust, and Javier's body responded to the advances while a distinct unease settled into his mind. He'd certainly had this exact fantasy a few times already, but the rapid escalation of intimacy didn't fit with any emotionally realistic progression.

When her hands began to play with the button of his fly, Javier's inner alarm bells demanded he stop this runaway train before it derailed. Pulling his head back, he let his hands rest on her wrists, a gentle stall.

"Whoa, Mina, hang on. Let's just talk for a minute. How... are you even here?"

She looked up at him, hurt clouding her glassy eyes. "I thought you wanted this."

"No, Mina—trust me, I do. But last time I saw you, that woman—"

"She's gone. So we can be together now."

"Be together?" Javier's confusion only deepened as he tried to piece together Mina's nonresponses. "Where did she go?"

Mina didn't answer. Instead, she unzipped her hoodie and let it fall to the floor before grabbing the hem of her own shirt and yanking it over her head. Then her hands were on him once more, insistent in their exploration. Javier's breath caught at the touch of her bare skin—God, she was gorgeous. And here. And... something was still terribly off.

"Mina, stop. Is that blood?" Javier asked, taking a step back.

Half of her torso was smeared with flaking russet. Despite her proximity, he didn't dare touch her right now. Mina looked down with a foggy expression, her own fingers delicately touching the streaks of ruddy stain.

"Lian is dead." Her voice sounded vacant, as if trying to grasp at a memory that wouldn't coalesce. And then her expression contorted into the kind of grief he'd only encountered at funerals. Her voice wavered. "I killed her." Mina turned away from him, and he watched her rib cage spasm around the sobs she fought to suppress.

Javier clenched his jaw, weighing the best way to comfort her. He'd seen this woman dazzle at a ball, take down a clan of mobsters, and endure unfathomable abuse to save his life. Yet he'd never seen her broken like she was now.

"Hey, it's going to be all right." He put a hand on her shoulder tenderly.

She shrugged it off at once and bent down to grab her shirt. "You don't want this. I shouldn't have bothered you. I—"

Javier threw his arms around her from behind, squeezing tightly as an unbidden surge of emotion prickled at his own eyes. "You're not going anywhere. I can't let you leave me again."

After several minutes, her stiffness finally dissolved. Her head hung forward like a marionette whose strings had been cut. Javier held her like an injured bird, tightly so that she wouldn't hurt herself more with her frantic, ineffective wingbeats.

"When I left Beijing," she said, "the only place I wanted to go, the only place I thought I might feel safe, was with you. I was so worried you'd left." Mina's head inclined toward his suitcase. "It looks like you're headed that direction, in any case."

A warmth spread through Javier's chest, followed by crushing guilt. "My sister—well, it sounds like you might have been there to see the wreckage firsthand—but I need to get her out of the city. I was going to come back for you. I couldn't imagine not knowing what happened to you after... that night."

"You were going to come back for me?" Mina twisted her head toward him.

Javier loosened his grasp, and she turned to face him, still held in his arms.

"Of course. I couldn't just abandon you."

She sniffled as she laid her head on his chest tenderly. "Thank you, Javier." Her voice was meek—exhausted, it occurred to him.

"Hey, I don't mean to be rude, but you have some interesting smells going on right now. Maybe a shower is in order? I'll rustle up some food. I have ingredients for fried rice with chicken... or fried rice with an egg. Lady's choice."

Mina stared up at him, and he was worried for a second that she was going to tell him to go fuck himself. Instead, her face cracked into a small grin, half of a chuckle.

"I mean, I'm a little cleaner than I was after the Federovs, at least."

"That's a good point. Maybe we should work on finding you some new social circles, ones that don't leave you caked in blood after a night out, hmm?"

Mina shook her head, her smile fading. Javier would be lucky if she even had the energy to shower.

"Come on. I'm not cleaning your ex-lover's blood from your body. I have boundaries. But. I also have a clean towel, so you're in luck." He knew his gallows humor was probably pushing up against a hard edge, but that was the coping mechanism that came to him most naturally. Maybe it would work for Mina, too, at least for tonight. They would have time for a serious conversation after she rested.

"You know, it might not even be her blood," Mina said with a strange shudder.

Well, that was concerning. Was it Mina's? A... third party's? Javier realized he didn't actually want to know.

Mina floated to the bathroom, her face blank and her limbs slack. Maybe he should help her after all?

No. Let the woman shower, and be here for her when she gets back.

Javier folded her clothing and laid it on the bed—his *good* folding, not the folding he'd used on his suitcase T-shirts. Next, he threw together his version of a chef's special: fried rice with chicken *and* an egg, with two dashes of an unlabeled hot sauce Wenshi had left behind. The flavor was exceptional, but man, did it burn. Javier was laying the two heaping plates on the table as she walked out from the bathroom, wearing one of his button-down shirts and toweling her hair. Under any other circumstances, Javier wasn't sure he would be able to keep his hands to himself. As it was, his own moral code wouldn't let him even acknowledge how cute she looked. Sometimes, being the good guy sucked.

They ate without much conversation. Mina seemed to be having a difficult time keeping her eyes open as she sluggishly chewed about half of the food.

"Um, are you hungry for something... *else*? I can—"

The last time he'd slit his wrist, her reaction had been a little frightening. Even under considerably less trying conditions, she'd struggled to keep herself together.

"No," she said firmly. "Thanks."

Javier pressed his lips into a line. "Why don't you go lie down, then? I'll sleep on the couch tonight, and we can work on a plan tomorrow." He stood and pushed his chair in.

With a sigh, Mina nodded her head. She stayed seated though, staring at her rice.

"Javier? Why are you so nice to me?"

The way she asked that question—like she honestly didn't know—hit him harder than he expected. The answer wasn't a difficult one.

"Because you fight even when it wrecks you. Because you keep coming back to me. Because you *deserve* someone to be nice to you."

Her hand rested on his as he reached for her bowl. "Thank you."

Javier smiled at her warmly, and Mina opened her mouth with an inhale like she might have something else to add. In the end, she flashed a small, sad smile of her own before scuffing off to the bedroom in his oversized socks.

Javier did the dishes after shoveling the rest of Mina's portion into his mouth—easier than trying to store the leftovers. Just as he settled on the couch with a book, hoping to decelerate his dizzy mind before trying to sleep, his bedroom door creaked open.

"Javier? Sorry, just... Could you lie with me? Like we did that one time." Though her voice was timid, she was actually asking for something she wanted. Progress.

"There's nothing I'd rather do." He leapt off the couch and snapped off the living room lights before she had a chance to change her mind. Now that she suggested it, he realized how much he needed to be close to her too.

In the darkness, Mina slid under the duvet once more, and Javier had an awkward moment of hesitation. Should he stay on top of the covers? He usually slept in his boxers, but that seemed awfully forward.

"You're overthinking. Just get in here." Mina flapped back the covers, and Javier did as he was told, wrapping an arm around her as she snuggled into his body. Beneath the sharper scent of his man shampoo, he still caught a whiff of whatever made her hair smell like orange blossoms.

"Promise me you'll still be here when I wake up? Otherwise, I'm going to have to hunt you down." He didn't know if he could take her vanishing again.

"I promise."

Javier let himself relax into the pillow. There was absolutely nowhere else he'd rather be. He could finally sleep easy, knowing she was here. Safe. In his arms.

33

Mina blinked her eyes open in a darkened room, light creeping in around drawn curtains at the end. Her fingers dragged over the rough cotton sheets beneath her.

Where am I?

Her nose detected the smell of coffee overtop the musty bedding. A man hummed beyond the closed bedroom door.

Javier. Mina shot upright with a bolt of icy panic. *Lian is going to—*

She paused. Lian wasn't going to do anything. Ever again. A small thrill cut through the torrent of unprocessed grief. Mina was in Javier's apartment, and there wasn't any reason she shouldn't be. No threat of consequences for either of them. A strange smile tugged at her lips. *Is this what freedom feels like?*

Mina threw back the covers and padded over to the door. Dim light greeted her on the other side.

"Good morning, sunshine." Javier beamed, bustling to the table with a steaming cup of coffee and a plate of toast, a kitchen towel slung over his shoulder. "I was wondering if this might rouse you. You've been asleep for nearly twelve hours."

She accepted the cup, cradling it with her fingers so that she might absorb its warmth, inhaling the comforting smell. The smile on her lips widened, and a devious thought crept into her mind.

"Do you know how insensitive it is to call a vampire 'sunshine'?"

Javier froze, his mouth opening to apologize, no doubt. Mina chuckled into her cup, and Javier caught onto the joke with an eye roll.

"I see someone is back to their sarcastic snark. Must mean you're feeling better."

He set a plate of toast on the table and took a seat with his own mug. "This is probably not up to the princess's standards, but it's what I had. You know, you have a peculiar habit of showing up unannounced."

Mina wrinkled her nose and took a seat, grabbing a piece of bread. It was smeared with a thick layer of butter and a ruby-colored jam. Raspberry? She crunched into it, sending flakes of crust back to her plate. Yup, raspberry. Combined with a swallow of strong coffee, this was the best breakfast she'd had in a long time. Homey and familiar compared to the formal affairs at Zhang Manor. *I never have to go back there again,* Mina thought gleefully.

"You better stick to calling me sunshine. I don't think I'm rightfully a princess anymore—and thank the fucking gods."

"Fair enough, *sunshine.* So, I'm supposed to meet Eva in an hour at her place. She arranged a private flight for us to Japan— she thought it would be safer than trying to get her research through airport security. Then in Tokyo, we'll book flights back to the States. You can absolutely come with us, or I can stay here and help you figure out your next plan. What are you thinking?" He looked over his coffee cup with such an earnest, expectant gaze that Mina faltered.

"A plan?"

"Yeah, you know. You decide on the thing you want to happen and then take steps to make it happen... Not ringing any bells?"

Mina set her cup of coffee down and rubbed the crease between her eyebrows. It wouldn't kill Javier to just let her have one tranquil meal before thinking about the future.

"I don't know. I hadn't thought beyond... None of this was part of a *plan*. It just happened."

"Well, the good news is you can start a plan at any time. So, Mina, what would you like to happen next?"

Her shoulders slumped, the weight of the exhaustion she'd been outrunning settling in her spine with an ache. Every plan she'd ever made had ended in such a catastrophic dumpster fire. What business did she have even *trying* to envision a future?

"It's been so long since I..." She shook her head. She didn't have Lian anymore to make her decisions for her, and that was a *good* thing. The thought of starting over was petrifying, and yet a small voice in the back of her head made a good point: *You've been through worse.*

Did she want to go with Javier? Yes, she decided, but not because he was the next person to control her life or because of some metaphysical vampire attraction. He had taken care of her when she was beaten down, and he gave her space to make her own decisions. Lian's power and charisma had been intoxicating, but Javier's traits were the ones that actually made a good partner in life, she realized with lucid clarity.

"You know, I don't think I want to stay in this city for one more fucking day. But... are you sure you really want me to come with you? I'm fresh out of a really fucked-up relationship, no money, no job skills, *not* human—"

Javier came over to her side of the table before cutting her off mid-sentence with a quick stolen kiss.

"You're perfect."

Her heart melted into a puddle of molten happiness, and she met his eyes with a genuine smile. Why did he always make her feel like anything was possible? Like his entire world rested on whether she would be in it?

"So, logistics," Javier said, clearing his throat and pivoting his hips away from her.

Mina smirked at his poor attempt to hide his excitement. She didn't know what she had been thinking, tearing her clothes off yesterday. Then and now, she was grateful Javier had the good sense to not push the physical intimacy. Not until her head cleared, at least.

"Do we need to swing by your place to pack anything? Maybe get your passport? I might stay in the car this time, if that's all right."

Fuck. A passport.

"I have no idea where it might be, and in any case, it's a Korean passport that expired at least ten years ago. I used to have a fake until..."

Australia. The plane. The boy and the teddy bear.

"Javier, I can't go with you." Mina hung her head so he wouldn't see her watering eyes, the realization crashing down on her timid happiness.

"Hey, a passport is a stupid booklet of paper. I'm sure we

can work out a temporary one or maybe even apply for some sort of asylum status."

"I'd interfere with the plane's electronics," she choked out.

"No, you wouldn't."

Mina lifted her head. Javier stood with one hand on his hip, his soft brown hair messily tousled from sleep. Damn him for being so wonderful before they'd have to say goodbye for good. And damn him for making her explain the obvious.

"You're the one who proved just how dramatically I fucked with your gizmos."

"Exactly. I know your impact is limited to high-speed data signals for wireless communication. We'll keep you away from the cockpit, maybe hold your in-flight meal. I promise it will be fine."

Mina swallowed, wrapping her hands around her cooling mug once more. He wouldn't lie to her about that, not when his own life would be on the line too. Lian had mentioned special shielding on the private jet's electronics—had that been a fabrication to guilt her into thinking the woman saved her from herself? *Gaslight number 823 in the Lian Zhang playbook.*

"I'm pretty sure Dr. Robles isn't going to be thrilled with the idea of traveling with me, either. Last time we spoke, we didn't end on good terms," Mina said—a last-ditch effort to get Javier to back out of this while he still could.

Javier rolled his eyes. "Eva can get over herself and her fixation on her damn research. Besides, what kind of little brother would I be if I couldn't guilt her into getting my way? Now, knock it off with the 'woe is me' trauma-queen act. Either you want to come with, and we'll figure out the details, or you don't. Which is it?"

How did he have such a no-bullshit way of framing everything? The perspective was amazingly good at getting to the crux of the question and leaving her little room to hide behind an excuse. That made it seem easy to just do the thing she wanted. Could it be that life was really that simple?

"Fine, I want to go. I'm warning you, though. You keep being this nice, and you're going to have a clingy vampire to get rid of on the other side of the ocean."

Javier tossed the kitchen towel on top of her head as he scuttled off to the bedroom. "I have five more minutes of packing, and then we're leaving, so finish your breakfast."

Mina peeled the damp towel from her hair, feeling giggly despite the slight mildew smell. Who was this wonderful stranger who made her feel accepted? Safe. Like she had nothing to apologize for.

Was it possible she was standing on the edge of something good? A future where she could just be Mina? How had she gotten so lucky?

"ABSOLUTELY NOT." Eva crossed her arms and glared at Javier with his packed suitcase. Mina stood behind him, trying not to point out that she knew this would happen.

"Eva, you're being rude," Javier whispered. "Invite her into your apartment. The three of us need to talk."

"There's nothing I want to say to her."

Javier leaned forward and dropped his voice. "Stop pretending you don't want to help the *broken vampire*."

Was that supposed to be a whisper?

"I'll just wait in the car," Mina said and turned to leave.

"Why are you here, anyway? Did Lady Zhang finally get tired of her *pet project*?"

"Eva!"

Mina froze mid-step, a spike of anger hitting her in the chest. Gods, that woman could make some pretentious assumptions.

"No. She's dead." Mina turned back around to face the pair, trying to keep the irritation from turning her irises red. "Javier said I could come with you. If that's not the case, fine— but I'm done being talked down to."

Eva's brow furrowed as she considered Mina with a skeptical seriousness. "When's the last time you ate?" she asked, more softly.

Javier took a step forward. "I fed her toast this morning. She's not going to get hungry. Right, Mina?"

Mina's nostrils flared, wanting to tell both the siblings to back the hell off. But things would be better if they could get their travel journey off on the right foot. Eva was an ally, Mina reminded herself, which helped cool some of her anger.

"The last meal that stayed down? A few days ago. But I'm not hungry, and I've had more practice fasting than most. I really could use your help if you're willing."

Eva finally unfolded her arms and opened the door wide enough to see the interior. Clothing and papers were strewn over every flat surface in sight, a few open suitcases half filled with knickknacks. "Fine. Come in."

"Eva, the flight leaves in a few hours. Why aren't you packed yet?" Javier wheeled his suitcase in and propped it up against the wall to prevent its unbalanced cargo from toppling. He immediately went to one of Eva's cases and started unceremoniously cramming more stuff in.

"I've lived here for over a decade. It's not that easy to just bundle everything up and move on." Eva took a framed picture out of the suitcase and started polishing the glass with a corner of her shirt.

The sentiment felt dissonant. Mina had been in Shanghai just as long and couldn't think of a single thing she cared to take with her. Every item she'd "owned" in Shanghai had been on loan from Lian, its possession conditional on Mina's good behavior. Even the items that felt personal—the phoenix coronet from her turning ceremony, the briefcase with her initials, her books of poetry—none of it would carry to a new life.

"So, if Lady Zhang is truly gone..." Eva prompted.

"She's gone." Mina closed her eyes, chest tight with the memory of the hairpin grazing the woman's sternum on its way to her heart. Her unmoving body surrounded by a lake of blood. Ignoring her shaky hands, Mina sat down next to a pile of clothing and started folding.

"Then who is taking over House Zhang?"

Mina paused holding an umber cardigan. "One of my elder siblings, I guess. I really don't care. It's not my house anymore."

"That's not how vampirism works. You carry the lineage in your blood, and someday, you'll have to reckon with your remaining family."

"Pretty sure I know how 'vampirism works,'" Mina grumbled, tamping down the pile of clothing with more force than necessary. It gave her a petty satisfaction to think of the wrinkles the bossy woman would have to iron after unpacking.

"Fine, it doesn't matter. But if House Zhang is under a different regime, maybe they'll back the research again and stop the blood dilution. Maybe I don't need to leave after all." Eva removed a stack of papers from one of the suitcases and took a seat on the couch between a shoebox of toiletries and a stuffed elephant.

"Evelina Cecilia Robles, you are getting on that plane." Javier's tone was firm as he put both hands on his hips. Mina felt an odd shudder run down her spine, staring up at the taller man wearing a button-down with jeans. The black leather belt and the authority in his tone gave her an eerie impression of Lian for half a second before the sibling banter continued, breaking the illusion.

"Stop trying to sound like Dad." Eva stuck her tongue out before caving and throwing the papers back into the suitcase.

The three worked together for the next half hour, packing the rest of Eva's belongings while talking her out of the necessity of a rice cooker in her carry-on. Mina sat on suitcases while Javier wrestled zippers that groaned as they rounded the overflowing corners. Eventually, four overstuffed bags stood next to the door.

"We need to swing by my office to get rations for Mina. I'm not risking her hunger on a flying tin can."

"I said I was fine." Mina didn't need to spend the rest of her life with a babysitter chasing after her with a snack.

"And I'm sure you think you are. Ignoring your dietary requirements won't make them go away. If you're going to be a rogue vampire, you're going to have to come up with a better plan than avoidance."

Mina opened her mouth to argue then closed it again. *Maybe this is what sibling concern is supposed to feel like,* she thought with a strange contradiction. Good gods, it was annoying.

Javier grabbed the rickety handle of his suitcase along with one of Eva's. "Enough squabbling. Even a fancy private plane won't wait forever." He took off down the hall, leaving Mina and Eva standing by the door. A distant look of tension clouded Eva's face as she surveyed her depersonalized apartment.

"For what it's worth, it's strange leaving for me too," Mina offered.

Eva met her eyes and gave a slow blink—a mutual truce for the time being—and Mina grabbed one of the remaining cases and set off after Javier.

AT THE SANGUIS INSTITUTE, Mina and Eva went into the building together, leaving Javier to guard the bags in the cab. He had given them precisely fifteen minutes to fetch supplies, warning that he was willing to leave without them. Both women saw through the outstandingly bad lie.

A single emergency light illuminated the lab space as Eva crouched to raid the fridge labeled "Test Samples—Don't touch. That means you, Dr. Yi!"

"Drink one now," Eva said, handing Mina a pouch. "And then we'll grab a couple for the road. Hopefully, the plane will let us use their refrigerator. This will buy you a few days of leeway until you figure out your next plan. Cow's blood is fine for a while, but it will eventually lead to chronic fatigue and possible episodes of rage feeding."

"Thanks." Mina was reluctant to take advice on being a vampire from a human... but if there was any human who would know, it was this one. The packet of cold blood squished in her hand. There couldn't possibly be anything less appetizing. With grave determination, she drank most of it. When she gagged at the end, Eva gave her a strange look.

"Are you sure you're okay?"

"I'm not okay at all," Mina snapped back. "But what am I supposed to do? Just give up?"

Eva paused, her reusable grocery tote filled with blood bags dangling absurdly from the crook of her arm.

"So, you and my brother. Are you serious about him?"

Mina coughed on a reflux of blood. Was this really a conversation that needed to be had now? Eva's expression was expectant and solemn.

"Look." Mina sighed. "I'm not making any long-term commitments, but yes, I genuinely hope I can get to know him. He makes me feel like... like I'm not worthless. Like possibilities exist that I can't even conceive of yet."

Eva chewed on her lip for a second. "Promise me you'll be careful. For his sake. Not only with the blood thing, but... our dad passed away when he was pretty young, and then I disappeared a few years later. Javier likes to play things down with jokes, but he's sensitive, and he deserves someone who's not going to abandon him. If he's your lifeboat out, I get it. Just don't let the illusion linger too long if you don't mean it."

"I promise I'm not just using him," Mina said soberly.

Maybe Javier deserved someone better than her—no, he *definitely* deserved someone better than her. Someone normal. Someone without a decade of damage to unpack. But that was a decision *he* got to make. And as far as she could tell, he seemed just as curious about the possibility as she was.

"What will it take for you to start trusting me, Eva?" Her words felt shaky. Foreign. Cathartic.

"Me?" Eva scoffed. "I'm not the one you need to convince. Focus on my brother, and we'll be fine."

Despite the gruff response, Mina felt something shift in Eva's gaze. Something honestly appraising instead of skeptical. It was a start.

Begrudgingly, she had to admit the blood was helping her feel more grounded. More capable of pulling this off. And like maybe having a well-meaning older sister wouldn't be the worst thing.

A LOUD *CLICK* echoed through the empty concrete parking structure as the stairwell door opened and Mina and Eva emerged. They strolled casually, looking terribly unfazed for having a bag of stolen blood in their possession while running dangerously late for their flight.

"Come on! Hustle!" Javier urged, waiting outside the open car door, nervous sweat prickling at his skin.

The driver had been giving him dirty looks for the past thirty minutes even after pocketing the extra bills Javier slid his way. Eva and Mina both gave him the same raised eyebrow. They were two creatures so similar in their stubbornness, Javier knew they would like each other in time.

After they packed Mina carefully into the middle seat, hoodie drawn and slathered in sunscreen against the non-vampire-rated window tint, the group trundled off to the airport against the late afternoon traffic.

Javier glanced at his watch for the hundredth time, itching for a smartphone with a navigational ETA. A hand buried within a sweatshirt sleeve came up to rest over his.

"Everything will be okay," Mina said.

"I'm the one who's supposed to be comforting you," he grumbled in return, staring out the window at the stopped traffic.

"You know, even if you two date, you won't be able to have kids. And you know I'm not going to either, so Mom is going to be extra pissed," Eva added, arms folded.

"Eva!" He heard a small snicker from beneath Mina's hood. The outrage!

Switching to Spanish, he cut back, "Could you lay off just a little bit?" Even as he spoke, he realized her implicit acceptance of a relationship between him and Mina. Interesting. "There are a lot of things we need to figure out before we would ever even get to the 'kids' conversation. Plus, there are lots of other ways to have kids these days."

"Just saying." Eva shrugged. "I think Mom will like her, though. Once she gets over the whole bloodsucker thing."

Javier swallowed. Yeah, that was going to be an interesting conversation. "Maybe if you explained how you've been working with and studying them..."

"Not a chance. I know you want a happy family reunion, but it's not going to happen."

Javier rolled his eyes. They still had at least ten hours of flight time left. He was pretty sure he could wear her down by the time they landed.

"For what it's worth," Mina interjected in the same language, "I'm excited to see your vineyard. As far as your mom goes, even if I can't have kids and even if I'm a vampire, I think I can get her to like me—I'm good with older women."

Eva snorted.

"*You speak Spanish?*" Javier yelped. "And *eww*. You didn't actually just say that, did you?"

"I like languages. I speak many tongues," Mina replied theatrically, reminding him of Eva's useless boss, Lord Vespa, or something.

Eva dissolved into a giggle fit on her side of the car. Javier sank down into his seat and didn't speak for the rest of the ride to the hangar. For once, he truly didn't have a comeback.

Despite the facts that Eva and Mina were definitely ganging up on him and that he stood no chance once they discovered that they did, in fact, like each other, this was the most weirdly normal moment of togetherness he'd had since arriving in Shanghai. Ironically, on the way to the airport. He kept the smile off his face, just to avoid encouraging them. Whatever Eva said now, he was absolutely getting the three of them to the vineyard together to enjoy a nice glass of pinot noir at sunset.

When they pulled up to the guard gate at the smaller tarmac outside the main Shanghai airport, Eva consulted with the guard in Mandarin. The chain link clanked as it parted for them, and the car lurched forward through the opening.

"What did he say? Did we miss the flight?" Javier asked. They drove along the periphery of the airstrip with smaller planes taxiing close enough that the airwaves shook the car. The roar from their engines caused Mina to wince with each takeoff.

"I told you before. We are the only ones on the flight. It's not leaving without us." Eva shook her head. "We're going to a hangar where we can unload before they bring a different plane around. There was a mechanical issue, apparently."

"What kind of mechanical issue?"

"*Javier*. It doesn't matter. There will be a plane. It will take us to Tokyo. End of story."

He rubbed his clammy palms on the thighs of his jeans. Once they were in the air, he would feel better. It had never been the flight part of air travel that made him anxious—it was the scramble with bags, the uncertainty about customs, and the fear of being late that drove him nuts. After an hour in the car, his nerves were frayed, Mina had slipped into nonverbal contemplation, and Eva seemed more annoyed than ever. They were all ready to be out of this city.

As promised, the hangar at the end of the long line of open doors held no plane. Sunlight cut in viciously from the western sky, illuminating the full length of the cavern as they pulled in. The poured concrete floor was dotted with I-beam columns that supported the flat corrugated roof. A solitary black car was parked at the back of the building, perhaps an out-of-service limousine, but otherwise the structure was empty. Javier paid it no mind as their own vehicle shut off.

He reached for the handle of the door, ready to exit the claustrophobia of brooding women in the back of the taxi. "How long is the wait going to be? Maybe we can shut the door for Mina if it's going to be longer than—"

Mina caught his arm in a painful grip as he tried to leave the car. "I have a bad feeling about this."

He couldn't see her eyes behind those sunglasses, but the tremor in her voice chilled him to the bone. Of course she would get cold feet. Flying *was* scary, especially if you'd been made to believe that you could take out the engines.

"Hey, I told you, there's no reason to be afraid. You said you wanted to leave the city, right? Here's your escape. Right here. All you have to do is keep going a little longer, and I *promise* there are good things to look forward to on the other side of the ocean."

Their driver hit an oversized red button on the wall, and the door to the hangar clanged its descent, gradually shading the empty space until it was a vampire-safe zone. Slowly, Mina's grip on his arm relaxed enough for Javier to offer her his hand. He helped her out of the car, where she finally pushed down her hood and removed her sunglasses. Her eyes kept darting to the car in the back, but if she could see anything through the blackened windows, Javier couldn't tell.

"Javier, a little help here?" Eva hollered as she attempted to wrestle an overstuffed bag from its wedged position in the trunk.

He reluctantly left Mina's side to give her a hand. Together, they finally dislodged it, the car's suspension groaning before they hoisted it to the ground. One suitcase down, three to go.

"I told you, if you hadn't packed so much stuff—"

A mechanical *kachunk* ruptured in the hangar, and Javier whipped around to find its source. His eyes crossed as they focused on the steely barrel of a gun a few inches from his nose. The beady-eyed driver's arm was locked straight, the man unmoving. Javier's brain scrambled to make sense of why this was happening.

"We don't have any valuables," Javier started, slowly raising his hands and enunciating clearly. "But you're welcome to the rest of my cash. Maybe just lower that thing a touch?"

The car door of the black limousine at the back of the hangar opened, the sound echoing through the space. A stiletto-toed foot emerged. A soft "no" came from Mina as she brought a hand to her mouth, her eyes wide with panic.

Lian emerged from the distant car, her clothing rumpled,

her makeup smudged, and a murderous expression on her face. The sight of her made the threat of the gun fade away. Lady Zhang was by far the more terrifying presence in the room.

They'd been ambushed.

Mina tried to warn me. And I didn't listen.

A visible tremble overcame Mina's entire body as Lian glided toward them, heels striking the concrete with menace. The shorter woman backed until she collided with the car, nowhere left to run.

Lian approached her directly, a predator locked in on its prey.

"You didn't think escaping eternity would be this easy, did you, pet?"

34

"H-how are you alive? I stabbed you. You were d-dead," Mina stammered as if she could logic this reality into the one she expected.

"That was a feeble assassination attempt, even for you. No forethought whatsoever." Lian crowded her, coming to stand a few inches away. "Did you really think a sliver of soft wood was enough to kill one as ancient as I? Stun, perhaps. At least until my precious Peach pulled it from my heart. Truly a shame I needed her blood to recover my strength—that is one death you can rightfully claim responsibility for."

Mina's fingers scrabbled against the unyielding metal of the cab, arching her spine to keep as much distance between their bodies as possible. Javier watched as the person who was just beginning to think through her own wants and needs disintegrated before this tyrant. A furious heat swelled in his chest. This is what Mina had known of love—no wonder she was a goddamn mess.

"Now, pet." Lian leaned in close, brushing a strand of hair away from Mina's face.

The smaller woman flinched as violently as if struck.

"I told you what would happen if you saw that boy again."

Mina's head snapped up in a panic. "No!" She tried to shove Lian away, tried to get to Javier in time as Lian grabbed her wrists and pinned her against the car, a sadistic smirk on her lips.

The gun jabbed against Javier's forehead as the driver adjusted his grip, settling his finger on the trigger. *No,* Javier thought. *This is not how it ends. We are too close to freedom to let her take it from us.*

He didn't think—he reached. Grasping at the fury within himself, the energy that burned like a flame. A flame that couldn't be contained. That night he'd started a kitchen fire, he'd imagined what he would do if he saw Lian again. This was his chance. *Let her burn.*

Javier felt it when it happened, like a tearing sensation in his core. An explosion of magic intent on exothermic destruction. A flash of light blinded him before the smell of melting polyester hit his nose. The top of Eva's suitcase was ablaze with a noxious orange-and-black flame. Okay, it would have been better if that had hit Lian directly, but he could use the diversion nonetheless.

With the driver's attention distracted, Javier ducked his head to the left, knocking the muzzle out of the way before throwing all his weight behind a punch to the driver's face. The man hit the floor, knocked out cold, and Javier scrambled for the gun. He instinctively aimed it toward Lian as soon as it was in his hands. The woman leered at him from where she stood, pressed against Mina. She hadn't even moved. His heart thudded so hard in his chest that the sights on the firearm wouldn't stay lined up with her torso.

"Let. Her. *Go!*" he roared with as much menace as he could muster.

Eva used her jacket to stifle the flames on the suitcase.

Lian responded with a quirked eyebrow and an incredulous smile before turning back to Mina. "This is who you chose over me? A mage so incompetent he nearly set himself on fire?" Her hand closed around Mina's throat, cutting off her reply.

Shame burned within Javier—shame at failing to listen to Mina, to protect her. Loathing for failing to recognize the magical part of his family and himself for so many years. If he had, maybe he could have saved her the first time.

This needed to end. Here and now.

Javier centered himself, lined up the sights on the gun, and braced for the recoil.

The shot exploded from the gun—*BANG*—deafening his ears as the recoil jammed into his swollen wrist. The bullet sailed through the empty air where Lian had stood, a lone Mina staring at him with a mixture of shock and grief. A metallic ring sounded as the bullet ricocheted off the building structure before the murmured hiss of a deflating tire could be heard.

Javier spun, searching for any trace of Lian. The woman had vanished. A second later, the gun was ripped from his hand, and the butt came down against the back of his head with a dizzying thud. Javier careened to the pavement. An immovable weight pressed down on his spine, pinning him to the floor as Lian's voice boomed above him.

"*Foolish* boy. Perhaps your most egregious embarrassment

is the fact that you even thought you had a chance. A chance with Mina. A chance to kill me."

Javier's fingers scrambled over the smooth concrete, looking for any purchase. Anything that might be used as leverage as his cheek was pressed against the cool stone. *I can't fail*, he kept repeating, while the logical part of his brain recognized that was exactly what was happening.

Then, miraculously, the immovable weight was gone from his back. He rolled to the side, hopping to his feet as quickly as he could, ignoring the wooziness from the blow to the head. Mina and Lian were wrestling on the asphalt a dozen feet away, toward the center of the hangar. Eva jogged toward him, her face a blurry double image until she stopped moving.

"Hermano mío," Eva said, her voice brimming with a decade of buried emotion as she yanked hard on the chain around her neck. The condor pendant broke free, and her thumb caressed it once before she pressed it into his hand, tears slipping from her eyes. "*Tómalo*. It's all the protection I have." She glanced over toward the vampires, Lian straddling Mina, her fist coming down on Mina's face. A small whimper was Mina's only response to the impact that landed with a wet crunch. "This is not a fight," Eva continued. "This is a slaughter. I will buy you time—and you will run."

Javier's stomach dropped as the jagged edge of the pendant's wings bit into his palm. This couldn't be happening. She wasn't saying goodbye. She wasn't.

"Eva, no—I'm not—"

"Lady Zhang!" Eva bellowed.

The woman's fist hovered in the air, poised for yet another blow against Mina's battered face. A single trickle of blood ran down Lian's temple.

Eva continued, "You're known for nothing if not your unfaltering pragmatism. Trying to control this woman is anything but." Eva took slow steps toward the vampires, while Javier stood frozen in place with uncertainty.

Lian slowly rose, her pristine image finally showing some signs of the struggle. The neck of her blouse had been torn, revealing a dark stain on her chest with purple-black veins radiating outward.

"Mina and Javier are not the problem you should be concerned with," Eva continued, her voice remarkably steady. "*I am.* I know what you've done in Shanghai, and I have the evidence to prove it. Let them go, and you can have me. I'll help you take this city for House Zhang if you spare them."

Javier thought Lian might speak, thought she might deliver another lecture on her own superiority or condemn Eva's scientific accusations once more. Instead, in another flash of vampire speed, Lian was standing before Eva. Everything happened in one imperceptible motion: Lian moving and then her claws dripping with Eva's blood. The three deep gashes over Eva's throat only revealed themselves a second later as a gush of crimson blood that slowly bathed the woman's front as a wet choking noise emanated from her mouth.

What?

Javier's thoughts were a jumble of confusion as he watched the blood pour from his sister's neck. Eva's own expression echoed the confusion as her shaky hands rose to press themselves against the source of the bleeding. Eva was the doctor—she wasn't the one who was supposed to get hurt. How was he supposed to help her when she was the healer?

Lian licked her lips where a few droplets of Eva's blood had landed. "Mmm, now, you would have been the more powerful magician, wouldn't you?"

Eva sank to the floor, a wild desperation in her eyes. The wounds were too great. The blood flowing too freely.

Lian grabbed the front of Eva's shirt, hoisting her up half-way, their noses nearly touching as Lady Zhang craned over her.

"Is this how you've been keeping Vasa alive all this time? Sneaky girl. I should have suspected."

Only choked, incoherent sounds escaped from Eva's gaping mouth, her face draining of its color.

"Never mind. He'll be gone soon, anyway. Just like you." Lian jammed her hand inside Eva's stomach and reached upward with a sickening crunch as a sharp gust of air left Eva's lungs. Lian's arm emerged from Eva's chest cavity slowly, pulling out Eva's glistening heart as the doctor's eyes glazed over. Lady Zhang sank her teeth—now rows of completely jagged menace—into the organ, and she made a noise of pleasure as she chewed. Lips smacking. The entirety of her eyes suffused a deep garnet, trails of blood trickling down to her elbows.

Eva's body slumped to the floor. Motionless. Javier tried to keep his focus on her head as it lolled to the side, refusing to look at the bloody wrongness of her desecrated torso.

How could she be gone? He'd just found her—only just begun to get to know the courageous, brilliant person she'd become. He had no breath, had no words, had no action as Lian stood in the middle of the hangar, consuming his sister's heart.

"Delicious," she said with a seductive chuckle. "I doubt

you'll taste half as sweet." She winked at Javier before tossing the remainder of Eva's heart on top of her body.

Deep inhalations rebuilt his strength from a raw fury.

"*You!*" he yelled. "I'm going to *kill you.*" He launched himself toward the cackling vampire before his path was blocked by a second one.

Mina stood before him, one eye swollen, shoving him back. "Run, Javier. I'll hold her off as long as I can. Go!"

Then Mina's body jerked sideways as Lady Zhang tossed her into the air. She sailed a few dozen feet before bouncing hard on the pavement.

"You never could have taken care of Mina the way I have." Lian raised her claws and made the same slicing motion she had against Eva. It happened so fast, and the warmth that suffused his throat convinced him that he would shortly follow his sister to the grave.

And just that quickly, it should have been over.

Except he could still breathe. Could still swallow. The condor talisman Eva had given him burned itself into his palm with nascent magic. He clutched it even tighter, its edges searing into his hand.

Lady Zhang held up her hand, the tips of her claws gone, a trail of purple smoke rising from each. She frowned, her silken cool finally cracking.

"Your protections won't last forever. Nor will they stop a bullet." Her voice rasped monstrously, an octave lower than before.

Mina was on her feet at once, in a race for the gun with Lian. She got there first and tossed it back into the depths of the hangar. "Javier, *go!*" she shrieked before Lian delivered a backhanded blow that landed with a sickening crunch, knocking her back to the floor.

He was done playing by these dumb vampire rules and ultimatums. Time to get some leverage back on the side of the human. The last human. *Cover me just a little longer, Mina.* As he raced toward the door to the hangar, he turned his head over his shoulder to see her tackle Lian around the ankles, mere feet from the weapon. He could hear the scrape of metal sliding on concrete. Felt the whiz of a shot sail past his ear.

His hand slammed down on the red button by the hangar door, and the garage opener thrummed to life overhead, the springs creaking as the door rose. Sunlight flooded into the cavern, the two vampires still wrestling in the center for control over a stupid firearm. When the rays met them, both women shrieked in agony, Lian darting off to one side of narrow shadow while Mina scrambled to the other, leaving the weapon in the center. Smoke billowed from the skin of both vampires anywhere the beams of light had touched. The side of Lian's face resembled a melted wax figurine, blistered and angry red. Mina looked only slightly better as she trembled in a ball, cradling one arm that had a protrusion that looked eerily similar to bone. Javier's lungs ached for oxygen as he ran to her.

"Mina," he sobbed, falling to his knees beside her and smoothing the hair from her face. Bruises and abrasions mottled her flesh with a rainbow of colors, her smooth complexion distorted by swelling and peeling skin from the burns.

"Javier," she murmured, resting her head against his shoulder as she sniffled. "I'm so sorry."

He held her in his arms, refusing to think about Eva.

About her sacrifice. None of it was Mina's fault to be sorry for. It was his own for not listening.

After a quiet moment, she pushed herself back from him, her eyes darting to the other side of the hangar before settling back on his. Mina cupped his face with her functional hand.

"The sun will set soon—you have twenty minutes at most. Leave while you still can."

"I'm not leaving you," he said fiercely. There was no world in which he simply walked away from this, Eva dead and Mina destroyed. "I'll bring the car over here, and we'll go together."

Mina gave him a smile so sad he wanted to weep himself. "She'll never stop coming for me."

"I don't care. I'm not letting you—"

"I'm really sorry I didn't get to see your vineyard. Goodbye, Javier."

The irises of Mina's eyes shifted in a mesmerizing burgundy miasma. Javier blinked, trying to clear the illusion as something within him unraveled. He couldn't tear his focus away.

I need to be somewhere. The sole thought emerged from his foggy mind with salient clarity.

He stood from his crouch, his eyes drifting from Mina's collapsed form to Eva's lifeless body to the shadow pacing the other wall. None of it registered. None of it mattered right now. He had somewhere to be. The car. Yes, he needed the car.

Javier went to the cab driver and rummaged in his pockets until he found a key ring. The man groaned as he fished them out. Javier heaved the burnt suitcase into the back seat of the car before settling in behind the wheel. He stuck the keys in the ignition and paused.

Why did it feel like he was forgetting something?

You'll be late if you don't drive. Now.

Was that his voice?

But I'm forgetting—Ah, of course. The seat belt. Javier fastened it across his chest, feeling relieved to resolve the mystery of the forgotten item. He started the car, shifted it into drive, and peeled out of the hangar, a serene sense of numbness overtaking his mind.

IT TOOK ALL of Mina's fractured willpower to maintain the compulsion as Javier walked away. The first few steps were the hardest—only then did she realize how much she'd needed to hear him say goodbye in return. Of course, he couldn't. That wasn't a luxury she'd earned. This was about survival. Javier's survival. As the car pulled out with an emphatic tire screech, a nauseating quiet suffused the space, interrupted only by the occasional takeoff or landing from the jetway beyond.

It had been such a foolish dream that had led her here in the first place. Of course she hadn't really killed Lian, the immortal vampire goddess of Shanghai. Mina would never be strong enough to kill her. And thinking she might have a future with that kind man had gotten his sister murdered. A fate that still might follow Javier, depending on how far Lian was willing to chase him. Mina had done the only thing she could for him, knowing how much he would hate her for it. She'd made her choice to become a Shanghai vampire. These consequences were hers alone to endure.

Lian paced the edge of her shadow boundary, the noise of her footfalls maddening in their easy cadence. The sun dipped ever lower in the sky, the warm light that separated them a fleeting comfort against the impending twilight. As it neared, Mina used the corrugated metal wall at her back to help herself stand. She refused to kneel for this woman anymore, if it was the last conscious act of defiance she was permitted. Propped against the wall, her body heaved with each labored breath, her body a fractured jumble of pain. Mina glared across the wedge of waning light before a shadow finally overtook the space between.

The monster on the other side smiled broadly, pointed teeth gleaming against a bloodstained mouth. Lian's injuries had healed remarkably during the respite, her face only flushed pink on the side that was previously melted. Mina could boast no such recovery, and she knew the damage would likely get much worse before she was allowed to heal.

"You really made quite the mess of things this time," Lian said as she finally neared. Mina held her mouth stubbornly closed. She could say nothing to deter the repercussions she would face. Lian gave a small snort before grabbing her by the upper arm, leaving the broken lower half dangling painfully as she hauled Mina to the black sedan parked at the back. She forced herself to look hard at Eva's defiled body as they passed, etching the memory into her brain. The memory of a woman who had died a gruesome, undeserved death for her mistakes. A woman she might have called sister in a different life.

"Don't worry, we'll make sure your poor decisions don't result in anymore... casualties," Lian said in a mocking tone. When they got to the car, she flung Mina roughly to the ground. The ache in her kneecaps as they collided with the concrete was nothing compared to the piercing fear of what would come next.

From the interior of the car, Lian withdrew the ornamental box. The same box she'd shown Mina in the bank vault on her return to Shanghai. Mina knew this had been coming, and yet to be faced with the inevitable conclusion of her errors still took her breath away. *Maybe I should have... Maybe I could...* There was no answer for this. Nothing left to do.

The pin was removed from the clasp, and the box opened to reveal the serpentine collar, already slithering angrily in its track. The woman sliced a long gash on her own arm and slathered the metal scales messily with it. It writhed in the slippery liquid. Mina sat petrified by the promise of the collar: a life without free will.

"I regret that you've forced me to take such drastic measures, pet. I really do." Grasping the snake behind the head, Lian spoke a litany of words, the flowing, melodic syllables of the language sounding wrong on her tongue. It released its own tail, which thrashed wildly in freedom. Lian held her wrist above its head, forcing more of her lifeblood down its throat. Its slithering tongue darted out to lap at the cut, becoming more sedate as it drank.

Finally, as the snake hung with only the barest twitch to its movements, Lian knelt next to Mina, her face devoid of all expression. A fleeting moment of panic gripped Mina's limbs. She should be fighting. She should be trying to run.

It won't matter. This is what you bargained for. Just don't let her make you forget your name. You're Mina. You're—

Lian's cold hands brushed against her neck before the collar slithered into place, the snake devouring its own tail once more and, with it, Mina's sense of self. A numb compliance washed over her mind, and she blinked up at her creator.

"Mistress?"

"You will not speak unless addressed." Lian's voice was pure icy control.

Mina bowed her head, gasping at the short breaths she managed. Even though the collar rested loosely, the constricting effect on her psyche was undeniable as it squeezed her into obedience. *Unless...* Mina's thoughts struggled against the magical straitjacket.

You can fight this. You're stronger than you realize.

"I—" A single syllable was all she managed before an unimaginable pain traveled from the base of her spine down to the tips of her toes, shocking in the totality of its agony. The ache was so deep, so inescapable, that she couldn't even scream. Only endure until it mercifully relinquished, leaving her sobbing against the concrete floor.

When Lian knelt beside her and brushed her hair from her face tenderly, Mina shied away.

"This fight in you won't persist much longer. You'll succumb to the collar's conditioning soon enough. As I did."

Mina's eyes flickered up toward Lian's. Still, nothing. Not even a glimmer of emotion as she stared down at her broken prize.

"Now. I'm going to take you home and teach you the full price of your betrayal. And in the end, you'll thank me for it and resume your rightful place at my feet. Is that understood?"

The words escaped her lips before Mina could even think.

"Yes, mistress."

Somewhere beneath the haze of the collar's superimposed will, a smaller voice screamed.

Was it her own?

Mina wished it would stop.

35

The haze of Mina's compulsion didn't lift from Javier's mind until the wheels touched down on the San Francisco jetway. Strapped into his seat, he became aware of the lights dinging and passengers starting to move around, and visions of Eva's last moments, of Mina's broken body flashed in his mind.

I left them there. I left both of them there.

The heels of his palms came up to squeeze at his temples as he grappled with the realization of what he'd done. What he *hadn't* done. How not one, but two women had sacrificed themselves for his escape. Which he'd managed with nothing but a bruise on the back of the head to show for it.

"I'm going to be sick," he said, his throat tightening as he tried to choke back the vomit. An observant seatmate handed him a sick bag just in time for him to relieve the contents of his stomach. When he was finished, he leaned his head against the seat in front of him, the tears flowing like a busted water pipe.

A hand rubbed his back as the old woman next to him said,

"Don't worry, dear. You're almost home. Everything will be better once you're off the plane."

No, he wanted to argue. *Nothing will ever be better again.* Certainly, nothing would be better for Eva or Mina. He stayed in his middle seat, desolate and motionless, as everyone else deplaned. Finally, a uniformed employee approached, a no-nonsense voice commanding, "Sir, I'm going to need you to leave the plane."

Javier looked up at this unfeeling person, unsure he could bring himself to move through these perfunctory mechanics. With numb hands, he unlatched his seat belt and stood to shuffle into the aisle.

"Sir. Your bag."

Javier looked back at his messenger bag shoved under the seat. He leaned down to collect it before continuing his journey down the aisle. Christ, he had a headache.

At the baggage carousel, he loaded each of the massive suitcases onto a trolley he'd begged off another family unloading. The charred suitcase was the last to arrive. He let it take two full laps before he could bring himself to pull it off the belt.

He hadn't even said goodbye. To either of them. In the end, he'd just walked away. Left Eva's body to rot in an industrial warehouse. Left Mina alone with a viper. How could he ever live with himself again?

You'll do it by going back for her. That was the plan all along, remember?

Javier blinked with clarity. Right. That was what he needed to do. He needed to go back for her. But not yet. Not before he had a chance at winning. Eva had been right—the standoff in the hangar hadn't been a contest. It couldn't be, against an opponent so powerful. And Lian had been right—he was a sorry excuse for a magician. Someone in his family had to be able to help him understand his absurd ability to arbitrarily set things on fire.

But before contending with his magical heritage... he needed to go home. With a resigned sigh, he wheeled the trolley out to the taxi stand, an impossibly bitter taste in his throat. An hour later, he climbed out from the yellow car in front of his mom's house at the vineyard and handed over the absolute last of his cash. He unloaded the bags, choking on the dust churned up by the cab as it tore down the road. The sun was high in the sky, and he squinted to make out the tips of the mountains along the skyline.

Home.

Under any other circumstances, he would've been racing to the front door, ready to give his mom a bear hug and recount his adventures. This was the longest he'd ever been away from home. As it was, Javier stood surrounded by suitcases in the dusty driveway, uncertain he had the strength to even approach the door let alone knock.

The sky was nearing sundown by the time the door opened. The wind whipped his mother's curls around her face. She shoved them aside, squinting in his direction.

"Javier?" she asked, disbelief in her voice.

He felt miserable with the comfort it brought to hear her say it again. Dread settled atop his shoulders at the impending confession.

"Javier!" She ran to him in sock-covered feet.

"Mamá... Discúlpame. I..." Javier bit his lower lip, his chin a quivering mess. "I couldn't save her." The words tumbled out in a disorganized jumble, absent the context he couldn't bring himself to share.

"Save who, mijo?" She grabbed him by the shoulders and placed a hand on his neck as she looked him over for injuries, her expression brimming with concern.

His mouth twisted with grief as he braced himself to say it. To burden his mother with the cost of his failure. To reopen the wound of her daughter's loss all over again.

"Eva. I found her, and then I lost her." Javier took a hitching breath. "Eva is dead."

"No, Javier," Gabriella said, her chin trembling as she took in the sincerity of his anguish. "No, it can't be," she insisted.

"I'm so sorry, Mamá. This is all my fault."

Was this the guilt Eva felt at losing Dad? Javier thought, another layer added to his grief.

Tears sprang to Gabriella's eyes, and she crumpled to her knees, her cotton dress a tangle beneath her. "Dios, no... not my baby. Not my Eva. Why did you need her too? God, *why?*"

Javier sank down beside her and grabbed her hand. It was unfair, but saying it aloud—sharing the tragedy with someone else—eased the pain in his chest from a suffocating pressure to a deep ache. He sat with her in the driveway until the sun set, letting the dirt steal each shed tear. The evening autumn air carried a chill, one that left his mother shivering as soon as the light disappeared.

"Come on, Mamá. Let's go inside. I'll make some coffee." He needed it—for what came next and just to stay upright.

He led her back to the house before retrieving the cases. They lined the entryway precariously, leaving just enough room to pass through. Javier didn't have the stamina to start unpacking anything that reminded him of Shanghai or his sister just yet. He found Gabriella clutching a picture in the living room, one of the last of their family together. With a heavy heart, he turned into the kitchen.

After dumping the morning's coffee grounds into the compost, he replaced the filter and scooped four heaping measures of fresh grounds into the basket. He rinsed the carafe and used it to fill the reservoir with water before clicking the button that would start the machine's sputtering brew. While it worked, he opened the fridge. A half-eaten flan sat beneath a film of plastic. He couldn't imagine a more perfect consolation.

Javier sliced two pieces and slid them onto plates. From the drawer with the loose front, he fished out two thin stamped forks, the silverware from his childhood that his mother refused to replace. When the coffee was finished, he poured two steaming mugs. Gabriella sat wordlessly as Javier stood on the kitchen side of the bar.

The first dulcet bite of cinnamon-laced confection greeted his palate like an honest welcome home. He followed the silky bite with a scalding swallow of coffee, and even that tasted good.

"How was she?" Gabriella asked with a sniff. "Before..."

"Eva was incredible. Of course." He said it with enough conviction to almost hide the chasm of sorrow beneath. "Did you know she became a doctor? Her research was some of the most renowned in Shanghai. And I..." Javier glanced over at the suitcases. Tomorrow he would go through her belongings and find the next direction for her research. It was the only way he could honor her legacy. "I think she was happy."

Gabriella smiled down at her plate, and Javier could tell she was doing her best not to dissolve into tears once more. She didn't ask any more questions as they ate their dessert, for which he was immensely thankful. Explaining how Eva had died would be its own separate hell—one he could face on a different day.

After Javier rinsed the dishes and set them in the dishwasher, he rounded the counter. His mother was still perched on the stool, her shoulders slumped forward like a marionette with cut strings. He placed a gentle kiss on her forehead before she pulled him into a fierce embrace.

"You'll never leave me, will you?" she asked, her voice a meek plea.

"Te prometo," he vowed, hugging her back.

When he pulled away, Gabriella wiped tears from her face. "Shower. Now."

"But, Mom—"

"No buts. Go. Then bed. We will talk more tomorrow."

Javier bit back his response. Mom's house, Mom's rules—even if he'd just faced a vampire queen and barely escaped with his life. Sure. Mom could still make decisions about bedtime.

By the time he was done with the shower, though, Javier was exhausted beyond any conceivable measure. He flopped onto the bed with the towel still wrapped around his waist, and that's where he stayed for the next fourteen hours.

Two weeks later, Javier sat in the cramped office inside the barn, surrounded by binders of barely contained paper. His mother's haphazard accounting skills had run awry during his absence, but he nearly had the books rebalanced. He rechecked the math on his sketchpad for the second time, trying to discern whether the numbers could possibly be legitimate. The vineyard's yield for the summer showed a fifteen-percent improvement over last year, and a late-summer distributor contract for next year made the cash flow actually solvent for once. They wouldn't even need his savings to bridge the spring-season start-up costs.

Javier tugged at the too-short cuff on his suit jacket, trying to cover the overexposed shirt sleeve as he flipped the page. He was waiting to find the ledger that listed a defaulted loan or some lopsided equipment sale, but so far, he'd come up empty-handed. The sole year he'd been absent for the harvest, the vineyard was doing better than ever. *Figures.*

"Javier!" His mom hollered sharply from outside.

He grimaced. "Yeah, Mom. I'm coming."

He closed the books and yanked the pull chain on the light before stepping out of the barn. The crisp air of the November morning had slicked the outdoors with dew. Gabriella marched over to him, wearing her black veil and accompanying formal mourning attire, an angry frown on her face. She hit him on the arm with her purse.

"You make your mother look for you on a morning like this? *Vamos.*"

Javier trudged to the car behind her. After a slight respite in her animosity after his return, she'd been irascible these last couple weeks, planning Eva's memorial. He'd tried to tell her Eva wasn't Catholic and wouldn't have wanted a big thing, but that only made Gabriella angrier. Then they'd had a whole disagreement about the photo for the program. He'd wanted to use the one from Eva's professional bio, but Gabriella insisted they use her senior photo from two decades before so that people would "recognize her." Whatever.

Roberto was waiting with the engine on already—he seemed to be the only person who could temper Gabriella's swings between despondency and wrath. The man gave Javier a sympathetic nod as he wriggled into the back seat of the pickup. Gabriella climbed into the front, complaining about having to hoist herself into the cab wearing a dress. People—especially mothers—were entitled to their own grief process. Javier just wished hers weren't so loud.

When they arrived, the church was already filling up with black-clad family and friends. Javier stared up at the Gothic spires, trying to remember the last time he attended Mass. After Dad's death, church had kind of lost its luster.

At least the Catholic memorial services had a structure for the grief proceedings. He nodded his head at the condolences offered by tearful relatives. He stood next to his mother in the pew. He listened dutifully as the priest presided over the memorial Mass. He took communion, aware of the sacrilege he was committing. Between the wrath of God and the wrath of Gabriella, the choice was easy. And when the priest stepped down from the altar and invited him to speak, Javier went.

The smell of incense and floral arrangements was stifling in the pulpit. Javier unfolded the piece of paper from his pocket and smoothed it over the lectern. The entire morning had been remarkably emotionless. In fact, being back in California had provided a stark clarity, compared to the chaos of his last days in Shanghai. Here, he had tasks to accomplish—disseminating Eva's research to every colleague he could track down, writing letters to his legislative representatives that read like crackpot conspiracy theories, and double-checking the vineyard's logbooks. Those were all things he could do. Facing the congregation, he felt the dam start to give way.

Keep it together. Eva would call you a baby if she saw you crying in front of all these people.

Javier cleared his throat. "I have two readings today. The first is from the book of Revelation." The edges of the paper crumpled beneath his fingers as his mind flashed back to his monstrous last image of Lady Zhang—her face half melted, her front stained with Eva's blood. "'Render to her as she has rendered to you: pay her back double for what she has done. In the cup where she mixed her draught, mix her double.'"

He looked up to a sea of blinking eyes. A solitary hacking cough sounded. His mother scowled as her gloved hand marked the sign of the cross—likely a prayer for his ungodly soul invoking the unconventional verse. But from somewhere on the balcony, for just a second, he thought he heard a tinkling laugh, one that sounded uncannily like Eva's. Javier shook his head. Probably just some AV tech. Sound always traveled strangely in these old stone cathedrals.

Remembering himself, he continued with the rote phrase, "The word of the Lord."

The congregation replied in unison, "Thanks be to God."

"The second reading comes from the Book of Sirach: 'Honor the physician, for the Most High created her; her gift of healing comes from God. Through her, the sick are cured and their pain taken away.'"

At a serious nod from the priest, Javier stepped down from the pulpit and returned to his seat by his mother. She tutted quietly at him—a promise of a stronger rebuke coming later, when they were on less sacred ground, where she could unleash a less-than-devout lecture on his failings as a son. Javier couldn't wait.

The car ride home went about as expected, full of shrill commentary on the audacity of his remembrance and that he'd gone to Shanghai in the first place. Bad Things happen when

477

you lie to your mother. When they reached the vineyard, Javier offered to help her with food in the kitchen.

"No, you've done enough already" was all he got as he watched the back side of Gabriella disappear down the walk.

Roberto tipped an ibuprofen into his hand. "She'll come around, eventually. I'll talk to her."

"Thanks, Berto," Javier said as the man clapped him on the shoulder and followed Gabriella, small clouds of dust puffing up beneath his freshly polished boots.

Javier skirted the rambler-style house to the back patio, where several of the vineyard employees were setting up long buffets of food. A few early family members hovered at the fringes, chatting quietly. Javier went straight to the table of the wine and poured himself a hefty glass.

He raised it, thinking, *Here's to you, Eva. Just had to be stubborn about not coming back to the vineyard, didn't you?* He took a large swallow and then another, and then the glass was gone. Javier poured more before anyone could stop him. One hand rubbed the outline of the condor pendant beneath his shirt. He hadn't taken it off since getting back. He couldn't. He needed a way to remember his sister and the sacrifice he couldn't talk about.

"Hey, primo. Mind if we join you?"

Javier turned to find a young woman with a flouncy skirt and mischievous eyes. She was joined by a gangly man with black rectangular glasses and severely parted hair. They both looked strangely familiar, yet—*No... it can't be.*

"Inés? Pascal? You came all the way here for this?"

"Of course! We are still family, after all, even if you haven't bothered to visit since Tío Pedro died," Inés said.

Javier gave her a hug and Pascal a handshake, trying to

reconcile the memory of his pain-in-the-ass twin cousins with the young adults before him.

"So, were you really in Shanghai? Did you see any vampires?" Inés poured herself an even larger glass of wine than Javier, leaving Pascal to pour his own.

Javier's mouth went dry, so he wet it with another sip.

"One or two."

"What do they look like in person?" Her lips quirked into a devilish smile, some twisted fantasy probably playing in her mind.

"They look like people. Pale people." Man, he didn't have the energy for this.

"So, how did Cousin Eva really die?" Pascal cut in, direct as ever.

Javier spluttered the next sip of wine. "There was an accident."

"You used that one for Tío Pedro. Gotta at least pick a new excuse."

"Um, I think I should go help my mom in the kitchen. It's good to see you. Let's catch up before you leave."

"Wait, Javier." Inés caught him by the arm. "We're older now—you don't have to keep things from us. We heard our parents talking about how volatile Eva's gifts were. Is that what happened? We didn't even know she was in Shanghai. The elders are pissed that she may have exposed our family."

Javier blinked. Were they really having this conversation?

"You know about *magic*?" he asked them, feeling ridiculous as soon as he said the word aloud.

"Duh. They teach us all when we're old enough to use it. We had to wait until fourteen because Pascal was such an idiot."

Pascal gave a wry smile. "But then, Tío Pedro would have died before teaching you, didn't he?"

Inés looked between Pascal and him like she'd been presented with a delectable treat. "Oh, Javi, you should come back with us! Reconnect with your heritage and all." She grabbed him by the hand and swung it merrily. "We'll need to double-check with Abuela and Abuelo, but I'm sure they'd be fine with it."

Silvio and Lucia were two people from his childhood he could barely remember. Javier had been working himself up to reach out to them. But he didn't know how to phone up his relatives and say, "Hey, remember me? So, about this ancestral magic..."

And maybe part of him was scared—scared that he didn't have what it took to do magic or the courage to go back to Shanghai. The price of his failure had been so high the first time. How did a sane person convince themselves it was a good idea to go back for more?

Javier ran a hand through stiffly gelled hair. "Let me think about it, all right?"

Inés patted him on the chest, right on top of Eva's pendant, with a wink. "Whatever you say, primo."

Pascal tipped his head to Javier, and the pair of them bounced off.

More relatives had shown up by then, including the afore-mentioned abuelos. They stood at the edge of the crowd with stern expressions, wearing clothes that looked like they'd seen more funerals than Javier had seen years. Children too young to know better chased each other in the field. Someone played ranchera music. The occasional laugh could be heard as people shared memories of his sister, of being family.

Javier sighed. If he didn't launch himself into this now, he might never get the momentum again. He owed it to Mina and owed it to Eva to finish what he'd started. The guilt and regret would eat him over time if he did nothing—that much he knew.

Dammit.

"Inés! Pascal! Wait up!"

CONVINCING his grandparents to bring him back to Mexico City had been easy. Getting Gabriella to let him go had nearly broken him.

"You promised you wouldn't leave me!" she'd shouted, and Javier had nearly given up on the entire endeavor. The dream of rescuing Mina after such a crushing defeat seemed so depressingly out of reach. Still, the thought of her never truly left his mind, like a ghost he couldn't shake.

Javier hadn't had the nerve to attempt anything magical since that day, either, even going so far as to avoid the anger that seemed to set off the random bursts of flame. But Pedro's journal still warmed when he pressed his hand to the cover, and he couldn't shake the memory of Eva conjuring a thunderstorm in a water glass. He knew that magic lived within him, and that demanded some follow-up in its own right, whether it held the key to saving Mina or not.

Boarding his flight south tangled his stomach in impossible knots. The smell of recycled air, the scratch of economy seats—everything brought back too much. This time, though, he was there by choice, and he knew what awaited him at his destination: not some mad search for a long-lost sister, not a doomed vampiress that would turn his world upside down, but family and, he hoped, knowledge of a legacy bequeathed by his father.

As the engines fired up, propelling the craft into the sky, Javier clutched the pendant hanging around his neck. He wasn't giving up. He was regrouping. And one day—when he was ready—he would return to Shanghai. For her.

36

August traversed the long courtyard of Zhang Manor, leaving crisp footprints in the dusting of snow. He hadn't planned to be back in Shanghai so soon with the Vasa integration in Buenos Aires in a frenzied state of transition. However, enough peculiar events had aligned to justify an in-person visit to his dear sister, and her annual lunar New Year's party was a capital excuse to drop by uninvited.

After a cryptic missive from Dr. Robles three months ago, the woman and her research had seemingly dropped off the face of the earth. August had choice words for Lian about the stunt she'd pulled reneging funding; also, his lawyers would be in touch regarding violation of contract. In addition, his covert information trail out of Beijing had all but completely stalled out.

But the more persuasive reason for his visit was a lack of contact from Mina, along with a very worried fledgling who wouldn't stop nagging him about her. After Lian and August's last encounter, he prayed the woman would see reason and reverse course. If anything, it seemed she was only steering harder into the gales.

Guests in fur-trimmed coats oohed at the acrobats and dancing lion in the inner courtyard. They clutched their steaming mugs of spiced beverages as fireworks bombarded the sky with acrid displays of dancing light. August nodded at those who glanced at him though he was hard-pressed to find a familiar face.

He shrugged out of his cashmere coat and scarf at the door and picked a stray piece of lint off his jacket. A separate couple approached to retrieve their outerwear—finally, faces he recognized.

"Lord Quezada, Isabella, pleasure to see you both. Leaving so soon?"

The vampires glanced at each other before Lord Quezada gave him a polite nod.

"We have another engagement, unfortunately. It's been... an *eccentric* gathering." They both gave their regards before parting. The former Spanish inquisitor's assessment of the party atmosphere Lian had cultivated only agitated August further. He braced himself as he pushed forward into the heart of the foyer.

Zhang Manor was splendid, with yards of red silk. Lavish floral arrangements featured orchids and chrysanthemums. Trays of cocktails imprinted with gold-leaf serpentine designs celebrating the year of the snake drifted through the guests. All was in keeping with Lian's traditional celebration. Yet something was off. August felt it as a subtle hum in his fingers, an out-of-place resonance.

A silken laugh floated over the din of the crowd, and August traced it to the sitting room. Lian sat in a regal-looking chair, wearing a crimson blouse beneath a tuxedo jacket, cuffs casually unbuttoned and turned up. A diamond-encrusted snake pin swirled on her peaked lapel. And on the floor beside her, atop a satin pillow, sat Mina.

The young woman's appearance evoked the beauty of a porcelain doll. A slip of a red dress clung to her form in a vulgar sort of way. August's instinct was to look away in deference to her modesty. But he couldn't. Because wrapped around her neck was the one thing he thought he would never see in person: the ouroboros collar that had once enslaved Lian.

Nervous energy tingled down his spine as August pushed through the crowd with a brusque determination. Though Mina gave no overt reaction to his presence, he caught the twitch of a tendon in her neck. The collar came to life, slithering a turn, tightening perhaps, before the beast settled its head at the vertex of her collarbones, a sickening sight to behold.

"Lady Zhang," August started, not bothering to hide the displeasure in his tone. "I don't mean to rob your guests of your magnanimous presence, but I need a word. In private."

The gentlemen comprising her circle of confidants all considered him openly as though appraising his net worth. Who the hell were these people, anyway?

She chuckled, swirling the sphere of ice around her whisky glass. "Lord Vasa, how marvelous you could make it," she said, not bothering to stand. "It's funny, though—I don't remember inviting you."

August opened his mouth, a biting reproach on the tip of his tongue. But too many eyes were on him, too many outsiders' eyes. Before the end of the night, he promised himself, he would get his answers.

"I had local business to attend to—some unexpected deviation in research plans. I thought it only polite to stop in. I do hope we can catch up before the evening is over." His tone was clipped, far from the suave nonchalance he'd been trying for. Lian smirked at him before going back to her previous conversation.

August grabbed a cocktail of his own and sank into the backdrop of the party, pretending to mingle with others while staying close enough to overhear the conversation Lian carried on with her small group of rapt acolytes—five of them dangling on her every word.

"And, of course, you know what the bureaucracy is like in France," a man in a pinstripe suit was saying with arrogant charisma. "My dear Lady Zhang, I hope you don't mind me saying, but your... companion is quite stunning. Is she your..."

"My fledgling, yes." Lian let her hand slip beneath Mina's chin, tilting it up as if inspecting a prize.

Mina kept her hands in her lap, her expression placidly demure.

"Exquisite, isn't she?"

"Certainly. My curiosity is piqued—are all fledglings this... dutiful to their sires?"

Lian released Mina's head and took another swallow of whisky. "Most have significant attachment to their *creators*," she corrected gently. "A recent lesson in humility has done wonders for this one's overall demeanor, though. Wouldn't you agree, pet?"

"Yes, mistress." Mina's mask remained perfectly in place— not a hitched breath, not a tug at those glossy lips, nothing but flawless adherence to a preordained script. August sneered at the absolute malice it must have taken to break the resilient young woman to such a soporific state.

"Incredible," another gentleman murmured, just as sartorially inclined, his jet hair shiny with pomade. There was money in that circle, to be certain. "She's a testament to your mastery." He raised his coupe glass in toast as Lian simpered shamelessly.

"Yes, I maintain high standards for the things I allow into my domain."

A guffaw came from one inebriated gentleman. "If you'd be willing to share her for a night, I'd pay a pretty sum to have someone that perfect fawn over me."

The joviality in the conversation died along with the humor on Lian's lips.

The gentleman, to his credit, recognized the error immediately. "Apologies, Lady Zhang. I intended no offense. Only, she is a compliment to your command. A truly rarified beauty."

Lian took a slow sip of her drink, considering the man for a tense moment. "I suppose I can't blame you for coveting something so dear. But Mina is mine and mine alone," she finally replied, her hand resting on Mina's shoulder possessively. Black-tipped claws emerged a centimeter—just enough to make their presence known.

"Naturally," the man said before quietly excusing himself, a wise move.

"Pet? Go fetch us a bottle of the single-malt Brae Morven from my study. This is a celebration, after all."

Two bottles left in existence, and she was opening one for sycophants?

Mina daintily rose from her pillow, a picture of grace. After making sure Lian was fully engrossed in the conversation with her other guests, August trailed up the stairs after her. If Lian wasn't going to talk to him, he could at least get a straight story from Mina, if that collar would permit her to speak. Of all the vile things he'd known the woman to do in their time, this was one boundary he hadn't fathomed her crossing.

He slipped into the study, closing the door with only the subtlest of clicks. Mina jumped violently, bumping her head on the top of the cabinet it was stuck in. She withdrew, a dusty bottle clutched beneath white knuckles, her brows gently drawn together.

"What has she done to you, child?" August closed the distance to her. Mina backed to the shelf of vases behind the desk, her chin dropping.

"Please, Lord Vasa, you shouldn't be here." Her voice was the barest whisper. She tried to hasten past him, but he grabbed her shoulders, the skin icy beneath his touch. The bloodstone scales of the monster glistened in the soft glow of the desk lamp. He lifted a hand to stroke the beast, but his fingers curled into a fist as he thought better of it, a deep regret settling in his chest.

"Forgive me, älskling. I didn't realize how entirely this obsession consumed her."

Mina wrenched out of his grasp, a flash of indignation ghosting over her face before she schooled it into the serene mask.

"Lord Vasa, you are mistaken. Lady Zhang is merely enforcing the discipline I'm due."

His eyes traced her form, the absolute stillness of her composure, the certainty in her voice. Seeing the extent of her self-suppression broke his heart. Mina was a resilient girl, but no soul could survive such a trial unscathed. Lian had endured the collar's cruelty for several decades, but she was already centuries old, her mettle well forged by adversity. Even then, the woman was but a wraith by the time she found freedom. He wondered how long Mina had before it erased her entirely.

"Tell me you're still in there, älskling," August said softly. He waited several tenuous seconds before the woman spoke, her eyes trained on his shoes.

"Do you remember the movie we watched with Dmitri? The black-and-white one?"

Surely she meant *Dracula*. "Yes, I remember."

Her eyes danced from one floorboard to the next. "I am no longer Mina, and she... she is a different kind of villain entirely." Mina looked up at him, just for a moment. "Take care of Dmitri. Tell him I'm sorry I couldn't say—"

The door to the office banged open, causing them both to start. Mina stepped away from him, a renewed tension present in her posture.

Lady Zhang stalked into the room, glaring at both of them in equal measure.

"You know better than to keep me waiting, pet." Her voice dripped with threat, a complete reversal from the saccharine hostess she had been portraying downstairs. "And you"—she rounded on August—"know better than to harass my fledgling."

"What you've done to this girl, Lianna..." He gestured at the mute fledgling, a hot rage crawling beneath his skin. "You will undo it immediately if there is to be any redemption for your wicked soul."

Lian tilted her head at him, a wry amusement on her lips. "The girl is a danger to herself and others, left unfettered. What I've done isn't only justified—it's *necessary*. Isn't that right, pet?"

"Yes, mistress."

"*Mistress?* Lianna, I've always known your tastes leaned more sadistic than most, but this is beyond the pale."

"Perhaps you'd feel differently if you knew what she'd done." Lian folded her arms across her chest. "Pet? Would you care to inform Lord Vasa whose fault it is that his bright young scientist is dead?"

A shiver overcame Mina's shoulders as she meekly said, "It's mine."

The words were an icy deluge down August's spine. "Tell me it's not true." He directed the challenge at Lian; there was no question about who the real perpetrator of any wrongdoing was.

The commotion of the party below was the only response as the ancient vampire turned to face her quarry instead. Mina remained implacably still, at least outwardly. August could sense wild tension in her muscles, the tautness a learned response to an unpredictable pursuer.

"I think you ought to be punished for your dalliance. Don't you agree?"

"Yes, mistress."

"Lianna, don't," August bit out hoarsely.

"You will *not* interfere with the methods I choose to maintain discipline in my home. This lesson is partly for you too. If you speak with her again, it is she who will suffer the consequences." Lian's slender fingers went to the encrusted ornament on her lapel and unpinned it. "Your hand."

Mina offered her hand, not a tremor to be seen. Lian grasped it and set the point of the pin where the skin met the fingernail of Mina's index finger. With painful slowness, she drove it underneath the nude lacquered nail, the pin burrowing until it met the crescent nail bed. Mina endured this with only the faintest flare of a nostril. August paled to imagine the tortures she'd been subjected to that this treatment could be tolerated with such sangfroid.

When Lian withdrew the pin, she lifted Mina's hand and caught the solitary drop of blood with her tongue then brushed a gentle kiss against Mina's knuckles.

"Good girl. Now, go rejoin the guests. Show them how charming Zhang vampires can be."

With a single bow toward Lian, Mina vanished from the room. August waited for the door to close before unleashing his rebuke.

"This behavior will not stand. I will call a council of the eight houses and tell them what you've done. You will be deposed for this."

The laughter that came out of Lian's mouth was maniacally joyous. "Oh, August. You're going to call a *meeting*? That's your power play?" She poured herself a glass of whisky. "I suppose it would be. You were never a match for me alone, even before the rabies."

At the mention of his illness, the specificity of the name, claws extended from August's hands, his fangs lowering at the visceral threat the woman posed.

"How did you find out?" he asked gruffly. Even under duress, he couldn't imagine Dr. Robles giving up his secret, and she'd sworn the diagnosis would remain undocumented and undisclosed.

"Find out?" Lian said, a vicious enjoyment in her expression. "My dear brother, I had you *infected*. Based on the rate of your progression, and knowing your darling doctor is gone, I give you another six months before you succumb to the madness. At most."

Instinct took over. A feral snarl erupted from August before he lunged at her. She neatly sidestepped him, and he crashed into the dense shelf of books behind. Dusty volumes tumbled to the ground as he braced himself against the woodwork, a disorienting lean to his vision. Lian merely refreshed her glass with amber liquid.

"Get out of my house, August. You've embarrassed yourself enough for one night."

August straightened himself and tugged his jacket back into place. She was right—he couldn't beat her here in her domain, in her city. It had been foolish to try.

Forcing his vampire aspect to recede, he struggled to reconcile the image of the partner he'd once cherished with the woman he was sharing the room with. He wanted to leave her with some parting words, something that might remind her of her humanity.

As their eyes met for a last time, August searched for any trace of the creature he'd spent the last three centuries admiring. Nothing but obsidian hunger stared back. Lian was lost, and he needed to stop pretending her redemption was within reach.

So he did as she suggested. He stalked past her without another word. Out of the office, down the stairs. He pushed through the party, which had only grown rowdier in their absence. Raucous laughter boiled over from a group. Someone bumped into him without so much as an apology.

He spotted Mina in the sitting room, putting on a gallant show for the lascivious men cornering the recondite young vampire. All the while, the collar monitored her actions. Any misbehavior would trigger an excruciating attack against her magical core itself. Just imagining the stringent captivity made August's skin crawl.

Where had Lian been before crash-landing into him in Sweden? It was somewhere mountainous in the Middle East, maybe Persia. He would need to investigate the collar's thaumaturgic origin if he stood a chance at disabling it long enough to spirit Mina away. It was a daring heist he was likely to get one shot at; there would be no missteps in its execution. If the Robles boy still lived, August would find him. The magic in his veins just might buy enough time to accomplish what was necessary.

A last glance around the room revealed Lian standing at the top of her staircase, an empress surveying her court. She winked at him, and a splitting pain cracked down the middle of his skull. August raised a hand to his head to ensure it was still whole. It was. Perhaps the heat of the room had gotten to him.

He stumbled out into the biting night air, forgoing his coat. Snow floated from the sky in slushy clumps, wetting his hair and face as he fled the courtyard. Slowly, his resolve coalesced into clarity.

He would direct his remaining energies where they counted: stopping the monster he'd helped bring to power. He would live long enough to rescue Mina, long enough to show the world what Lian Zhang had become.

Her delusions of absolute power had given her a weakness. She would underestimate him from now on. Let her bask in her empire a little longer, thinking herself untouchable.

In the end, that would be her undoing.

AUTHOR'S NOTE

This book took on a life of its own through the writing process. It tore itself from my brain without my consent, keeping me sleep-deprived for weeks on end. While I've tried to analyze why this story demanded so fervently to be told, the best I can do is offer you an evocation.

It began as a simple conjecture: surely, if immortal creatures existed, they would not be content to watch as humankind continues in its destructive course. From this solitary idea Lian was born—a woman intent on single-handedly rectifying modern humanity's moral and political failings. Mina was the natural consequence of someone so magnetic—and gods, do I feel bad for putting her through this book. It gives me some solace to know that Javier is waiting for her, a person who will finally give her the space and support to become herself, after he does some growing up of his own.

It was the dynamic between these characters that kept me writing, revisiting old wounds while inventing new ones for my own twisted enjoyment. If you've made it to the end, then likely part of you understands.

Thank you, dear reader, for walking through the blood and the

fury with me. This story, above all else, wanted a voice—
wanted not to be quiet anymore. It wanted to resonate with
others who might understand its heart. Because you are here, it
is complete.

I promise: this is not where the journey ends. Mina has a self to
reclaim, Javier has a legacy to unearth, and August has ghosts
to reckon with.

As for Lian... she will inform us of her plans when she deems us
worthy of the knowledge.

Until next time,
K.M.

GLOSSARY OF NON-ENGLISH WORDS

Korean

gwaenchanha - it's all right

haejang-guk - oxblood soup

halabeoji - grandfather

Mandarin Chinese

āyí - auntie

duì - yes, correct

gānbēi - cheers

hǎo - fine, good

nǐ shì gè hǎo xiǎohuǒzi - you're a fine young man

shénme shì? - what is it?

tā hǎokàn ma?/hǎokàn - is she pretty? yes.

xiè xiè nǐ - thank you

yī, èr, sān - one, two, three

zhōngqiū jié kuàilè - happy Mid-Autumn festival

zǒu ba - let's go

Russian

zdorovye - cheers

Spanish

abuela/abuelo - grandmother/grandfather

discúlpame - forgive me
Dios - God
hermano mío - my brother
leyendas - legends
lluvia - rain
los tacos están en la mesa - tacos are on the table
mijo - son
nombre - name
pero no te preocupes - but don't worry
primo - cousin
tía/tío - aunt/uncle
te prometo - I promise
tómalo - take it
vamos - let's go

Swedish
allt var bra - all was well
hej - hi
skål - cheers
älskling - darling

ABOUT THE AUTHOR

Katherine Mercer writes dark fantasy and gothic horror about people caught between love and ruin. By day she's a software engineer; by night she's responsible for whatever's happening to her characters. She lives in Minnesota, drinks her coffee black, and has strong opinions about tragic ballets. *Vampires of Shanghai* is her debut novel.

Her next release, *Magicians of Mexico City,* is anticipated in 2027.

For a free short story from the night of Mina's turning ceremony, visit **katherinemercer.com/newsletter**